@Micha~~el~~

@MichaelWoodBooks

Also by Michael Wood

Stolen Children

Michael Wood

One More Chapter
a division of HarperCollins*Publishers*
The News Building
1 London Bridge Street
London SE1 9GF

www.harpercollins.co.uk

This paperback edition 2020

First published in Great Britain in ebook format by
HarperCollins*Publishers* 2020

A catalogue record for this book
is available from the British Library

ISBN: 978-0-00-837486-0

Set in Birka by Palimpsest Book Production Ltd, Falkirk
Stirlingshire

Printed and bound in Great Britain by
CPI Group (UK) Ltd, Croydon CR0 4YY

To Chris Simmons.
For starting the ball rolling all those years ago.

Prologue

Monday 10th September 2018
Avenue de la Corse, Marseille, France.

9am

He walked down the road with cars parked either side. It was early morning, but the sun was already high in the bright blue sky. Up ahead was a golden sandy beach and beyond that, the warm crystal waters of the Mediterranean Sea.

There was a breeze blowing which cooled him down slightly. He was nervous. No, he was petrified. Sweat was running down his face and his Adidas T-shirt was sticking to his back.

He kept turning around and looking over his shoulder. He had no idea how he had managed to leave his hotel room without awakening his "parents" in the adjoining room. He'd crept down the back stairs and scurried through the kitchens. He'd gone unnoticed as breakfast for more than two hundred guests was busily being prepared. He'd dodged shouting chefs and hurrying waiters, stolen a banana and a croissant from a tray, and bolted out of the fire escape. Once he was out of sight of the hotel, he'd sat on the steps of a closed shop and eaten his meagre breakfast. It had tasted foul.

Yesterday evening, while alone in his single room, he'd looked on his phone for the nearest police station. It was less than a five-minute walk, yet he'd been walking for more than half an hour now and he still couldn't find it. He'd been down the Avenue de la Corse twice and there was nothing resembling a police station at all.

Then he saw it. Above a black door, next to barred windows was a sign which read Police Nationale. He'd thought it was a closed down shop when he'd passed it before. How could such a small building be a police station?

His heart quickened. He glanced around him once more to check he wasn't being followed, then pushed open the door and stepped inside.

He didn't know a word of French apart from *bonjour*. Marseille seemed like a very touristy place, so, fingers crossed, someone in here would speak English and understand him. He approached the desk. A dishevelled man in his mid-fifties with grey stubble and a dark tan looked down at him.

'Bonjour. Comment puis-je vous aider?'

He looked up at him with wide, terrified eyes. 'Do you speak English?'

'Non.'

'Is there someone here who speaks English?'

The policeman looked to the door then back at the young boy. 'Où sont vos parents?'

He only understood the word *parents* and took a step back. He looked at the door. This had all been a terrible mistake. He should leave. Run. But where to?

'Please. I need your help.' His eyes filled with tears.

The policeman didn't say anything to him but stepped away from his desk. At the back of the room, he spoke to another man in an identical uniform. Their voices were low, and they kept looking over at him. He still had time to run.

'Hello. I speak a little English,' the second man said in a heavily accented voice when they both returned to the front desk.

From his back pocket, the boy took out a sheet of A4 paper that had been folded into fours. He opened it up, placed it on the desk and flattened it out. It was a missing persons poster.

Underneath the red headline was a photograph of a young boy, smiling, with blond hair and blue eyes.

The boy pointed at the photograph and then at himself. He did this a few times.

'This is me,' he said. 'This boy is me.'

'This is you?'

'Yes.'

'You are this missing boy?'

'Yes. I'm him. I'm Carl Meagan.'

Chapter 1

Monday 10th September 2018
Stannington, Sheffield

4pm

Linda Armitage opened the door to the bathroom and stepped out into the bedroom. She was pale and a sheen of sweat glistened on her forehead. She'd been sick. Again.

She looked at her son, Riley, in his bed. He was lying on his side, mouth agape, breathing deeply. He was finally asleep. She turned off the television which was showing an episode of *Pingu* she had seen thousands of times before and turned on the monitor on the bedside table. Not that she needed to. When Riley woke up, he screamed the house down. However, Linda always needed to be able to hear him breathing. A slight deviation from the norm and she was in his room like a shot to make sure he was still alive.

Hopefully, he'd sleep for an hour or so and she could get some time to herself before she had to start making the evening meal. She flicked the kettle on in the kitchen and sat down at the table. She was tired. She needed a shower; her hair was greasy; her skin was dry, and she hadn't changed her clothes for a couple of days.

The front door opened and was kicked closed with a bang. Linda braced herself but it didn't wake Riley up.

Her fourteen-year-old daughter, Jodie, struggled under the weight of the shopping bags and heaved them onto the counter in the kitchen.

'Are you all right?' Jodie asked.

'Yes. Fine. Why?'

'You're pale. Have you been sick again?'

'Just a bit.'

'Have you eaten anything?'

'Yes. I had that sandwich you made me for lunch. I managed to keep it down for an hour or so, but . . .' she tailed off.

'Maybe you should go back to the doctor.'

'I will. Did you get me some ibuprofen?' she asked, changing the subject.

'No. Mrs Mortimer wouldn't serve me. She said it was more than her job's worth.'

'Oh for God's sake. She knows they're for me.'

'I said that,' Jodie said as she began to unpack. 'They didn't have any ham for Keeley's packed lunch either, so I bought chicken. Is she here? I could have done with a hand carrying all this.'

'What are you talking about?' Linda asked as she rummaged in the drawer looking for any ibuprofen that may have been missed.

'I told her to wait for me outside the Co-op. She knew I was buying milk. I came out and she'd buggered off. You're going to have to have a word with her, Mum. I don't mind helping around the house but she's old enough to take on a bit more responsibility too, you know.'

'I will. Found some,' she said, ignoring Jodie and pulling out a blister pack with two tablets left. 'I wonder how long these have been in there. They should be all right, shouldn't they?' She poured a glass of water from the tap and swigged them back.

'Mum, did you hear what I said?'

'Yes, I did. I'll have a word with her when she comes in.'

'You mean she hasn't come home yet?'

'No. I mean . . . she was with you.'

Jodie sighed. 'I've just told you that she wasn't there when I came out of the Co-op. I assumed she'd run on ahead.'

'Well, she hasn't.'

'Then where is she?'

'I don't know.'

Mother and daughter stood glaring at each other.

'I suppose that means I've got to go out and look for her then, doesn't it?' Jodie said, irritation evident in her voice.

'Well I can't,' Linda said, nodding towards Riley's bedroom.

Jodie threw the pack of apples she'd been unpacking down onto the table and stormed out of the kitchen towards the front door. She was muttering under her breath, but Linda couldn't hear what she was saying. She slammed the door behind her. This time, Riley woke, and his screaming began.

So much for having five minutes to relax with a cup of tea.

Linda went into Riley's room. He was sitting up in bed. His face was red and screwed up as he cried. He was trying to pull at his hair, but he had his mittens on, so he wasn't able to inflict any injury to himself.

Linda flicked on the light and the disco ball in the ceiling began rotating, casting its soothing colours on the walls as they danced around the room. She picked up the remote and put the TV back on, back to that annoying penguin making that awful noise and pissing on the ice.

The landline in the hallway started to ring.

Linda ignored it and picked Riley up. He started to relax immediately. He felt safer in someone's arms.

She made soothing noises and rubbed his back gently. The phone continued to ring.

'Shall we go and see who's ringing us, Riley?' she asked in a sing-song voice. 'It might be your nana to tell us all about her bunions again. Or maybe a nice gentleman will ask if we want to claim back PPI.'

She struggled to move Riley to her other arm. He was getting heavier by the day, and she seemed to be getting weaker. It wouldn't be long before she'd be unable to pick him up at all.

'Hello?' She answered the phone.

'Mrs Armitage?'

'Yes.'

'Linda Armitage?'

'Yes,' she strained to hear. With Riley gurgling on one side and a barely audible distorted voice coming through the phone line, she struggled to concentrate.

'We have your daughter.'

'What?'

'We've got Keeley. Pay fifty thousand pounds if you want her back.'

'Who is this?' Linda gripped the receiver hard. Her eyes widened, her mouth dried, and her heart thumped loudly in her chest. This was a joke, surely.

'We'll ring back in twenty-four hours.'

The line went dead.

Linda remained frozen to the spot, the phone still next to her ear. All she could hear was the dial tone. Had she just imagined that call? She hadn't been sleeping too well lately.

She hadn't left the house for six days. Was her mind playing tricks on her? People didn't get kidnapped for ransom in this country. Well, there was that little boy, Carl something. He was from Sheffield. She couldn't remember what had happened to him though.

Riley started to struggle in her arms. He flailed his legs, kicking her in the stomach and his glove-covered hands slapped at her face. She didn't feel it. She ran back into his bedroom, dumped him in his bed and lifted up the railing on the side so he couldn't get out. He began to cry and scream again, but she ignored him and left the room, closing the door behind her.

She ran into the living room for her mobile and scrolled through the contacts for her daughter's number. Her fingers were shaking, her eyes were blurred, but she somehow managed to make the call.

The phone began to ring in the kitchen. She ran in and saw Jodie's mobile on the work top.

'Fuck.'

In a full-blown panic, Linda dropped the phone and hurried to the front door. She opened it and ran out into the autumn sunshine. At the end of the garden path she looked left and right. There was nobody around.

'Jodie!' She called out. There was no reply. She ran to the end of the road. 'Jodie!'

Tears were streaming down her face. She had no idea what she was supposed to do. She felt completely alone. Alone and desperate.

Curtains began to twitch in neighbouring houses as people wondered as to the commotion.

'JODIE!' She screamed at the top of her voice.

'Linda, what's going on?'

She turned around and saw her next-door neighbour had come out of her house.

'Amanda, have you seen our Jodie or Keeley anywhere?' Linda asked.

'Jesus, Lin, what's happened? Are you all right?' She asked, looking her up and down and taking in her dishevelled appearance.

'No. I need Jodie.'

'I saw her leave your house not five minutes back.'

'Where did she go? Which direction?'

'I've no idea. What's going on?'

'Someone's got our Keeley,' she cried.

'What?'

'Someone's just called. They've got our Keeley. They've taken her.'

'Who has?'

'I don't know,' she screamed.

'Come on,' she put a comforting arm around Linda's shoulders and slowly walked her back to the house. 'Let's get you inside. We'll call your Craig and the police and let them sort it out.'

'I can't lose her. I can't lose my baby,' she cried.

'You won't lose anyone. I promise. Everything will be fine.'

More neighbours had gathered onto the small street to stare at the commotion.

Since Riley was born and because of his subsequent illness, Linda had hardly left the house. She felt embarrassed if he yelled or cried in public and people looked at her as if she was an unfit mother, unable to control her child, so she simply stopped going out. Months went by without her having her hair cut. She no longer showered daily. The weight had dropped off her and she'd stopped sleeping. Her life revolved around the twenty-four-hour-a-day care Riley needed.

Amanda led Linda into the living room and sat her on the sofa.

'Now, tell me what's going on?' she asked.

'Keeley's gone,' she said through the tears. 'Someone's taken her.'

'Are you sure?'

'What are you talking about? Of course I'm sure.'

Amanda took Linda's hand in hers. 'Look, it's obvious you've not been looking after yourself, and I know you've not been sleeping too well lately. Are you sure you haven't just nodded off and had a bad dream?'

'What? Don't you believe me?'

Amanda looked away.

'Jesus Christ! Are you saying I've made it up? Do you think I'm going mad or something?' She ranted, snatching her hands back.

'I'm not saying anything like that, Linda. It's just . . . well, you are under a lot of strain at the moment. Craig's working all hours and you're trying to look after three kids on your own. It's going to have some kind of psychological . . .'

'You think I'm cracking up,' she interrupted. 'You think I'm imagining things.'

'There are places Riley can go, respite, so you can get some rest.'

'I can't believe this. Haven't you heard what I'm saying? Keeley has been kidnapped and they want fifty thousand pounds, or they'll kill her.'

'Linda, listen to yourself. This is Sheffield, not New York. People don't get kidnapped for ransom here.'

'You're not listening to me,' she screamed, pulling hard at her hair.

'Ok, ok, calm down. I tell you what, I'll phone Craig, he can come home and sort it all out.'

'You need to call the police.'

'I'll call them too,' she lied.

4:45pm

'Mum, I'm back,' Jodie called from the hallway. 'I've been right back to the school and nobody's seen . . .' She stopped in the entrance to the living room when she saw her mother on the sofa with Amanda Raine comforting her. 'What's up?'

'Did you find her?' Linda jumped up from the sofa.

'No. I even knocked on a few of her friends' doors as I passed. Nobody's seen her since she left school.'

'Oh my God,' Amanda said.

'See, now do you believe me?'

'What's going on?' Jodie asked.

'Jodie, come with me.' Amanda turned Jodie around and pushed her out into the hallway, closing the living room door behind her. 'Jodie, your mum seems to think Keeley's been kidnapped.'

'What? That's ridiculous. She'll have just gone off with a friend or something.'

'That's what I said. She said she's had a phone call from someone demanding fifty thousand pounds.'

'What? But . . . oh my God.'

'What is it?'

'Keeley had PE today.'

'So?'

'She said that Mr Page . . .'

'What about Mr Page?'

A look of horror etched itself on Jodie's face. 'Have you called the police?'

'No. I called your dad but he's in Chesterfield on a delivery. He said he'll come back as soon as he can.'

'We should call the police.'

'Jodie, what is it? What do you know?'

'I think Mum might be right. I think Keeley might have been taken.'

Chapter 2

'I'm Detective Sergeant Sian Mills. This is Detective Constable Finn Cotton from South Yorkshire Police.'

'Come in,' Amanda ushered them both into the house and quickly closed the door behind them.

All three stood in the cramped hallway. Sian looked at the walls and took in the framed pictures of a happy family smiling at her. There were coats hanging on the wall and shoes haphazardly placed at the bottom of the stairs. This was a lived-in family home.

'Was it you who called the police?' Sian asked.

'Yes. It's Mr and Mrs Armitage's daughter, Keeley, who's gone missing.'

'Are they through there?' Sian asked, pointing to what she assumed was the living room.

'Yes. Linda's in a bit of a state,' she said in hushed tones. 'Craig's, well, he's a bit more controlled.'

'Ok. And you're saying Keeley has been kidnapped?'

'Well,' Amanda leaned closer to Sian. She dropped her voice even lower. 'That's what Linda says. I'm not sure if I believe her.'

'Right,' Sian said, exchanging glances with Finn. 'Let's go and have a word with them.'

The living room wasn't very large, and it was cluttered. The first thing Sian noticed was the giant bean bag in the corner. Jodie was sitting in it with Riley on her lap. He was wearing woollen mittens and a safety helmet. Linda was standing by the window, glaring out at the darkening street. She was biting her nails. Any hint of a noise, anything that caught her eye and she turned quickly towards it like a lion alert to its prey. On the sofa sat Craig. His face was expressionless. A large, solidly built man in his forties, he wore dirty jeans, an old sweater and a hi-vis waistcoat. There was a heavy atmosphere in the room, which was to be expected. Nobody spoke.

'Linda, the police are here,' Amanda said quietly as she ushered Sian and Finn into the room.

Sian proffered a sympathetic smile. 'Mr and Mrs Armitage, hello. I'm DS Sian Mills. This is DC Finn Cotton. Is it all right if I sit down?' There was no reply, so Sian perched herself on the edge of the sofa next to Craig. From her bag, she took out a thick form and a ballpoint pen. She tucked her red hair behind her ears and cleared her throat. 'I won't patronise you by saying I know how you're feeling right now, because I don't. However, I'm going to do everything possible to find your daughter.'

'Then why aren't you out there looking?' Linda said. Her eyes were full of tears. There were dark circles beneath them, and she already had the look of a defeated mother who had given up all hope.

'Linda, I need to know as much as possible about Keeley before I can get a team out looking for her. The more information you give me, the more likely we are to find her.'

'Ask your questions,' Craig said.

'Thank you. Now, how long has Keeley been missing for?'

'It was about four o'clock when I left her outside the Co-op,'

Jodie said from the corner of the room. Her voice was barely audible.

'Is that the Co-op on Oldfield Road?'

Jodie nodded and Finn made a note in his pad.

Sian looked at her watch. It was half past five. 'Have you called all her friends to see if she is with any of them?'

'I did,' Amanda chimed up. 'Linda's got her friends' numbers in her phone. I called them all. Nobody has seen her since she left school.'

'Which school is that?'

'Mary Croft Primary School on Hopwood Lane.'

'And have you contacted family members to see if she's with any of them?'

Craig nodded. 'She isn't.'

'Linda, what can you tell me about this phone call?' Sian asked.

Linda tried to speak but her emotions wouldn't allow it. Her bottom lip wobbled. When she opened her mouth, she choked and buckled. Craig jumped up and caught her. He towered over his wife and held her firmly against his chest.

Sian looked around the room. Bookshelves were full to bursting with paperbacks, DVDs and ornaments. Picture frames adorned the mantelpiece showing the children in various states of happiness.

Sian turned to Jodie. She decided to leave the matter of the phone call for a moment. 'Jodie, what was Keeley wearing when you last saw her?'

Jodie wiped her left eye with her sleeve. 'She was wearing her school uniform and a yellow jacket over the top. She had a pink backpack with her, too. It was a Frozen one.'

'Is there a chance Keeley may have run away?'

'No,' Jodie answered.

'No she bloody hasn't,' Linda exploded, pulling herself out of her husband's embrace. 'She's been kidnapped. Somebody has taken her.' She wiped her eyes. 'The phone rang. I answered. A man said he'd taken my daughter and wanted fifty thousand pounds. He said he'd call back in twenty-four hours and the line went dead.'

Finn was scribbling frantically in his notebook. 'What time was the call?' He asked without looking up.

Linda looked to Amanda.

'It was a little after four,' she said. 'Maybe ten past.'

'Was it definitely a man's voice?' Sian asked.

'I . . . yes. I think so.'

'You think?'

'It was . . . deep. Low.'

'Did you recognise it?'

'No.'

Sian turned to look at Finn who raised an eyebrow before scribbling back into his notebook.

'You don't believe me, do you?' Linda said. 'Why would I make something like that up?'

'Linda, nobody is doubting you. I'm just trying to get all the facts,' Sian said in as soothing a tone as she could. 'Now, has Keeley ever gone missing before?'

'No she hasn't,' Linda snapped again. 'She has no reason to go missing. Look,' she ran her fingers through her hair, pulling at it hard. 'She hasn't run away. She isn't with friends. She isn't in the habit of just taking off without telling us. She's nine years old for crying out loud. Some sick bastard has taken my daughter now will you do what you're paid to do, and fucking find her,' Linda screamed.

Craig grabbed his wife again and pulled her towards him. 'I think she might need to have a lie down,' he said.

Amanda opened the living room door, and everyone watched as Craig practically carried Linda out of the room. Even Riley had stopped fidgeting and was glaring at his mother.

'Jodie, does your sister have a mobile phone?' Sian asked.

'No. She wants one, but Dad says she's too young.'

'Do you have a recent photo of Keeley we can use?'

'There's the school one above the fireplace, but it was taken earlier this year. She's wearing her uniform in it.'

Sian went over to the mantelpiece and picked up the cheap silver frame. Keeley, wearing her blue cardigan and white polo shirt was beaming to the camera. Her wavy blonde hair was tied back in a neat ponytail. Her complexion was smooth and clear, her eyes a brilliant blue. Sian found herself smiling slightly as she gazed into the little girl's eyes.

'She wouldn't run away,' Jodie said. Her voice was broken as she tried to act the grown-up in the absence of her parents. 'Things aren't easy around here with Riley. We all muck in and help. She wouldn't do anything to add more worry.'

Sian looked down at Riley then back at Jodie. She nodded. 'I understand. We will find her, Jodie.'

The door opened and Craig sheepishly entered the living room. 'I'm so sorry about that.'

'There's no need to apologise,' Sian said. 'This is an extraordinary situation you're in. Now, I'm going to go back to the station, and we'll formulate a plan to find Keeley. However, if she has been kidnapped, it's just possible they may be watching the house. I'm going to have a Family Liaison Officer come out and spend the night here in case they make contact and to answer any questions you may have. I'm going to take this photo of Keeley,' Sian said, showing the framed picture. 'But I'll make sure you get it back. Now, Craig, I need you to sign this giving your consent for us to contact your local GP, dentist and Keeley's school. This is purely to help us gather as much information as we can to find Keeley. It also gives us consent to pass on information about Keeley to relevant media organisations should we need to put out a missing persons alert.'

She handed him the form and her pen. He scribbled where shown and handed it back.

'You will find her, won't you?' He asked, his voice level.

'We will absolutely do everything possible. I promise you,' she said, looking directly into his eyes.

Sian nodded to Finn and they left the living room. It wasn't until they were outside the house that they both visibly relaxed.

'Oh my God,' Finn said as they made their way to the car. 'That poor family. Do you know what it reminded me of?'

'I know what you're going to say and I'd rather you didn't,' she said as she climbed in behind the wheel.

'Do you think it's possible it's the same people?' Finn asked, putting on his seatbelt.

Sian sat in silence and thought for a while. 'Nobody knows what happened to Carl Meagan. We don't know if he's dead or alive. However, the kidnappers didn't get their ransom money. From their point of view, it was a failed kidnapping.'

'Maybe they've learned from their mistakes and are having another go.'

'Shit. I need to talk to Matilda before this gets out.'

Chapter 3

Detective Chief Inspector Matilda Darke had sneaked out of the police station and driven home. She turned from the smooth tarmacked road and down the bone-shaking dirt track that led to the former farmhouse. Daniel Harbison's dirty Ford van was already parked outside. She smiled as soon as she saw him and hoped she didn't make a pillock of herself as she tried to park the Range Rover in such a tight space. This was her second four-wheel drive in less than a year and she still couldn't get used to how much bigger it was than the Fiats she had previously driven.

'You're all done then?' She asked as she climbed down from the car.

'Yep. All done and dusted.' He held out his hand with a bunch of shiny new keys in his palm.

Daniel Harbison was an old friend of her husband's. They'd worked together as architects many times over the years, collaborating on projects and running ideas past each other. Following his death, Matilda had felt a change of house was needed in order to try to get on with picking up the pieces of her life. She'd fallen in love with the ramshackle farmhouse the second she stumbled upon it. It needed a great deal of work to make it habitable and Daniel was the first name that had come to mind.

Adjacent to the house was a building used as a double garage. Matilda was happy to leave it as it was. However, Daniel was itching to get his hands on it. The roof, although in urgent need of replacing, was structurally sound, and had enough space to turn it into a self-contained flat. Matilda was against the idea. The thought of having a tenant, especially one so close, was the antithesis of moving here in the first place. Daniel had told her, many times, that it would add thousands to the asking price, should she wish to sell in the future. She'd make a fortune. Eventually, she relented and gave him free reign to do whatever he wanted with it. His face had lit up like a five-year-old on Christmas morning. Now, after seven months, it was complete.

During his time at Matilda's house, showing her plans, asking her to approve materials and costs, they had grown closer. They had been out to dinner on a few occasions and he'd spent the night once when his van wouldn't start – in the spare room, of course. They'd shared a couple of kisses and although nothing had been said, there was an underlying agreement that things were moving, incredibly slowly, in the direction of them becoming a couple.

Matilda's husband, James, had died from a brain tumour in 2015. He was the love of her life and she missed him every day. She had no intention of marrying again, and there wasn't a single man on God's earth who could come close to replacing him.

Daniel had been divorced for five years. His wife packed a bag and left one day without warning. He'd returned home from work to find a note on the kitchen table telling him she was incredibly unhappy, and she was leaving in order to find herself. He didn't hear another word from her until nine months later when he received the divorce papers through the post. By that point, he was over her disappearance. He signed them without giving it another moment's thought.

'Would madam like to take a look around her charge?'

'My charge?' She smiled.

'Surely you're going to rent it out.'

'I told you, I have no desire to be a landlady.'

'You'll change your mind once you've seen what I've done with it. It'll be criminal to leave it empty.' There was a twinkle in his eye.

Matilda couldn't help but smile at his enthusiasm. He led the way to the double garage with Matilda following. As she looked at the ornate brick work and newly tiled roof, she had to admit he'd done an amazing job.

Daniel was two years younger than Matilda at forty-two years old. He was six foot three, broad shouldered and built like a rugby player. He was solid and it was all muscle. He didn't only design the buildings, he took a hands-on approach too and helped with the construction. He liked nothing more than getting his hands dirty on site.

He unlocked the oak door at the side of the building. They stepped in and Matilda inhaled the newness of freshly laid carpets and wood.

They were faced with a solid oak staircase with hand-carved spindles and newel post.

'I've stolen some of the garage space to make a small utility room behind the stairs. You don't need to see in there unless you have a fetish for boilers.'

'I think I can by-pass that room.'

'Up we go then.'

Daniel led the way. Matilda followed and had to bite her lip to stop her from thinking lewd thoughts when her eyeline landed on Daniel's firm bum tightly wrapped in a pair of torn, dirty jeans.

The kitchen was larger than she had expected. An oak work top and matching cupboard fronts. A fitted fridge and cooker. A small hallway led to a cosy living room and through there, another small hallway led to two bedrooms, one master, one box room, and a compact bathroom. It had all the mod cons. Every space was utilised perfectly.

'Daniel, I'm speechless,' Matilda said, staring in awe.

'It was a toss-up between fitted wardrobes in the master bedroom or a small en suite. I decided on the wardrobes.'

'Good choice.'

'You've got skylights, drop lights, sockets with USB ports, solar panels on the roof and the glass in the skylights is self-cleaning. I know the rooms aren't huge, but I've added some fun details here and there for it to stand out above the norm, and those views are stunning.'

'You've enjoyed spending my money, haven't you?' She smiled.

'I really have. So, what are you going to do with the place?'

'I have absolutely no idea.'

'You could put it on Airbnb. With those views, people will be queuing up to spend a weekend here.'

'And have complete strangers not ten yards from my bedroom? I don't think so.'

'Put an advert in the quality press then? I'm sure a junior doctor or a young lawyer would love to live in here.'

She thought for a moment. 'I'll think about it.'

'Good. Well, I think we should celebrate, and I just so happen to have a bottle of champagne in my van.'

'How convenient.'

'Would you like to do the honours?'

'What do you want me to do? Smash it over the front door like I'm launching a ship?'

'And waste all that lovely alcohol?' He stopped at the top of the stairs and turned to Matilda. 'I was thinking, how about I cook for us tonight?'

'Really?' Matilda's eyes widened. As much as she liked Daniel, she couldn't get used to having a man in her life again, even if the situation between them was so casual it was almost comatose.

'Yes. Nothing fancy, obviously, just a nice, light meal.'

He smiled and Matilda found herself unable to resist. His smile was infectious; it lit up his face and made his eyes sparkle.

'I'd like that.'

'Good. Erm . . .'

'Yes.'

'Would it . . . you know, I mean, would you mind . . .' he looked at his shoes, his face reddened in embarrassment as he spluttered. 'I'd like . . . if you don't mind that is . . .'

'Daniel, do you want to kiss me?' Matilda asked. Her mouth dried as she felt her heart thumping loudly in her chest.

He looked up at her. 'I would. Yes. Only if you want to.'

She took a tentative step forward and stretched her neck up, tilting her head until she was level with him.

He placed his hands on her arms and held her firmly. She felt a trickle of electricity run through her. He kissed her. His stubble pressed against her face. It was soft, gently passionate and awkward.

She felt a vibration in her pocket and pulled back.

'Something wrong?' he asked, a look of panic on his face.

'No. My phone's vibrating.'

'Oh,' he smiled.

She looked at the display and saw her colleague, DS Sian Mills was calling. Her pleasant evening with a handsome architect was ruined.

Chapter 4

2015 had not been a good year for Matilda Darke, profession-
ally or personally. Once James had been diagnosed with a
brain tumour, it had been a fast downward spiral. It wasn't long
before they were told his cancer was terminal and he had only
a few months left to live.

Matilda decided to keep the news to herself. She didn't want
sympathy from her colleagues, offers to make her a casserole, or
a bunch of flowers to cheer her up. Her sole task was to cherish
the little time she and James had together, and at work, that
meant acting as if everything was absolutely fine.

In the days before his death, seven-year-old Carl Meagan had
been kidnapped from his home in Dore. His parents were away
for the night in Leeds and he was being looked after by his
maternal grandmother who was murdered by the kidnappers
before they took Carl from his bed. The Meagans received a
ransom demand for two hundred and fifty thousand pounds.
As owners of a chain of successful organic restaurants throughout
South Yorkshire, they were able to collect the money together
and a date was fixed for the drop.

On the day of the trade, James Darke succumbed to his tumour
and died in hospital with Matilda by his side. She told nobody
and went to work in the afternoon as planned. Evening came,

and she set off alone to Graves Park with a heavy bag full of money on the front passenger seat.

Looking back, she should have told her boss what was happening in her personal life. She should have taken compassionate leave and handed the case over to someone else. Her mind hadn't been on the job and she had been in no fit state to work. Her eyes were blurred with tears as she drove through the dark streets of Sheffield and she headed for the car park, waiting for the call from the kidnappers. Unfortunately, she was in the wrong car park.

The kidnappers panicked and fled, taking Carl with them. Almost three years later, and neither Carl nor the kidnappers had been heard from since.

Carl would be eleven-years-old now and his mother refused to give up hope that one day he would be found. Matilda tried to continue, but it wasn't easy. She was a changed woman and she believed she had Carl Meagan's blood on her hands. There was no doubt in her mind that he was dead, that she'd failed the Meagan family. She would make sure it never happened again.

Following the phone call with Sian, Daniel realised tonight was not the night their relationship was going to take a leap in the right direction. He told Matilda to ring him and he left with the unopened bottle of champagne on the front passenger seat.

Matilda watched him go. She felt nothing for the ruined evening. There was only one thing on her mind – a child had been kidnapped for ransom. There was no way she could mess this case up. She'd let Carl slip through her fingers. She would stop at nothing to rescue a second child. Waiting for Sian to arrive was the longest twenty minutes Matilda had endured. Her mind went into overdrive as it came up with all kinds of scenarios based on the scant information her DS had given her. *A child has been kidnapped*. That was all Matilda needed to hear for the memories to come flooding back, to remove the hard work she had done over the past three years to restore her mental health. *A child has been kidnapped*. Who'd taken her? Why? What did they want? Was she already dead? Was Carl dead?

'Jesus Christ,' she said to herself as she bit down on her lip to stave off the tears. She wanted to cry. She wanted to scream. It was selfish of her to think this, but why was this happening to her again, just as she was getting her life settled. Finally.

A child has been kidnapped.

'FUCK!' Matilda screamed loudly. The expletive resounded off the walls.

The doorbell rang and she ran to the solid door and pulled it open. Sian was standing there. Her face was ashen.

'Are you all right?' Sian asked.

'No,' Matilda replied honestly. 'Come on in. The kettle's not long since boiled.'

Sian placed her bag on the oak table and pulled out the form she had filled in while at the Armitage house. Matilda told her to help herself to whatever she wanted in the fridge while she tore through the report.

Matilda looked at the photo. 'Blonde hair and blue eyes. Just like Carl.'

'That's what I thought too. Even Finn put two and two together.'

'Tell me about the Armitages,' Matilda said, pulling out a chair and sitting down.

'Well, they're a complete contrast to the Meagans. For a start, they don't live in a big house. They don't own restaurants and I doubt they've got fifty grand in the bank.'

'So why target them?'

'You tell me,' she shrugged. 'I didn't go into any details with them – the mother was practically hysterical; understandable, really – but they have a young son, Riley. He's severely disabled by the looks of him. I'm guessing any bit of money they have gets spent on caring for him.'

'So, they're not rich, and don't seem to have a lot of money?'

'No. The ransom makes no sense at all.'

'Have you contacted the phone company and checked that a call was definitely made?' Matilda asked.

'Yes. Finn did that. He emailed me when I was on the way over here. A call was made to the house at seven minutes past four. It lasted less than a minute.'

Matilda frowned. 'If you're going to kidnap someone for ransom, you target someone who has plenty of money.'

'Maybe the kidnapper knows something we don't.'

'But if you had money stashed away and had a severely disabled child, you'd be spending it on them to give them a better life, wouldn't you?'

'That's what I'd do.'

'Precisely. Like you said, either the kidnapper knows something about the family we don't, or, it's a hoax.'

'A hoax? Why would someone claim to have kidnapped a child when they haven't?'

Matilda returned to biting her bottom lip. Her eyes darted left and right as she tried to think. 'To cover up another crime, perhaps?'

Sian was about to take a sip of ice-cold water when she stopped, the glass touching her lips. 'Such as?'

Matilda looked away.

'Keeley already being dead?' Sian asked.

'It's possible.'

'What are the alternatives?'

'Children are usually kidnapped by a parent if the parents are divorced or a family member, for some deep-seated reason. If it's for ransom then the family are usually well off. If that's not the case here, and, as you say, it isn't, then someone is playing a very dangerous game.'

'Does that make our job easier or harder?'

Matilda ignored Sian's question. She went over to the window and looked out at the expansive garden, but she wasn't looking at the view. She was thinking of this poor girl. She was thinking of Carl Meagan, and she was thinking of herself. If Keeley was dead, then it had happened before the police had even become involved. Nothing they could do would bring her back to the family. She couldn't be blamed like she was blamed for Carl's disappearance.

She closed her eyes softly and shook her head, hating herself for thinking of her own reputation. Keeley may already be dead, but if that was the case, her murderer was out there and needed catching and Matilda would move heaven and earth to catch the sick bastard.

Chapter 5

The role of the Family Liaison Officer is that of an investigator. They gather evidence and information from the family to contribute to the investigation. It is important for the FLO to gain the trust and confidence of the family members who are their main source of support during such a difficult time.

Detective Constable Ellen Devonport was ideal for this role. An experienced and well-respected DC, she had taken further training in order to make her invaluable to South Yorkshire Police. Whenever an FLO was needed, she wanted her name to be the first mentioned by the senior investigating officer.

Sian had given her the basics of the Armitage kidnapping. It was imperative she was circumspect upon her arrival in case whoever was holding Keeley was watching the house. On her approach to the house, she pulled over in her battered Fiat Punto, and made a call to Craig's mobile, telling him who she was and to act like he knew her personally when she knocked on the door. She parked outside the house and headed up the garden path, taking long strides, and looking determined. She had purposely dressed down for the occasion. Ellen usually took pride in her appearance, always smartly dressed, enough make-up to look professional yet accentuate her best features, with her chocolate brown wavy hair glossy and shiny and bouncing with every step. For this occasion, she'd dressed in comfortable jeans, a baggy sweater and an old pair of Converse trainers. She'd tied her hair back into a loose ponytail and had a black rucksack that had seen better days over one shoulder.

She knocked on the door and stood back. It was opened almost straight away by a tired looking Craig Armitage.

'Craig, how are you? I've just heard. I thought you could do with a friendly face,' she said. She walked past him into the house and waited until he closed the door before she dropped the character.

'Good evening, Mr Armitage,' she held out a hand for him to shake and was surprised by how light his touch was. 'I'm DC Devonport. Ellen. I'm the Family Liaison Officer. How are you all doing?' Her accent was soft Geordie, friendly and light.

She turned around at the sound of a cough coming from the kitchen and saw Jodie standing in the doorway with her arms folded. Her eyes were red from crying.

Once Ellen had explained what her purpose was for being here, Craig and Jodie went their separate ways. Linda was in no fit state to talk. She had cried herself to sleep. Craig was keeping a constant vigil, while Jodie was taking care of Riley in his bedroom. Ellen went to join her.

'I'm guessing he likes penguins,' Ellen said, noticing the all the stuffed penguins and pictures of them on the walls.

'Yes,' Jodie replied as she changed his nappy. '*Pingu* is the only programme he seems to respond to. We're not sure why. When it's on, there's a change in his facial expression. It's like he's genuinely happy.'

'It must be difficult for you all.'

'Not really. Mum and Dad told us to think of it like we have a baby who won't grow up. He'll get bigger, obviously

– he's quite heavy now – but we have to feed him, change him, clothe him, bathe him, and we'll keep doing that for the rest of his life.' She turned to look at her for the first time. 'Our lives, too.'

Once she'd changed the nappy, Jodie dressed him in pyjamas. She struggled with the trousers as Riley kicked his legs, but she took control and he was soon ready for bed. She placed him in the specially equipped bed, put mittens on both hands so he wouldn't hurt himself during the night, and lifted the bars so he wouldn't roll out. She flicked a switch on the wall which turned on the soothing colour-changing light and left the room. Ellen followed.

'Does he sleep through the night?'

'No. He'll wake up three or four times, sometimes more. He'll scream and wail for hours. I sometimes think he's trying to talk to us, to tell us something but we're not able to understand him.' She headed for the living room and slumped down on the sofa. When she looked up, she had tears in her eyes. 'What are you doing to find Keeley?' She asked.

Ellen sat on the armchair opposite. 'At the moment, our primary concern is waiting for the kidnappers to make another call and give your parents more information.'

'What if they don't?'

'They will. They've asked for money. They've given your parents twenty-four hours to get it. They'll call back and arrange the exchange.'

'We don't have fifty thousand pounds,' she said, wiping her eyes with her sleeves. 'Every extra pound we get is spent on Riley. Dad has two jobs just to keep our heads above water.'

Ellen noticed how mature Jodie seemed for her age. She was fourteen years old, but acted and spoke like a woman double her age. She had a great deal to contend with at home; when did she had time to act like a normal teenager?

'Leave that to us to sort out. DCI Darke and her team know exactly what they're doing.'

'I just keep thinking that we're never going to see her again. That she's going to disappear like Carl Meagan did.'

'What happened to Carl was an extremely rare occurrence, Jodie.' Ellen leaned forward on her chair. 'There are still people looking for him. I'm very confident we'll bring Keeley home.' She smiled, hoping one would be returned. It wasn't.

Jodie was about to say something when a scream was heard from Riley's bedroom. She rolled her eyes, got up off the sofa, and dragged herself to his bedroom.

Ellen didn't follow this time. She sat back and looked around the living room. Framed photographs on the wall showed the family in happier times at the beach, in parks, on rides. They were all smiles for the camera, but the smiles didn't reach the eyes on any of them. The eyes told a different story. They'd gone to the beach for a fun day out as a whole family, but there was an underlying sense of something darker. Linda's smile looked painted on; Craig's looked painful. Jodie's was the usual glare of a sullen teenager while Keeley's was one of rote. Riley's stare was emotionless and distant. Even when they were all together, enjoying the sun, they were not a happy family. Why was that?

Chapter 6

Sally Meagan couldn't sleep. In the years since her only child had been missing, she had reached the very pits of despair, drowned herself in alcohol, contemplated ending her own life, anything to end the pain she was feeling that she'd failed her son in the one task a mother has – to protect her child at all costs.

She'd written a book about her experience of a missing persons investigation and the anxiety of not knowing where her child was or what had happened to him. She'd hoped it would be cathartic, to release all the pent-up emotions she was going through. It hadn't worked. The book had sold well in England, and around the world. Carl's picture was everywhere; surely someone knew where he was. All the book seemed to do was bring out the attention seekers, the so-called psychics, and the weirdos. Once again, Sally had hit rock bottom.

Earlier this year, she had received a series of phone calls from a child saying he was Carl and wanted to come home. They had, briefly, given her a glimmer of hope, but they stopped as soon as they had started. Were they really from Carl? At the time she'd thought so, but, looking back, the voice hadn't been at all like Carl's. Once again, it was some sicko looking for a laugh. As much as she relied on the public to help her find her son, with each passing day she loathed them more and more.

Help had come from an unlikely source. Matilda Darke. The very woman who had screwed up the ransom drop and allowed her son to disappear from the face of the earth had offered words of comfort, and an ally in the form of retired detective Pat Campbell. Between the three of them, they spent their spare time formulating ideas, plans, features, anything to keep Carl in people's minds in the hope of finding him and bringing him home.

There had been many reported sightings of him in Sweden. Sally wanted to fly out there, scour the country for him, but Pat and Matilda, and her husband Philip, were against the idea. Carl was a blond-haired, blue-eyed boy. He fitted the Swedish make-up. It would be a futile journey and would do nothing for Sally's already fragile mental health.

Philip was the stronger of the two. He always had been. He coped with the loss of his son by diving into work. Philip was always behind the scenes, creating menus with the chefs, keeping the books in order and making sure they had the best suppliers, while Sally was front of house. She kept the staff in line, ensured the restaurants were clean and tidy and the customers happy. After Carl's disappearance, she lost interest and stayed at home, waiting for the phone call that would tell her Carl had been found, or an email with a clear image of her son, a few years older, but perfectly healthy and in the hands of officials who were bringing him home. Days went by, then months, then years, and the call didn't come. Sally realised she would have to move on. She could not spend the rest of her life looking for one child in a world of seven billion.

She flung back the duvet and swung her legs out of bed. It was a little after two o'clock and she hadn't been to sleep yet. She'd finished reading the David Nicholls book she'd enjoyed but wasn't in the mood to start another. She put on her dressing gown in the dark and headed out of the room. There was no need to tip-toe; after a long day at work Philip could be in the paddock of a Formula One track and he'd still nod off.

The bedroom door was always ajar. Woody, their golden Labrador, bought for Carl as a birthday present, slept on the floor in their bedroom. However, the next morning, they'd find him outside Carl's room, curled up. He missed him immensely and hadn't barked once since his best friend had gone.

As Sally left her room and headed for the stairs, there he was on the floor, keeping guard.

He opened his eyes and lifted his head at the sound of movement.

'Hello Woody, can't you sleep either?' Sally said in a loud whisper. She bent down and scratched behind his ear. 'I'm going for a cup of tea. Would you like a Bonio?'

He seemed to understand the B-word as he jumped up and trotted downstairs, tail wagging.

In the kitchen, Sally turned the light on above the oven to give the room a warm glow and flicked on the kettle. From the small cupboard next to the fridge, she took out a Bonio. Woody sat, gave her a paw without having to be asked, took it gently from her, and ran to his bed in the corner of the room. The sound of his teeth demolishing the biscuit filled the silence.

Sally had left her phone plugged in to charge in the kitchen. She unplugged it and began to scroll through the news stories on the BBC News app. There was nothing of great interest. She logged on to Facebook. Her heart sank at the lack of notifications. This was the third day in a row without some form of communication about a sighting of Carl, or even a well-wisher saying she was in their prayers. People were forgetting all about him. She opened the Twitter app and saw that Sheffield was trending. That rarely happened.

> **@JoArm**: *My 9yo sister was kidnapped this afternoon around 4pm. We've had a ransom demand. If anyone knows anything, tell us. We love her. We miss her.* **#FindKeeley #Sheffield**

> **@SusieQT**: *Girl missing in* **#Sheffield** *is Keeley Armitage. My kid is in her class at Mary Croft. Parents in pieces.* **#FindKeeley**

> **@JillRice**: *Girl in* **#Sheffield** *missing since yesterday. Really eerie out there right now.* **#FindKeeley #Sheffield #Stannington**

> **@Blades379**: *Keeley is a lovely girl. Always happy and smiling. Why can't people let kids be kids?* **#FindKeeley #Sheffield**

> **@SheffGirl21**: *I saw Keeleys mum. She was screaming for her in street. Heartbreaking.* **#FindKeeley #Sheffield**

The kettle boiled. Sally ignored it. It was happening again. Another child had been kidnapped in Sheffield. She had no idea what this meant, but suddenly, the hope of finding Carl grew a little stronger.

'Philip,' she said. She looked up, remembered it was dark and the middle of the night. 'Philip!' she shouted and ran out of the room. She took the stairs two at a time, almost falling over Woody who was following, and ploughed into the bedroom.

She turned on the main light and jumped on the bed.

'Philip. Philip.' She shook him hard. 'Wake up.'

He mumbled under the duvet and eventually scrambled his way out of his comfortable cocoon. He opened his eyes and squinted at the brightness.

'What's up? What time is it?'

'It doesn't matter what time is it. Look at this,' she showed him the phone.

'Hang on. I can't see a thing.' He took his time sitting up and picked up his glasses from the bedside table. He noticed the time on the alarm clock. 'Sally, it's not even half two yet.'

'I know.'

'Have you even been to sleep?'

'No. Look, Philip, please, just look at this,' she said, annoyed.

He scrolled through the phone, reading the postings on Twitter while Sally provided him with a running commentary.

'A nine-year-old girl has been kidnapped in Stannington. Her sister has been posting on Twitter asking if anyone's seen her. She's put up pictures of her too. The family have been asked for a ransom. She hasn't said how much, though.'

'So?' Philip said, looking up at his wife.

'Don't you see what this means?'

'No.'

'Philip, how many people get kidnapped for ransom in this country?'

'I've no idea.'

'Not very many. Yet here we are, in Sheffield, and we have the second kidnap for ransom in four years. That's not a coincidence.'

'You don't seriously think that the same people who took Carl have taken this . . . what's she called . . .?'

'Keeley. Keeley Armitage, and yes, I do.' Her face had lit up.

'But . . . why?'

'I don't know. But don't you see, this is fresh evidence. If the police find Keeley, they'll find Carl.'

'You don't know that.'

'I do.'

'Sally, please, don't get your hopes up.'

'It's too late for that,' she said, jumping down off the bed.

'Where are you going?'

'To phone Matilda. She's bound to be working on this.'

'You're not phoning her at this time of night.'

'Oh. No, you're right. She'll need her sleep so she's fully alert. I'll wait until morning.'

'No,' he said firmly.

'What?'

'Matilda is going to have her hands full. If you have to call anyone, ring Pat. Let her deal with this.'

Sally thought about this for a moment. 'Fine. You're right. Pat will be able to get to Matilda much sooner than I can.'

'Good. Now, come on, get back to bed.'

Reluctantly, Sally placed her phone on the bedside table and got into bed.

'Philip, just think, we could have Carl home in a few days.'

Chapter 7

Ellen Devonport was struggling to get comfortable on the sofa bed in the living room. She was used to a king-size bed, a memory-foam mattress and a hunky paramedic to snuggle up to. A rickety aluminium frame that squeaked every time she turned over and a mattress the thickness of a cream cracker was not ideal for a good night's sleep. It didn't help that she could hear Riley wailing in the next room.

She wondered why nobody got up to tend to him, or were they supposed to leave him in the hope he'd tire himself out and fall asleep? She turned over, put the thin pillow over her head and closed her eyes. It was going to be a long night.

A noise woke her up. She wasn't fully asleep, but the sound of a door opening and closing made her sit up. She looked at the time on her phone: it was a little after three o'clock. She sat in silence and listened intently. Riley had fallen asleep. But there was something else, too. Somebody was moving around downstairs.

It was only natural that the family wouldn't be able to sleep. They'd be worried sick about where Keeley was, what had happened to her, and who had taken her. Maybe Linda or Craig had got up to make a drink. They might appreciate a stranger to talk to, a friendly shoulder to cry on.

Ellen pushed back the duvet. She felt the cool night on her

bare legs. She pulled on a pair of tracksuit bottoms and slipped her feet into the slippers she'd brought with her. She put a sweater on over her T-shirt and crept out of the room.

The kitchen was in darkness. She didn't turn on the light and tried not to make a sound. She hoped Riley was a heavy sleeper and didn't want to wake him up in case he didn't go back to sleep and spent the next few hours crying out.

The dining room and kitchen had once been two separate rooms but had clearly been remodelled to accommodate Riley and his wheelchair. The sound of whoever was up was coming from around the dining area. Ellen carefully walked through the kitchen and flicked on the light.

Linda jumped. 'Jesus, you scared the shit out of me,' she said in a loud whisper. She was bent over the dresser, rummaging through the drawers.

'I'm sorry. I heard movement. I thought someone might be up and want to talk.'

'No. I'm fine,' she said, turning back to the open drawers.

'What are you doing?'

'Just looking for something.'

'Can I help?'

'No.'

'Would you like me to make you a cup of tea?'

'No. Ah, here it is.' She pulled a folder out of the drawer and sat down at the dining table. 'Can you pass me a pad and pen from the top drawer in the kitchen? It's the drawer under the kettle.'

Ellen obliged. 'What are you doing?'

'I'm wondering how we can raise the fifty thousand pounds for the kidnappers. We've got three thousand in the holiday account and just under four thousand in a savings account.

Craig did a sponsored run a few weeks ago. He raised over a grand. That's about eight thousand.' Linda's eyes were wide and staring. She wrote quickly on the pad with a shaking hand. She was frantically flicking through the folder of bank statements. 'There's two grand in the current account, that's ten. See, it is doable.'

Ellen pulled out a chair and sat down. 'Linda, stop. You need to go to bed and get some sleep.'

'I can't sleep. I need to be doing something,' she tucked her greasy hair behind her ears. 'We could sell something.' She looked at her hand. 'Craig's grandmother gave him this wedding ring to give me. It's an antique. What do you think it's worth?' She held out her hand to Ellen. 'Do you know much about jewellery?'

'Erm, no. Perhaps I should go and get Craig.'

'It's got to be worth a couple of thousand, at least,' she said, ignoring Ellen. 'I'll put down fifteen hundred to be on the safe side and anything extra is a bonus.'

Ellen got up from the table and edged out of the dining room.

'Now, what else have I got? My mum gave me a necklace for my twenty-first. It's not old but it's real gold. We might get a couple of hundred for it. Where are those premium bond certificates?' She said, pulling sheets of paper out of the folder and scattering them around the table.

'Linda, what are you doing?' Craig asked. He stood in the entrance to the dining room wearing a black T-shirt with a tatty dressing gown hanging off his shoulders.

'Craig, how new is your van? What do you think you'd get for it in a quick sale?'

'Linda, I need that van for work.'

'We need the money to get Keeley back.'

He pulled out a chair and sat down next to Linda. He took her hand. 'Linda, listen to me, we don't have that amount of money.'

'We have things to sell?'

'Not fifty grand's worth of stuff.'

'We can empty the bank accounts, cash in the premium bonds and the life insurance policies. I'll phone our Adam in Dublin; he'll lend us some money. We can easily raise fifteen, maybe even twenty grand that way.'

'And where are we going to get the other thirty?'

Her eyes darted rapidly from side to side as she thought. 'I don't know. Maybe we can get a loan from the bank, or a second mortgage on this place. Maybe we can release some equity.' She reached out and grabbed for Craig, pulling on his sleeves.

'There's no equity left in this place. We released all we could when we did the alterations.'

'Aren't there some companies who buy your house and rent it back to you? I know we won't get anywhere near the market value, but it'll be more than fifty thousand.'

'Linda don't do this,' Craig said softly.

'We need her back, Craig,' she said urgently. 'I don't care how we do it, but we're getting her back.'

'We advise people not to pay ransom demands,' Ellen said, stepping forward. 'If you pay and they disappear with the money, they'll do it again, and who knows how much further they'll take it next time. Kidnapping is a form of terrorism and we don't negotiate or give in to terrorist's demands.'

'So why are you even here then?' Linda shouted, jumping up from her seat. 'What's the fucking point of you if when the kidnappers call we tell them to stuff their money and hang up? You're supposed to be on our side and if we can get the fifty grand we'll pay it.'

'Linda, calm down,' Ellen said quietly.

'Calm? Calm? How the fuck do you expect me to be calm?' she exploded. 'My daughter is missing. She's out there, some-where, terrified to death because some pervert's got his hands on her. She's never spent a night away from us before. She'll be scared, frightened, and all you're doing is telling me to calm down and have a fucking cup of tea.'

Ellen opened her mouth to say something, but Linda cut her off.

'Don't tell me what to do,' she screamed. 'Don't tell me how to behave and how to feel. I want my little girl back. I don't care what the police say.' Tears began to stream down her face. She choked on her words.

Craig held his arms out and Linda fell into them.

'I want her back, Craig. We need to do whatever we can to get her back home.'

'I know, sweetheart. We will.'

'Mum?'

Ellen turned around to see Jodie standing in the doorway. Her face was a map of worry. Her eyes full of tears. In a nightie and dressing gown, with her hair a tangled mess, she looked younger than her fourteen years and vulnerable.

'I can't stand not knowing where she is,' Linda cried. 'I can't . . .' Her words were lost to her tears as she fell out of her husband's arms and onto the floor. She opened her mouth and let out a scream so loud and painful the whole neighbourhood must have heard it.

'What do I do?' Craig asked, looking, helplessly to Ellen.

'I think we should call a doctor. She may need sedating.'

'I don't need sedating,' she screamed. 'I just—' She stopped dead.

'What is it?'

Her eyes were darting left and right. It was as if a switch had been flicked inside her brain. 'Nothing,' she said before standing up and heading out of the room. 'I just . . . you're right. Ellen. I'm sorry for snapping. I need to get some sleep. We all do.'

All three watched, open-mouthed, as Linda went from hysterical to calm in record time.

'What just happened?' Craig asked, mystified.

'I've no idea,' Ellen frowned.

'There is a way,' Linda said to herself as she padded back up the stairs. 'They'll let me have the money. They won't want to see someone go through what they went through. They'll be only too happy to help.'

Chapter 8

Tuesday 11th September 2018

Linda tried to stay awake. Ideally, she wanted her husband to fall asleep so she could get up and sneak out of the house. They lay in bed next to each other, not touching, and she listened intently to his breathing, waiting for it to slow and deepen. It didn't, and she fell asleep before Craig did.

When she eventually woke, daylight was creeping behind the curtains and Craig's side of the bed had already been made. She looked at the time on her phone. It was a little after six o'clock.

She threw back the duvet and swung her legs out of bed. The clothes she had been wearing yesterday were littering the floor where she had dropped them after undressing. As silently as possible, she pulled on the jeans and the wrinkled sweater, slipped into a pair of Converse and padded carefully down the stairs.

In the hallway, she could hear Craig and Ellen chatting quietly in the kitchen. How long was she going to be here for? She checked her pocket for keys, mobile phone and her purse, then headed for the front door. Once she was at the end of the road and out of sight of the house, she'd call for a taxi.

* * *

Sally Meagan ate her muesli and drank her black coffee under the watchful eye of her golden Labrador. He knew that as soon as she was finished, she'd fetch his lead, put on her walking shoes, and they'd head out for half an hour or so. He patiently sat by her side, ears alert, eyes wide, waiting. Waiting.

The moment Sally stepped down from the stool at the breakfast table, Woody jumped up and followed her out of the room, tail wagging, tongue lolling and as excited as a child in a chocolate factory.

As usual when Sally left the house, she locked the door, looked up to the concealed camera above the entrance, and headed for the gates at the bottom of the drive. The Meagans were very security conscious and following Carl's kidnapping they'd surrounded the property with a high wall and cameras. She entered the code on the keypad that only she and Philip knew and waited until the gates were closed behind her before setting off on her walk.

Woody was a well-behaved dog. He missed Carl so much, but he had adapted to Sally being his primary carer, his replacement owner, and he listened to her commands as she kept him on a short lead, and they walked down the quiet, narrow pavement.

It had been a long, hot summer, but as soon as August dissolved into September, it seemed that nature had decided to be begin autumn straight away. It was noticeably cooler in the area and the leaves had lost their shine. They were already beginning to die. It wouldn't be long before they turned brown and dropped off. Sally loved the autumn; the colours, the crisp, cool smell in the air, the nights drawing in, fewer people out and about smiling and enjoying themselves. People tended to stay indoors as the weather turned. There was a sense that life was on pause until next spring.

'Mrs Meagan?'

Sally jumped at the sound of her name. She turned around and saw a woman a few feet behind her in jeans and a sweater. Her hair was pulled back into a loose ponytail. She wore no make-up and looked unwashed and shattered, as if sleep had eluded her for weeks. She looked haunted, frightened.

Sally didn't say anything. She had no idea who this woman was, but she obviously knew her. Woody, placid and playful, would, hopefully, come to her aid if needed.

The woman stepped forward.

'I'm sorry to confront you like this. I hate myself for coming to see you, but I have nowhere else to go and I'm desperate.'

'I'm sorry, I don't think . . .'

'Please,' she interrupted, again, taking another step forward. 'Please, let me say what I've got to say, or I'll never say it. I'm Linda Armitage. My nine-year-old daughter was kidnapped yesterday. The kidnappers called and said they want fifty thousand pounds. We don't have that kind of money. We don't have anywhere near that amount. I spent most of the night making a list of what we could sell, but I only totalled it up to around twenty thousand, if that. I need my daughter back,' she said, wiping away tears. 'I'm not asking you to give me the money, but I was hoping you'd lend it to me. I'll pay you back, a little each month, with interest. I don't know who else to turn to.'

Linda was desperate, that much was obvious. Her rambling, her tears, her knotting her fingers together were all signs of a woman on the edge.

'I read about your daughter on Twitter last night. I'm terribly sorry for what you're going through.' Linda proffered a weak smile. 'If there was anything I could do, I would.'

'You could let me have the money,' she said, holding out her hand as if Sally had fifty grand in her back pocket instead of a roll of poop sacks.

'I don't have it.'

'The kidnappers wanted two hundred and fifty thousand for your Carl. You had that in a bag for the ransom drop. I've read the book.' Linda's face turned red with rage.

'I know. We did that against the police's advice. They told us not to pay the ransom. Kidnapping for ransom is a form of terrorism and the police don't give in to terrorist demands. We went against their will and look how that turned out for us. We lost Carl.'

A tear rolled down Sally's face and she didn't wipe it away.

'The worst thing you can do is pay the ransom demand.'

'But I need my Keeley back.' She fumbled for her phone, unlocked it and swiped through the menus until she found a photo. She held it out for Sally to see. 'Look how beautiful she is. Look how sweet and innocent she is. Do you have any idea what may be happening to her right now?'

'Yes, I do, because I've thought of the exact same things happening to Carl.'

'I'm begging you, Mrs Meagan, as one mother to another, please, help me.'

'I'm sorry. I can't.'

Sally turned to walk away. She wanted to go back home. The one shred of hope she'd felt last night had been obliterated as the memory returned of walking into her home, seeing her mother dead and her son missing. It never really went away, but it was locked up, deep in the recesses of her mind. Now, the door had been flung wide open, and everything came back.

'We've got your son, Sally. We want two hundred and fifty thousand pounds or we sell him to the highest bidder.'

'We don't have that kind of money.'

'Let's not play these games, Sally. Stop listening to the police and listen to me. Get the money sorted or your pretty little boy ends up in some paedo's basement.'

'You can't?' Linda screamed. 'What do you mean, you can't? I've seen the house you live in. I've read about all the restaurants you have and the number of staff you employ. You seemed to come up with the quarter of a million for your son easily enough, but you won't give me fifty thousand?'

'You need to talk to the police, Mrs Armitage,' Sally said, walking quickly away. 'They will advise you every step of the way. I'm sorry.' The tears were rapidly falling. She wanted Carl back more than anything in the world. She'd sell the house, her jewellery, the restaurants, everything, but she couldn't get caught up in someone else's drama. She wasn't strong enough for that.

Linda didn't give chase. 'You're heartless, do you know that?' She shouted after her. 'You're hurting and in pain because you didn't get your son back, I understand that, but to put other families through the same thing when you're in a position to help makes you one evil bitch.'

'I'm sorry,' she said quietly to herself as she pulled hard on Woody's lead for him to keep up with her. 'I'm sorry. I'm sorry. Please forgive me.'

Chapter 9

Matilda looked at herself in the mirror in the hallway. She was looking old. A sleepless night of tossing and turning, her mind a whirl of missing children and the dark nightmare of what they were going through, had taken its toll. She had black circles beneath her eyes, more wrinkles seemed to have appeared during the hours of darkness, and it didn't matter what she did with her short dark hair it stuck out in random places.

There was a knock on the door. She opened it to see Sian standing on the doorstep, looking in a similar state of distress.

'The more I look at myself in the mirror, the more I see my mother staring back at me,' Matilda said.

'I've given up looking in mirrors. When you've got four kids – five if you count my Stuart – then people expect you to look a mess,' she said with a half-smile. 'You don't look like you've slept much.'

'I haven't.'

'No. Me neither. I had a call from Ellen Devonport about half seven, too.'

'Oh.'

'Linda Armitage sneaked out of the house. She came back, slammed the door behind her and went straight upstairs. She wouldn't talk to anyone.'

Matilda frowned. 'Where had she been?'

'They don't know.'

'How long had she been out?'

'They don't know that either.'

Sian drove with Matilda in the passenger seat, looking at her reflection in the small mirror in the visor.

'You'd think people would prepare you for old age, tell you about the lines on your forehead and crow's feet.'

'You're only forty-f—'

'Don't say the f-word,' Matilda interrupted.

'My Stuart says wrinkles are a sign of a life well lived.'

'Do you believe him?'

'I believed him when he said having four kids would be fun. Silly sod. I also believed him when he said he'd help out if we had a big party for our silver wedding anniversary.'

'How are the preparations going?'

'Slowly. He's full of ideas but he expects me to put them into action.'

'Typical.'

'I'm on the internet all night trying to find someone to make an ice sculpture while he's flicking through Sky. He's about as much use as a condom machine in a monastery.'

'An ice sculpture? Really?'

'I know. Tacky isn't it? I'm trying to put him off the idea.'

They turned off Stannington Road into Acorn Drive and pulled up outside the Armitage House. Craig's dirty Mercedes Sprinter was parked in the driveway.

Sian made to get out of the car while Matilda stayed and stared at the house.

'What's wrong?' Sian asked.

'This doesn't look like the house of someone who has fifty grand to spare,' she said, taking off her seatbelt.

It was still only early, and the pavements were littered with mums and dads taking their children to school. The faces of the parents were drawn and full of worry. It appeared that word had got out about Keeley's disappearance.

Matilda and Sian received strange looks from passers-by as they made their way up the garden path. As much as they tried not to look like detectives, it wasn't easy when everyone was glaring at them. Their job seemed to emanate from them. A few lingered to see how distressed Linda was when she opened the door. They were disappointed when it was Ellen – a face they had never seen before.

'How are they all?' Matilda asked.

'As you'd expect. Craig's decided to stay off work today and Jodie isn't going to school.'

'Good idea,' Sian said.

'Do you know where Linda went yet?'

'No. She won't tell us.'

'Is she still in bed?'

'No. She's in the living room. They all are.'

'Right. I'd better go and introduce myself,' Matilda said.

Outside the living room door, Matilda paused and braced herself. She took a deep breath and knocked lightly before entering.

She was hit immediately by the dense atmosphere. Grim faces turned to look at her. Craig was sitting with Riley on his lap. Jodie was cross-legged in the armchair wearing her pyjamas and dressing gown. Linda was on the sofa, staring into space, her eyes wide and full of tears. It was happening all over again.

'This is DCI Darke,' Ellen said, making the introduction. 'She's going to be leading the investigation into finding Keeley.'

'Darke?' Linda asked. 'As in Matilda Darke?'

'That's right,' Matilda nodded.

'Jesus Chris! We're never going to get our Keeley back,' she sobbed, pulling another tissue out of the box on the coffee table in front of her and wiping her red eyes. The table was littered with crumpled tissues. She stood up and went over to the window.

'Linda!' Craig admonished.

'I mean it. Have you read this?'

From a bookcase behind her packed with paperbacks, Linda picked one from the third shelf and threw it with force at her husband. He batted it away so it wouldn't hit Riley. It landed face up on the sofa. Matilda looked at it and saw the book written by Sally Meagan about her missing son. The smiling face of Carl in happier times looked up at her. Matilda's heart sank. Neither she nor the South Yorkshire Police were painted in the best light. Since the book had been released, tensions between Matilda and Sally had eased slightly. They would never be best friends but there was a mutual respect for each other as they worked together to try and find out what had happened to Carl.

'Yes, I've read it. Not every case can be solved, love, you know that. That doesn't mean to say she can't find our Keeley. I'm sorry,' he said to Matilda.

Matilda gave a pained smile as she shrunk into herself and edged back towards the door.

'Don't apologise for me,' Linda said. 'Can we request another detective?' She asked, looking to Sian.

'Linda,' Ellen began, her voice quivering slightly. 'I can assure you that DCI Darke is the best person to be working on this case. She is the finest detective within South Yorkshire Police, and she will leave no stone unturned in finding your daughter.'

'Then why isn't she then? Why aren't any of you out there

turning over these stones?' She turned to look out of the window. 'Where are the police cars? Where are the helicopters?'

'It's not as simple as that, Mrs Armitage. We need to go through exactly what happened.'

'I explained all this last night. Don't you lot communicate with each other?' she asked. She was visibly shaking, and beads of sweat were forming on her forehead. 'My daughter is missing. She's been taken, kidnapped, and you need to find her.'

'We are doing everything—'

'In our power,' she interrupted. She spoke with pure venom.

'Linda, why don't you come and sit down,' Craig said.

'I don't want to fucking sit down,' she exploded. 'I can't sit around here drinking tea while God knows what's happening to my daughter. If you're not going to do anything, I'll find her myself.' She stormed out of the living room.

'Mum,' Jodie whimpered, tears streaming down her face.

Craig stood up. He handed Riley to Jodie and followed his wife out of the room.

Matilda, Sian, and Ellen stood awkwardly in the living room while voices were raised out in the hallway. Linda was spitting venom and saying harsh words about Matilda. She'd heard them all before, but it still hurt to hear them again.

Craig opened the door and stepped back in on his own. 'She's gone for a lie down,' he said. 'I really am sorry for what she said. She's not usually like this.'

'It's perfectly understandable,' Matilda said, though she would be lying if she said it hadn't hit a raw nerve. Matilda sat on the sofa next to Craig. 'I know you and Linda answered a lot of questions with DS Mills last night, but I'd like to ask some of my own.'

'That's fine,' he nodded. Craig looked shattered. His eyes were barely open and fatigue was evident in the slow way he moved.

'The kidnapping,' Matilda began. 'As I'm sure you're aware, kidnappings don't happen very often in this country. Is there a chance someone could be playing a prank?'

'A prank? No. No. Of course not. Who would do something like that?'

'Ok. Is there anyone you can think of who may have a grudge against you?'

'No,' he replied quickly.

'Have you had any arguments or fights with anyone lately?'

'No.'

'Has anything out of the ordinary happened to any of you recently to bring unwarranted attention?'

'No!' He snapped.

'Have you, or anyone, noticed anyone hanging around the house, any strange phone calls, emails or texts?'

'No. Nothing.'

Matilda adjusted herself on the uncomfortable sofa. It was infuriating the way people lived in their own bubble, unaware of what was happening in the real world. Until something outlandish like a kidnapping happens, the signs of a stranger lurking in the shadows are rarely seen. Why didn't people open their bloody eyes more? 'Craig, do you have the fifty thousand pounds asked by the kidnappers?'

'No, we don't,' he said, running his fingers through his messy hair.

'In cases like this, when someone is kidnapped for ransom, the kidnappers know the family is able to raise that kind of money.' She immediately thought of the Meagans and their lavish lifestyle. 'Can you think of anyone who would think you can get your hands on fifty thousand?'

'No,' he said, getting up from the sofa and going over to the window. He turned back to Matilda. 'Look, we're just a regular, normal family. We're not rich. We don't go on expensive holidays. We don't drive big cars. I'm working two jobs to try and keep us solvent. I work seven days a week to provide for my family. There are times when I don't see my kids for days because I'm out before they get up and I don't come home until they're in bed,' he was struggling to keep hold of his emotions. 'We don't have a spare fifty quid let alone fifty grand.'

'Dad,' Jodie whimpered. She held out her hand and he took it, perching next to her on the armchair.

'We're not rich. We're not famous. We're just an ordinary family trying to survive in this bastard of a world,' he cried.

Matilda looked at Ellen and nodded slightly towards Jodie.

'Jodie, why don't you and I go and feed Riley. It must be past his breakfast time by now.'

'Dad?' She asked, looking at her father with wet eyes.

'It's ok, love, you go and feed your brother.'

Matilda waited until they were all out of the living room before she spoke. Sian had joined her on the sofa.

'Craig, I'm sorry for the questions I'm asking. I'm just trying to find out who would have taken your daughter.'

'It's fine. I know you're only doing your job. It's just . . . I feel so helpless.'

'That's understandable. Craig, where were you when your wife called you yesterday to say Keeley had gone missing?'

'It was Amanda from next door who called me. I was in Chesterfield making a delivery. I've got an app on my phone that will confirm it.'

Quick with an alibi. 'Thank you. I hope you didn't mind me asking.'

'No.'

'Where did your wife go this morning?'

'I don't know. She wouldn't tell me.' Again, he replied too quickly for Matilda's liking.

'Ok. Is Keeley the type of person to go off with a stranger?'

It was a while before Craig answered. 'I'd like to think not. We've told her about the danger of talking to strangers, but, some of these sick bastards are very manipulative, aren't they?'

'I'm afraid so. Are your daughters on any social networking sites?'

'Isn't everyone? Jodie's on the lot, I think. Facebook, Twitter, Pinterest, Instagram, Snapchat. I keep telling her, it's called social media, which means you have to be social and not spend the evenings staring at your tablet.'

Matilda smiled. 'And what about Keeley?'

'She's on Snapchat. Our Jodie got her interested in it. She keeps taking selfies and putting dog ears on them or something. I don't see what all the fuss is about.'

'Me neither,' Sian butted in. 'I've got four kids and they've all tried to get me on Instagram and Twitter. I can't think of anything worse.'

'Have they mentioned being contacted by anyone they didn't know?' Matilda asked Craig.

'Everyone's a stranger on social media. I've told the girls time and time again that they don't know who they're talking to. Their profile picture might be that of a fourteen-year-old girl, but that doesn't mean it's not a fifty-year-old pervert typing the messages. Wait, you don't think Keeley's been contacted through these sites?'

'At this stage, I've no idea. We will need to look at all their activity online.' Matilda leaned forward. 'Craig, I know I'm probably the last person you and your wife want to look for your daughter after the Carl Meagan investigation. However, I am very good at my job and I have an exceptional team of officers around me. We will do everything in our power to find Keeley and bring her home.'

Craig nodded and offered a weak smile. 'Thank you.'

Matilda paused as she studied Craig. His face was a map of angst and worry, and he seemed genuinely distraught at not knowing where his daughter was, but there was something niggling away at Matilda's brain telling her there was something odd in this household. When Carl went missing, there was no doubt in her mind he'd been kidnapped and the request for a ransom was genuine. Here, she couldn't quite work out what was going on. Not yet, anyway.

'We'll need to look at any laptops, computers, tablets and phones that belong to you all.'

'Of course. Take anything you think will help.'

'Thank you. Would it be possible to look around Keeley's bedroom before we go?'

'Sure. Listen, can I ask you a personal question?' Craig asked.

Matilda knew what was coming. She took a deep breath. 'Of course.'

'Why didn't you find Carl Meagan?'

Matilda led the way with Sian following. As they reached the first floor landing, they could hear muffled sobbing coming from one of the bedrooms, obviously Linda. The atmosphere in the house was heavy and was getting darker as each minute ticked by without them knowing where Keeley was.

Keeley's bedroom door was wide open. The carpet was a plush pink and the walls – what could be seen behind the posters of Disney films – were painted a warm pink. This was the bedroom of a typical nine-year-old girl. The single duvet cover was from *Frozen*, showing a beautiful princess and a smiling snowman. There were fairy lights around the headboard, soft toys on the bed, and Disney books on the shelves. Beneath the window was a desk. Her pink tablet was plugged in and charging.

'I thought you answered Craig's questions very well,' Sian said quietly. 'It couldn't have been easy for you.'

'It wasn't. I thought he deserved the truth. I'm sure his eyes glazed over once I started waffling.'

'Mat,' she said, putting her hand on her arm. 'Are you going to be ok leading this investigation? I mean, it's going to bring back memories of Carl, but it'll bring back memories of James, too.'

'It already is. I like to think I'm a stronger person than I was three years ago. However, if I find myself not coping, I'll step down. I promise you.'

Matilda had no intention of stepping down and handing over the case to a lesser detective. In the years since Carl disappeared she'd studied kidnapping cases and read dozens of psychological reports on kidnappers and their motives. If anyone understood why someone stole a child, it was Matilda. It was time to put what she'd read to good use.

It wasn't a large bedroom and due to the amount of stuff Keeley had, it was cluttered, but it was clean and tidy.

In the top drawer of the desk, Sian took out a sketch pad and began to flick through it.

'Wow, she's good,' she said. 'Her attention to detail is amazing for a girl so young. Look at these dresses.'

Matilda joined her at the desk. She looked over her shoulder at the drawings which looked more like something a fashion designer would create rather than a nine-year-old girl.

In the same drawer were packs of coloured pencils, all different shades and grades. She had all the tools needed to sketch her fashions. Matilda pictured her spending hours at this desk, looking out at the sprawling countryside from her window as Sheffield dissolved into Derbyshire, gaining inspiration for her designs.

'She writes stories too. Listen to this: "Princess Keeley was locked in the tower. She spent her days sewing the gowns for her sisters to wear and plaiting their hair. She was sad and lonely and only ate what little food her nasty sisters gave to her through the small gap under the door. At night she looked out of the window. If the moon was full, it lit up the whole kingdom and she could see the big boats on the sea. She often fell asleep leaning against the windowsill as she waited for her prince to rescue her." Oh dear,' Sian said.

'That's very sad,'

'Do you think that's how she feels?'

'It certainly sounds like it. Are there more like that?'

Sian flicked through the pages. 'There are a few other stories. I'll read them back at the station. These drawings are a bit worrying, though.'

'In what way?'

'They're a bit . . . what's the word . . . mature,' Sian said. 'Look at this one.' The picture was of a dress; nobody was wearing it, but it was very low cut, the breasts were full and the split up the side was very revealing.

Matilda took the pad from her and studied the pictures. 'A nine-year-old really shouldn't be drawing clothes that reveal so much flesh. I mean, who is she designing these for? Is she picturing herself as having huge breasts?'

'I'm not sure. Mind you, have you seen some of those Disney films? The animators certainly pay a lot of attention to putting the curves in all the right places,' Sian said. 'She's probably only drawing what she's watching on TV.'

'She shouldn't be sexualising herself at this age.'

'Unless someone was telling her to.'

They both looked at the tablet in the centre of the desk.

Craig was waiting for them at the bottom of the stairs.

'Craig, does only Keeley have access to this tablet?' Matilda asked in the hallway downstairs. She held up the tablet.

'Yes. Well, it's hers. We keep an eye on her while she's using it.'

'Does she use any other device in the house?'

'No.'

'We're going to take this with us to go through, analyse social media, see who she was talking to. We're also taking her story book too. She may have written something that could be useful. Sian's writing you out a receipt.'

He nodded, biting his lower lip.

'What do we do if the kidnapper calls before the twenty-four hours?'

'He won't, but we're setting up a tap on your phone line. If there is anything you think of that might help in finding Keeley, please mention it to Ellen.'

'Thank you,' he said. He held out his hand for Matilda to shake.

She looked down at the large hand and placed hers inside his. His large fingers wrapped tightly around hers.

'I know you'll find her,' he said, looking at her with wet eyes.

Matilda couldn't reply. She nodded, removed her hand and headed for the hallway. She pulled open the front door and almost fell out. She inhaled deep breaths and slowly breathed out. It had been years since she'd had a panic attack. Try as she might, she couldn't get Carl Meagan and everything she went through three years ago out of her mind. She didn't want to return to those dark days.

'Are you all right?' Sian asked.

'No.' She shivered as a gust of wind blew around her. 'No, I'm not.' She headed for the car.

'I'll get Rory and Scott to search online and on social media,' Sian said as she lowered herself in behind the wheel and put her seatbelt on. 'We need to find out everything we can about the family. Like he said, they're just a normal, regular, everyday kind of family. Why them?'

Matilda didn't reply.

Sian started the engine. Matilda looked out of the window and back at the house. Craig was standing at the large living room window looking out at her. They made eye contact. Matilda offered a sympathetic smile, but it wasn't returned. Craig continued to stare.

'What are you thinking about?' Sian asked when she glanced at Matilda and saw a heavy frown on her face.

'It's nearly always the father, isn't it?'

'What is?'

'When a child goes missing or dies or something happens, it's nearly always the father. What do you think of him?'

'Craig? I get the feeling he's screaming on the inside but trying to remain calm for Linda and the kids.'

'You don't suspect him?'

Sian thought for a moment. 'No. I don't think I do. Do you?'

Matilda remained silent. Until she found evidence to the contrary, she suspected everyone.

Chapter 10

While Matilda and Sian were at the Armitage house, DI Christian Brady was setting the Homicide and Major Enquiry Team to task. Until the kidnappers made their next move, there was very little they could do. However, in case the kidnapping was a hoax, a contingency plan was set up for the investigation into a missing child to begin. The first step was to contact everybody on the child sex offender's register and find out their movements for the time Keeley disappeared.

'Sir, I've been scrolling through Twitter and Jodie Armitage has been tweeting quite a bit since last night,' DC Scott Andrews said. He stood in the doorway to Christian's office.

He sighed. 'I bloody hate social media. Thanks Scott, I'll give Ellen a ring.'

'I've just seen Sian's car pull up in the car park.'

'Right. We'll need to get the briefing started. I'll be right out. Scott, keep an eye on social media. Anything that sounds a bit dodgy, let me know.'

'Will do.'

Christian stepped out of his office as Matilda and Sian entered the HMET suite.

'How did it go?' He asked.

Matilda rolled her eyes. 'Don't ask. Listen, is the ACC here yet? Her car isn't in the car park.'

'Oh. I'm not sure.'

Sian had made two strong coffees and handed one to her boss. It was greatly needed, and Matilda inhaled the caffeine before taking a sip. She could feel herself relaxing immediately.

She looked up at the whiteboard on the wall behind her. Keeley's school photo was already at the top, smiling at the whole room.

'Ok then, let's begin . . .'

DS Aaron Connolly's mobile rang. He pulled it out of his pocket, looked at the screen and silenced it. He mouthed 'sorry' to Matilda.

She continued. 'We have a missing child to find. Keeley Armitage is nine years old. She lives in Acorn Drive, Stannington with her family. Parents are Craig and Linda and she has an older sister, Jodie, who is fourteen and younger brother Riley who is four. Keeley looks more or less as she does in the photo on the board. She's four feet tall with shoulder-length curly blonde hair which she wears tied back in a ponytail. She is slim, has blue eyes and a fresh complexion and wears size two and a half shoe. When she went missing, she was wearing her school uniform, as seen in the photo, and a yellow lightweight coat and carrying a pink backpack with characters from the film *Frozen* on it.'

Scott was stood by the board adding the details as Matilda spoke.

'The last person to see Keeley was her sister who told her to wait for her outside the Co-op on Oldfield Drive while she went inside to do some shopping.'

DC Rory Fleming, with a mouth full of Snickers, raised his

hand and waved it about to get Matilda's attention. He quickly chewed and swallowed. 'Sorry, I missed breakfast. I've got the CCTV footage from the Co-op,' DC Rory Fleming said. 'Do you want to watch it now?'

'No. Shall we wait until Keeley's been found?' Scott said. A ripple of laughter ran around the room.

Matilda pulled down a white projecting screen while Scott turned off the lights. Rory hammered away at his laptop and the image from the Co-op's CCTV camera above the entrance appeared.

The picture was of high quality and showed shoppers entering and leaving the store. At 15:39, Jodie and Keeley walked towards the automatic doors. Keeley was licking an ice cream. Jodie knelt down, held her by the shoulders and said something to her before going into the store. A few minutes later, Keeley had finished her ice cream and walked off, disappearing out of shot.

'Play it again,' Matilda instructed.

The officers watched the footage for a second time in silence. When finished, Scott turned the lights back on.

'It's like she had no intention of waiting for her sister,' Sian said.

'That's what I thought,' Rory said.

'Is she heading in the direction of home?' Matilda asked.

'She is.'

'But she didn't make it.'

'No.'

'Are there any other CCTV cameras on the route she should have taken?'

'I'm afraid not.'

'I didn't think so. So, is this all we've got of her?'

'Yes.'

'Rory, take this to the tech department. See if they can zoom in on the people, clean it up and get some decent images. We can see most of the kids are wearing school uniform. If we can show this to the teachers, they may be able to identify the kids and we can ask them what they saw.'

'Will do. Can I finish off my breakfast now?'

'You may.'

Rory nodded then bit off another chunk of chocolate.

'One more thing Rory.'

He almost choked which made the room roar with laughter. Even Matilda smiled.

Aaron's phone rang again. 'Sorry. I'll turn it off.'

'Someone's popular,' Sian said with a hint of a smile.

'Scott, what did you manage to dig up on the family?' Matilda asked.

'There is a lot about the family online, especially the father, Craig Armitage.' He went over to his laptop and projected images onto the screen showing various newspaper articles. 'Craig does a great deal of charity work. He runs marathons, half-marathons, bike rides, abseils buildings, anything to help raise money for charity.'

'Which charity?'

'Well, at first it was to buy the specialist equipment they needed at home for Riley. They've had the doors widened downstairs to accommodate Riley's wheelchair. The garage has been turned into a bedroom and en suite wet room for him, the garden has had to be adapted, and various other pieces of equipment he needs. None of it is cheap.'

'Do we know what happened to Riley?' Sian asked.

'Yes. He developed epilepsy not long after he was born, and the seizures grew in strength. When he was one, he had one during the night while everyone was sleeping. He banged his head on the side of his cot, knocking him unconscious. His brain was starved of oxygen for too long for the damage to be repaired.'

'The poor boy,' DC Ranjeet Deshwal, who had recently become a father for the first time, said, putting his head down.

'How did the family react to all this?'

'According to the article I read, Craig talked about his wife and daughters rallying round and helping out. They come across as a close-knit family, but he's going to say all that for a newspaper article, isn't he?'

'True. We need to chat to the neighbours, close friends and family; find out as much as we can about them,' Matilda said.

'I expect Linda feels guilty,' Sian said.

'How do you mean?' Scott asked.

'Well, when you've got young children, especially when they're babies, you want to protect them, look after them. They're vulnerable and rely on you,' she said from experience as the mother of four children. 'When they're ill, especially with the condition Riley has, you're even more protective. On the night his injury occurred, she'll have been asleep and will have berated herself more than once for indulging in sleep while her child had stopped breathing. It's natural.'

'But it wasn't her fault.'

'That doesn't stop her feeling guilty. You ask any parent of a child who injures themselves.'

'So, how is Linda going to be feeling now?' Scott asked. 'Will she blame herself for allowing Keeley to be kidnapped?'

'Judging by the state she was in yesterday and this morning, yes,' Sian said. 'She's tried to protect all her kids, but most of her effort goes on Riley so she relies on Jodie to pick up the slack. Keeley's gone missing, so Linda will be hating herself more.'

Matilda gazed out of the window overlooking the car park. She saw the dirty Land Rover belonging to ACC Masterson arrive. Matilda watched through the slats of the vertical blinds. The diminutive Valerie jumped down from the driver's seat, slammed the door behind her and walked, lazily, towards the building. There used to be a bounce to her step. She was the assistant chief constable of South Yorkshire Police, a role she coveted. Now, everything had changed. Matilda recognised that look, that strolling gait.

The room had quietened. They were all waiting for Matilda.

'Sorry,' she apologised. 'Now, as I was saying, we need to know everything about their routine, what's going on in their lives. I know we don't like to think this, but facts don't lie, and the majority of the time, when a child goes missing, or is killed, it is by someone they know. Just because Craig does all this charity work and Linda is a doting mother doesn't mean we don't investigate them. I want everyone's movements known for around the time Keeley went missing. Not just of the parents, but of the entire family too, that includes aunties, uncles, cousins, grandparents, great grandparents and third cousins twice removed. Until we know what happened to Keeley Armitage, everyone is a suspect. Is that clear?'

There were nods of ascent from around the room.

'Good. Now, Sian, I'd like you to pay a visit to Keeley's school. Find out what kind of child she was there – is she different from when she's at home, was she being bullied, the usual. While you're at the school, get a spare uniform and get it photographed. We need to try and get a similar jacket to the one she was wearing too. I'll try and get Craig and Linda to do a television appeal later if this ransom demand doesn't play out like it should.'

'You don't think she's been kidnapped for ransom, do you?' Aaron asked.

'No, I don't,' she said, sitting on the edge of a desk. 'When you kidnap someone for ransom, you choose a family who has plenty of money, like . . .' She swallowed hard. 'Well, like the Meagans. Yes, Craig has raised over half a million pounds, but you only have to read all these stories of him in the paper to know that he hasn't put the money in his own bank account. It's to buy special equipment for his son, or for the Children's Hospital. He works two jobs, Linda doesn't work. They don't have that kind of money.'

'Why would someone pretend they've kidnapped her when they haven't?' Scott asked.

'To cover up what really happened to her,' Matilda answered.

The room went silent while they all took in the implications of Matilda's statement. Had Linda Armitage invented the kidnapping because she had killed her daughter?

'But we're not discounting the kidnapping completely?' Aaron asked.

'No. Nothing is being discounted until we have firm proof. I hope we're monitoring all their calls.'

'We are.'

'Can I ask a very sensitive question?' Rory asked.

Everyone turned to look at him, and his face reddened at the attention.

'Go on,' Matilda prompted.

'I'm only asking this as we're keeping an open mind on the whole kidnap thing, but, say she was kidnapped and there is someone out there waiting for fifty grand, do you think, that . . . well, what I mean is . . . is there . . .?'

'Is it the same people who kidnapped Carl Meagan?' Matilda finished his question for him.

'Yes. Sorry.'

'Don't apologise, you've every right to ask. I've spent most of the night thinking that myself. Kidnaps for ransom are very rare in this country. Is it possible the people who kidnapped Carl are having another go? I really don't know.'

'But Carl's kidnappers didn't get their ransom money,' Scott said.

'No. But we don't know what happened to Carl. I screwed up the ransom drop, and they got away with Carl. After that, who knows what they did to him. Maybe they sold him on and made their money that way. We don't know.'

Matilda's brow had wrinkled, and her face took on a look of sadness. The Carl Meagan case haunted her on a daily basis, and now it was happening again, just when she was getting her life back on track. This was a cruel twist, and Matilda knew she had to get it right. She could not allow her emotions to get the better of her, and if that meant upsetting the already fragile parents of Keeley Armitage to get some answers, then she was perfectly prepared to do so.

She looked up to find the whole room staring at her, waiting to hear what she was going to say next.

'Right then,' she clapped her hands together. 'You've all got things to be going on with. Christian will give you your tasks. Get out there and find Carl—' Then, 'Fuck,' she muttered under her breath.

'Come on everyone, away from your desks. This is a police station, not a call centre,' Christian said, covering his boss's error. 'I don't want to see any of you in here until the evening briefing.

Matilda turned away from the room and headed for her makeshift office. She closed the door behind her and pulled the blind closed.

Her small office was a mess, as always. Every available surface was cluttered with files and paperwork; open cases, closed cases, cold cases, any information relating to a missing person somewhere in the world who bore a striking resemblance to how Carl would look now.

She slumped in her leather chair and pulled open the top drawer of her desk. A fragile envelope, coming apart at the seams from permanently being opened, sat on top of a notepad. She lifted it up carefully, opened it and pulled out the five photographs from inside. They were all of Carl with his family; playing in the back garden, on his father's shoulders at the beach, opening presents on Christmas morning, playing with the puppy in the park, snuggling with the same dog in bed. In each picture, he was smiling, he was happy, he was content.

'Where the bloody hell are you, Carl?' She asked as tears began to form.

Chapter 11

The sound of hammering drew Ellen into the living room. The coffee table had been moved to one side and the carpet pulled away from around the window. Craig was on his hands and knees thwacking a hammer down onto the exposed floorboards.

'Craig!' She called out over the din. 'What are you doing?'

He turned around to face her. His face was expressionless. 'I hate not having anything to do. I can't just sit around here waiting for the phone to ring at four o'clock. I thought I'd do a few jobs I've been putting off.'

'I think maybe you should leave that for a while, at least until Linda gets up. I've made a fresh pot of coffee.'

'If I drink any more coffee, I'll be bouncing off the walls.'

'It's better than tearing up the living room,' she smiled.

He smiled back. His face seemed to light up for a brief moment.

In the kitchen, Ellen poured them both a coffee from the cafetière. They sat at the heavily scratched pine table.

'I like the garden,' she said, looking out of the window. It had been designed with wide walkways for Riley's wheelchair to go down, raised patches of grass for him to sit on without too much trouble getting out of his chair.

'Thanks. I did most of it myself. It took me ages.' He added a splash of milk to his strong coffee and poured in three heaped spoonfuls of sugar. 'Riley loves it. He enjoys the fresh air.'

Ellen cleared her throat. 'Tell me about Keeley. What sort of a child is she?'

'She's a good child,' he replied without giving the question any thought. 'She's never given us any worry. She dotes on Riley and I think she listens to Jodie more than she does me and her mum,' he laughed nervously.

'How's school? Does she have any favourite lessons?'

'Maths. She's good at it, too. I don't know where she gets it from. I'm useless with numbers. She got a certificate last year for one hundred per cent attendance. She loves school.'

'Any best friends?'

He frowned as he thought. He took a deep breath. 'I don't know. I think Jodie would be your best bet to answer that one.'

'What does she like doing out of school?'

'She's a big Disney fan. She's got all the DVDs. I've lost count of the amount of times I've sat through *Frozen*. She enjoys drawing too. She's always drawing pictures of clothes, especially dresses. She designs dresses for Elsa to wear. She even drew a wedding dress once. She said it was going to be the one she'd wear when she was old enough to get married.'

'Does Keeley think about things like that? Getting married?'

'No. I think it's the whole Disney princess thing? I expect she's waiting for Prince Charming to ride up on a white horse and whisk her off to his castle.' He smiled.

'Craig, if someone acted the Prince Charming to Keeley, a stranger, is she the type of girl to go off with them?'

He paled instantly as if all the blood had been drained out of him. 'You mean, grooming her?'

Ellen nodded. 'It's not easy to hear, I know, but I'm afraid I have to ask these questions.'

'To be honest, I've no idea. When we bought her the tablet, we told her all about not talking to people she didn't know. We go through it from time to time and it's got all those protection locks on it, but these people are sneaky fuckers, aren't they? I like to think she's sensible, but at the end of the day she's only nine. If somebody told her they had a castle and horses, I think she may fall for it.'

'I'm sorry, I had to ask,' she leaned forward and placed her warm hand on his.

'That's ok. You need to know these things. If some sick bastard has laid one finger on her, though, I swear to God, I'll rip him apart.'

'She wouldn't.'

They both jumped at Jodie talking from the doorway. Ellen quickly removed her hand from Craig's.

'Sorry?' Ellen asked.

'What you said, about Keeley falling for someone who said they had a castle and horses, she wouldn't. I've told her all about the internet. I've explained, in detail, what people are like on there. Whenever anybody new starts chatting to her on Snapchat, she tells me, and I sit with her, and watch the conversation play out. She's a good girl. She wouldn't go off with a complete stranger.'

'You seem very confident about that.'

'When I started picking her up all the time from school, we came up with a safe word that only me and her knew so if I had to arrange for someone else to collect her, I'd give them that word and she'd know it was ok to go with them. I never had a reason to use it.'

'I didn't know that,' Craig said.

'That's very sensible of you, Jodie,' Ellen smiled.

Jodie went over to the fridge, took out a can of Coke and pulled out the chair at the top of the table. She swiped a speck of fluff from her father's jumper, closed a magazine left open, and sat down.

'We've had lessons in school about strangers approaching you online and how predators try to groom you. I wanted to make sure Keeley was safe without frightening her.'

'Would Keeley go off with someone she knew if they turned up at the school, without seemingly needing a safe word?' Ellen asked.

Jodie's bottom lip began to wobble. 'I can't protect her all the time,' she cried. 'I've warned her against strangers, but how do you warn someone against people they're supposed to trust?'

'Like who?' Ellen asked.

'I think we should leave it there,' Craig said. He leaped from his seat and went over to his daughter. He held her firmly in his arms, pulling her tightly to his chest, and stroked her hair as she cried loudly.

'Jodie, is there someone . . .?'

'Please. Can we leave it for now?' Craig demanded.

'Of course. I'll just . . .'

Ellen left the room and closed the door on Jodie's cries and Craig making reassuring noises.

She stood in the hallway and ran her fingers through her greasy hair. She looked into the living room and saw Riley strapped into his highchair. He looked back at her with a vacant stare. She went in and picked up the small penguin he'd been playing with that had dropped on the floor. She handed it back to him.

'Here you go, sweetheart.' Over her shoulder, she saw an episode of *Pingu* playing on TV. The sound had been muted. She looked back at Riley. He was smiling. 'What happened here last night, Riley?' She asked him quietly.

Chapter 12

Matilda knocked on ACC Masterson's door and waited for Valerie to tell her to come in. It was a long wait.

'Come in.'

Matilda pushed opened the door and carefully entered, closing it behind her.

Valerie wasn't behind her desk, as usual, buried under a mountain of paperwork and reports. In fact, her desk was relatively tidy. The ACC was standing by the window, her back to the room, gazing out at the sprawling view of Sheffield in autumn. Beyond the double glazing, new buildings were rising as Sheffield continued to go through its seemingly endless regeneration process. The high street was facing the same hardship as others up and down the country. People didn't seem to want to shop on the street anymore, preferring to do it online. Shops were closing, footfall was easing, and city centres were turning into ghost towns. Sheffield seemed to have the solution. A new cinema had recently opened, and a bowling alley and pool hall were scheduled to open sometime next year. New restaurants and coffee shops were popping up, and, thanks to the new HSBC headquarters opening next summer, the city centre would hopefully start to see people return, if not to shop, then to be entertained.

Valerie's eyeline followed a crane as it turned, carrying a heavy slap of concrete high up above the streets of the city centre.

'Do you think Sheffield needs any more hotels?' She asked, not turning around.

'I don't know. I haven't given it much thought,' Matilda said, stepping further into the room.

'Apparently there's going to be one where the old market was and there's talk of an Ibis at the bottom of the Moor, right next to the Premier Inn. Who knew Sheffield was in such high demand.'

'It's not exactly a holiday destination,' Matilda sniggered.

'No.'

'Is everything all right?'

Valerie turned from the window. She looked smart in her crisp uniform. Her grey hair was swept back. She was a small woman, barely over five feet tall, but her personality was titanic, as was her reputation as a powerful leader. However, recent events had taken their toll. Her face was heavily lined and there was an air of sadness about her which filled the room.

'Fine,' she quickly replied, taking her seat behind the enormous desk.

'How's Arthur? Any news?'

Valerie visibly sank in her seat. Her head bent down to her chest. She sniffled. She wiped away a tear before looking up.

'Not good,' she managed to say, her voice cracking. 'He's regained consciousness, but . . .' She shrugged. She couldn't speak.

Matilda sat down in front of her desk. 'Is there anything I can do?'

'You could make him remember who I am.'

'He doesn't remember you?'

She shook her head as the tears fell. Matilda ran around the desk to comfort her boss.

Earlier this year, Valerie had been all smiles and full of plans as she and her husband, Arthur, a retired dentist, were charting their route through Europe in a motorhome. Valerie was taking early retirement and they were going on the trip of a lifetime. A month ago, their plans had been thrown into chaos when Arthur suffered a massive stroke. He was unconscious and in intensive care for three weeks. Valerie had taken a few days off work but wallowing alone in their large house in Derbyshire made her feel worse, so she made a quick return to work, one eye permanently on her phone, waiting for the call from the hospital.

'He's lost all feeling down his left-hand side. He's lost his speech, he can't feed himself, or dress himself. He doesn't recognise me, or the children. It's like talking to a complete stranger who just happens to look like Arthur.'

Matilda plucked a few tissues from the box on the desk and handed them to Valerie for her to wipe her eyes and nose.

'What are you going to do?'

'I've no idea.' She blew her nose loudly. 'What can I do? It could take years for him to get any form of movement back. He may not even get his memory back. All our plans, all our dreams, everything we've both worked for, ruined.'

Matilda didn't know what to say. She hoped that wrapping a comforting arm around her shoulders would help her to open up. When she was grieving for James, she had her best friend, Adele, to talk to, and crying and screaming at the world really did help.

'He'd hate this,' Valerie continued. 'We always talked about what we'd be like as old people. I'd laugh and joke about us causing havoc in a nursing home, but to Arthur, it wasn't a joke. He hated the idea of growing old, of not being able to do the things he's always been able to do. That's what this trip was all about; visiting all the places we've only seen on TV before it's too late. Now look at him.

'You know, I sit in the hospital room and I watch him. He looks so sad. He's got tears in his eyes and I know that he'll be screaming inside, screaming at me to help him, to do something so he's not feeling like this. It's so unfair, Matilda.'

It really was unfair, and Matilda knew exactly how she felt. James was only forty-five when he died. A brilliant man at the top of his field, handsome, caring, loving, and he was taken from her.

'You need to be strong for him,' Matilda eventually said. 'Physiotherapists can help with his speech and movement, but you, and your kids, need to help with his memory. You've been married for such a long time, you'll have thousands of stories and photos to show him, to help him unlock the door to help him remember. It'll be hard, I know it will, but you can relive everything together again. His will to get better will be strong; you have to match that strength.'

'You're right. I know you're right. It's just . . .'

'When you feel low, when you need to scream and shout and cry, come and visit me. I've got a huge garden you can stand in the middle of and scream and nobody will hear you. You helped me when James died. Please, don't go through this on your own.'

Valerie placed a clammy hand on top of Matilda's. 'Thank you. You're a good friend, Matilda. Now,' she wiped her eyes. 'We've got a kidnapping on our hands, I hear.'

'Yes. A nine-year-old girl. Keeley Armitage.'

'Any clue as to who might have taken her?'

'Not so far. I've got an FLO at the house. I'm going to see her in a bit.' She stood up and went around to the other side of the desk. 'The kidnappers said they'd call back in twenty-four hours. That's around four o'clock this afternoon. We've no idea if they're watching the house or not so we can't go knocking on doors. We're just having to wait.'

'I've been told it's all over social media.'

'Yes. The eldest daughter, Jodie, put something on Twitter last night. I'm guessing she thought she was helping.'

'And I see our favourite journalist has reared his ugly head again,' she turned the open laptop around to face Matilda. The screen was showing the home page of the local newspaper, the *Sheffield Star*, and a brief breaking news story written by Danny Hanson.

'Ah,' was all Matilda could think of saying after she read the short article.

'I knew he'd bring up the Carl Meagan case at the mention of a kidnapping,' Valerie said. 'Are you thinking . . . you know . . . similarities with Carl?'

'I'm trying not to.'

'I can assign someone else to this case if you'd rather not get involved. Nobody would think badly of you for taking a step back.'

I'd think badly of me.

'That's fine, thank you, but I can do this. A year ago, probably not, but I'm stronger now.'

Valerie smiled. 'Yes. You are, aren't you? I suppose now is as good a time as any to tell you.'

'Tell me what?' Matilda frowned.

'There's a restructuring process planned for South Yorkshire Police to begin late next year. I've been asked to recommend officers who I believe would be suited for more demanding roles. I already see Christian Brady as a future DCI and Sian Mills should have been an inspector years ago. Have you considered being Superintendent Matilda Darke?'

Chapter 13

Matilda had never considered being a superintendent. She loved her role as detective chief inspector and enjoyed being in charge of a major crime unit. Valerie had chastised her on more than one occasion for going out to attend interviews and crime scenes when she should be behind a desk supervising and coordinating. Becoming a rank higher would mean an end to all of that. She couldn't imagine the rest of her career being trapped behind a desk. The very thought of it made her shudder. However, if she was reluctant to move up, that would be blocking Christian and Sian in achieving bigger and better things. This would require some thought.

On her way out of the station, she sent a text to Adele asking if she was free to come round for a meal tonight. She received a reply almost straight away saying she was. Matilda's text back told her it was her turn to pay for the takeaway and she voted for Chinese. The sarcastic gif she received as a reply made her laugh out loud.

Detective Constable Ellen Devonport answered the door and let Matilda in.

'How's it going?' Matilda asked in a whisper while they were in the hallway.

Ellen shook her head. 'You're not going to believe this,' she said, lowering her voice. 'Linda only snuck out of the house earlier and went to see Sally Meagan and asked her for the ransom money.'

Matilda's face hardened in anger. 'What? What happened?'

'She didn't give it to her. She's been crying non-stop since she got up. Craig managed to get it out of her and when he did, well, you should have seen him. He had a right go at her. I thought he was going to hit her at one point.'

'He got violent?'

'Not physically, but he turned red and I saw him clench his fists a few times.'

'Bloody hell. Where's Linda now?'

'Craig put her to bed.'

'Jesus,' Matilda pinched the bridge of her nose hard. Sally had been growing stronger in recent months, but something like this could be a setback. 'I'll have to go round and see Sally later, check on how she's doing.'

'Don't blame Linda, ma'am, she's desperate. Craig said she'd never asked anyone for anything before in her life. All the special stuff they need for Riley, they've bought it all themselves, or raised the money. They've never asked for loans or handouts.'

'I won't. But she needs to be one hundred per cent focussed for this afternoon.'

'She will be. I'll talk to her,' Ellen said with a placatory smile.

'Any phone calls or emails?'

'A few from family members. They've been using their mobiles though. I told them to keep the landline free. Oh, before I forget, the next-door neighbour came round earlier, Amanda Raine. She remembered Jodie said something to her last night and thought we should know. Apparently, when Jodie found out

Keeley had been kidnapped, she asked her mum if Keeley had had PE yesterday with Mr Page.'

'And had she?'

'Yes.'

'Why's that significant?'

'Jodie wouldn't say.'

'Ok. Let's go and have a word with Jodie then.'

Riley's bedroom had been adapted from the garage attached to the house. In one corner was an en suite wet room and opposite was a large framed bed with foam protectors so Riley wouldn't hurt himself while he was asleep.

The room was equipped with soft lighting. The blind at the window was closed and in two corners were large colour-changing LED sensory mood bubble water towers which cast a soothing glow around the room.

On the carpet, Riley was sitting in a large bean bag. He was wearing jeans and a long-sleeved T-shirt with a penguin on the front. His favourite toy, a penguin, was nestled in his lap. Opposite him, Jodie was blowing bubbles towards him. When they hit his face and burst, he giggled. This made Jodie smile. Other toys and teddy bears were strewn around the floor.

'Are they tickling you, Riley?' Jodie asked as he gurgled loudly. 'Do you like the bubbles?'

'Jodie, can we have a word?' Matilda asked quietly from the doorway.

She looked over her shoulder and nodded. Riley didn't register their presence.

'This is a nice room,' Matilda said.

'It's relaxing. Riley can get stressed at times. The changing colours, the bubbles, and the music help to calm him.'

'How old is he?' Matilda asked, even though she knew the answer.

'Four. He goes to school in the new year. Only a couple of days a week. I'll miss him.'

'You look after him a lot, don't you?'

'No. Mum looks after him more.' Jodie blew more bubbles. Riley giggled and clapped his hands.

Matilda sat down on the floor next to Jodie. 'Jodie, I want to ask you about something you said yesterday. When you found out Keeley was missing, you mentioned a teacher. Mr Page? Who is he?'

'He's a teacher at Keeley's school.'

'Why did you mention him?'

'I don't know,' she shrugged, blowing more bubbles. 'Oops, Mr Penguin is getting wet,' she said to Riley.

'Jodie, do you think Mr Page might have something to do with Keeley going missing?'

'I don't know.'

'Then why bring him up?'

'It's . . . I don't know.'

'Jodie, you're not going to get anybody into trouble. If you think you know something, you really need to tell us so we can find your sister. You might not think it's important, but we need to find out.' Matilda wondered why Jodie would bring Mr Page up in the first place if she didn't think it important. It may be something and nothing but right now it was the first sign of a hint of progress. Matilda wasn't going to let it slide.

Jodie continued to play with Riley. She reached for a plastic spiral tower all in different bright colours which she placed in front of her brother. She handed him a ball. He placed it on the top of the tower and as the ball ran down, it made a jingling sound. He gurgled and smiled.

'He loves this game,' Jodie said, copying his smile. 'He loves the sound of the bell inside the balls.' She handed him another ball.

'You love Riley, don't you?'

'Of course I do.'

'And you love Keeley?'

'Yes.'

'Then tell us about Mr Page, Jodie.'

She let out a heavy sigh. 'Mr Page is Keeley's PE teacher. She's said a couple of times that he's been a bit too . . . close.'

'What do you mean by close?'

'She said he puts his arm around her, and he helps her get changed after PE. She said she thinks it's weird.'

'Does he do this with other girls?'

'She didn't say.'

'Other boys?'

'She didn't say.'

'Who else has she told?'

'Nobody.'

'Why did she tell you? How did it come up in conversation?' Matilda asked quickly.

'She's not wanted to do PE a few times and I asked her why not. She loves PE, loves going outside and running. For her to suddenly not want to do it, I knew something must have been wrong. I thought she was being bullied at first.'

'What advice did you give her?'

'I told her that if she was uncomfortable, she should either tell the head teacher or Mum and Dad.'

'Did she?'

'No. I don't think so.'

'How long ago was this?'

'Towards the end of last term. Before the summer holidays.' She handed Riley another ball and he giggled as he watched the ball roll down the spiral tower.

'Was she still not looking forward to PE again this term?'

'No.'

'Thank you, Jodie. You've been a big help.'

Matilda stood up to leave the room when Jodie called her back.

'Will you be here, at four o'clock, when the kidnappers ring again?'

'Yes.'

'What will we do when they call?'

'I don't know. It depends what they have to say.'

'We're not going to get her back, are we?'

'You will. I promise. We will do everything we can to bring her home.'

If any of Matilda's officers had made such a promise, she'd have chastised them at the earliest opportunity. Every time she entered this house, saw the torment Craig, Linda, and Jodie were going through, she was reminded of Carl and his parents. She didn't remember making them a promise, but her mind had been all over the place with James's cancer weighing on her mind. Now, she had one task and one goal. She felt she could make a promise and make good on it.

'Do you think the same people who took Carl Meagan have taken her?'

Matilda took a deep breath. She could feel Ellen Devonport's eyes burning into the back of her neck. Suddenly, the dull lighting and the warmth of the room were becoming too much for her. She needed air. She needed light. 'No. I don't,' she replied firmly.

'Keep playing with Riley. Leave us to worry about everything else.' She gave her a smile, waved goodbye to Riley, even though she knew he wouldn't wave back, and left the room.

'Should we promise her we're going to bring Keeley home?' Ellen asked once they were back in the hallway.

'No, but what else could I say?'

The landline started to ring. Everything in the house fell silent. Even Riley seemed to stop giggling.

Craig bolted down the stairs and ran into the living room. He picked up the phone. His shaking finger hovered over the green button. He took a deep breath.

'Keep calm, listen to what they have to say, and ask to speak to Keeley,' Matilda said. 'We're recording this call.'

'Hello?' Craig answered. His voice was high and filled with panic.

'Mr Armitage?'

'Yes.'

'Have you been in an accident in the past twelve months that wasn't your fault?'

He ended the call without answering and slumped on the sofa. He sobbed loudly. Ellen went over to him and put her arm around him.

'I can't do this,' he cried. 'I can't bear not knowing where she is. This is killing me.'

'What's going on?' Jodie came running into the room. 'Dad?'

Ellen moved to one side to allow Jodie to comfort her father. As Craig sat up and lifted his daughter onto his lap, Matilda noticed that although Craig was making the right noises, he wasn't producing any tears.

Chapter 14

Matilda arranged to meet DC Scott Andrews outside Mary Croft Primary School on Hopwood Lane. She was there before him and spent the time scrolling through social media. She didn't use Facebook and Twitter but had accounts so she could monitor what other people were up to, especially during investigations.

Linda Armitage had a Facebook account and it wasn't protected either. She was able to look at all of her posts and photos. Most of them were of Riley playing in his bedroom or snuggled up asleep. Her posts were of how much she loved her son, how proud she was of him, and how she thought he was finally interacting with her after years of one-sided play. The comments were mostly positive. She had around two hundred friends and most of them seemed to be mothers judging by their profile pictures of them posing for selfies with their kids.

Craig wasn't on social media. There was, however, a Craig Armitage page on Facebook which detailed all of his fundraising events. Most of the posts were signed 'L' so Matilda assumed Linda had set up the page for her husband. The photos showed Craig in action – abseiling down the side of the Arts Tower in Sheffield city centre or taking part in the London Marathon dressed as a penguin. Again, all the comments seemed to be

positive and congratulated Craig and Linda on all the hard work
they were doing to make Riley's life as comfortable as possible.

Matilda logged on to Twitter. Sheffield was still trending. She
scrolled through and read Jodie's comments about Keeley being
kidnapped. She'd updated the posts by saying there was no more
news, she was still missing, and the whole family was frightened
of what might have happened to her.

The comments on Twitter were not as polite as on Facebook.
Mostly people said how sorry they were and had retweeted
Jodie's post with the photo of Keeley. There were a few who were
vile and blamed the parents. If they'd kept a closer eye on her
in the first place, she wouldn't be missing. One predatory post
said Keeley looked cute in her uniform and he wished he'd got
to her first. Another said she was probably at the bottom of the
River Don. A few stated the father had most likely killed her.
Matilda felt sick just reading them. She took several screen shots
and emailed them to Ranjeet back at the station. These people
would need contacting, as would Twitter. People like that
shouldn't be allowed an account.

There was a knock on the passenger seat window making
Matilda jump. She looked up and saw Scott's smiling face looking
at her. She unlocked the door. He got in beside her. She caught
a whiff of his strong fragrance and opened the window a crack.
Scott was in his mid-twenties, had a tidy mound of blond hair
and a complexion that looked as if a razor had never been
scraped across it. Since telling the whole station he was gay
earlier this year, and finding a boyfriend, his confidence had
grown. He was no longer the shy, quiet one of the team. Matilda
loved seeing her team happy. She hoped she would be again,
one day, too.

'You looked engrossed,' he said.

'Just reading some of the things people have been saying on social media. Are you on any of these?'

'God no. I can't stand them. Everyone is so fake saying how perfect their lives are, what they're having for tea and how their children are the best in the world. What a load of crap! I think it should be banned. And I certainly don't think kids should be allowed on there. It's poisonous.'

Matilda smiled. 'I'm starting to agree with you there, Scott. You haven't got a charger for an iPhone, have you? I'm running on fumes, here.'

'No. I'm Samsung.' He looked at the school. 'I thought Sian was coming here.'

'She was but as I was passing I thought I'd go.'

'I hate schools,' he exaggerated a shudder. 'They always make me feel like I've done something wrong.'

'Guilty conscience,' she said with a smirk. 'There's something I want to ask you. Correct me if I'm wrong, but a few months ago, Chris had a temp job at Mary Croft Primary School, didn't he?'

'He's had temp jobs in practically every school in Sheffield. He was thrilled when this permanent one came up at Stannington Secondary.'

'But he did work at Mary Croft, didn't he?'

'Yes. I think he was covering sick leave.'

'Good. I want you to ask him about a Mr Page. He's a PE teacher here. Hopefully we'll be able to have a word with him now, but I'd like to know what other teachers thought of him.'

'Sure. No problem.'

'While you're at it, ask him if he knows Jodie Armitage. Does he teach her?'

'Are you trying to turn Chris into a detective?'

'No. I'm using my contacts to the best of my ability, that's all,' she said with a twinkle in her eye.

'Should he get paid for this?'

'No he bloody shouldn't. It's his civic duty to help the police.'

'That won't help us save for a deposit.'

'You're thinking of living together?'

He failed to hide his smile. 'We'd like to.'

'Wow. I didn't know you were that serious. What about Rory? He won't be able to afford that flat on his own.'

'I've spoken to him about it. He's fine. He said he'd ask Natasha to move in with him.'

'Bloody hell, look at you two settling down. Finally.'

Scott blushed.

They stepped out of the car and into the autumn air. Scott was dashing off a text to Chris, asking him about Mr Page, while Matilda locked the car. Scott and Rory's situation made her think. They had both faced difficulties in the past few years; both had been seriously injured in the line of duty yet had managed to drag themselves out the other side and were getting on with their lives. All Matilda seemed to do was work. She had resigned herself to the fact that nobody could ever replace James, but that shouldn't stop her meeting someone new and having fun. Maybe she should ask Daniel Harbison over one night and see about pushing whatever it was they had a bit further forward.

Standing in the corridor outside the head teacher's office, Matilda looked at a wall of children's drawings. The children had written their names on the bottom of their pictures and she recognised Keeley's name straight away. She stood up and went over for a better look at the picture.

The drawing was of a princess at the top of a high tower. She was leaning out of a window looking out over the sprawling countryside. Her face was sad and there were tears rolling down her face. In the background, a large white horse with a knight on its back came charging towards her. The princess had blue eyes and blonde curly hair, exactly like Keeley.

'She's a very talented girl.'

Matilda jumped and turned around. The head teacher, Sheila Croft was standing in the open doorway to her office. A small, round woman in her mid-fifties, Sheila had an uncontrollable mound of mousey hair in tight curls. Her cheeks were red, and she had a slight smile on her face.

'Sorry, I didn't mean to startle you. Sheila Croft,' she said, holding out her hand. 'No relation to the great Mary Croft.'

'I'm sure you're asked that all the time,' Matilda said, shaking her hands.

'About once a day,' she smiled. 'Come on in. Can I get you a coffee or something?'

'I'm fine. Thank you.'

Sheila's office was small and warm. There was a large photograph of the school on one wall and a bank of filing cabinets running along another. Matilda and Scott took a seat in front of her desk.

'I'm guessing you've heard about Keeley going missing.'

'I have,' her smiled dropped. 'Shocking news. We'll help out in any way we can.'

'Thank you. What can you tell us about Keeley?' Matilda asked.

Scott perched a notebook on his lap, a pen poised, ready to take notes.

Sheila looked at her computer screen. 'She's an exemplary pupil. She reads two years above her age level, and she scores highly in maths. Her attendance was one hundred per cent last term.'

'I'm guessing you only come into contact with pupils whenever they've done anything they shouldn't.'

'Usually, yes.'

'Is there anyone I can talk to who knew Keeley better – her teacher, perhaps?'

'Of course.'

'Was Keeley bullied?' Matilda asked.

'Not that I'm aware of. The children of Mary Croft are like one big family,' she smiled.

'Ms Croft, I've been a detective for more than twenty years. I know what kids are like when they're together; they can be complete shits. You're not telling me you don't have bullying going on here.'

'We operate a zero-tolerance approach to bullying at Mary Croft,' the smile grew.

Matilda took an instant dislike to her. How could she be so blind to the behaviour of children. 'I'm sure you do, but if you tell me there are no bullies at this school, I'll call you a barefaced liar. Now, perhaps I could speak to a teacher who actually knows Keeley.'

Lauren Beech was a tall, slender woman in her late twenties. Her features were small, as if intruding on her elfin face.

She'd arranged for a teacher to cover her class while she, Matilda, and Scott talked in the staffroom. Lauren set about making them a cup of tea.

'I'm guessing Mrs Croft tried to tell you there isn't a bullying problem here.' Lauren spoke in a light voice that was almost a squeak.

'Something like that.'

'Mrs Croft is a good head teacher, don't get me wrong, but she does view things with rose-tinted glasses from time to time.'

'Was Keeley being bullied?'

Lauren's shoulders dropped. 'I'm afraid she was.'

'In what way?'

Lauren brought the drinks over to her and sat down. Matilda noticed the teacher was drinking out of a pink mug with a unicorn on it. From the many non-descript mugs available on the side, she had chosen this one purposely. Lauren, a primary school teacher, didn't seem much older mentally than her pupils; she wore her hair in bunches tied with furry bobbles.

'The other kids knew of Keeley's situation at home. Some said cruel things about her brother.'

'Riley? Like what?'

'I'd rather not say,' she said, looking away.

'Whatever you tell me isn't going to shock me. In fact, I've probably heard much worse.'

She took a breath. 'They call him names like spastic and window-licker,' she said barely above a whisper. 'It really upset Keeley.'

'Did Keeley report this to you herself?'

'Yes. I had a word with the pupils, and we did an assembly on tolerance and how people are different to us but they're still people. I reported it to Mrs Croft on a number of occasions, too.'

'How did Keeley react to the name calling?'

'I found her crying a couple of times. I tried to reassure her as best as I could. I told her that Riley was none of those things, that he was her brother and she should love him as such.'

'What did she say to that?'

Lauren smiled. 'Keeley is very grown up for her age. She smiled and said she already knew her brother was special, and she loved him. She said she didn't care what people called him, but she liked to have a cry from time to time as it helped her.'

'Helped her how?'

'She didn't say.'

'Is Keeley a happy girl?'

Lauren thought for a long while before answering. 'I want to say yes, but I'm not sure. I always get the impression she's hiding something.'

'Like what?' Scott asked. He didn't look up from his notepad.

'I don't know. There are many layers to Keeley. She smiles all the time, but it's not a genuine smile. I think she's unhappy. I've spoken to her about it many times, but I can never find out. She always changes the subject.'

'Does she ever speak about her home life?'

'No.'

'So, you don't know if she was having problems at home with her parents, perhaps?'

'No. Occasionally, I catch her yawning when she should be working. She says Riley kept her awake during the night. I assume that's all it is.'

'What impression do you have of her parents when they come for open nights?'

'Ah. I've never actually seen them.'

Matilda and Scott exchanged glances.

'Really?' Matilda frowned.

'Keeley's parents are incredibly busy. I believe her father works two jobs, and her mother is Riley's carer so it's not easy for her to get away. When it comes to the open evenings, it's her sister who's turned up.'

'Jodie?'

'Yes.'

'But she can't be responsible for her; she's only fourteen.' Matilda had a great deal of sympathy for Keeley and this made sense of her fascination with all things Disney. Was she feeling left out at home? Did she hope her Prince Charming would take her away from her ignored life? Worst of all, had someone used Keeley's situation to their own advantage?

Ms Beech shrugged. 'That's not the way her parents see it, evidently.'

'Huh,' Matilda said. 'Thank you. You've been a big help.'

'It sounds like Keeley's left to bring herself up,' Scott said once they were out in the corridor.

'That's what I was thinking. A nine-year-old girl needs her parents. I get that their time is consumed with Riley and his needs, but they shouldn't neglect their other children, too.'

'You think that's what they're doing, neglecting her?'

'I don't know. It's possible. I understand that Riley needs twenty-four-hour care and Craig has two jobs, but Keeley is at a very important age. Being neglected like this by her parents could seriously damage her development into adulthood.'

'What if someone showed an interest in her? If she was feeling neglected at home and bursting into tears at school, it wouldn't take much for someone to try to talk her into going with them if they offered her what she wanted,' Scott said.

'If that's the case then it's someone who knows the family and their circumstances.'

'Like . . . a teacher perhaps?'

Sebastian Redford Page, to give him his full name, was a tall, thin man in his late twenties. He had spiky ginger hair with matching designer stubble. He was pale and his eyes were a very cool blue. He entered the head teacher's office and smiled at Matilda and Scott before taking a seat. He had a worry frown on his forehead which made him look like a naughty schoolboy brought in for being caught smoking. He wore a tight-fitting black Adidas tracksuit.

'Shall I leave you to it?' Sheila asked.

'If you wouldn't mind,' Matilda smiled. She waited long after the door was closed before she began. She wanted to make sure she could hear the heavy footsteps of the head teacher disappear down the corridor.

'Mr Page, I'm sure you've heard the rumours about Keeley Armitage going missing.'

'I have, yes. It's true then?'

'I'm afraid it is, yes.'

'Oh God,' he looked down.

'Obviously, we have to ask the family a lot of questions to find out how and why someone has gone missing; some of these questions can be difficult and awkward, as can some of the answers. I'm afraid your name has come up as someone we should talk to.'

He looked back up at Matilda. 'In what way?' His eyes darted between the two detectives.

'You teach Keeley, yes?'

'Yes. I teach all the children here.'

'You taught Keeley on Monday?'

'Yes. It was the last lesson of the day.'

'Keeley's sister, Jodie, has told me that Keeley didn't like attending PE classes anymore. She said you made her feel uncomfortable.'

'Uncomfortable? In what way?' His worry lines deepened.

'Apparently, you're very tactile, always putting your arms

around her, helping her get dressed after the lessons. Is that true?' Matilda leaned back in her chair and crossed her legs.

'What? Of course it isn't true,' his eyes widened. 'I'd never do anything like that. Besides, as a male teacher, I'm not allowed in the girls' changing rooms. Look, we're taught not to have any physical contact with the children. We're never alone with them. We don't do anything that could be misinterpreted. I stick by those rules.' He looked frightened.

'Are you saying Keeley made those stories up?'

'Yes I bloody am,' he said, exasperated.

'Why would she do that?'

'I don't know. I take her for two lessons a week. I don't know the girl. I wouldn't—'

'Ok, Mr Page, please try to calm down,' Matilda said.

'Calm down? You're practically accusing me of molesting a nine-year-old girl and you're telling me to calm down?'

'Nobody is accusing you of anything. I'm simply asking a question.'

'I can't believe this,' he leaned forward and put his head in his hands. 'I have done nothing wrong. I haven't touched anyone.' He looked up. There were tears in his eyes.

If Sebastian had been a drama teacher she'd think he was giving a wonderful performance. However, she found herself feeling genuine sympathy for him. His wide-eyed rabbit-caught-in-the-headlights stare was not an act.

'Mr Page, there is one more question I have to ask you.' Matilda waited while he composed himself. 'Where were you yesterday evening around four o'clock?'

'I was here.'

'Whereabouts?'

'I was clearing away the hall. We'd been playing badminton.

I was packing the nets away. Then I went into the staffroom and wrote up some notes for today's lessons.'

'Did anyone see you?'

'No. It was empty. Most of the teachers do their work at their desks in their classrooms. I'm PE so I don't have one.'

Matilda and Scott exchanged glances.

'You don't believe me,' Sebastian said. 'You think I've taken her, don't you?'

'I don't think anything, Mr Page. I just follow the evidence.'

'Well you're barking up the wrong tree because I have absolutely nothing to do with that girl going missing,' he said, standing up.

'Mr Page—'

'No,' he interrupted. 'You're not fitting me up. I know what you're doing. You're fucking clueless so you go after anyone who seems a bit dodgy, any tenuous link. We can't help who our families are. If you want to accuse me of anything else, then you'll have to take me down to the station and I'll bring my solicitor with me.'

He stormed out of the office, slamming the door firmly behind him.

'Wow, that was something,' Scott said to fill the awkward silence. He was fishing his phone out of his trouser pocket.

'I wonder what he meant by not being able to help who our family are.'

'Dunno. I've heard back from Chris. He said he vaguely remembers a Mr Page but there's a woman he works with who knows him better than he does.'

'Who?'

'A Ruth Harrison,' he showed Matilda the text message.

'Aww, he signed off with three kisses,' Matilda smiled.

'Give over, you'll make me blush.'

The door opened and the statuesque Sheila Croft came back into her office.

'May I ask why my PE teacher has just stormed out of the building and driven his car out of here like he was leaving the pit stop at Silverstone?'

'He's gone?' Matilda asked.

'Yes.'

'Can you give me his home address?'

She hesitated. 'Erm, yes, I suppose can. I'm guessing this is about Keeley going missing?'

'Yes.'

'And you think because his brother is in prison, he's got something to do with it?'

'I don't know anything about his brother.'

'No, of course not,' she scoffed, not believing her.

'Honestly, I don't. What about his brother?'

Sheila let out a heavy sigh. 'Oh. Perhaps I shouldn't . . . shit,' she uttered under her breath. She took a deep breath. 'Sebastian's brother is Calvin Page who was sent to prison for raping three girls.'

'I didn't know.' His reaction to being accused was suddenly understandable. People would assume he was like his brother if a similar incident occurred. It was a sad fact that a lot of people were narrow-minded about these things. Matilda wondered how close the brothers were. Was it possible that Sebastian pointed out the more vulnerable pupils to his brother for him to groom? That was a disturbing thought that made Matilda shiver.

'Evidently. Look, do you have any idea of the damage you're going to do to this school? I accept members of staff here on their merits and a very vigorous background check is done on each and every one of them. That's not going to count for anything once the parents put two and two together and come up with nine. They'll not want Sebastian anywhere near their kids, and he's done nothing wrong.'

'I'm just doing my job. Sometimes it isn't very pleasant.'

'No. And neither is the aftermath when you've left and others have to pick up the pieces.'

'I'm trying to find a missing girl . . .'

'And my heart goes out to her and her family,' Sheila interrupted. 'I will do everything I can to help in your investigation, but your bull-in-a-china-shop approach is not the way to go about it.'

She looked at her computer, scribbled an address down on a note pad, tore off the piece of paper and thrust it out towards Matilda. She took it, thanked her, and left.

'I didn't handle that very well, did I?' Matilda asked once they were out in the car park.

'We weren't to know his brother was a rapist. If we'd have had any other information than 'Mr Page' we'd have been able to look him up.'

'True.'

'Where to now?'

Matilda looked at her watch. It was one o'clock. Three hours until the kidnappers were due to ring. She felt a headache coming on. Her head was full of dark thoughts and the disturbing acts people did for their own enjoyment. She needed time out. If she continued like this, she'd be a basket case by the end of the day. She let out a sigh. 'Let's go off grid for a couple of hours. I'll buy us something unhealthy for lunch and you can tell me about your sex life.'

'I'd rather not do that, if it's all the same to you.'

'I don't want to know any details, Scott. I just want to know that someone is actually happy in this frightening world we're living in.'

They both climbed into the car and Matilda started the engine.

'I'm very happy,' he said, beaming.

'That's good,' Matilda found herself smiling back. 'That's very good.'

From the window of her office, Sheila Croft watched as Matilda and Scott drove away. She turned back to her desk and took her iPhone from the top drawer and scrolled through the contacts until she came to one she wanted. She made a call and waited impatiently, drumming her fingers on the desk. After a dozen rings, the voicemail kicked in.

'Sebastian, it's me. Listen, I need you to ring me as soon as possible. I'm afraid I've ballsed up.'

Chapter 15

'Sian, can I have a quick word?' Rory sidled up to her desk in his chair.

'If you can get my sandwich out of this hermetically sealed packet, you can have several,' she said, handing him the pack. 'I see you're growing your hair again.'

'Yes. Natasha likes it long and curly. She says I look like Jon Snow.'

'The newsreader?'

'The character from *Game of Thrones*.'

'Oh. I'll take your word for it.' She turned away and her eye caught DS Aaron Connolly on the other side of the room. 'What's wrong with Aaron?'

'I've no idea. Why?'

'He's just sitting there staring into space. He's got a face like a slapped arse.'

'He's always got a face like a slapped arse.'

Sian frowned as she studied her colleague. It was true his face belied what he felt. He had the original poker face. However, more than usual he seemed to have the weight of the universe on his shoulders.

'Maybe he's having personal problems,' Rory said.

'Really? Him and Katrina? I thought they were solid.'

'Not everyone can be like you and Stuart. Speaking of

which . . .' He handed her the open packet. She took out the first sandwich, looked at the limp bread and sparse filling and took a disappointing bite. 'You know your anniversary party at the end of the month?'

'I should do, I'm planning the whole bloody thing.'

'I was wondering if I could bring Natasha along with me.'

'Well, the invitation does say Mr Fleming and guest.'

'Cheers,' he beamed.

'Things getting serious with you then?'

'I think so.'

'How long have you been seeing each other?'

'Five months. I know it's not long, but when you know you just know.'

'Yes, Rory. Your generation didn't invent romance.'

'She's just so . . . I don't know, I can't describe it. If I had to write a list of everything I wanted in my ideal woman, I would be describing Natasha. It helps that she's bloody gorgeous, too. Have you seen her out of uniform?'

'I can't say that I have, Rory, no,' Sian said.

'She has an amazing body. You should—'

'Erm, Rory,' Sian interrupted. 'I think you're probably better off waiting until Scott or Ranjeet gets back before you continue that sentence.

'Oh yes, sorry. I'll just go and grab a coffee.'

'Maybe a cold shower as well,' Sian said. She was about to take another bite when her phone rang. She rolled her eyes.

'Homicide and Major Enquiries. DS Mills speaking.'

'Sian, it's Tony,' the sergeant on the front desk said. 'I've got a bloke on the phone who says he's from the British Embassy in France. He's asked for DCI Darke but she's not in and DI Brady isn't answering. Can you take it?'

'Sure. Put him through.' She took a sip of cold tea to rinse out her mouth while the call was being transferred. 'Hello, I'm afraid Detective Chief Inspector Darke is out at the moment. I'm DS Sian Mills. May I help at all?'

'I hope so. I'm Adrian Moorhead. I'm with the British Embassy Paris. Early yesterday morning a young boy presented himself to Police Nationale in Marseille. He said his name is Carl Meagan. Does that mean anything to you?'

Chapter 16

'You're not serious, surely,' Valerie said, looking up at Sian with wide-eyed amazement.

'I am,' Sian said. 'This young lad just walked into a police station and said he's Carl Meagan.'

'Where is he now?'

'He's in police protection. He says he was kidnapped, and a couple have been looking after him. They said he was to call them Mum and Dad.'

'And where is this couple now?'

'I don't know. He doesn't know where he's been living. They brought him to France for a holiday. They've been staying in a hotel, but he doesn't know which one.'

'Jesus,' Valerie said, squeezing the bridge of her nose.

'According to Adrian Moorhead at the British Embassy, the police have told him that this boy is in a very healthy condition. There's no sign of abuse or mistreatment.'

'Does Matilda know?'

'No,' she said. 'Her phone is going straight to voicemail. I've left a couple of messages.'

'Where is she?'

'I don't know.'

'So, what's happening now?' Valerie asked.

'Adrian is liaising with Police Nationale. They're going to send through photographs of this boy, and they've taken a blood and hair sample from him so we can check the DNA we have on record for Carl Meagan to make sure it is him.'

'Ok. In the meantime, this stays between us. We tell Matilda, and that's it until we have proof. Clear?'

'Perfectly,' Sian said.

It wasn't possible for Matilda to go off grid. She was never able to leave work behind. It was with her every waking moment of the day, and depending on the case she was investigating, it occupied a great deal of her sleeping time too. As they headed away from Stannington they had to pass the secondary school. She slammed on the brakes.

'It seems pointless to go for a bite to eat then come back. We may as well pop in for a chat now,' she said with a smile.

'How convenient,' Scott rolled his eyes.

Matilda and Scott held up their identification to a camera at the gates and then again at the main entrance. When they were buzzed in, they were greeted by the head teacher, Alan Fitzgerald, an incredibly tall and wafer-thin man with large ears, who bore a striking resemblance to the BFG.

Chris met them in the corridor. His smile was large and spread across his face. He wore tight black trousers and a fitted white shirt, open at the neck. He took them to the staffroom where Ruth was making coffee for them all.

Chris Kean was the son of Matilda's best friend, Adele. She had known Chris since he was a toddler, and often brought up stories of changing his nappy when the urge to embarrass him was too great to ignore. He was tall, sporty, and very handsome. His once unruly mop of curly hair had been shorn to a stylish dark blond buzz cut. He was clean-shaven and carried himself with an air of confidence. His colleague, Ruth Harrison, was a complete contrast. She was in her late thirties and looked every inch the defeated woman. Her brown hair was straight and lifeless. Her skin was dry and had patches of acne. She looked tired, drawn, and sad.

'Ruth, this is DCI Matilda Darke. And, you've met Scott, haven't you?'

'Yes I have,' she smiled, but it seemed painful. 'Nice to meet you both.'

Pleasantries over, and coffee made, they all sat around a low round table by the window, looking out over the school's playing field.

'Chris says you know Sebastian Page from Mary Croft,' Matilda said. She took a sip of her coffee and tried not to show how bad it tasted.

'Bloody awful, isn't it?' Ruth said. 'Yes, I do. Well, I did. I worked at Mary Croft for two years. I left last summer to come here.'

'Why did you leave?'

'It was nothing to do with Sebastian. I just can't stand kids that young.' Again, she proffered a smile, but it was false, as if she'd forgotten how to smile and was uncomfortable with doing it.

'Tell me about Sebastian.'

'I liked him . . . at first. He's a good teacher; it's just, he has a very quick temper.'

'In what way?'

'Not with the kids or anything,' Ruth quickly added. 'I remember once, he used to always come to school on his bike, and he was going home when he saw he had a puncture in one of the tyres. Well, he really flew off the handle, blaming the kids for sabotaging it and how he was going to have to walk and it was raining. He went way over the top.'

'Maybe he'd had a bad day?' Scott offered.

'No. He was like that with everything. If there was no milk left in the fridge for his coffee, he'd moan about how it was always when he wanted a drink that there was no milk left and never anyone else, like the world was out to get him. He'd get quite volatile.'

'Was he ever violent?' Matilda asked.

'I never saw any signs of it, but I wouldn't be surprised. He asked me out once. I said no as I'm married. Well, I'm separated, but, well, it's complicated. Anyway, I turned him down. He's not my type anyway, but he asked me why. You don't ask that, do you?'

'What did you say?'

'I just told him that I was recently separated and wasn't looking for anyone yet.'

'How did he take it?'

'He said fine, but, a couple of times when I was out, just the local pub with friends, you know, he'd be there. He'd make it seem like it was a coincidence, but I knew he'd followed me there.'

'How did you know?'

'Just a feeling. I always felt like he was watching me out of the corner of his eye. He creeped me out.'

'Did you say anything to him?'

'No.'

'To anyone else?'

'No. This job came up and I was happy to leave. I wasn't in a good place when I worked there. This was a fresh start for me.'

'What about you, Chris?' Matilda asked. 'When you worked at Mary Croft, did you notice anything strange about him?'

'You mean apart from his casual racism, homophobia, transphobia and anti-Semitism?'

'Really?'

'We had these parents come into the school and said their son wanted to be a girl and asked for the school's policy on allowing him to wear a dress to school. Well, you should have heard him on the subject. He was saying the child should be taken into care because the parents were forcing their ideas onto him and what kind of six-year-old knows they're in the wrong body. Then we had a Polish family move into the area. The two kids came to the school, but they didn't speak much English. It was embarrassing the way he kicked off.'

'Were complaints made about him?' Scott asked.

'Only by the other teachers to the head. The thing is, like Ruth said, he's good at his job. He makes his lessons fun for the kids, which is what they like, and he never showed any of this side to the parents. He's a real Jekyll and Hyde character.'

'Why are you asking about him?' Ruth asked, a painful looking frown on her forehead. 'Is it to do with this girl going missing?'

'His name has come up in our enquiries,' Matilda said. 'Do you know the Armitage family?'

'I know Jodie. I take her for maths.'

'How is she?'

'Quiet. Intelligent. A bit of a loner. I never see her with any friends. I know she has to do a lot at home with her brother like he is.'

'Chris, do you teach Jodie?'

'Yes, for English. I'd echo what Ruth said.'

'What I'm going to say now is in the strictest confidence,' Matilda began, leaning forward. She caught a whiff of the horrible tasting coffee so sat back. 'If I told you a complaint had been made about Sebastian Page possibly touching a pupil, inappropriately, would you be surprised?'

'Not in the slightest,' Ruth said instantly.

All eyes turned to Chris.

He thought for a moment. 'I don't like to say it, but I don't think I'd be surprised either.'

'We need to find him,' Matilda said, taking large strides back to the car. 'Where does he live again?' She fished in her pocket for the piece of paper with his address on it. 'Pitsmoor. I'll get a uniform to go round and pick him up. We'll get a search warrant for his house too.' She took her phone out of her inside jacket pocket. 'Bloody battery's gone. Scott, can I borrow your phone.'

'Sure,' he took it out and looked at the screen. 'Oh.'

'Something wrong?'

'I've had a few missed calls and about a dozen texts from Sian.'

'I didn't hear it ring.'

'No. I always have it on silent and the vibration thing stopped working. I'm due to upgrade next month so didn't think it was worth getting fixed.'

He quickly scanned the texts then listened to the voicemails. 'They're asking if I know where you are. Sian says something's come up and you're needed straight away back at the station.'

Matilda looked at her watch. 'I haven't got time to go back there and get back here for four o'clock. Give her a ring, ask her what she wants.'

She got in the car behind the steering wheel and started the engine. 'Ruth Harrison looked like she had the weight of the world on her shoulders,' she commented while Scott waited for the call to connect.

'Problems with her ex. He won't leave her alone, apparently. Chris was asking the other night about how she goes about taking out an injunction against him.'

'That bad?'

'Must be.'

'Men! I don't know why people are so interested in having a partner. Life is much simpler with a box of Maltesers and a good book.'

Scott was about to reply when his call was answered. 'It's me. You've called several times. Anything wrong? . . . Yes, she's here. Do you want to speak to her?' He handed the phone to Matilda.

She listened for a while. Her face paled. Her eyes widened. She ended the call without saying anything.

'What's the matter? Has something happened? Has Keeley been found?'

'No, but it sounds like Carl Meagan has.'

Matilda turned to look at Scott with a look of genuine happiness on her face.

Chapter 17

Ellen Devonport entered Riley's bedroom with a mug of tea in her hand. Linda had been out of bed for less than half an hour and she was busy with a cordless vacuum cleaner. She'd woken just after lunch time and felt drained, tired, and sick. A quick shower hadn't helped. There was so much she had to do.

'I've made you a cup of tea,' Ellen said.

Linda jumped, not realising there was anybody in the room with her. She turned around. 'I bet you spend a great deal of your time making tea,' she said, putting the vacuum cleaner down and taking the mug.

'It's part of the training course,' she said with a smile. 'How do you feel?'

She thought for a moment, both hands wrapped protectively around the mug. 'Numb. I want to cry but I don't think I have any tears left.'

'I know it doesn't sound like much, but we really are doing everything we can to find Keeley.'

'I feel sick for going to see Sally Meagan like that. Do you think I should apologise?'

'I'm sure she understands what you're going through.'

'Will you apologise for me?'

'I'll mention it to DCI Darke.'

'I was horrible to her as well. I bet you all think I'm a complete cow.'

'Not at all.'

Linda began tidying the room, putting toys away and folding up clothes. 'Do you have kids?'

'No.'

'When you have children, you want to do everything to protect them from what's happening in the world. You do your best, but you can't wrap them in cotton wool forever.'

'I think you've done a wonderful job with Jodie and Keeley. They're model children. And Riley,' Ellen turned to look at Riley in his bed. He was sitting up in the corner wearing his protective helmet so he wouldn't bang his head against the bars. He was playing with a book made out of fabric, each page making a crinkling sound as he scrunched it up. 'Well, he's just lovely,' she smiled.

'I love him to pieces,' Linda said quietly. 'I blame myself for the way he is.'

'Why?'

'When I discovered I was pregnant, I was shocked. I didn't want a third child; two was enough. It took me a long time to get used to the idea of three kids. When he was diagnosed with epilepsy, I blamed myself. It was my fault he was ill because I had thought such horrible things.' Her voice began to crack.

'That's rubbish, Linda. You can't manufacture an illness.'

'The night he had the big seizure that caused him to stop breathing was the first night since he'd been born that I'd had a drink. Well, I'd had a few drinks actually. I woke up to go to the toilet; I've no idea what made me go and look in on him. He was so still. I thought he was dead.' She put the mug down on the windowsill and went over to the bed. Riley looked up and held his arms out to her. She reached down and heaved him up. 'He's suffered for what I've done. I'm a bad mother.'

Ellen was on the brink of tears. 'You're not, Linda.'

'And now Keeley's been taken. They're being punished because of me.' She cried and held Riley close.

Ellen leaned out of the bedroom and called for Jodie. She appeared almost instantly. Ellen asked her to take Riley which she did without question. Ellen took Linda and led her into the kitchen where she sat her down at the table.

'Linda, none of this is your fault. You love your children and you're doing the best for them. You and Craig are wonderful parents. You're not to blame. What happened to Riley is just . . . well, it's nature. There's nothing we can do about that. However, we can do a great deal for Keeley, and we will.'

Linda reached for the kitchen roll on the unit behind her, tore off a few pieces and wiped her eyes and blew her nose.

'If I ask you a question, will you tell me the truth?'

'Of course I will.'

'What is the likelihood of you finding Keeley?'

'I don't know percentages, but I can tell you every police officer in Sheffield is working on this.'

'But you don't know where she is or who's got her?'

'Not right now we don't, but we're talking to so many people who know her or who were in the area at the time she disappeared. In this day and age, with all this technology, somebody will have seen something.'

'I don't know what I'd do without her. She's always smiling. She always cheers me up when I'm feeling a bit low.'

'Linda, can I ask you a few questions about the call from the kidnapper?'

'Ok.'

'What was their voice like? Was it male or female?'

Linda sniffled and wiped her nose as she thought. 'I'm not sure. He didn't say much.'

'Are you certain it was a man you spoke to?'

'I think so,' she frowned.

'What about any accent? Did he sound local?'

'No. It was sort of . . . flat, monotone.'

Ellen thought for a moment. 'Did he seem anxious or scared?'

'No. He was very calm, neutral, almost like . . .'

'Go on.'

'Like it was a recording.'

'A recording?'

'Yes, as if, the words had been typed into something and a computer was reading it out. Like, if you ask Siri a question and it gives you a reply, it was like that, but not.'

'Would you say it was like the caller was speaking through a voice changer?'

'Yes,' she said, animatedly. 'I'd say exactly that.'

'Right.' Ellen took a notebook out of her pocket and made a note.

'Is that helpful?'

'Yes. I think it might be.'

'Why would the kidnapper do that, though? It's not like calls are recorded, is it?'

'No.'

'So why go to all that bother?'

'I don't know. Maybe they thought you might recognise them.'

'Do you think it's someone we know?'

Ellen hesitated. She took a deep breath before answering. 'Personally? Yes, I do.'

* * *

Matilda was sitting in front of Valerie's desk while she explained the scant details from the British Embassy in Paris. Matilda looked drawn. Every time she thought of Carl, she thought of the nightmare she had lived through at the time with her husband dying. All the dark memories came flooding back and she realised how much she missed him. If Carl could be found, maybe she would finally be able to close a door on that whole period and move on.

'I'm afraid the French police don't seem to see this case as urgently as we do,' Valerie said. 'You'd think a simple task of emailing a photograph over wouldn't take long, but I'm still waiting.'

'What do we know of the people who took him?'

'Nothing.'

'How can that be?'

'Police Nationale in Marseille are dealing with it. I've no idea if any arrests have been made or who they're talking to.'

'Bloody hell! Where is this boy now?'

'He's in police protection but I don't know where.'

'How long is all this going to take?' Matilda asked, getting flustered.

Valerie shrugged. 'Matilda, are you all right?'

'I'm fine.' *Liar*.

'Would you like to take the rest of the day off?'

Matilda frowned. 'How is that even possible with a kidnapped girl on our hands?'

'Christian can take over.'

'No,' she took a deep breath and composed herself. 'Look, if this boy is Carl, then that's amazing. It's the best news in the world. Why should I want to take time off? We can't do anything until it's confirmed.' She looked at her watch. 'Shit. I should be getting back to Stannington.'

'How are the family doing?' Valerie said, standing up.

'Not good.' Matilda headed for the door. She turned back to look at her boss. 'Will you call me the minute you hear anything from France, or when they send you the photo?'

'I will.'

'Any news on Arthur?'

'No change,' she said, looking down.

'We seem to spend most of our lives waiting around for things to happen, don't we? We're not as in control of things as we'd like to believe.'

'You can say that again. Go on, get back to Stannington,' she said, rushing her out of the office.

Valerie turned her back on Matilda and looked out of the window.

Matilda stood in the hallway, her back pressed firmly against Valerie's closed door. She felt a prickle of heat creep up her back and her vision began to blur. She looked ahead and the corridor appeared to be closing in. It seemed like her panic attacks were returning.

'Walpole, Compton, Pelham,' she said under her breath.

When Matilda first went off work following her husband's death and Carl going missing, she had been assigned a therapist to talk through her issues with. A coping strategy for the panic attacks was to control her breathing by concentrating on a single topic. For Matilda, that was reciting the names of the British Prime Ministers. It worked, too. It had been a good couple of years since she'd had to manage her focus. She'd thought she was back in control, able to face anything life threw at her. She was wrong.

'Pelham-Holles, Cavendish, Pelham-Holles, Stuart, Grenville. Oh for fuck's sake,' she chastised herself as she stormed off down the corridor.

* * *

One girl missing and one boy possibly found. Such a cruel twist of fate that one family's suffering might be coming to an end while another's was just beginning. And in the middle of it all was Matilda Darke.

Matilda thought she had her emotions under control; that she was a strong and independent woman. However, all it took was one piece of bad news to bring her back down to the wreck she was in the early days following James's death. She was reminded of this fragility as she made her way back to Acorn Drive.

Carl's return would be headline news across the world, but the flip side of the coin would see the story of Keeley's disappearance. Two missing children. One found. One lost. Matilda vilified by the press once again. At the time it had happened with Carl Meagan, she had been numb to the onslaught, away from work on an enforced sabbatical. This time . . . it didn't bear thinking about.

There were more cars parked on Acorn Drive than last time. As soon as Matilda pulled up, she knew why. Out of the Skoda in front stepped Danny Hanson. Matilda rolled her eyes. She wished that man would fall down a hole somewhere.

'What are you doing here?' She barked at him, harsher than she expected.

'Don't panic!' He held up his hands in surrender. 'I haven't been knocking and upsetting anyone. What can you tell me?'

'Nothing.'

'Oh, come on. A missing girl. A ransom demand. Sound familiar?'

'You're a parasite, do you know that?'

'I've been called worse.'

'Look, Danny, you really need to piss off. The kidnappers could be watching. If they see press outside the house they might panic and not call.'

'Whereas seeing the famous DCI Darke pull up isn't conspic- uous at all,' he said flippantly.

Matilda stopped halfway up the pavement, turned and leaned in close to him. She had no idea how old Danny was but his smooth skin, lack of stubble and large puppy eyes made him look as if he was barely out of his teens. She imagined him using his smiling eyes, his little-boy-lost act on interviewees to extract any kind of information for a story. 'Danny,' she said calmly. 'I don't like you and you don't like me. Now, I don't give a shit what you write about me in that printed toilet paper you call a newspaper, but in that house is a family going through hell. Give them some consideration.'

He thought for a moment before nodding. 'Ok. I'll back off. But only for tonight. I'll be back tomorrow.'

'Jesus!' Matilda cursed, turning back to the house. How can someone so young and inexperienced ooze such confidence and pugnaciousness? *Wanker*.

Ellen opened the door before she had time to ring the bell. 'He's been out there for about an hour.'

'Whichever dickless president presses the nuclear button first, the only creatures left roaming the planet will be cockroaches and journalists,' Matilda said, entering the house.

'And I'm sure they'll be very happy together,' Ellen said with a smile.

In the living room, Craig was sitting on the sofa next to the coffee table where the phone was. He was dressed in a mismatched tracksuit. Linda was curled up next to him. She looked shattered despite having slept for more than fourteen hours. Her hair was knotted and dry. Her skin was blotchy, and her half-open eyes were red.

Matilda gave them both a wan smile and sat on the edge of

the armchair opposite. In the background, she could hear the sound of Riley giggling. She guessed Jodie was with him. Sian and Ellen hovered at the side of the room.

The clock was ticking.

The atmosphere in the room was dark and heavy. Apart from the noise from Riley's bedroom, the silence was palpable. Linda kept wiping her eyes and rubbing her red nose with a soaked tissue. Craig was biting on his bottom lip and drumming his fingers impatiently on the arm of the sofa. He was a seething mass of emotions which threatened to erupt at any moment.

Four o'clock came and went.

'How long do we leave it?' Craig asked, breaking the silence like a hammer to a window.

Matilda looked at her watch. It was three minutes past four.

'What was the exact time the call came through?' Matilda looked to Sian.

Sian flicked through the pages of her notebook. 'Seven minutes past four.'

'They're not going to wait until bang on seven minutes past four for fuck's sake,' Craig said, his face reddening in anger.

'We don't know that, Craig,' Ellen said. 'We don't know how their minds are going to work. At the end of the day, they want their money, so they'll stick to their plan.'

'But we don't have that kind of money,' Linda said, struggling to keep hold of her tears.

'We need to take this one step at a time,' Matilda said. 'When that phone rings, you need to speak calmly and slowly. Ask to speak to Keeley. If they ask if you have the money, tell them yes. Then we'll go from there.'

'I don't know if I can do this,' Linda said. She was a physical and emotional wreck.

'You have to,' Craig said harshly. He put his thick, muscular arm around her and pulled her close to him. She sank into his embrace and smiled when he kissed the top of her head. 'I'll be with you. We'll get through this together. I promise.'

Matilda watched them. Two doting parents who had done nothing wrong forced to endure the nightmare of one of their children being stolen from them. It broke her heart to witness them falling apart. She turned away quickly to look out of the window. She had to stop thinking of them as Philip and Sally Meagan. This was a completely different case. She knew the Meagans. She didn't know the Armitages. One of them could be responsible for Keeley's disappearance. They both could.

Linda's face was blank. Her eyes were red. She looked genuinely anguished. Craig was more difficult to read. He was being the caring husband and father, trying to be strong for them all. Trying. Matilda didn't like that word. It smacked of someone putting on a performance.

Time ticked by agonisingly slowly. Seven minutes past four came and went. As did ten past. As did half past.

'They're not calling, are they?' Craig asked.

'It doesn't look like it,' Matilda said reluctantly.

'Oh my God, they've killed her,' Linda cried. 'They've killed her. They've killed my baby. Oh Jesus Christ, Craig, they've killed her.' She collapsed into her husband and he held her tight, rocking back and forth on the sofa to try and calm her down.

Linda couldn't manufacture all those tears.

Matilda gave the nod to Ellen while she and Sian stepped out of the living room.

'You knew there wasn't going to be a phone call,' Sian said quietly.

'I didn't know for sure, but I'm not surprised the phone didn't ring.'

'Why?'

'Simply because they don't have the money. If someone kidnaps a child for ransom it's from someone who obviously has the means to pay. And these people don't.'

'What now?' Sian asked.

'I want Sebastian Page found.'

'Uniform are outside his flat, but he hasn't come home.'

'Run his registration number through ANPR, get it picked up and hunt him down,' Matilda said through gritted teeth. She took a deep breath to calm herself. 'Tomorrow, at first light, we start a search. I want a full team out here looking in every park, alley, field and wood. We're on the outskirts of Sheffield. There's farms and woodland close by; they all need to be searched. I want dogs out here and a helicopter in the sky. We rip this whole place apart until we find her.'

'She's dead, isn't she?' Sian asked.

Matilda took a deep breath. 'It would appear the kidnap was a hoax to cover up what's really happened. In my opinion that can only mean one thing.'

They heard movement and turned around to see Jodie standing in the doorway to the kitchen. She'd overheard every word.

'She's dead?' she asked. Her voice was fragile. Tears were streaming down her face. 'You think she's dead?'

'Jodie, we're hoping and praying that Keeley is alive and safe, but we have to think of every eventuality,' Sian said, running over to the girl and holding her by the shoulders. 'I know you may think we sound heartless, but we're just doing our job. It's not easy. I'm sorry.'

Jodie sniffled. 'I don't want . . .'

'What? What don't you want?' Sian asked.

'I don't want this to drag on. Mum won't survive. If she really is dead, you need to find her body. Mum isn't strong like Sally Meagan. She won't be able to cope with not knowing what happened.'

Matilda stood back and watched as Jodie fell apart and Sian tried to placate her. In the living room, Linda was sobbing loudly, and Ellen was making all the right noises to try and make her feel better, but her words were falling on deaf ears.

It was happening all over again. A child had been kidnapped. The ransom demand had gone awry and Matilda was standing in the middle of the fallout. The sensation of her phone vibrating in her jacket pocket made her jump. She pulled it out and saw it was an email from Valerie. The subject line read 'Carl Meagan'. There was no message, just an attachment. Matilda knew what it was. She opened it and looked at the face of the boy who was calling himself Carl Meagan.

Chapter 18

There was a great deal of work to be done – so much to organise for the search to begin at first light tomorrow morning, and Matilda wanted a press conference as soon as possible so Craig and Linda could get the whole country looking for their daughter. However, for once, she was going to listen to what Valerie kept telling her: delegate. She told Sian to get the search set in motion and sent an email to DI Brady to set up the press conference. Matilda needed some time away from the Armitage family.

She drove at speed through Sheffield and, as usual, was caught up in traffic in Woodseats. By the time she arrived at Pat Campbell's house in Bradway, dusk was setting.

Pat was a former detective inspector with South Yorkshire Police. She had taken early retirement for health reasons, but that wasn't the true story. Only her husband, Anton, knew the real reason why she had given up the job she loved so much.

Matilda knocked on the door and waited. It was opened by a short woman with unruly grey hair. She wore black casual trousers and an oversized comfortable woollen sweater. She looked fashionable and elegant without really trying. She smiled.

'Hello, I didn't expect you to call.'

'Not interrupting anything am I?'

'No. Anton's playing bowls. He asked me to go and watch but

I don't think I can handle the excitement,' she said, her reply laced with sarcasm. 'Come on in. Coffee?'

'I'd love one.'

'Come through to the kitchen.'

Pat's home was neat and tidy. It was decorated in neutral colours and had a minimalist style. Pat wasn't a fan of ornaments and walls covered with prints and framed photographs. The odd one of the grandchildren was fine, but all they amounted to was extra time dusting.

They took their coffee through to the conservatory which faced a very organised-looking garden.

'My garden could do with your magical touch,' Matilda said as she stood by the window.

'It's got nothing to do with me. It's all Anton. I love looking at a nice garden, but I hate doing it. He can spend all day in there pottering. I generally stay in here with my feet up and a magazine,' she smirked. 'You look harassed.'

'I feel it.'

'How's the search for the young girl going?'

'It isn't. The kidnappers didn't call back.'

'Oh.'

'What does that say to your detective brain?' Matilda asked as she sat on the wicker padded sofa next to Pat.

'That she wasn't kidnapped in the first place.'

'That's what I was thinking. Meanwhile, twenty-four hours have gone by and we're no further on.'

'Alibi for the parents?'

'Mother was at home, father was working. They're clean.'

'Uncles, cousins, grandparents?'

'We're working on it. Look, Pat, the reason I came round was because of another matter.'

'Go on.'

Matilda filled her in on the latest developments surrounding Carl Meagan. She pulled out her phone and showed her the photograph.

'Oh,' Pat said, slightly deflated. 'I'm not sure. I wasn't expecting him to look like that.'

'Neither was I.'

The photo emailed from the British Embassy showed a young boy with a mess of dirty blond hair. He was pale and clean, but his eyes were drawn and sad. They were blue, like Carl's, but had a dullness about them. His lips were thin and chapped and his cheek bones were prominent whereas Carl had a chubbier face.

'I suppose it could still be him,' Pat said, not taking her eyes from the screen. 'People can change a great deal in, what is it, just under four years. Don't forget, for a child, four years is a long time. He'll have had a growth spurt. He's been living in a different climate, different foods, different weather. He's bound to look drawn; he's been away from his parents for four years.'

'I know.'

'What are you thinking?'

'I don't know. I want this lad to be Carl so much.'

'He doesn't look like the composite you had done of how he'd look now, does he?'

'The ageing program can only take in so many factors. They generally show you what he'd look like now if he'd been living a healthy lifestyle.'

'Well, he looks like he has been. There are no bruises. He doesn't look like he's been poorly treated. He looks older than eleven, but, being kidnapped is bound to age a child.'

'Do you think we should show this to Sally and Philip?'

'Yes,' she replied firmly. 'We promised Sally we'd be upfront with her every step of the way. What's happening next?'

'Police Nationale are sorting out a DNA sample from the boy. They're going to send it to us and we'll see if it's a match for what we have on file for Carl.'

'And what about the people who kidnapped him?'

'I've no idea what's happening there at the moment.'

'You do know that Sally's going to want to fly straight out to Marseille.'

'I know. We need her to be rational about this. Yes, it's a step in the right direction, but we need to keep an open mind.'

'Would you like me to come with you?'

Matilda visibly relaxed. Although the atmosphere had thawed between her and Sally, things were still strained when they were in the same room together. Pat was the perfect buffer. 'If you don't mind.'

'Of course not. When?'

'Some time tomorrow? I need to get home, have something to eat and a long shower. I'm knackered.' Her voice broke as the relentlessness of the day's dramas were taking their toll on her on.

'You can have something to eat here if you like? I've had my tea but you can have what I've saved for Anton.'

Matilda smiled. 'I don't think he'd like that.'

'Probably not, but it'll teach him for dropping taking me out for a bite to eat for playing bowls.'

'No thanks. I'm not going to be a pawn in your weird little squabble. Besides, Adele said she'll pop over with a Chinese.'

'Ok. I'll see you out.'

* * *

There was something infectious about being with Pat that always made Matilda leave her house with a smile on her face. Since retiring, Pat had lightened considerably. She was approachable, good humoured and a pleasure to spend time with. They hadn't worked together much when Pat was still a serving DI, but her reputation was of having been a ball-breaker. She stood no nonsense and she wasn't shy about sharing her feelings, frustrations, and disappointments towards members of her team. The retired version was a complete contrast.

Matilda waved goodbye from behind the wheel of her Range Rover and headed for home. Hopefully, Adele had let herself in and was already spooning out the chow mein.

As Matilda drove up the makeshift driveway, she saw a car parked outside her house and the lights on inside. For a brief moment, it felt like she didn't live alone. She even smiled. Then she recognised the car as belonging to Adele, and the smile faded. She'd have company for a couple of hours and then she'd be alone again. Matilda used to enjoy being on her own with a book and memories of her husband, but it was no longer enough.

'Hi honey, I'm home,' Matilda called cheerily from the hallway.

Adele came out of the kitchen, hands on hips and a stern look on her face. 'Where the bloody hell have you been? I've been slaving over a hot stove for hours. A phone call would have been nice. You've been with that floozy again, haven't you?'

Matilda smiled. 'I'll tell Sian you called her a floozy.'

'Don't you dare. She may be small, but she's frightening when her temper's up.'

Adele and Matilda were the same age and had known each

other for more than twenty years. When Adele first moved to Sheffield she had been in a mess and Matilda had helped her pick up the pieces of her shattered life. When the tables were turned after James died, Adele had reciprocated. They were more than friends. They were closer than sisters, which irked Matilda's sister, Harriet.

Adele was a good-looking woman. She wore her dark brown hair at shoulder length, tucked behind her ears. She had warm brown eyes, soft skin and full red lips. She always dressed elegantly, and her attractiveness was boosted by her confidence.

The large kitchen was warm and welcoming. There was a strong aroma of Chinese food and the wine was in the cooler waiting to be poured. After the day Matilda had had, she needed this more than ever.

They piled their plates high. They rarely over-indulged like this so a treat once in a while was fine.

With a vegetable spring roll in her mouth, Matilda visibly relaxed in her seat.

'Rough day?' Adele asked.

'You could say that.'

'You?'

'One post-mortem, one court appearance, two reports written, and one parking fine.'

'Sounds like a fun day.'

'Oh, it was a hoot. That DC Cotton looks very young. How old is he?'

'Too young for you,' Matilda said, looking at Adele over the top of her wine glass.

'I wasn't asking for that reason,' she said with a twinkle in her eye.

'I think he's about twenty-four. He's also married.'

'At twenty-four? Idiot.'

'You married young.'

'Exactly. That's why I can call him an idiot.'

'Who was the PM on?' Matilda asked after a few mouthfuls of crispy duck.

'A woman was found in Stanley Street. Early twenties. She'd been strangled.'

'Prostitute?'

Adele nodded.

Matilda frowned. 'That's three in the past couple of years. I'll need to have a word with Bev.'

'Who's Bev?'

'An ageing prostitute who's been walking the streets for as long as I can remember. She knows all the girls.'

'I hear you may have found Carl Meagan,' Adele said, changing the subject when she saw the tell-tale sign of sadness in Matilda's eyes.

'How do you know?'

'Scott told Chris who told me.'

Matilda rolled her eyes. 'Nothing is certain until we get the results from a DNA test. I have my doubts.'

'Let's have a look at the photo.'

'What photo?'

'Of the lad in France who says he's Carl.'

'Bloody hell, doesn't Scott keep anything private?' Matilda wiped her hands on her napkin and pulled her phone out of her pocket. She opened the attachment in the email and pushed the phone across the table.

Adele picked it up and angled it so the light was right, and she could have a good look at the photo. She studied it for a while.

'You're not convinced, are you?' Matilda asked.

'It's not what I was expecting.'

'I said that.'

'I didn't think he'd look so thin.'

'That's what I thought too.'

'I mean, if he'd been living rough or been hidden away, I'd say fair enough, but he looks clean and healthy.'

'Again, I thought similar.'

'Have you shown Sally yet?'

'No. Me and Pat are going along tomorrow.'

'I don't envy you,' she said, pushing the phone back across the table.

'Neither do I.'

The case of Carl's disappearance may have left the newspapers, but it still affected those involved, primarily Philip and Sally. However, Matilda was deeply affected, too. She often had an unsettling dream where she received a phone call revealing the whereabouts of his body. Or, when she woke with a start, sweat causing her pyjamas to stick to her, she knew her sleeping had been haunted by visions of Carl. While the Meagans continued their search, she had understood the endless features in the press. However, they were easily avoided and had soon disappeared. Now, the case was back in the forefront of her mind. This would make the newspapers. The spotlight would return. The dark dreams would increase.

'I can't believe how close Scott and Chris have become in such a short space of time,' Adele said. 'They look good together.'

'Sorry?' Matilda asked, looking up from the plate she hadn't touched for a while.

'Scott and Chris. They seem to be doing well together.'

'Yes. Did you know they were thinking of getting a place together?'

'Ah. Yes, I did,' she wiped her mouth with her napkin and pushed her plate away. 'I was going to bring that up later.'

Matilda frowned. 'Why? Anything wrong?'

'No. It's just . . . well, Chris has mentioned something to me and asked if I'd ask you to, you know, sound you out.'

'I'm not sure what you're talking about and something tells me I'm not going to want to know.'

'Well,' she began after taking a large gulp of wine. 'You know what house prices and rents are like these days and you know how little a teacher and a DC earn. Money is very tight.'

'If they're looking for help with a deposit, I'll gladly help. As long as the others at work don't find out.'

'No, it's not that. I've offered, but they want to pay their own way.'

'So, what are you trying to say?'

'They were wondering if they'd be able to rent your flat above the garage.'

Rory was in bed with Natasha. The room was lit only by the low wattage of the bedside table lamp. Beneath the creased duvet, they were both naked and breathing heavily following their second love making session in less than half an hour.

Rory lay back with his hands behind his head. He had a look of contentment on his face. Natasha, petite, pretty, pale skinned with pitch-black hair, snuggled up to him and rested her head on his smooth chest.

'Do you talk about me at work?' she asked in her soft Liverpudlian accent.

'What do you mean?'

'Has anyone said anything about me to you?'

'No. What are you going on about?'

'It's just . . . well, I've been getting some strange looks and I overheard a couple of the girls talking in the toilets about how I'm sleeping with you to try and get into CID.'

'What? That's shit.'

'I know. I didn't want you to think that's what I was doing.'

'I didn't think that. Besides, I have no influence over promotions.'

'You know what people are like though. It sometimes feels like being back at school with some of them.'

Rory sighed. 'I used to be a bit like that myself. When Faith was going out with Steve, me and Scott were very childish. If we'd spent less time mucking about and opened our eyes a bit more, we might have seen him for what he really was, and Faith could still be alive today.'

Natasha looked up at him. 'Do you really believe that?'

'I do, yes.'

'You can't blame yourself for what happened. It still upsets you, doesn't it?'

He nodded. 'She was a good detective. She was young. She didn't deserve what happened.'

'Rory, can I say something?'

'Of course you can,' he looked down at her.

Her eyes were wide. She licked her lips. 'I think I'm falling in love with you.'

Rory swallowed hard. 'Really?'

She nodded. 'Do you mind me saying that?'

'No. I'm glad you said it. I feel the same way.'

Her face broke into a huge smile. 'Oh, thank God. For a moment there I thought you were going to flip.'

'Don't be silly.'

They kissed. His hands swept over her body, down her

back, and cupped her bum. He pulled her up so she was sitting on him.

'Wow, someone's happy,' she said, feeling him press against her.

'I bloody am now.'

In the next room, Scott and Chris were in bed together. Scott was scrolling through his phone while Chris was looking at affordable flats on his tablet.

'Bloody hell, are they at it again?' Chris asked.

Scott nodded.

'How many times is that now?'

'Third, I think.'

'I'm obviously going out with the wrong flatmate.'

Scott looked over at him and saw he was grinning. 'You were the one who had a headache last night.'

'What do you think of this one?' Chris showed him the tablet.

'Nice. Where is it?'

'Dronfield.'

'That's miles away. Long commute to work for both of us.'

'But it's cheap and it's in a nice area.'

'It's not usually so cheap in Dronfield.'

'It does need a bit of work doing to it.'

'What do you call a bit of work?'

Chris swiped across the screen a few times before showing Scott a photo of the master bedroom.

'It doesn't have a floor.'

'I know.'

'That's not "a bit of work". Since when did floorboards become an optional extra?'

Chris looked at his watch. 'Do you think my mum will have asked Matilda about her flat by now?'

'Probably.'

'Do you think she'll rent it out to us?'

'I'm not sure. She really likes her solitude.'

'Yes, but we won't be living in the house with her.'

'No, but she'll be able to hear us. I don't think I like the idea of my boss hearing me have sex.'

'We're not as loud as Rory and Natasha.'

The headboard in the next room was banging rhythmically on the wall.

'I like Rory, I really do,' Chris said, 'but we need our own place. It's weird now I've seen him naked.'

'When was this?' Scott asked.

'Last week. I got up to make a drink and he was coming out of the bathroom wiping himself. I got a right eyeful.'

'Oh, I'm sure that was terribly distressing for you,' Scott mocked.

'Well, I didn't mind the view, obviously. He's got a great body on him. It's just, well, it's awkward.'

'Fuck, Rory, you're an animal,' Natasha called out from the next room.

'Are they doing this on purpose?' Chris asked.

Scott smiled. 'If your mum hasn't asked Matilda, I'll ask her myself at work tomorrow. If she doesn't want to rent to us, then, I don't know, I suppose we'll have to go shopping for floorboards.'

Chris put his tablet down. He took the phone from Scott and placed it on the bedside cabinet.

'What are you doing?' Scott asked.

'We're going to show them they don't have the monopoly on banging headboards.'

He lay on top of Scott and kissed him passionately, grabbed his legs and pulled him down the bed.

'Fuck Chris, you're an animal,' Scott shouted. They both struggled to stifle their laughter.

Adele was slumped on the sofa, half-filled glass in hand, with an empty bottle at her feet and one just open on the coffee table. Matilda was standing by the living room window, looking out at the garage.

'I suppose it wouldn't be so bad having Scott and Chris living in there. It might even be nice having a neighbour again.'

'Is this you finally admitting you made a mistake moving out here?'

'No. I love it out here.'

'You don't like being so alone though, do you?'

She turned back from the window. 'Everybody seems to be moving on, settling down, and showing how happy they are. You've got Chris and Scott and then there's Rory and Natasha. Sian and Stuart are celebrating their silver wedding anniversary and Christian is the perfect family man.'

'And you're feeling left behind?'

'Kind of.'

'It sounds like you're ready to start dating again.'

'I'm not,' she said, glancing at her wedding photo on the mantelpiece.

'What about that architect who did this place, and the garage. You said he was tasty.'

'He is.'

'Is he single?'

'Yes.'

'Well, go out with him then.'

Matilda smiled coyly. 'We've been out for a couple of meals.'

'What?' Adele sat up. 'You never mentioned this. Matilda Darke, you're keeping secrets from me.' She patted the sofa next to her. 'Come on, tell me all the details.'

She went to sit down. 'There are no details.'

'Have you kissed?'

'We may have.' Matilda felt herself warming as she thought of the few kisses they'd shared. Daniel was an incredibly handsome man. He made her feel . . . she wasn't sure *happy* was the correct word, but something close to happiness. When she was with Daniel, she realised that life hadn't stopped just because James was dead. There was more to life than work.

'Ooh, exciting. What was it like?'

'Awkward.'

'Oh. Why?'

'Well, the first time, we were on this sofa. I opened my eyes and I saw James looking at me. Daniel noticed it too. They were good friends.'

'Just take things slowly, one step at a time.'

'We're taking things incredibly slowly. In fact, I think they're going backwards.'

'There's no need to rush into things.'

'I know. I'll never forget James. He was the love of my life. I'm worried that any new partner, I'll compare to James or treat him like a replacement.'

'Cross that bridge when you come to it. If you take things slowly, you'll see the signs and be able to avoid them.'

'Do you think?'

'Definitely.'

'Daniel's asked me out for this weekend. Do you think I should go?'

'No. I think you should come round to mine so we can watch *Strictly Come Dancing* together and cry into a bag of Kettle Chips. Of course you should go, you silly cow.'

'I will,' Matilda beamed.

'Oh,' Adele said, looking sad.

'What's wrong?'

'Now I'm feeling sad and lonely. You don't happen to have a spare hunky architect for me, do you?'

'No. But I'll buy you a bag of Kettle Chips.'

Chapter 19

Not long after one o'clock in the morning, police were called to a disturbance in Sheffield City Centre. A group of four men were involved in a drunken brawl. A shop window had been smashed and one man was relieving himself into the fountain in the Peace Gardens. The micturater gave his name as Sebastian Page. He was immediately arrested and sent to South Yorkshire Police HQ, where he was charged with disturbing the peace, drunk and disorderly behaviour, and the possible abduction of Keeley Armitage.

By the time Matilda arrived for work, he was sober enough to be interviewed but suffering a massive hangover. She allowed him to stew in his own self-pity for a little while longer. She had a search party to organise.

'Who's our land search manager?' Matilda asked as she strode into the incident room.

'I think it's Aaron,' Sian said, looking up from her computer.

'Where is he?'

'Not in yet.'

'Typical. Sian, get the search team out to Stannington now. I want as many PCs and DCs as we can spare. Christian, get a team together and get knocking on all the doors on Acorn Drive and the surrounding areas. I want to know everything about the Armitage family. Ask the usual questions: what are they like, any rows or arguments? What's Keeley like as a child? Is she happy, smiling, or sad and lonely? Any friends? Have they seen anyone suspicious or new hanging around lately? Any strange cars? I want the head teacher of Mary Croft spoken to again. Have any other kids or parents reported strangers hanging around lately?'

'Ok. By the way, I've liaised with the press officer. They're good to go whenever you are.'

'Right. I'll need to have a word with Craig and Linda about that.'

Matilda went into her office and pulled a waterproof jacket from the hook on the back of the door. She wanted to go out to Stannington herself and see the search in action.

'Christian, before you go,' she called out to him as he was leaving the office, 'I want an Armitage family tree. I need to know whether they have family living close by, cousins, aunts and uncles, that kind of thing.'

'I've already started with that. Ellen's finishing it off for me.'

'Thanks,' she put her hands on her hips and looked around the room. 'Where the sodding hell is Aaron?'

DI Christian Brady was a dedicated and trustworthy detective. Matilda had welcomed him into her team with open arms and, like Sian, he gave one hundred per cent. His only distraction was the ravages of age. He was balding slightly, and was getting a little soft around the middle. His once fitted shirts were now worn loosely, and he'd taken to arriving for work wearing a designer flat cap.

He was heading down the corridor, phone in hand, when he almost collided with Aaron who was conducting a private phone conversation behind a vending machine.

'Jesus, Aaron, you scared the— What's wrong?'

Aaron was frequently asked if anything was wrong. He had a permanent look of worry on his face, a brooding brow, and slouched shoulders; he was a dead ringer for Idris Elba's Luther but without the cool coat.

'Nothing, why?'

'There is. Has something happened? Is Katrina all right?' he asked, referring to Aaron's wife.

'Fuck,' he said, kicking the side of the vending machine.

'Come here.' Christian grabbed Aaron by the elbow and led him to an office. He opened the door and poked his head through to make sure it was empty before pushing Aaron in.

The small room was dark, cold, and there was an underlying smell of damp. It took a while for the lights to warm up.

'I've fucked up big time,' Aaron said, sitting on the edge of a desk.

'What have you done?'

'It's nothing work related. Well, it kind of is in a way.'

'Spit it out, Aaron.'

He took a deep breath. 'Remember the Mercer case earlier this year?'

'I'm hardly likely to forget it. I still see blood sometimes when I close my eyes.'

'Me too. Anyway, I've sort of been seeing Leah.'

'Leah?' Christian thought for a moment. 'Leah Mercer? Isn't she married?'

'No. She got the marriage annulled.'

'Even so, you're married.'

'I know,' he said, looking down.

'I don't get it; didn't she leave Sheffield?'

'Yes. She moved in to her brother's place in Liverpool. I've been seeing her at the weekends.'

'What about Katrina?'

'I've said I've been working extra shifts.'

'Jesus Christ, Aaron.' Christian looked on his colleague with scorn. A committed family man, Christian could never contemplate having an affair. He loved his wife and his children far too much.

'Leah's pregnant,' Aaron blurted out.

'Oh my God.'

'I'm know. I'm fucking idiot.'

'What are you going to do?'

'I have no idea. I've been trying to end it with Leah for a couple of months. I love Katrina so much. I hate the fact that I'm hurting her, and she doesn't know it.'

'It's not hurting you that much if you're still sleeping with Leah.'

'What do I do?' Aaron asked, looking up with pleading eyes.

'If I knew the answer to that I'd tell you. You're going to have to bite the bullet and admit what you've done. You're going to hurt a lot of people, but you're going to have to accept that.'

'Shit.'

'Come on, Matilda's looking for you. You're our land search manager and you're needed in Stannington.'

'I don't think I'm up to this.'

'You don't have an option,' Christian said, his voice stern. 'You're at work, you leave your fucked-up life at home. There's a missing girl out there relying on us to find her. Now, I'll gladly have a pint with you and try to help you sort out your mess, but right now, we've got a job to do.'

He took a step back and held the door open for Aaron to go through.

'You're right.' Aaron said.

Stannington was on the edge of the city of Sheffield, on the border with the Peak District National Park and, beyond that, Derbyshire. Up the road from Acorn Drive, where the Armitages lived, was the B6076 Stannington Road which ran straight into open countryside. Farms and fields lay either side and there was a direct route to the Damflask Reservoir.

Matilda had to cover all the bases. It was possible that Keeley had been kidnapped, and, for whatever reason, the kidnappers hadn't called back. Maybe Keeley had died in an accident; maybe they'd murdered her. Or, maybe, Linda or Craig Armitage had made the whole story up and they'd killed her. She'd spent the majority of last night tossing all the scenarios around in her mind but couldn't settle on one. It was little wonder she'd only managed four hours' sleep. If she was dead, there was a strong possibility her body was around here somewhere, and Matilda would find it at any cost.

It was eight o'clock when the first minibus containing uniformed officers in all-weather gear turned up. DS Aaron Connolly had a map of the areas to be searched and dispatched officers in teams.

Matilda climbed out of her car and watched as officers were split up and dispersed. She shivered as a gust of cool wind whipped around her. According to the weather forecast, a storm was predicted for later this week. Hopefully Keeley would be found before the bad weather set in.

There were many areas in and around Stannington where a small girl could be hiding, lying injured or dead. Stannington

Park and patches of green for children to play on were dotted about, all of which had to be searched.

Vanloads of uniformed and specialised officers with trained dogs descended on the area. They were all given maps and targeted areas to search. It was co-ordinated chaos. Matilda watched as Finn Cotton began his first case as a fully qualified detective constable after several months as a trainee. The wind was nipping at his face, turning his cheeks red. He zipped up his coat and pulled the hood up, covering his strawberry-blond hair. He was in a team with Scott and Rory. They were to search the grounds surrounding Underbank Unitarian Chapel and Townhead Farm, up to Riggs High Road. Finn took a laminated map from Aaron and they headed off, heavy boots resounding on the broken road.

Beyond Stannington Park, the houses disappeared and the horizon opened up to farms and countryside and scattered copses of trees. All of these needed to be searched. Well House Farm, Oldfield Gate Farm, Parkside and Little Parkside Farm and Goodyfield Farm would all have outbuildings and fields, all of which would need to be searched. Beyond those was the River Rivelin, and a specialised underwater search team were dispatched to the area in the hunt for the missing girl.

Above Stannington, SY99, the force's helicopter, was flying low as it looked from the skies for anything they could relay to the officers on the ground.

Matilda looked up and squinted in the sunshine. She didn't hear Sian approach.

'We're like an occupying force,' she said.

Matilda turned around and saw what she meant. The police had taken over Stannington. Marked cars and vans were haphazardly parked everywhere. Uniformed officers were knocking on doors, talking to people on the street, handing out leaflets. The campaign to find Keeley Armitage had begun. It was more than forty hours since she had gone missing. Matilda hoped all this effort wouldn't be in vain.

'Is this the most up-to-date map we've got?' Matilda asked.

'I'm not sure. Why?'

'It's still showing Dyson Ceramics on here. If you look over the hill, you'll see the whole site has been levelled and they're building houses on there. How can we search for someone when the fucking map is wrong?' she said in frustration, thrusting the map at her DS.

She turned and took large strides up the steep incline. Sian quickly followed.

'The search teams aren't stupid. They'll know these maps aren't one hundred per cent accurate. They'll search the areas they're designated to do whether it's a factory or now a housing estate.'

'Is there any wonder the Armitages don't have faith in us when they see the rag-tag bunch we've got looking for their daughter?'

'What are you talking about?'

'Didn't you hear Rory? He asked Aaron to give him and Finn the area down near Hill Top as that's close to Our Cow Molly and they can pop in for a Ferrero Rocher ice-cream cone.'

Matilda came to a rest at the side of the road and leaned against a brick wall.

'Mat, it's just gallows humour. He didn't mean it. Everyone is committed to finding Keeley,' she said, putting her arm around her. 'Look, why don't you take an hour or so off? There's not much you can do here.'

'No. I need to be doing something. I just . . .'

'What?'

'I just can't believe this is happening again,' she said, looking out at the swarm of officers searching for a missing child. Matilda had a lump of emotion stuck in her throat that was making her feel sick to her stomach. She'd always believed history repeated itself but this was cruel.

'It's not happening again. It's completely different. If you treat every missing person case like Carl Meagan's, then you're going to drive yourself insane. We'll find Keeley. I know it,' Sian said defiantly.

'I wish I shared your optimism,' Matilda said. She relaxed slightly.

'Now, what's this you were saying about Ferrero Rocher ice cream? Is that actually a thing?'

Chapter 20

It was time for school to begin.

There was an eerie feeling in the close-knit community. Anxious parents held on tight to their children as they took them to school. On a normal day, kids would be running in front, laughing, screaming, and parents would be gossiping. Today, the atmosphere was sombre. Children walked silently, gripping their mother's hand. Faces were grim, and everybody tried to avoid eye contact with the heavily wrapped up police officers who made their way along Stannington Road.

Police cars drove slowly, and a helicopter circled high above. None of this felt real.

Head teacher Sheila Croft watched the growing crowed of worried parents and made her way to them. She offered a sympathetic smile.

'Good morning.'

'Miss Croft, these gates will be locked, won't they, once all the children are inside?' a worried parent asked.

Sheila tilted her head. 'The gates are locked every morning at nine o'clock and not opened until school ends at three-thirty. This happens every single day. Your children are perfectly safe here.'

'Have you heard anything about Keeley yet?' asked another parent.

'No, I haven't. I have a detective coming round later today. I expect I'll be updated then.'

'I heard the police were here yesterday and they spoke to Mr Page who's since done a runner,' one parent shouted above the sound of a helicopter.

'Is this true?' Someone called out from the back of the small crowd of parents, which seemed to be growing with every question directed at Sheila Croft.

She held up her hands to quieten the crowd. 'Mr Page was questioned because he was the last teacher to teach Keeley before she went missing. As for him doing a runner, that is simply not true,' she said, hoping her poker face would hold.

'My Phoebe was very upset this morning,' one woman said as she stroked the golden blonde hair of a grim-faced child in front of her. 'Will you keep an eye on her?'

'I'm going to be holding a special assembly this morning. You've nothing to worry about. Come along Phoebe, let's get you into school and let Mummy go off to work.'

Sheila held her hand out to Phoebe, who looked to her mother for permission to take it. She eventually allowed herself to be led away.

Mary Croft Primary School was one of three primary schools in the Stannington area, but it was the largest and held over seven hundred pupils. Many parents had elected to keep their children away from school today as gossip and rumour spread around social media like wildfire. *There was a kidnapper on the loose. A van had been seen slowly circulating the area seeking vulnerable children walking on their own. There was a known paedophile living near the school, the police knew about it, and were keeping it to themselves. At least one teacher had a criminal record.* Every stranger was a suspect. Every unknown car had their registration number written down, and suddenly, everyone was frightened.

All the children assembled into the hall. They sat quietly on the floor in rows, their legs crossed. Teachers stood at the side of the room. They tried to act normally for the sake of reassuring the pupils, but they were equally fearful. Would the finger of suspicion be pointed at them? The profession of teacher was no longer a rewarding one. They were blamed for a great many things: low test results, showing too much interest in a student, not showing enough interest. Placing a hand on the back of one child if they were upset was suddenly no longer a symbol of comfort, but a sign of a teacher grooming the child. They couldn't maintain eye contact with a child for too long in case it was seen as intimidation or as if they were being somehow suggestive.

Sheila Croft walked down the centre of the room. Her sensible shoes clacked loudly on the parquet flooring as she walked with her shoulders back, head high, and ample bosom on display. She was wearing a beige ankle-length skirt and a white shirt buttoned up to her fat neck. She dressed conservatively for a reason: protection against any unwanted or unwarranted attention from parents and teachers alike.

'Good morning everyone. As I'm sure you all know by now, one of our fellow pupils, Keeley Armitage, who is in Miss Beech's class, has gone missing. Now, on your way here this morning, you will have seen a lot of policemen and police-women who are doing everything they can to try and find her. I know it looks scary, but it's not. Police officers are there to look after us and keep us safe. There is nothing for any of you to worry about. However, if any of Keeley's friends know where she might be, or if they've seen anything strange, or if Keeley has mentioned anything strange lately, then you can tell me, or your teacher. Nobody is going to get into trouble. All we want to do is find Keeley.'

Sheila looked out at the sea of blue sweaters with the yellow logo on the left breast. All the faces were blank as the children, aged from seven to eleven, had their first glimpse of reality; the world wasn't all about learning the alphabet, times tables, and playing games. Outside of the school gates, beyond their back gardens, there was fear, dread, and horror.

Chapter 21

Craig and Linda Armitage had no interest in being famous or on television. They were both perfectly content to live their lives being the best parents they could be and, hopefully, raising three happy and healthy children. When Matilda mentioned a press conference, Linda burst into tears.

'Oh God, do I have to?' She asked once Ellen had calmed her down.

'It would help.'

Linda stood up and went over to the mirror above the mantelpiece. 'I look a mess. I can't remember the last time I had a haircut. My face is all blotchy. And what do I wear? I can't go on television; people will talk about me. What will happen if I don't cry or if I cry too much and can't talk? Can't someone else do it?'

'Linda, we need both of you to be there,' Matilda said firmly. 'We'll prepare a statement for you to say. Craig can speak if you don't want to, but you'll get more sympathy from the press, and the public, if you both make an appearance.'

'Craig?'

Craig was sitting on the sofa. Riley was asleep on his lap. He was unshaven, his hair was knotted, and he looked shattered. 'I'll speak,' was all he said.

At South Yorkshire Police HQ, the press was assembled and waiting in a packed conference room. Cameras were pointing towards the platform and the gathered journalists were chatting animatedly among themselves.

Craig and Linda looked petrified. They were sitting on an uncomfortable-looking sofa, holding hands, with grim, pale faces. They gave the impression that at any moment a judge was going to sentence them both to death.

Ellen Devonport was sitting next to them, talking them both through the press conference, what was expected of them and how it would unfold. They didn't seem to be paying any attention. Linda was wearing blue jeans and a navy sweater. Her hair was combed and pulled back into a loose ponytail. She wasn't wearing any make-up and had taken her earrings out. Craig wore black trousers and a white shirt with a grey sweater over the top. He'd shaved and ran his fingers through his hair. They both looked presentable, given the situation.

'Do I look all right?' Linda asked for what seemed like the hundredth time.

'You look fine,' Ellen replied, patting her hand.

Valerie entered the anteroom in full uniform, with Matilda following. She introduced herself to Craig and Linda before shaking their hands and reassuring them that South Yorkshire Police were pulling out all the stops to find their daughter.

'Is there anything you'd like to ask me about the press conference?' Valerie asked.

Linda's bottom lip was wobbling. She breathed in hard and swallowed her emotions. 'Will I have to speak?' She asked, her voice breaking.

'The press will direct their questions to you, Linda. They always like to hear how the mother is coping. However, myself or DCI Darke will step in if the questions become too much for you.'

'We're ready,' Ellen said.

Craig stood up first, still grasping his wife's hand. He had to help her up as all energy seemed to drain from her. The door was opened, and they stepped out.

The cameras began to flash. Linda gripped Craig's hand tighter. Ellen led the way and pointed out the seats for them to take. They sat behind the desk and looked ahead at the sea of reporters and cameras.

Matilda took a seat at the end of the table. Linda was in the middle with Craig and Ellen either side, both were holding one of her hands for support. She was pale and looked as if she was about to throw up all over the table. In front of Craig was a single sheet of A4 paper with the prepared statement he was to read out for the reporters.

Once the flashing had stopped and the murmurs had subsided, Matilda took a deep breath and opened the proceedings.

'On Monday 10th September, nine-year-old Keeley Armitage disappeared on her way home from school. Around four o'clock, Mrs Armitage received a phone call from someone who said they'd kidnapped Keeley. We now believe this was a hoax. However, Keeley remains missing. The photograph on the screen behind me shows Keeley wearing the uniform of Mary Croft Primary School in Stannington. She was wearing this, along with a yellow jacket, when she went missing. Officers are currently searching around the Stannington area for Keeley. If anybody out there has seen her or knows of her whereabouts, they're to call the number on the bottom of the screen immediately.'

More cameras flashed. Despite Matilda doing the talking, all the cameras seemed to be centred on Linda and her husband.

'Craig Armitage, Keeley's father, is going to say a few words.'

Craig remained still and silent for a long moment. He let go of his wife's hand and picked up the sheet of A4 paper on the table in front of him. His hands were shaking. He cleared his throat.

'Keeley is a bright and happy girl. She's our middle child and her older sister, Jodie, and younger brother, Riley, miss her terribly, as do her mum and me. She was last seen outside the Co-op on Oldfield Road. At the time she went missing, there were a lot of other schoolchildren and parents about. Somebody must have seen where she went or if anybody took her. If you've taken her, for whatever reason, we need her back home. Please, take her to a police station, or phone us. We just want her back home with us.'

Finished, he put the paper down on the table and reached out for Linda's hand. She grabbed for it and wrapped her fingers around his.

'DCI Darke and ACC Masterson will now take a few questions from the press. Please state your name and the organisation you're with before your question.' The press officer said clearly from the side of the room.

'Rose Cartwright, *BBC Look North*. How do you know the kidnapping was a hoax?'

'The ongoing investigation and evidence we've gathered has led us to believe it was a hoax,' Valerie said.

'Bob Rogers, *Sheffield Telegraph*. According to social media, a ransom demand of fifty thousand pounds was made. How can it be a hoax, yet you still have a missing child?'

'We believe that whoever has taken Keeley used the kidnapping ploy to mislead police.'

'So she was definitely taken? She hasn't simply wandered off?' Bob asked.

'That's our understanding of the situation,' Valerie said.

'Greg Levy, *The Sun*. Linda, if whoever has taken your daughter is watching this, what would you personally like to say to them?'

More cameras flashed followed by a silence, as all eyes turned to Linda.

Craig squeezed her hand tighter. She opened her mouth, but nothing came out. She grabbed for the plastic cup of water and took a large gulp.

Linda looked deep into the television camera in front of her. 'Keeley's my youngest daughter. I love her so much. She makes me smile. I miss her. I need her home. I don't care why you've taken her. I just want you . . . I *need* you to give her back to me. Please.'

Craig wrapped his left arm around Linda's shoulders, and she sank into him. The silence around the room grew.

'Any other questions?'

'Danny Hanson, *Sheffield Star*.'

Matilda's ears pricked up.

'DCI Darke, this must bring back memories of Carl Meagan's disappearance four years ago. There are similarities with a ransom demand. Do you believe the two are connected?'

Matilda leaned closer to the microphone in front of her. She tried to speak but her dry mouth wouldn't allow her. She cleared her throat. 'We've established that, in this case, the ransom demand was a hoax. We have no evidence to suggest that the cases are connected.'

'Two children going missing, money demanded in both cases. How confident are you that you can get Keeley back where you failed with Carl?'

'South Yorkshire Police are working around the clock to find Keeley . . .'

'You said the same about Carl going missing.'

'Mr Hanson,' Valerie jumped in. 'Your questions are not helping. Every case is different. There were circumstances beyond our control in why Carl was never found. However, the case remains open and we remain active in looking for him. Looking for Keeley is in the very early stages and we are confident we can bring her home. Now, unless you have a more pertinent question, I believe you can sit down.'

'Do you have a suspect?' he asked quickly.

'At present, we haven't identified one suspect, but we are following a number of leads.'

'There are rumours you have a teacher from Keeley's school under arrest.'

'Mr Hanson, I'm aware that the majority of what goes into your newspaper is based on rumour, innuendo and gossip, but at South Yorkshire Police, we only deal in facts. I suggest you look that particular f-word up before you continue,' Valerie said.

There was a ripple of laughter from around the room.

The press officer chose this moment to bring the conference to an end. Linda couldn't stand up fast enough. She and Craig were led off the platform by Ellen Devonport. Matilda refused to break eye contact with Danny Hanson until he blinked first. A flash of a camera caused Matilda to turn her head.

In Dore, Sally Meagan was sitting on the sofa in the living room. She stared, wide-eyed, at the television watching the press conference live. She was taken back in time to when she and Philip had been led out onto the same platform and had given a tearful plea for Carl to come home. She had no memory of what she'd said or of the questions asked of her by the press.

Every time she'd looked up, she'd been blinded by the flash of the cameras.

'It's happening again,' she said, choking on her tears as Woody looked up at her from his position on the sofa next to her. 'That poor family. I wouldn't wish this on anyone.'

Philip came into the living room, snatched up the remote from the coffee table and turned the TV off.

'I told you not to watch it.'

'I know. I had to, though.'

'Why?'

'Phil, do you think we should have given her the money?'

'No. How many times have we had people coming to the house or emailing us asking for money? If we give something to one, we have to give to them all. We can't do that.'

'But . . . she looks like a female version of our Carl,' she sniffled.

Philip squatted next to her and took her bony hands in his. 'No she doesn't, Sal. You just think she does. Don't do this to yourself.'

Craig and Linda were whisked to Valerie's office. It was quieter and had more comfortable seating. The ACC had arranged for a tray of coffee to be waiting for them. Nobody spoke as they made their way along the corridor. Linda, with her head down, never let go of her husband's hand.

Matilda waited until they had entered the office before she dug out her mobile and made a call.

'Christian, how did it go?' She asked quietly.

'We've searched their shed and Craig's van. We found nothing.'

Matilda relaxed. *It doesn't mean he's in the clear. Keep your guard up*. 'That's good. Did Jodie see you searching?'

'No. Sian was chatting to her in Riley's room.'

'Ok.' She ended the call and went to join the others in Valerie's office.

They were all sitting awkwardly around a small table on comfortable chairs. Ellen placed a tray of coffees in the middle and handed one to Linda. She took a sip and pulled a face.

'Do you have anything to put in this?'

'I do,' Valerie went over to her filing cabinet and took out a bottle of whiskey. She poured a small measure into Linda's coffee. Craig refused.

'What happens now?' Craig asked.

'The press conference was filmed by all the main news channels. It'll be shown on their bulletins and I believe a news crew from *Look North* are going out to Stannington this afternoon to film some of the search,' Matilda said. 'It will feature heavily in their programme tonight.'

'What happens if nothing comes of it? I mean, I know you'll get calls, you're bound to, but what if there are no leads?'

'We take it one step at a time,' she said. 'Obviously, we hope we find Keeley through this. If not, we'll stage a reconstruction, another press conference, we'll get you on breakfast television being interviewed, double page features in national newspapers. There is so much we can do.'

Craig smiled and leaned back in his seat, suitably placated. Linda was perched on the edge, her hands wrapped around the mug, her knuckles white.

'I don't think I can go through another night without her. Why would someone do this? Why do people take children?'

Nobody could reply. The clock on the wall ticked loudly. Everyone in the room knew why a person kidnapped a child, but saying it out loud would not be helpful, especially to Linda.

Chapter 22

Matilda picked Pat up from her home in Bradway. She was smartly dressed in black trousers and a cream jumper, heeled shoes and a long black cardigan. She'd styled her hair and put on a touch of make-up. Her fragrance was sweet and not too overpowering. Beside her, Matilda felt like she'd spent the night sleeping in a bus shelter.

'Without sounding too much like a young World War II bride, any more news from France?' Pat asked as they set off from outside her home.

'No. They won't tell us where the boy is or if they've found the couple he was travelling with.'

'What about the DNA samples?'

'We're still waiting. I'm hoping they're going to mark them as urgent and not post them second class,' she said, giving a slight chuckle.

'I saw the press conference on the news. How are you doing?'

She shrugged. 'I'm trying not to think about Carl too much, to focus on finding Keeley, but it's not easy.'

'No. I saw that leech Danny Hanson asking you questions about Carl. He's got one of those faces you'd like to smack with a hot frying pan.'

'Pat!' Matilda admonished.

'Sorry. I'm right, though. How are Keeley's parents coping?'

'Her mother isn't. She's a mess. Craig's trying to be supportive and strong for her, but he's just bottling it all up; you can see it in his face. I dread to think what's going to happen if we find a body.'

'Have you ruled them out?'

It was a while before Matilda answered. 'I'm not ruling anyone out.'

Pat gave a hint of a smile. 'Good to hear. This is a difficult case for you, Mat, don't let your heart rule your head.'

They pulled up outside the black gates at the bottom of the Meagan drive. Neither of them had called ahead. Secretly, Matilda hoped they'd gone out for the day, or better still, had decided to go on a world cruise and wouldn't be back in Sheffield for another six months. By then, hopefully, France would have sent the DNA samples over.

Matilda wound down the window and pressed the intercom button. It rang several times. Matilda's heart thumped loudly in her chest. She wished and prayed and hoped it wasn't answered.

'Hello Matilda,' Sally's distorted voice came out of the speaker. 'Come on in.'

Sally's voice: soft, a light Yorkshire accent, a hint of a lisp; it was a voice Matilda had heard many times overlaid by an array of harrowing emotions, but despite a warming in their strained relationship, Matilda always felt she could hear an accusatory tone. It made her feel guilty all over again. The gates slowly began to open. Matilda looked over to Pat and gave a nervous smile.

'I'm dreading this,' Pat said.

'So am I.'

She drove up the drive and parked the Range Rover outside

the front door. As they climbed out of the car, the door opened and out bounded Woody. He headed straight for Pat who took a Bonio out of her pocket. He immediately sat down and offered a paw. He took the biscuit gently from her, allowed her to scratch behind his ears and ran back into the house, snack in his mouth.

'He's a wonderful guard dog, isn't he?' Pat said.

'A burglar wouldn't need to bring any tools, just a box of Bonio,' Sally said with a smile. 'Come on in, kettle's on.'

Matilda and Pat followed Sally into the large house. The hallway was spacious and tastefully decorated in whites and creams. The kitchen was warm and cosy – a large range at the top of the room, solid oak cupboard fronts and worktops giving the room a country-cottage feel.

Sally went about making the coffee while Matilda and Pat sat on the stools at the island. In the corner of the room, Woody chewed loudly in his bed.

'Philip in?'

'Yes, he's just getting changed. I had a feeling you'd be visiting. I saw the press conference. Is the ransom thing really a hoax?'

'We think so.'

'My heart goes out to the parents. I know exactly how they feel.' Sally had her back to them. Matilda heard a slight catch in her voice.

'Sally, Linda wants me to pass on her apologies for—'

Sally quickly turned and held her hand up to silence Matilda. 'There's no need for an apology. I was absolutely petrified when she approached me, but looking back, I could see in her eyes she was acting out of desperation. If there's anything I can do, maybe talk to her, offer some advice, I'll gladly do it.'

Matilda smiled. 'That's very generous of you.'

Sally shrugged. 'Not generous at all; just practical.'

'Hello you two,' Philip said, entering the room. He was wearing skinny black trousers and a black polo shirt. Philip was tall and thin. His hair was grey and receding. He looked healthier than the last time Matilda had seen him. He no longer looked gaunt and had a bit of colour in his cheeks.

Matilda watched as Philip went over to Sally. He put his arm around her shoulder and kissed her on the cheek. They smiled at each other. She poured him a coffee from the cafetière and as he reached for a sugar cube from the bowl, she slapped his hand. They giggled.

Matilda smiled. It was heartening to watch them as a normal, happy couple. She hoped they weren't acting, and that this was a genuine display. She knew they both still missed their son and they hadn't forgotten him and moved on, but they'd adapted to a life without him, for now.

The four of them sat around the island and engaged in point-less small talk. Matilda noticed Sally kept stealing glances towards her. She knew their visit wasn't a social one, that Matilda had news, but was waiting for the perfect moment to say it.

'I'm sorry,' Sally said, placing her cup down in its saucer. 'I don't mean to sound rude, but you've obviously come here for a reason.'

'We have,' Matilda said.

'It's about Carl, isn't it?'

Matilda gave the smallest of nods. Sally reached out and grabbed Philip's hand.

'On Monday, a young boy walked into a police station in France and showed the officer a missing persons poster. He said he was the boy in the picture. He said he was Carl Meagan.'

'Oh my God,' Sally said. Her entire body shook. 'He's alive. I knew he would be.' Tears began to roll down her face. 'How is he? Is he well? Is he all right?' She couldn't speak fast enough; her words were tripping over each other as they fell out of her mouth.

'We've been told he's been well taken care of.'

'This is amazing news. This is wonderful.' She slapped a hand to her chest and took a deep breath. 'I can't believe it. When's he coming home?'

'Right now, he's in a secure location and being looked after by Police Nationale,' Matilda said. 'They're sending over a DNA sample so we can test it against the sample we have of Carl's to make sure it's a match.'

'You don't think it's Carl, do you?' Philip asked, looking intently at Matilda.

'What?' Sally butted in. 'Of course it'll be Carl. He'll know we've been looking for him. He'll have seen the poster and gone straight to the police. He's a good boy. He's done the right thing.' She couldn't stop smiling.

'I'm keeping an open mind,' Matilda told Philip. 'I genuinely hope it is Carl, but I'm not getting my hopes up until the DNA results come through.'

'This is amazing,' Sally beamed, not listening to a word Matilda was saying. 'Do you think we should go out to France?'

'Hold your horses, Sal,' Philip said, trying to calm her down. He turned to Matilda. 'Did the police in France send a photo through of this boy?'

'Yes, they did.'

Matilda took her phone out of her pocket and unlocked the screen. She went into the photos app and scrolled through until she found the one of the boy claiming to be Carl. She placed the phone on the island, turned it around and slowly edged it towards them.

Sally cried. She wrapped herself around Philip's skinny right arm and rested her head on his shoulder while looking at the phone through eyes blurred with tears. Philip's face remained blank.

'He's grown,' Sally eventually said. 'He's lost his chubby cheeks.' She wiped her eyes with her sleeve. 'He looks well,' she smiled.

'Philip?' Matilda asked.

'He looks nothing like Carl.'

'What?' Sally said firmly. 'How can you say that?' She grabbed the phone and held it up to him. 'Look at him. Look at his eyes. How can you not tell he's your son?'

'Because it's not him, Sally,' he said quietly, tears forming in his eyes.

'You're wrong. It's Carl. I know it is.' She looked deep into the photograph. 'I'll admit he's changed, but it's been almost four years, he's bound to have changed. He's eleven now. He's had a growth spurt; it's what happens with kids. It's him. I know it is. I can feel it in my heart.'

'Sally,' Philip said, looking down at the floor.

'What happens now? I know you said you have to wait for the DNA results, but how long will they be? When can we bring him home?'

'I'm hoping the results will be with us any day. It shouldn't take long to have it confirmed or not.'

'I'd better prepare his room. Do you think we should get the decorators in or do you think he'd prefer it the way it was?' Sally asked her husband but didn't wait for a reply. 'No. I think we should leave it and let him choose how he wants his room to look. We can decorate it together. This calls for a toast.'

She jumped down from the stool and ran into the utility room where the wine fridge was.

'Why don't you think it's Carl?' Pat asked.

'His eyes are wrong. His lips are thin. Why did you have to tell us? Why couldn't you wait until you have the DNA results?'

'It's the French police who are dealing with this. They could release the information to the press that they've found a child who claims to be Carl. I didn't want Sally hearing about it on the news.'

He nodded. 'I understand. She's seeing Carl because she wants it to be him.'

'Children do change,' Matilda said, placing a hand on top of his. 'There is every possibility this is Carl.' Of course, Matilda knew the opposite was true, too, that this boy might not be Carl. It didn't matter how many times Matilda looked at that photograph on her phone, she couldn't make her mind up.

'Matilda's right,' Pat said. 'What would be the point in lying? In this day and age, we'd find out soon enough if he was lying, and then he'd been in so much trouble. I can understand your reaction, Phil, but there is a chance.'

'Let's just wait until the DNA results come through before—'

Matilda was interrupted by the sound of a champagne cork popping.

Chapter 23

Normally, a detective sergeant and constable would conduct the interview with Sebastian Page. As all of them were out at Stannington taking part in the search for Keeley Armitage, there was only Matilda and Christian left to do it.

Matilda was in her office when Christian knocked lightly on the glass door. He didn't wait to be asked to enter before pushing the door open.

'Do you want the bad news or the bad news?'

'If one of those pieces of bad news is that Sian's run out of Maltesers in her snack drawer I'm going to scream this building down,' she said with a twinkle in her eye.

'It's worse than that.'

'Go on.'

He sat down in front of Matilda's desk. 'It's about Sebastian Page's brother, Calvin. He was released from prison in January.'

'What? Why didn't we know about this?'

'I don't know.'

'Where is he?'

'I don't know.'

'You don't have an address?'

'His home address is listed as a house in Hillsborough.

Uniform officers have been round and there's a different family living there.'

'For how long?'

'Since the spring.'

'So, where's Calvin then?'

'I don't know.'

'Shouldn't he have been in a halfway house or something?'

'He was, but according to the report his brother found him somewhere to live and offered to keep an eye on him.'

'Shit,' she said, slamming her hands down on the desk. 'Get Sebastian in an interview room now.'

'Will do.'

'Christian, what's the second piece of bad news?'

At the door, Christian turned back to look at his boss. 'Oh, right, that. Erm, I don't think you should look at any news reports today.'

Matilda waited until Christian had left the HMET suite before she lifted the lid on her laptop and went online. Most of the national newspapers led with the story of a child going missing in Sheffield. They all linked the case with Carl Meagan's disappearance with one newspaper even pointing out the similarities between Keeley and Carl – the blonde hair, the blue eyes. Were there child traffickers operating in Sheffield? If so, what were South Yorkshire Police doing about it?

'I bloody hate journalists,' she seethed.

Sebastian Page seemed to have aged twenty years over night. That's what a night in the cells could do to a man.

He sat in interview room one wearing a white paper suit. His clothes had been ruined by him vomiting all over them. His eyes were red and rheumy, and Sebastian seemed to be in great pain by keeping them open.

Matilda slapped a thick file down on the table, causing him to jump.

'Mr Page. Let's ignore the fact you were caught drunk and disorderly in Sheffield centre last night. Let's pretend you weren't arrested while pissing in a fountain in the Peace Gardens and I'm not even going to mention the smell coming from the cell you slept in after you vomited all over it and missed the toilet by a mile. What I do want to know is, where is your brother and where the hell is Keeley Armitage?'

Matilda remained standing. Her arms were folded across her chest and the steely look on her face showed she meant business and was in no mood for wasting time when Keeley was still nowhere to be found.

'My brother?' He looked up, his eyes barely open. 'What's Calvin got to do with this?'

'He's out of prison and he's not at the address he gave his parole officer. Where is he?'

'I've no idea. I haven't seen him for a few months.'

'Why not?'

'Why do you think? I'm a teacher and my brother is a child rapist, for crying out loud. That's not going to look good, is it?'

'You told his parole officer you'd vouch for him.'

He looked down at the table. 'Mum didn't want him living in that halfway house. She wanted him to get back to normal life as soon as possible.'

Matilda rolled her eyes. 'Why did you run after we interviewed you?'

'I don't know,' he said, his head sinking as if it was too heavy to hold up.

Matilda pulled out a chair and sat down. She stared at him, waiting for an answer. Christian remained standing by the door.

'I panicked.'

'The reactions of a guilty man.'

'I'm not guilty.'

'Then why panic?'

'Because . . .'

'Because is not an answer. Keeley Armitage is missing. I need to find her.'

'Honestly, hand on heart, if I knew where she was, I'd tell you.'

Matilda exhaled loudly. 'And Calvin?'

He shrugged.

'What about his friends, family, fellow child rapists?' She asked, clearly angry with his answers.

'I feel sick again.'

'I don't care. You're not leaving this room until you tell me where your brother is,' she shouted.

'Ma'am,' Christian said, as a way of telling her she was taking this too far and she should allow him a comfort break.

'Oh for fuck's sake. Put him back in his cell.'

'What shall we do with him? We can't hold him for much longer without charging him.'

'Whatever you can charge him with, do it; drunk and disorderly, criminal damage, concealing a convict, kidnapping and seriously pissing off a DCI.'

Matilda stormed out of the interview room and headed for her office.

By the time she'd climbed the stairs and entered the HMET suite she hadn't calmed down. Her face was still thunderous and she could feel the blood pounding in her ears. She felt faint and needed something to eat. She pulled open the bottom drawer in Sian's desk and grabbed a handful of chocolate bars before storming into her office and slamming the door so hard behind her the glass rattled in the frames.

Sian entered the suite, heard the banging, and headed for Matilda's small office in the far corner of the open-plan room. 'Is everything all right?'

'No. A nine-year-old girl is missing, and everybody keeps asking me if everything is all right as if I'm going to break into a thousand pieces.'

'I'm sorry.'

'And stop apologising.'

Matilda looked at Sian. 'I'm sorry, Sian. I know you're only trying to help.' She sank into her chair, tore into a Mars bar and ate half of it in a single bite. 'Why haven't we found her yet?' she asked with her mouth full.

'I don't know. I've had the results back from her iPad if you're interested.'

'And?'

'You're not going to like this.' Sian swiped her own iPad into life and opened the email she'd received from forensics. 'It seems that Jodie was mistaken. Keeley wasn't only on Snapchat; she was on Facebook and Instagram. The photos on Instagram are . . . very grown up.

'How do you mean?'

Sian showed her the iPad. The photographs showed Keeley fully made up, her hair stylishly arranged. Her clothes were tight and revealing and Keeley was seductively pouting into the camera.

'Oh my God. She looks like a completely different girl,' Matilda said.

'I know.'

'She looks older than nine too. Who is she sending these pictures to?'

'Nobody. She's posting them online. And she's received some very unsavoury comments.'

'Do we know who's posting these comments?'

'Yes. We're following them up. It's going to take time though.'

'I don't care how long it takes. I want every single person questioned. We're going to need to talk to Craig and Linda about these pictures too, see if they knew she was taking them.'

'Ellen did say that Riley got a lot of attention,' Sian said. 'Maybe Keeley has felt left out. The middle child often does. Maybe she's getting the validation she needs from elsewhere.'

'But this kind of validation?' she asked, showing Sian a photo on the iPad of Keeley wearing only a bra and sucking on a lollypop, staring into the camera with heavily made up, sleepy eyes.

'Why would a nine-year-old feel the need to dress like this and take these kinds of pictures?'

'Maybe somebody asked her to pose like that? Sian, we really need to find Calvin Page. He seems to have gone missing. Get on to his parole officer and see what they're doing to find him.'

'Will do,' she turned to leave.

'Hang on a minute,' Matilda said. She enlarged a photo of Keeley looking seductively over her shoulder, into the camera. She held the iPad up and showed it to Sian. 'What do you notice about this photo?'

Sian studied it. There was a look of sadness on her face. 'I'm not sure.'

'It's not a selfie.'

'What?'

'She's got her back to the camera; she has her arms wrapped around herself and she's looking over her shoulder into the camera. Someone took this photo. Someone asked her to pose like this and she complied.'

'Who?'

'I know who my first guess would be.'

'The father?'

'Well, look at the background. That's definitely Keeley's bedroom. I want the whole family interviewed separately.' The iPad was shaking in her hands.

'Mat, do you think you should take a step back from this?'

Matilda's bottom lip wobbled. 'No. I need to do this. Sian, if I don't find Keeley Armitage, I'm going to resign.'

'What?'

'I can't have a second missing child on my conscience. The press are already making comparisons with Carl. They'll turn on me next, I know it. If we don't find her, it'll kill me. I won't be able to do this anymore. It'll finish me.'

Chapter 24

Everything to the east of Stannington Road within a twenty-mile radius had been searched: Stannington Park, farms and their out buildings, open fields and the new housing estate, but to no avail. To the west of the main road lay more open fields and pockets of woodland. These were the areas now being targeted. If Keeley Armitage wasn't found here, the search would have to be widened and continue over the border into Derbyshire. With nothing but sprawling acres of green land, the search would be arduous. More officers would need to be drafted in and other forces asked to join.

DC Finn Cotton and PC Natasha Tranter had been paired up and were tasked with searching the small copse of trees known as Storrs Brook. Light was beginning to fade, and it wouldn't be long before the sun disappeared behind the looming clouds slowly edging their way across the horizon. Following a hot, dry summer, it would appear that autumn was about to bite; a storm was coming.

Throughout the day the wind had steadily increased. The heavy-duty waterproof trousers and matching coat, hat, and insulated gloves were not flattering, but they helped keep the officers warm.

'I bet we've done more than ten thousand steps today,' Natasha said as she and Finn left the brightness of farmland behind and entered the shadowy cover of trees. The temperature was noticeably cooler in the Brook.

'My feet are killing me,' Finn said. 'I bet I've got blisters when I eventually take these off.'

'Do you think we'll find her?'

Finn turned to look at his partner. He saw the worried expression on her face. 'I kind of hope we don't. If we find her out here then we're finding a dead body.'

'The only alternative is that she's been taken for . . . God only knows what. It's a no-win situation.'

'Don't let DCI Darke hear you say that. There's a lot riding on her finding Keeley alive.'

'What's she like to work for, DCI Darke?'

It was a while before Finn answered. 'I don't really know her that well. I generally take my orders from DI Brady, but she seems fair. She's a little screwed up, obviously. Every now and then I feel like I'm being stared at. I look up and she's glaring at me and then I remember I'm sitting at DC Easter's desk.'

Searching the copse would require more intricate techniques than open space. There were many places a body, or clothing, or a scrap of fibre could be hiding. Finn took a torch from the pocket of his oversized coat and switched it on. It wasn't dark yet, but twilight was setting in. It wouldn't be long before the search was called off for the evening and they'd be brought back out here again tomorrow.

They looked around trees, up trees, swept undergrowth and scrambled through thickets. The ground was uneven and bone dry. Twigs snapped underfoot, the sound echoing in the silence.

'Finn, can I ask you a question?'

'Sure.'

'Has anyone mentioned me in the HMET?'

He thought for a moment. 'I don't think so. Why?'

'I just wondered if people were talking about me going out with Rory.'

'I haven't heard anything.'

'That's good. I'm being talked about by some of the uniform officers,' she said, looking downbeat.

'Really? Why?'

'A female PC going out with someone in plain clothes; I'm obviously trying to further my career by sleeping my way to the top.'

'Is that what they're saying?'

'Yes. When Harry Blythe went out with DS Hobbs last year, nobody said a dicky-bird. In fact, he received pats on the back all round.'

Finn noticed how suddenly distracted Natasha seemed. She'd lost all impetus in the search as she dwelled on the taunts she was receiving.

'Have you spoken to your sergeant about it?'

'What's the point? She's just as bad.'

'I could have a word with DS Mills if you like. She can't stand all this bullying in the workplace. She'd know exactly what to do.'

'I'm frightened of looking into promotion in case people think I've only been accepted because of who I'm dating. I really like Rory. I've been out with a few headcases in my time, and I've got the scars to show for it, but Rory, well, he's . . .'

She didn't get to finish as she tripped on the root of an oak tree, lost her balance and fell. She slipped down a small embankment and into a dried-up river bed.

'Natasha? Nat?' Finn called from above. He didn't receive a reply.

He edged his way down slowly, taking extra care where he stepped, and using each tree to steady himself so he didn't take the quicker, but more painful route, to the bottom.

He found Natasha sitting upright, leaning against the truck of a mighty oak. She was nursing her ankle and looking straight ahead. Her face was muddy and grazed where she'd collided with a branch on her way down.

'Natasha, are you all right? Have you hurt yourself?'

She didn't reply. She stayed staring straight ahead, her expression blank, her eyes wide. He turned around to see what she was fixated on and almost fell over at the shock.

Upside down, legs entwined in the roots of a tree sticking out of the embankment, head almost touching the dry riverbed, was the cold dead body of Keeley Armitage.

Chapter 25

By the time Matilda Darke arrived at Stannington, dusk had fallen, and a stiff wind was blowing the storm straight for Sheffield. She edged her way down the embankment towards the awkwardly positioned white tent protecting what little trace forensic evidence nature hadn't already destroyed. The surrounding area was lit up like an alien invasion as blue-suited forensic officers began fine-tooth combing the vicinity.

Matilda's heart sank. This was not the result she had envisioned. She wanted nothing more than to drive to the Armitages's house on Acorn Drive, open the back door and have Keeley jump out and run into the arms of her tearful parents.

'Are you all right?' Christian asked her as he handed over a forensic suit for her to put on over her clothes.

'No. This wasn't how it was supposed to be.'

He gave a sympathetic smile. 'I know I shouldn't say this, but at least it's a result. There'll be no endless anxious waiting for the phone to ring or a police car to pull up outside. They'll be able to grieve.'

'I've failed,' she said, struggling to hold on to her emotions. She turned her back on the forensic tent. She didn't want anyone from her team to see her cry like this.

'You haven't failed.'

'She's dead, isn't she?' she said, raising her voice. 'This isn't a positive result, Christian. It may be a conclusion, but it's the wrong one.'

'Look, you don't know what happened. Until we have all the facts of the case, we can't say how we could have performed any better. Nothing is straightforward. She could have been dead before her parents called us. We've already said the whole kidnapping thing was a hoax; maybe it's the parents who killed her and wanted to throw us off the scent.'

She looked up at Christian. He was upset by the situation, that was obvious. He also had children of a similar age to Keeley, he would feel it more than anyone, but he was being the consummate professional as always, and keeping his emotions in check.

Matilda took a deep breath and headed towards the tent. The flaps were pulled back for her and she ducked as she entered. She couldn't see the body as Adele Kean and her technician, Lucy Dauman, were bent over it. A part of her was clinging to the hope that this body did not belong to Keeley Armitage and perhaps another child had fallen and succumbed to an accident. A few more seconds of ignorance were bliss.

Adele stood up and revealed the body. Matilda wanted to be sick. There was no denying it now. Keeley had been left in the position in which she had been found, and it wasn't dignified. She was upside down, her legs painfully wrapped around the exposed roots of a tree. Her black tights were torn in several places, her grey, pleated skirt was up around her waist, showing her pink underwear. The blue sweater with the yellow Mary Croft school logo on the left breast was pulled up, revealing the white polo shirt beneath which was muddy and ripped. Her yellow coat was hanging off her shoulders. Keeley's blonde hair was a tangled mess and had twigs knotted into it.

Nobody said anything as Matilda remained frozen to the spot, looking deep into Keeley's dead blue eyes.

'The poor child,' she eventually said.

'I've been doing this for twenty years and it never gets any easier when a child's involved.'

'What can you tell me?'

'There's a heavy blow to the back of the head. I've no idea if it was from when she fell or was pushed down the embankment or if it was a deliberate blow to kill her. I'll know more when I get her back to the mortuary. However, I can tell you that she was strangled, and her neck was broken.'

'Any sign of . . . you know?'

'Sexual assault?'

Matilda nodded.

'She's still wearing her underwear and tights, so on the face of it, it doesn't seem like it. I'll know more after the PM.'

'I don't suppose you can estimate a time since death?'

'No. *Rigour mortis* has passed. However, she's wearing exactly the same clothing she went missing in and it doesn't appear to have been disturbed. We'll take soil samples and analyse stomach contents, but I wouldn't be surprised if she was killed shortly after she went missing on Monday evening.'

'Why take her just to kill her?' Matilda asked, almost to herself.

'I'm so pleased I don't have to answer that question.'

'Are you finished here?'

'Almost.'

'When will you do the PM?'

'Is first thing tomorrow morning all right for you?'

'Yes. I'll be there. I want Claire to do a full digital autopsy too.'

'I'll give her a call. Are you all right?'

'No. But I will be,' she said, giving her a brief smile. She couldn't take her eyes from Keeley's broken body. It was an image she would be seeing for many sleepless nights to come.

Christian was waiting for Matilda outside the tent. She nodded, confirming the body was that of Keeley Armitage.

'Would you like me to give Ellen a ring?'

'No. I need to do this.'

'Why do you put yourself through such hell?' Christian asked.

'Because it's my job.'

'No, it isn't. You can delegate duties, you know. That's the whole point of being a DCI.'

'No. I need to tell Linda myself.'

She started to walk away but Christian grabbed her arm and pulled her back.

'I know I shouldn't be saying this, but I'm not talking as a DI, I'm talking as a friend,' he took a deep breath. 'This is not the Carl Meagan case. You can't atone for what happened in the past. This was never going to end well, and you are not to blame for her dying.'

'I've let her family down.'

'No, you haven't. You haven't let anyone down. Look how many people have been involved in searching for Keeley. Do you think they're all going to go home tonight and blame themselves? No. I won't. Sian won't. Rory and Scott won't. It's not about blame. It's about finding the person responsible and making sure they pay for their actions.'

'You're right,' she said, struggling out of her forensic suit. 'I know you're right, Christian. It doesn't stop me beating myself up, though.'

'That's why you have supportive people around you. We can help. We will help. You don't have to go through all of this on your own.'

'I should go.'

'Where?'

'To break the news to Linda and Craig.'

'I'll come with you.'

'You don't have to. Ellen's there.'

'No. She's there for them, not for you. I'm coming with you,' he said with determination as he headed up the embankment.

Matilda smiled to herself. As much as she hated delivering the death message, as difficult as the job was at times, she was thankful she was surrounded by people who looked out for each other and cared so much.

Chapter 26

It wasn't far from Storrs Brook, where Keeley's body was found, to the Armitage house in Acorn Drive, but there was no direct route. The easiest way was to drive up Rowel Lane, over the River Loxley, onto Spout Lane and turn on to Acorn Way leading to Acorn Drive. It would take less than ten minutes.

Matilda asked Christian to take the longer route, pass Wisewood Cemetery and up the long Stannington Road. What was the rush to deliver the worst news possible? Delaying the inevitable would give the Armitages a few more minutes of hope before destroying their entire world. It also gave Matilda time to compose herself and decide what she was going to say once she'd knocked on the door.

At the back of her mind, she kept picturing the sexualised photos of Keeley found on her iPad. Who had taken them? And why? The father was the number one suspect. She'd watch his reaction closely when she told him of Keeley's fate. On the other hand, if he had killed her, why had he left the iPad on display?

As Christian drove slowly and carefully towards Acorn Drive, Matilda looked out of the window and watched life continue as normal. It was dark, and there were few people out on the streets – the odd dog walker, people coming home late from work, or back from the shops with an emergency bottle of wine.

Matilda didn't have a clue what to say. How could she tell parents their nine-year-old daughter was dead? It was almost inhuman.

'We're here,' Christian said, turning off the engine.

Matilda looked up at the house. The curtains were closed but lights were on in almost every room.

She took a deep breath, closed her eyes and breathed out slowly.

'Do you want me to do it?' Christian asked.

'No. I'll manage.' She looked over to him. 'Thank you, though,' she said.

As she walked up the garden path, she looked around her, and felt as if every curtain in the road was twitching. People were ghouls and wanted to be in on the moment when a family's life was destroyed. She rang the doorbell and stepped back.

Ellen opened the door. Her smiling face dropped as soon as she saw Matilda and Christian's grim expression. She knew that look. She knew what they had come to say.

'Oh my God, no,' she said in a whisper. Her bottom lip began to wobble, but she managed to swallow her emotion. She stood to one side to allow them both in.

'Where are they?' Matilda asked.

'They're all in the living room. We've had a full house this evening: Linda's parents have been round. So have Craig's and his sister.'

'They're not here now, are they?' Matilda asked quickly. The last thing she needed was an extended audience.

'No. They went home about an hour ago.'

'Where's Jodie?'

'She's in the kitchen making tea.'

'Ok. I'd rather she wasn't there while we speak to the parents.'

'Right. I'll go and sit with her.'

Ellen headed for the kitchen while Matilda and Christian entered the living room. Linda was sitting in the corner of the sofa, cradling a cushion. Her eyes were red from crying. She was biting her bottom lip raw. Her face was devoid of emotion. She looked physically and mentally drained. At the other end of the sofa, Craig was scrolling through the channels with the remote. He wasn't paying the television any notice, flicking from one channel to the next before seeing what programme was showing. He looked up first when he heard them enter the room and turned the television off.

'Is there any news?' he asked.

Matilda sat on the armchair opposite while Christian stood next to her for support. She leaned forward, hands clasped in front of her.

'Craig. Linda,' she began. Her voice was quiet, almost inaudible. She cleared her throat and started again. 'I'm afraid there's no easy way for me to say this . . .'

She didn't get a chance to finish. Linda opened her mouth and let out a blood-curdling wail that sounded like a wounded animal. Craig reacted, leaping across the sofa towards her and taking his wife in his arms as she collapsed into his embrace. Matilda shot back in her chair. She'd never heard anyone make such a noise before. Christian placed a hand on her shoulder. The door to the living room opened and Jodie came running in followed by Ellen.

'Mum?' Jodie asked, tears streaming down her face.

'No. No. No. It's not possible. It's not,' Linda screamed through the tears.

Craig tried to hush her. He held her tight, rocking back and forth. Jodie sat beside her father and placed her arm through his. She didn't say anything as she nestled in and clung on.

Craig looked up to Matilda. 'Are you sure?' he asked quietly. 'There's no doubt or anything?'

'I'm afraid not.'

Linda continued to scream. Her face was red, and her entire body shook as if the devil himself was trying to escape from within.

Matilda studied Craig. He had both arms wrapped around his wife and daughter. His face was blank, his eyes full of tears just waiting to fall.

'I really am terribly sorry to have to tell you such news,' Matilda said, her words lost over the sound of crying. 'I promise, hand on heart, that I will not rest until I've caught the person responsible.'

Craig gave her a sympathetic nod and smile.

'If there's anything you want or need, please, ask Ellen, and she'll get in touch with me straight away.' Matilda stood up. Her legs felt wobbly and she edged slowly to the door, not taking her gaze from Linda, whose heart was literally breaking before Matilda's eyes.

In the hallway, Matilda told Ellen all she knew about Keeley's death so far. The details were scant but the fact she was still wearing tights and underwear was perhaps a sign no sexual assault had taken place.

Christian drove Matilda home in silence. He offered to come in, but she declined, saying she'd call Adele and ask her to come over with a few bottles of wine and maybe a chocolate cake.

'Go home to your wife and kids, Christian. Give them an extra hug tonight.'

'I will.'

'I always forget how difficult it must be, doing this job when you've got kids.'

'I'm usually not bad at keeping work and home separate. I go home, I play with the kids, help them with their homework, tuck them into bed, and that's it. Work seems to have stayed in the car. I don't think it will tonight. I don't think I'll ever be able to get that sound Linda made out of my head.'

'I know. It cut straight through me.'

'Me too.'

'Well, we've got a lot to do tomorrow. Early start,' she said, getting out of the car. 'Take care, Christian.'

'You too.'

She slammed the door and headed for her home. She looked around her, up at the apartment above the garage, took in the silence of the surrounding countryside, and, for the first time since moving in here, hated the isolation.

As she unlocked the front door, she sent a text to Adele:

Tell Chris he and Scott are welcome to move into my flat.

Once inside, she slammed the door closed with her foot and scrolled through the contacts in her phone. She paused as her finger hovered over the green call button before pressing the screen.

While waiting for the call to connect, she went into the kitchen, turned on the light, and pulled a bottle of wine out of the fridge.

'Hello?'

'Daniel? It's Matilda. If you're not doing anything, would you like to come over?'

Chapter 27

When news broke that Keeley Armitage had been found dead and it was PC Tranter who had found her, Rory and Scott raced to the scene and took her back to their apartment in the city centre. She'd cried, showered, cried again and now lay on the sofa in Rory's arms.

'How are you feeling?' Scott asked, handing her a glass of wine.

'I honestly don't know, Scott. I mean, I've seen dead bodies before, we all have, but I've never actually found one. She was . . . she didn't look real. It was like a prop from a horror film. I don't think I'll ever get over it.'

'You will,' Scott said, sitting on the edge of the armchair next to the sofa. 'It'll just take time, that's all.'

'Her poor family.' She wiped tears from her eyes.

The intercom buzzed. Scott got up and went to answer it. It was Chris. He buzzed him up. He opened the front door and waited. It wasn't long before the door was pushed open at the end of the corridor and a beaming Chris came bounding along with a bottle of supermarket prosecco.

'Matilda said we can have the flat,' he grinned. 'I know it's not champagne, but we'll save that for when we move in.'

'Are you serious?' he asked.

'Yes. I wouldn't spend a fiver on a joke,' he laughed.

'That's brilliant.' Scott pulled Chris into an embrace and held him tight. 'I'm so thrilled. I love you.'

They both froze.

'What?' Chris asked.

'Shit. I'm sorry. I shouldn't have said that. It just slipped out.' His eyes widened and he looked horrified that he'd gone too fast too soon.

Chris swallowed hard. 'Say it again.'

'Sorry?'

'Say it again.'

'Do I have to?'

'Please.'

'I love you.'

'I love you, too.' Chris broke into a smile.

DS Sian Mills was in bed with her husband, Stuart. She had come home late from work, deflated and defeated. The discovery of Keeley's body was the worst news they could have hoped for. Sian's four children were either in bed or in their rooms doing whatever it was teenagers did behind closed doors, out of sight of their parents.

Stuart had cooked a meal for the whole family and left Sian a plate for her to warm up in the microwave. She couldn't face a heavy meal, and went straight to bed.

After almost twenty-five years of marriage, Stuart recognised the signs of distress in his wife and gave her the space she needed. When he went into the bedroom half an hour later with a mug of tea each and a packet of chocolate biscuits for them to share, she was under the duvet and the lights were off.

He knew she wasn't asleep and turned on the light. There was movement beneath the duvet.

'If you want me to fit into that suit for the anniversary party, you're going to have to help me eat these biscuits,' he said.

Slowly, the duvet was peeled back, and Sian sat up.

'Are you all right?' he asked.

Sian's face was red from crying and her hair was all over the place.

'We found Keeley. She'd been strangled.'

Stuart sat on the edge of the bed and pulled his wife into his arms. Stuart had the solid build of a rugby player. His huge arms wrapped around Sian's thin frame and her head rested perfectly in his centre of his pillowy chest.

'Do you know who did it?' he asked.

'No. Not yet.'

'You don't usually let things get to you like this.'

'I know. It's just . . . it's never easy when it involves kids. Matilda's not coping too well. It's bringing back memories of Carl Meagan going missing and that reminds her of James dying. I'm trying to be supportive, but . . .'

'You need support too,' he finished her thought.

'Well, yes.'

'And I've not been much support with this party, have I?'

'I didn't mean that.'

'I know you didn't, but I could help out more. I'm sorry. Would you like me to make you something to eat? I could do you a sandwich if you don't want your tea.' He went to get up off the bed, but Sian refused to let go.

'Stuart, will you stay here with me?'

'Of course I will.'

She snuggled into his body and felt safe and protected while his arms were around her. It didn't matter what went on out in the real world – children being murdered, prostitutes going missing, car crime and knife attacks – Sian was being comforted in the strong arms of the man she loved. She never wanted this feeling to end.

For the second time in three days, Linda Armitage had to be sedated. She had cried so hard she'd vomited in the kitchen sink.

With Linda in a deep and unnatural sleep, Craig was left to deal with the fallout. Ellen looked after Riley in his bedroom, playing with his toys and keeping him occupied while Craig had some quality alone time with his only surviving daughter. Ellen strained to listen, but their voices were deliberately low. It was more than half an hour before she heard movement and Craig came in to Riley's room to get him ready for bed.

'Would you like me to make you something to eat?' Ellen asked when Craig entered the kitchen.

He slumped down at the table. 'No. Thank you. I don't think I could eat anything.'

'You need to keep your strength up. Linda and the kids will need you to be strong.'

He looked up at her. Tears were heavy in his eyes. 'I haven't cried yet. I'm being strong for Linda and Jodie, but who's strong for me?'

Ellen sat in the seat opposite it. She reached across the table and took his hands in hers. 'Me. That's what I'm here for.'

The tears began to fall. 'She was my little girl, my little princess,' he sobbed. 'Why? Why would someone do something so . . .?'

'I don't know,' she interrupted. 'There are some people in this world who are just evil for the sake of it.'

'Do you know what happened to her?'

'Not everything, no. There will need to be a post-mortem.'

'Do you know if she was . . . you know?' He gripped her hands tighter.

'It doesn't look like it, no.'

He gave her a weak smile. 'Thank you. What happens now?'

'Our work is just beginning really. We will do everything in our power to find whoever did this. DCI Darke will not rest until she's arrested the killer. I can promise you that.'

Their eyes remained locked on each other. Ellen turned away first and let go of his hands.

'I should probably go up and check on Linda.'

In the doorway, he turned back and went over to Ellen. He wrapped his arms tightly around her. 'Thank you for what you said.'

'It's my pleasure.'

He released her then left the kitchen, leaving Ellen watching him go, a look of bewilderment on her face as to what had just happened between them. She heard voices from upstairs: Craig talking to Jodie.

Ellen sat down at the kitchen table and sent a text to her boyfriend. They didn't live together and as they both worked unsociable hours, they rarely saw each other. Ellen decided that was something that was going to have to change, and soon. When she saw Jodie heading for the kitchen, she quickly squirrelled the phone away and went back to washing the dishes.

'Is there anything I can get you?' Ellen asked.

'No. I just want a drink of water.'

The sound of Homer Simpson saying 'D'oh!' came from Ellen's pocket. She'd forgotten to put her phone on silent and quickly grabbed it to silence the embarrassing text tone.

'What was that?' Jodie asked. There was a hint of a smile on her lips.

'Just a text. Sorry.'

'Was that Homer Simpson?' The smile grew.

'Yes.'

'That's so cool. Can you Bluetooth it to my phone?' Jodie pulled her own mobile out of her back pocket. Riley started screaming from his bedroom. 'We'll do it later. His nibs has woken up.'

She went into the bedroom while Ellen turned back to the sink. She plunged her hands into the hot water and quickly pulled them out as a finger ran along the side of a sharp knife, slicing it open. Blood dripped from the shallow cut into the soapy water. She grabbed for the kitchen roll and wrapped a couple of sheets around it to stem the flow.

There was muffled talking coming from Riley's room. Ellen edged closer to the slightly open doorway.

Jodie was holding her brother in her arms and standing in front of the mirror. Riley was reaching out to his reflection and giggling.

'You'll never know about what happened to Keeley,' Jodie said. 'All this fuss, everything that's going on around you, and you haven't a clue, have you?' He was resting on her hip and she was jiggling him up and down. 'You don't need to worry about anything, little man,' she kissed him on the head. 'I'll look after you. I'll always be here to take care of you. I'm not going anywhere.'

Chapter 28

Amanda Raine was stood by the bedroom window looking through the small gap in the curtains she'd created. She'd been standing there for a while, watching the Armitage house next door. Ever since she'd heard a blood-curdling scream a few hours ago and seen the police leave it had been deathly quiet. It could only mean one thing: Keeley had been found dead. She hoped to God that wasn't true.

'What are you doing?' Grant said, coming into the bedroom and taking off his dressing gown.

Amanda jumped. She glanced to her husband then went back to glaring out of the window. 'Nothing.'

'You've been unsettled since teatime. Up and down at the slightest noise. Are you going to be like this all night?' he asked as he looked in the dressing table mirror and removed his contact lenses.

'The police came round this morning,' she said, fiddling with the crucifix around her neck.

'Well, they would do. They always talk to the neighbours when things like this happen. You haven't seen my silver cufflinks have you? I need my dress shirt for tomorrow.

'Top drawer. No, the other one. Grant,' Amanda said, stepping away from the window. 'Do you think I should phone the police up?'

'Whatever for?'

'Well, this morning they asked me about Keeley and what she was like as a child and if I knew the family, but . . . I didn't tell them everything.'

'Found them. What are you talking about?'

'I didn't tell them about Craig.'

'Look, Amanda, don't get involved,' he said sternly, looking up at his wife.

'But we are involved.'

'No, we're not. I'm not a fan of Craig Armitage, as you know, but they're going through hell right now and the last thing they want is the police looking into gossip and innuendo.'

'It's not gossip though.'

'It bloody is,' he said as he went over to the bed and pulled back the duvet. 'Are you coming to bed or not because I've got an early start in the morning and I'm turning the light out.'

'You've heard him through the walls as much as I have,' she said as she kicked off her slippers and started to remove her earrings. 'He has a temper on him. What if he's involved in Keeley going missing?'

'You've been reading too many Agatha Christie books.'

'No, I haven't. When something happens to a child the parents are nearly always involved. That's an honest-to-God fact.'

'Don't get involved, Amanda,' he reiterated, turning over in bed.

Amanda sat on the edge of the bed. Her face was a map of worry. She could feel herself getting cold as the temperature outside slowly fell. It was too early in the season to turn the central heating on. She climbed into bed and pulled the duvet over her, but she didn't lie down to sleep. Her mind was spinning with the events she had witnessed through her living room window today.

'Grant,' she said eventually. 'Grant,' she said louder when he didn't reply.

'What?' He sounded annoyed.

'The police searched Craig's van this morning.'

'They would have done. It's what they do.'

'That means they must suspect him, too.'

'No it doesn't. It means they're keeping an open mind.'

'I think I should tell them about him, about what he's really like.'

'For the last time, Amanda, it has nothing to do with us. Now, please, turn your light out and go to sleep.'

Amanda acquiesced to her husband's request. She lay in darkness with her eyes wide open as she contemplated what she should do. Craig was quick to temper – she'd witnessed it many times – but just because someone shouts at his family once in a while, does that make him capable of murder?

She let out a heavy sigh. It would be a long time before she fell asleep.

Chapter 29

Thursday 13th September 2018

The storm had broken overnight. It was as if nature had been waiting for Keeley to be found before unleashing a barrage of sixty-mile-per-hour winds and a month's worth of rain in six hours. Had Keeley's body not been found in time, vital forensic evidence might have been lost, and there was no telling what state the body would have been in when it came to identification.

Matilda hadn't heard the storm. The tall trees at the bottom of her garden had swayed in the gusts and shed most of their leaves. Her garden, landscaped to give it an intentionally wild look, had been given a serious hiding; pots had been tossed about and smashed, plants and flowers drowned, and the cushions on the garden furniture were beyond salvageable.

While the storm was raging, Matilda had been safely indoors with Daniel Harbison. He was knocking on her front door within ten minutes of her calling him. They stood in the hallway facing each other, eyes locked, standing almost toe to toe. Nothing needed to be said. The atmosphere was electric. Matilda made the first move. She grabbed the collar of his jacket and pulled him towards her, kissing him hard and passionately. She took his hand and led him upstairs.

Matilda didn't know if it was finding Keeley's body, her mood plummeting, the sense she didn't want to be alone, or the memories this case stirred up of Carl Meagan going missing, his subsequent return (maybe), or remembering the time in 2015 when she was happy, had a husband she loved and someone to go home to. Whatever the reason for calling Daniel, she was pleased he had come around. She'd forgotten how much she loved sex, the feeling of a hard body pressed against her and a man's huge, callused hands all over her. It was a pleasure she thought she'd never have again. She was happy she'd waited for the right man rather than a casual encounter she'd soon regret.

As Daniel was showering in the en suite he'd designed, Matilda lay in bed, the duvet wrapped around her. She was smiling. There was a general feeling of bliss and satisfaction about her. She looked across at the framed photo of James on the bedside table. She didn't feel guilty for sleeping with another man; she felt proud of herself for moving on, finally. After months of telling herself that was what she was doing, she'd actually done it, and it felt amazing.

Matilda hoped she wasn't grinning inanely as she entered the HMET suite. If anyone would pick up on the signs something wonderful had happened to her overnight it would be Sian, and once Rory found out, she'd be the talk of the whole station. Fortunately, everyone was occupied with the aftermath of Keeley's body being found and were all hard at work. Matilda was able to sneak in unnoticed.

There was a knock on the glass door of her office. She looked up and saw Christian standing on the other side. She beckoned him in.

'Morning. How are you feeling?' He asked.

'I'm ok.'

'Listen, I hope you don't mind, but I was talking to Jennifer about you last night,' he said, referring to his wife. He pulled out a chair and sat down. 'She can always tell when there's something niggling away at me. Anyway, we know you're on your own in that big house, no neighbours around, so, if you want to come over to ours for a meal or a few drinks, you're more than welcome. Open invitation, that kind of thing.'

Christian was obviously nervous at breaking down the professional walls with his boss. His moist brow and his reddened cheeks were testament to that. Matilda couldn't help but smile. She guessed he'd been badgered by his wife all night until he agreed to ask her.

'That's very kind of you, Christian, thank you. I may do that one day. Thank Jennifer for me, as well.'

'I will.' He seemed to visibly relax. Matilda hadn't accepted but she hadn't said a firm 'no' either. The invitation may be left open, but they both knew she wouldn't act upon it.

'How is Jennifer?'

'She's doing ok. She's increased her hours at work. More money coming in, finally.'

'More going out, too, unfortunately.'

'Tell me about it. Anyway, the reason I came to see you is because Jodie Armitage has been on Twitter again.'

'Oh?' Matilda looked to her computer. She hadn't turned it on yet.

'Yes. She announced late last night that her sister had been found dead. Then she put up a few photos of Keeley saying what a beautiful girl she was and that she'd miss her.'

'What kind of photos?' Matilda turned to her computer and logged on to the social networking site. Rather than posting several photos in a single tweet, Jodie had posted them all individually and almost flooded the site with smiling pictures of her younger sister. Matilda looked at the times of the tweets; they were all several minutes apart.

'What's she doing?' She asked herself as she scrolled through the teenager's timeline.

'I think she's attention seeking.'

'What?' Matilda looked up.

'I know it's a horrible thing to say, but her sister has just died; everything will be about her now. Then, after the funeral, when she goes back to school and the dust has settled, all the attention will be on Linda and Craig and Riley. Even then, Keeley will be thought of before Jodie is to keep her memory alive. This is Jodie's outlet for someone to acknowledge her and her grief.'

Matilda looked at the DI with a puzzled expression. 'That's very deep for you.'

'I think I might be maturing,' he said with a glint in his eye.

'Well, keep it up. We could do with more maturity around here. I'll get Ellen to have a word with Jodie about posting online and we need to keep an eye on what else she posts.'

'I can monitor that. Will you be attending the PM?'

'Yes. It's been pushed back until Linda and Craig have formally identified the body.'

'I can't begin to imagine what they're going through. To see your child on a mortuary slab must be the worst image possible.' He remained in his seat, staring into space.

'Do you want to get everyone ready for the briefing?' Matilda prompted.

'Sure.' He stood up and headed for the door. He turned back to Matilda. 'Have you changed your hair or something?'

'No. Why?' She asked, pushing her hair behind her ears.

'You look different.'

'In what way?'

'I'm not sure. There's something just . . . different.'

'Nope. Same old me.'

'Must be me.' He left the room.

Matilda smiled to herself. She stood up and was about to join the team when she felt her phone vibrate in her pocket. There was a text and an email waiting for her. The text was from Daniel:

Can't believe what we did last night. So happy. Free for dinner tonight?

She didn't reply. She didn't want to seem too eager.

The subject line of the email was 'DNA Sample'. She opened it and read that the sample from the boy in France claiming to be Carl Meagan was now in the hands of forensics officers working for South Yorkshire Police. It wouldn't be long before the truth was revealed.

Chapter 30

The viewing room in the mortuary had been designed with comfort in mind but missed the mark on every single level. The windowless room was depressing and oppressive. The cheap sofa was bland and uncomfortable. The decoration was tired and drab and the fake potted plant in the corner of the room had obviously been placed there in an effort to add a note of calm, but the dust-covered leaves made the room even sadder.

Craig and Linda Armitage sat on the two-seater sofa. Craig was sitting upright, facing the glass viewing window which had a closed curtain on the other side. Linda was leaning against him, sitting on the edge of the sofa, her left leg jiggling involuntarily. She was nibbling frantically on what was left of the nails on her right hand while her left was clinging on tightly to her husband.

They were both casually dressed – Craig in jeans and a creased rugby shirt, Linda in jeans and a black sweater she'd been wearing for the past two days.

The door opened and Ellen Devonport came in. She closed it quietly behind her. They both looked up.

'Are you all right?' Ellen asked, looking at a fragile and pale Linda.

'I'm fine,' she lied.

'She's been sick,' Craig said.

'Have you eaten anything this morning?'

'Jodie made me some porridge to line my stomach, but I couldn't keep it down.'

'Ok. We'll try and do this as quickly as possible so you can go home and get some rest. Now, I need to prepare you for what's behind this curtain,' she said, pointing to the window. 'Every effort has been made to make Keeley look as natural as possible. However, there's some bruising and grazes on her face which the doctor believes are from the surrounding trees and ground. They've cleaned them up as best they can.'

Linda nodded and smiled weakly. Her eyes were filled with tears. Craig remained impassive. They both stood up and joined Ellen by the window.

Ellen's hand hovered over a switch at the side. 'Are you ready?'

Craig didn't react. Linda simply nodded once.

'I'm going to open the curtain. I know it will be distressing but I need you to tell me clearly if the girl is Keeley or not.'

Another nod.

Ellen pressed the switch and the deep red curtain opened smoothly to reveal a small room behind it in which lay a single trolley. A girl lay under a white sheet which was pulled up to just beneath her chin. She had blonde hair which had been washed and combed. Her eyes were closed as if she was sleeping and her face was pale. Her right eye was slightly bruised and there was a graze on her chin.

Linda opened her mouth and let out a scream of despair as she clung on to Craig and fell to the floor. Ellen went to her aid and lifted her up. She dragged her over to the sofa and pulled a plastic cup from the water cooler in the corner of the room. She filled it and handed it to her.

'Here, drink this.'

She couldn't. She was crying and wailing and gasping for breath.

'No, no, no, no, no,' Linda said over and over again as she hugged her knees and rocked back and forth. 'No. Not my Keeley.'

Over at the window, Craig placed his hand on the glass. He was mouthing something to his daughter, but over the sound of Linda's cries, Ellen couldn't pick it up.

'Almond and raisin flapjack? That sounds disgusting,' Rory said as he squatted by Sian's desk, rifling through her snack drawer. 'What do you fancy?'

'I don't know. I want something sweet but I'm trying to be healthy. I'm getting a bit soft around the middle.' He picked up a Mars bar and contemplated it before putting it back.

'I don't see how you can be with all the bedroom gymnastics you're doing lately,' Scott said from the next desk.

'You're only jealous because your sex life went from cold to hot to cold again within the space of three months.'

'It has not. Me and Chris are very hot, thank you. We just don't want all and sundry to hear what we get up to.'

'Unfortunately, all and sundry are listening to every word,' Matilda said from the top of the room. 'Now, when you've quite finished, Rory, I'd like to get this briefing started.'

He picked up a Snickers and jogged back to his desk, playfully throwing a small packet of Maltesers at Scott's head as he went.

'Thank you. Now, I've had a text from DC Devonport. Craig and Linda have positively identified the body as belonging to Keeley.'

'How did they take it?' Sian asked.

'Ellen didn't go into any details, but I think we can guess. The post-mortem is in about an hour's time, so, where are we with the investigation? Any news on the whereabouts of Calvin Page?'

'Not yet,' Aaron Connolly chimed up, rifling through his untidy desk.

'Do you know where Calvin's living?'

'Erm . . . no,' he said, flicking frantically through his notebook.

'Have you considered contacting his parole officer?' Matilda asked. She looked at Aaron with a heavy frown.

'No. I mean, yes. Yes, I will. I'll look into it.'

'Is everything all right, Aaron? You seem distracted.'

'Yes. No, I'm sorry. Everything's fine. Leave it with me.'

'Aaron, we need to know where Calvin is. That is paramount. Not just in connection with Keeley Armitage but because he's broken his parole conditions. I'm aware this is different to what Calvin has done in the past, and, thankfully, Keeley doesn't seem to have been sexually assaulted, but he cannot be ruled out yet.'

'Ok. I said leave it with me,' Aaron almost snapped.

The room fell silent and all eyes turned to Aaron.

'Where are we with house-to-house and finding out everything about the Armitage family?' Matilda asked, bringing everyone back on topic.

'I've found something interesting,' Scott said. He flicked through his notebook. 'Here we are: Julia Aspinall lives across the road and just a bit further up from the Armitages, and she used to work with Craig before he had his own business. He used to be a delivery driver for Parcelforce and Julia worked in the offices. Now, Craig was dismissed because of a large number of items going missing from the rounds he was on. Customers would call whoever they'd ordered from saying they hadn't received their delivery, the company would investigate to see who the delivery bloke was, and Craig had a high percentage of so-called mislaid parcels.'

'What happened?'

'There was an internal inquiry and Craig left. Julia said it was all hushed up. However, Craig went on to set up his own business as a local courier, but he was bad-mouthed by a former colleague still working at Parcelforce. Craig had to change the name of his business several times before everything died down. But – and here's the interesting part—'

'About time,' Rory interrupted.

'Craig had a very public row with this colleague in a pub. Julia was there and overheard most of it. She heard the colleague say to Craig that if he ever went near his family again, he'd make him pay.'

'So, Craig did something to this other guy's family?' Christian asked.

'It sounds like it.'

'Do you have the contact details of this colleague?' Matilda asked.

'Yes. A Dean Oliver. He lives at Gleadless.'

'Great. Pay him a visit, Scott. See what you can dig up and find out where he was on the evening Keeley disappeared. Anything else?'

'Yes,' Sian said. 'A few of the neighbours aren't too complimentary about Linda.'

'In what way?'

'Some are saying she's quite unhinged, volatile, quick to temper. They often hear her shouting, even when it's only her and Riley at home.'

Matilda thought for a moment. 'I suppose we have to be careful here. Linda is in a difficult position coping with Riley twenty-four hours a day. It's going to get to her at some point. Maybe she cries and screams to let off a bit of steam.'

'Or maybe she's abusing Riley,' Aaron said.

'We don't know that,' Matilda castigated. 'Sian, have a word with their family GP. Nothing definite, just get their take on the family.'

'I found out something yesterday evening after the search,' DC Finn Cotton said, tentatively raising his hand. Finn was incredibly shy and still a new-ish member of the team. Although he seemed to get on well with everyone and joined in with conversations and having a laugh, he found it difficult to raise his head above the parapet when the whole team was assembled.

'Go on,' Matilda prompted.

'One of the neighbours, two doors along, Mrs Rita Clover, invited me in for a chat.'

'Is she fit?' Rory asked.

Finn blushed and cleared his throat before continuing. 'At first she didn't say anything bad about the Armitages. She was full of praise for how they raised the kids and the charity work Craig does, but then she threw doubt on the whole thing.'

'In what way?' Sian asked, hooked on his story.

'She said she and a few of the other neighbours often wondered if all the money Craig raised went to charity. She pointed out that Craig changes his van every eighteen months, the girls wear designer gear and seem to have the latest phones, and, around Christmas time, there's always loads of parcels delivered. Like Mrs Clover said, a courier can't earn that much money, so where is it all coming from?'

'So, what are they saying then, that he's defrauding these charities?' Scott asked.

'It sounds like it?'

'But is that a crime?' he asked. 'I mean, you run a marathon and collect donations and raise, say, two grand, but only hand over fifteen hundred to the charity. Is that fraud?'

'It is if the charity has sponsored you,' Matilda said. 'I mean, we were told from the start that Craig raised money to pay for the things Riley needs to make his home life as stable as possible. Once he'd done that, he continued to raise money and donated it to the local hospital. From time to time I suppose Riley is going to need new things.'

'In that case,' Sian said, 'the money should be going to buying Riley equipment, not designer gear for the girls and to make sure they all have a merry Christmas.'

'Maybe they're doing it for compensation,' Christian said as he sipped his coffee. 'Craig and Linda are going to spend a lot of their time and energy on Riley. The girls are going to feel left out. The only way they can think of to make it up to them is through material possessions. It keeps them quiet and happy at the end of the day.'

'But they're not happy,' Sian said. 'Look at the drawings and stories in Keeley's sketch pad. She wanted a prince to come along and take her away from all this. It's fine to wear designer clothes and have the latest Apple products, but a child of Keeley's age needs a hug from time to time.'

'I think what we can draw from this,' Matilda said, going over to the white boards which held photographs of the family, 'is that money is an issue with this family. If the rumours are true that Craig was stealing parcels, maybe he was selling them for the money. The same for the charity fraud too.'

'And what better way to get your hands on a large amount of money fast than by saying one of your kids has been kidnapped for ransom,' Finn said out of nowhere. 'There's already a GoFundMe page set up for them.'

'Is there?' Sian asked.

'Yes. I noticed it this morning. Someone posted a link to it on Twitter. I don't know who's set it up but it's to raise money to help the Armitages with the funeral. Already there's more than three grand raised.'

'Five grand now,' Rory said, looking at his laptop.

'And Linda went round to Sally Meagan quickly to beg for the ransom money,' Finn continued. 'Who knows how differently it would have played out if they'd handed over the fifty thousand.'

The whole room fell silent and everyone turned to face the DC who quickly blushed and sank in his chair.

'Sorry,' he said quietly.

'No. You're right,' Matilda said. 'Every line of questioning always seems to lead us back to Craig and Linda. I wanted them brought in yesterday but then Keeley was found so that went out of the window. While we're all here, what do we think of Craig and Linda?'

Everyone was silent. They obviously all had an opinion, but nobody seemed to want to speak up first. Eventually, Christian cleared his throat and began.

'Their reactions have been extremes of each other. Craig has remained staid, non-reactive, almost docile, whereas Linda has needed sedating. She's screamed and wailed and collapsed to the floor. They're complete opposite of each other. It's almost as if they've decided on who is going to play which role.'

'And Linda was at home on her own when the ransom demand came through,' Rory said.

'But BT confirmed that a call was made at the time she stated,' Scott added.

'Maybe Craig made that call from a burner phone,' Christian said.

'Craig was in Chesterfield delivering parcels.'

'Has the tracker on his van been looked at, or his phone?' Matilda asked.

'Yes. He was definitely there. CCTV confirms it, too,' Sian said.

'If this was just to get fifty thousand pounds, why kill her?' Christian asked.

'Maybe it was an accident. Fingers crossed the post-mortem will come up with something that can point us in the right direction,' Matilda said, turning to face the board again. She looked at the smiling face of the family in happier times looking down at her. She glared into the eyes of Craig, moved on to Linda, then back to Craig. It was difficult for her to work out how she felt towards the couple. In this situation, she wasn't seeing the true Craig and Linda. But if they were playing a cruel and murderous game, their real personalities would be deeply hidden beneath the guises they wanted the public to see.

Matilda squeezed her eyes tightly shut. She could feel the beginnings of a tension headache creeping up the back of her neck. She felt sick to her stomach with this case.

'If Craig and Linda are this calculating, are Jodie and Riley in danger?' Sian asked.

Sian's questions brought Matilda back from her reverie. She turned around. All eyes turned to Sian. That was a question nobody wanted to answer.

Chapter 31

Briefing has thrown up a few new lines of enquiry. C and L seem to have a lot of money worries. L asked Sally Meagan for 50k ransom money but was turned down. Could K's kidnap have been a ploy to get money gone wrong? Try and do some digging.

Ellen Devonport was in the kitchen of the Armitage home in Acorn Drive making tea for everyone when she felt her phone vibrate in her back pocket. She froze when she read the text from Matilda. Was it possible Craig and Linda had manufactured Keeley's kidnap for money and the whole thing had gone terribly wrong? Ellen's first thought was that she wouldn't be surprised. The disturbing fact was that the majority of people murdered were killed by a relative or someone they knew and trusted. What troubled Ellen was, if that was the case here, how could Craig and Linda be so cold as to act the grieving parents when they knew what had happened to their daughter?

Ellen composed herself. She finished making the tea and put the mugs on the tray to take into the living room. She walked slowly out of the kitchen, her hands shaking slightly.

In the living room, Jodie was curled up on the sofa next to her father who had his arm around her and was staring into space. Linda was in the armchair. She looked physically and mentally drained. Riley was in a large bean bag, his glassy eyes darting around the room.

'Would anybody like anything to eat?' Ellen asked quietly as she placed the tray on the coffee table.

Nobody replied.

'I'll be in the kitchen if you need me.'

She edged out of the room, closing the door firmly behind her. There was a dark atmosphere in the living room. She hoped to God it was genuine. What would happen to Jodie and Riley if their parents were arrested for Keeley's murder?

Ellen headed for the dining room. On the night Keeley went missing, Linda had been frantically looking through the drawers in the dresser for bank statements to see how they'd manage to pull together the fifty-thousand-pound ransom money. Ellen wanted to get a closer look at the statements. How financially solvent were they and what did they spend their money on?

The house was deathly silent. The only noise came from the dishwasher and the hum of the fridge. She was sure she'd hear anyone leave the living room. She opened the cupboard of the pine dresser and pulled out the red folder that contained the bank statements. Everything was neatly arranged: joint current account, two savings accounts, accounts for the children, mortgage statements and credit card statements. A quick look at the current account told Ellen they had more money going out each month than they had coming in. They dipped in an out of their overdraft on a monthly basis, yet still managed to transfer a few hundred to their savings accounts each month. How was that possible? They had six credit cards, all of them with high credit limits and each card was almost at its limit. They paid the minimum amount required each month.

Ellen went back to the bank statements and cast her eye quickly down the list of payments. Supermarkets and Amazon featured heavily, which wasn't surprising, but the amounts were. Around two hundred pounds was spent each week in the supermarket. Was that necessary for a family of five? Some of the amounts to Amazon were small, a tenner here, twenty pounds there, occasionally around a hundred, but they all mounted up to a great deal of money – money they didn't physically have.

Would fifty thousand pounds have been enough to lower the debts they'd accumulated? Ellen didn't think so. It would pay off a couple of credit cards and the overdraft, but unless they changed their spending ways, it wouldn't be long before another fifty grand was needed.

She put the red folder back in the drawer and pulled a buff cardboard file out. It was thick and filled with letters. The first was from a local firm of solicitors Ellen hadn't heard of. It was a demand on behalf of a building contractor for alterations to the house going back two years. The letter threatened legal action unless the debt of three thousand eight hundred pounds wasn't settled within thirty days. There was nothing in the file to show if the amount had been paid.

Ellen looked over her shoulder to make sure she wasn't being watched or that no one had crept up on her. She took her phone out of her back pocket and took a photo of the letter. It came out blurred as she couldn't keep her hands still.

Another letter from a different firm of solicitors demanded payment of four thousand two hundred and fifty-six pounds for a landscape gardener who had designed the back garden to make it more accessible for Riley. Again, there was no evidence to show if this had been paid or not. Ellen took another photo.

Craig had told her he'd done the garden himself. What was the reason for telling such a pointless lie?

The file was full of similar letters. Final demands, threats of court action and enforced bankruptcy. How had they got into such a financial mess? Ellen could understand them wanting to do the best for their children, but not to the point of financial ruin where the only solution was fake-kidnapping your own daughter.

She heard a noise from the living room. She stuffed the letter back in the folder, threw it into the cupboard and slammed the door closed.

She stood up and ran into the kitchen, breathless.

'Hello. How are you feeling?' she asked Craig.

'Numb,' was all he could say. He looked ready to drop.

'Would you like something to eat? A sandwich maybe?'

'I don't know what I want.'

Ellen went over to him, put her arm around his shoulders and guided him to the table. She pulled out a chair and sat him down. She squatted in front of him and placed her hands on his lap.

'Craig, I won't pretend to know what you're going through right now, but I'm guessing you feel like you're in hell. I'm here for you to talk to, about absolutely anything. If there's something you want to get off your chest, you can tell me. I'm not here to judge or take sides. I'm here purely for you.'

'I . . . I . . .' he choked. His mind was obviously wanting him to say something, but his mouth wouldn't allow it.

'What is it? What do you want to say?' Ellen pleaded.

'Dad?'

They both turned to see Jodie standing in the doorway to the kitchen.

'What's going on?' Jodie asked.

'Your dad's upset, Jodie. I was trying to get him to share his feelings. It's not helpful to keep things bottled up.' Ellen stood up. 'Is there anything I can get you, Jodie? A sandwich?'

Jodie ignored her. She went over to her father and sat on his knee, burying her head in his chest. Craig put his arms firmly around her and held her close, stroking her hair.

Ellen turned back to the sink. It was sparkling and shiny from her over-cleaning it, but it didn't stop her from picking up the Flash and squirting the draining board once again. How much longer was she expected to stay in this house? She knew the role of Family Liaison Officer was not an easy one, but Ellen was physically chilled to the bone in the company of this family. She frowned as she thought. On jobs like this, Ellen was full of sympathy for the grieving parents, but in this case, she couldn't warm to Linda or Craig. She felt great sadness for Keeley and Riley and it pained her to see Jodie's lost childhood, but why were the parents causing her such consternation?

Ellen looked up. Dark clouds loomed over the city and the light in the kitchen turned the window into a mirror. She could see Craig and Jodie's reflection reversed behind her. Jodie was curled up on her father's lap, more like a toddler than a teenager. Her eyes were closed, a faint smile playing on her lips. She was comforted. They were seeking solace in each other in a traumatic time. So why was a cold shiver running up Ellen's spine?

Chapter 32

Matilda pulled up outside the mortuary on Watery Street just outside the city centre in her Range Rover. She opened the door and felt a sudden gust of cool wind. She looked up and saw a heavy grey sky looming above her. Summer was definitely over. Autumn would quickly descend into winter which would be long, dark, and arduous. Adele was right; she had made a mistake in moving so far out of the city. Hopefully, with Scott and Chris moving in to the apartment and a potential relationship developing with Daniel, things wouldn't seem quite so lonely.

As she approached the building, the main doors opened and two women stepped out. She recognised the first woman straight away.

'Bev,' Matilda called out to her.

The taller of the two women turned at the sound of her name. Bev was in her late forties but looked at least a decade older. Years of working on the streets in all weathers and smoking like a chimney had ravaged her appearance. She layered herself in make-up to hide the wrinkles. She dyed her thinning hair light blonde and over-plucked her eyebrows. She was painfully thin with prominent cheekbones and a turkey neck.

'I told you this would happen,' she immediately launched into a tirade at the sight of the DCI. 'I warned you. You wouldn't listen and now a woman – a girl – is dead. She was nineteen, Matilda.' Bev's voice was hoarse and deep from a lifetime of cigarettes. Usually she sounded harsh and authoritative, but this morning there was a catch of emotion in her voice and tears in her eyes.

'Bev, I understand you're unhappy. We are dealing with it, I promise you.'

'Are you? I don't see any extra police cars patrolling the area. I don't see any coppers talking to us, asking how we are, if we've seen anything or anyone dodgy lately. Earlier this year that detective of yours promised there'd be more of a presence to make us feel safe. She lied. Who was she, Sarah?'

Bev turned to the smaller woman behind her. Sarah was always in Bev's shadow. Slightly younger in age, much younger mentally, Sarah followed Bev around wherever she went. They'd worked the streets of Sheffield together for more than twenty years and Sarah listened to everything Bev said. She didn't think for herself. She didn't talk for herself.

Sarah shook her head in reply to Bev's question.

'She gave us her card. It'll be in your purse.'

Sarah always carried a large shoulder bag around with her. It had seen better days and was only fit to be thrown away, but it contained everything both women needed – ID, make-up, hairbrush, mints, small bottles of mouthwash, even smaller bottles of vodka, prescription medication, and too many crumpled business cards to count.

She handed Bev a card.

'Detective Sergeant Sian Mills,' Bev read, holding the card at arm's length and squinting. 'Where is she, Matilda? Where's the help and protection she promised?'

'Bev, I know you're hurting, and I'm sorry for your loss, I truly am. If I had the officers and the budget, you'd have all the protection you need, but I don't. I'm being honest with you, Bev.'

'We've lost six girls in the last three years,' Bev said, ignoring Matilda. 'Don't try and tell me they've all moved on to different areas, because I'd call you a liar. They're dead. They'll be lying in an abandoned building somewhere, left to rot.'

'Bev, will you come and see me next week? Give me all the names of the missing women, the dates you last saw them, a description, and I promise I'll put a team on it.'

She thought for a moment, sucking her teeth. 'You're not just saying that to make me go away?'

'No. I'm not.'

'When?'

'Next week. Thursday.'

'Ok. Half past ten, but not at the station. We're not going in there, are we Sarah?'

Sarah shook her head.

'Fine. I'll meet you wherever you want.'

'You got a card?'

Matilda fished in her inside jacket pocket and pulled out a card and a biro. On the back she scribbled her mobile number. 'If you need me, call the number on the back anytime.'

Bev snatched it from her and handed it to Sarah to store in her bag.

'I know you're busy, Matilda. I also know you've had a bad couple of years, too. People think just because we're prostitutes, we're thick and we don't matter. I know all about police budgets and cutbacks and austerity. I used to work in accounts when I first left school. But just because we're further down the food chain doesn't mean we don't count. We have feelings. We're women. We're real women, just like you and this Sian and the bloody Queen. We matter. Come on, Sarah, you've got that check-up in an hour.'

They left Matilda behind, marching off in large determined strides up Watery Street. Matilda watched them. Everything Bev had just said was right. People took advantage of women like Bev and Sarah because of what they did to make a living, and it was wrong. Six women had disappeared from the streets of Sheffield in the last three years. They needed to be found. Matilda would find them.

Matilda sat in the small waiting area of the digital autopsy suite for radiologist Claire Alexander who was preparing the room to scan Keeley Armitage. It was stifling. It was always warm, and Matilda often left the building with her shirt stuck to her back. She helped herself to a plastic cup of water from the cooler. Deep in thought while she waited, she wondered about the conversation she'd had with Bev. Sheffield was awash with abandoned buildings and South Yorkshire Police didn't have the resources to search them all. Valerie certainly wouldn't commit to a team looking for bodies that may or may not exist. If only . . .

'Matilda.'

Matilda looked up to see Claire standing over her.

'Are you with us?' she asked with a smile on her smooth face.

'Yes.'

'Oh. I was calling you. You just sat there staring into space like you had the world's problems on your shoulders.'

'I feel like I have.'

'Which is it: Brexit, an overstretched NHS, a crumbling society, climate change, or an under-funded police force?'

Matilda stood up. 'Thanks for the reminders. You're a barrel of fun this morning.'

Claire gave a wide smile which lit up her face. 'Just reminding you of how bad things are to make your own small part of this world seem a touch brighter.'

'It hasn't worked.'

'I expected you to come in with a huge grin on your face with a new man in your life.'

Matilda frowned. 'How the hell did you know about that?'

'Adele told me.'

'She's a nosy cow.'

'So, who is he? What does he look like? What's he like in bed and does he have a brother?'

They set off through the myriad doors and down the narrow corridors to the digital autopsy suite. The further into the building they went, the warmer it became.

'I'm not answering any of those,' Matilda said. 'Besides, you always said you didn't want a man.'

'I don't. They're selfish, they're inconsiderate, they leave the toilet seat up and squeeze toothpaste from the middle of the tube. Why would you want one of those in your house?'

'That's true. Daniel did leave the bathroom in a bit of a mess.'

'So, he's staying over is he?' She asked playfully.

'None of your business,' Matilda said, failing to hide a grin.

The door opened and Adele entered the suite. Matilda slapped her on the arm.

'What was that for?'

'Telling people about me and Daniel.'

'I only told Claire.'

'And if you believe that, you'll believe anything,' Claire said, booting up the computer. 'Right, are we ready?'

The anteroom looked onto the digital autopsy scanner where Keeley Armitage was already laid out in a sealed and locked black body bag. There was so much empty space in the bag that it was obvious it was a child in there. It was sad. Digital autopsies and post-mortems were not pleasant things to do, but when the subject was a child, it was all the more difficult to get through.

Claire sat down at a bank of large-screen monitors. She hammered away at the keyboard and the scan began.

The machine was like an ordinary MRI scanner. The body moved slowly into the machine and was photographed from all angles in a spiral so a three-hundred-and-sixty-degree image was taken to allow a 3D model to appear on the screen. The scan took seconds to complete.

On the computers, Claire was able to turn the body over and look deep inside it at the condition of bones and organs without having to physically touch the victim and destroy any potential trace evidence that was on the outside of the body. If, for example, Claire discovered the hyoid bone was broken on Keeley Armitage, it would give Adele an area of the body to begin looking at when a full, invasive post-mortem began.

The digital autopsy was discreet, more respectful, and could often answer questions a senior investigating officer needed to know quickly to help their investigation before the full PM.

On the first screen, an X-ray image of Keeley was brought up. Once Claire was satisfied there were no broken bones, she changed the style of the image to show the internal organs and muscles in more detail.

'No hyoid bone fracture,' Claire said.

'Isn't that usually a common factor with strangulation?' Matilda asked.

'No. A broken hyoid bone only appears in around half of all strangulations. Besides, these fractures are rare in children as the hyoid components are not fully ossified and are more flexible than in adults. Now, if you look here,' she pointed to a small white patch on the image. 'You can see there is a lot of sub-cutaneous haemorrhage.'

'Meaning?'

'Meaning a great deal of bleeding beneath the skin.'

'What would have caused that?'

'There's pressure on the vagus nerve. This will have slowed the heart very rapidly so that it stopped.'

'How long would that have taken?'

'Consciousness is lost within ten seconds and unless pressure is released, death will have been within a minute. Although there are a lot of variants.'

All three women fell silent for a moment as they thought of the painful death of a child.

'If we look at the brain,' Claire began, bringing up a closer image of the brain on a different monitor. 'You can see evidence of cerebral oedema. This shows the brain was starved of oxygen for a long while. It was a slow death.'

'So, we're talking about death by manual strangulation?' Matilda asked. 'Someone actually put their hands around the neck of a nine-year-old girl and strangled the life out of her?'

'That would be my diagnosis,' Claire said. 'You can see there was massive loss of blood flow to the brain. Pressure on the neck leads to an obstruction of the carotid artery.'

'How much pressure are we talking about?'

'You'd need a lot of pressure to obstruct the flow and we can tell that took place by the injuries to the soft tissue in the neck,' she pointed to the relevant places on the images.

'Could a woman have done this?' Matilda asked.

'I'm not answering that question,' Claire said. 'However, bear in mind the victim here is a nine-year-old girl. She's young, slim, and wouldn't take much overpowering.'

'You're thinking the mother could have done this, aren't you?' Adele asked.

'I'm afraid I am,' Matilda eventually replied.

'Why?'

'We're getting a lot of information that Craig and Linda might not be the perfect parents they're making themselves out to be.'

'There's no such thing as the perfect parent,' Adele said. 'We all just make it up as we go along and hope we're steering our kids on the straight and narrow.'

Claire shivered. 'How a parent can kill their own child is beyond me.' Her voice began to break. 'Excuse me.' She stood up and left the room without making eye contact with Matilda and Adele. The door slammed behind her.

'Is she all right?'

'Claire can't have kids. She had ovarian cancer in her early twenties. She told me once – years ago – that all she wanted when she was young was to be a mother when she grew up. She puts on this strong, independent exterior, and she *is* independent, but she wanted a child more than anything in the world, and she can't have one.'

'Poor Claire.'

'Shall we take five minutes? Have a cup of a tea and a cherry Bakewell?'

Break time was a disappointment. Someone had brought in decaffeinated coffee, which, in Matilda's eyes, was an abomination, and the cherry Bakewells were a supermarket's own-brand

and filled with cheap ingredients. It delayed cutting open a child, however, so it was most welcome.

'Chris said he'd come round to the flat at the weekend and measure the rooms for curtains, furniture, that kind of thing,' Adele said.

'Bloody hell, let the paint dry on the skirting boards,' Matilda mocked. 'They can't wait, can they?'

'They're excited,' she smiled.

'What are you going to do in that big house on your own?'

'The same thing as you do in yours?'

'You don't have a dead husband to get depressed about.'

'No. I also don't have a hunky architect to share my bed with either.'

'I don't share my bed with him,' she said, reddening slightly.

'Well, share the kitchen table with then,' Adele winked. 'Have you heard from him?'

'Yes. He sent me a text earlier.'

'Are you seeing him again?'

'I feel like I'm back at school, here,' Matilda said, stuffing the rest of her disappointing snack into her mouth. 'We're two single adults who like each other. Let's just leave it at that for now, shall we?'

They were silent for a few seconds before Adele chuckled to herself.

'What?' Matilda asked.

'I was just wondering, as an architect . . .'

'No erection jokes,' Matilda interrupted.

'As if I would,' she held up her hands in surrender.

'I know what you're like.'

There was a light rap on the office door. It opened slightly and Claire Alexander poked her head around.

'Sorry, do you mind if I interrupt?'

'Not at all, Claire,' Matilda said. 'Please, add some sanity to the conversation.'

'I wish I could. I've discovered something on one of the scans that you're going to need to see.'

Claire led the way back into the digital autopsy suite. In the anteroom, the screen was still showing images of Keeley Armitage, only, now there were scans of the whole body rather than localised to her neck and head.

'First of all, sorry for rushing off like that,' Claire said. Adele placed a hand on her shoulder. 'Secondly, I've found this.' She zoomed in and pointed to shadowing on Keeley's lower torso.

'What is it?' Matilda asked.

'This is evidence of significant trauma with a large haematoma. The tissue in this region is incredibly soft. It's been severely damaged. These dark areas here are patterns of gas. We should not be able to see gas in this area because the tissue would keep it out.'

'I'm sorry,' Matilda began. 'I've no idea what I'm looking at here. What area of the body is this?'

Claire and Adele exchanged glances.

'It's the inside of Keeley's vagina,' Claire said quietly. 'This is evidence of a serious sexual assault.'

'But she was found fully clothed. Her knickers and tights weren't interfered with. You said so yourself, Adele.'

'The internal damage is sufficient to show bruising on top of old injuries that haven't had time to heal. This goes back longer than Keeley being kidnapped on Monday night. She was abused before she went missing,' Claire stated.

Chapter 33

ACC Valerie Masterson entered the HMET suite and stood in the doorway. She looked lost. Usually neatly turned out in uniform, her shirt wasn't tucked into her trousers, her jacket was unbuttoned, and her shoes were dull. Everyone knew of her personal situation; her husband was severely ill in hospital and her retirement plans had been thrown into chaos, so nobody drew attention to her slack appearance.

'Matilda not in?' she asked, approaching Sian's desk.

'No. She's at Watery Street. She'll be a few more hours yet.'

'Oh.'

Sian waited for her to go on, but she didn't. The DS followed Valerie's eyeline and landed on the framed photo on her desk of Sian with her husband and four children.

'I hear congratulations are in order,' Valerie said.

'Sorry?'

'Twenty-fifth wedding anniversary.'

'Yes. At the end of the month.'

'Arthur and I have been married for twenty-eight years,' she said, wistfully. 'We were hoping to be somewhere in Italy for the thirtieth.'

'It could still happen.'

'No. Not now.'

'You may not be able to go on the road trip like you planned, but you could still have a holiday. Two years is a long time. You don't know how he's going to respond to treatment until it starts. He could surprise you all.'

Valerie gave a weak smile. 'I wish I had your optimism, Sian. When Matilda gets in, will you give her this?' She produced a folder from behind her back. 'I've had an email from the embassy in France. They've sent through a transcript of the interview with the young lad claiming to be Carl Meagan. It makes for very interesting reading.'

'Oh.' Sian said, taking the folder from her. 'Any news on the DNA sample?'

'Not yet.' Valerie stood in silence, looking once again at Sian's family photo, before turning on her heel and heading for the exit. Her legs looked heavy as she walked, as if all life had drained out of her.

Sian picked up the framed photo and looked at her husband. 'Don't even think about putting me through what Valerie's going through right now, Stuart Mills. I won't hesitate in pulling the plug.' She didn't mean it.

She opened the folder Valerie left her and pulled out the four-page email. Her eyes quickly skimmed the first page and her mouth fell open. 'Jesus Christ,' she said to herself. Her phone rang, making her jump. She quickly closed the folder and put her keyboard over the top of it. 'Homicide and Major Enquiries. DS Mills,' she answered.

'Sian, it's Mat. Are you sitting down?'

'Yes.'

'Initial tests on Keeley Armitage show that she was sexually assaulted.'

'What?' Her eyes widened. 'How is that possible? She was fully clothed. Her tights were—'

'I know,' Matilda interrupted. 'I didn't mean she was assaulted when she was taken. There are old injuries. She was assaulted way before Monday evening.'

'Oh my God.'

'You know what I'm thinking, don't you?'

'Craig Armitage?'

'Exactly.'

'Shit. What do you want me to do?'

'We need to be incredibly sensitive about this,' Matilda said. 'If we go in like a bull in a china shop and we're wrong, we will not look good when the Armitages go to the press – which they will. Give social services a call, see if the family have appeared on their radar at all. Any news on Calvin Page yet?'

'No. Ranjeet left to meet his parole officer about half an hour ago.'

'I thought Aaron was dealing with that.'

'Erm . . . yes. I just heard Ranjeet was going.'

'Ok. Keep me posted.'

'Will do. Listen, Matilda,' Sian began, moving her keyboard and looking at the folder. 'I've received . . .'

'What? What have you received?' Matilda asked when Sian fell silent.

'Nothing. It doesn't matter. It can wait.'

Matilda hung up. She'd gone to her car to make the private call. When she looked up out of the windscreen, she saw DC Finn Cotton standing by her car, patiently waiting.

'Is everything all right?' she asked as she stepped out of the Range Rover. He looked ill.

'I've never attended a post-mortem before,' he said, barely opening his mouth.

'I thought you were at the one with DI Brady the other day, the prostitute found in Stanley Street.'

His cheeks reddened in embarrassment. 'No. DI Brady sent me back to Stanley Street to knock on a few doors.'

'You mean you were sick?'

He swallowed hard. 'I'm afraid so.'

'Ah. Well, I'm sorry to say this, but this one isn't going to be an easy one to watch. I mean, none of them are, but when they're on children, well . . .' She looked at him. He was petrified. She cast her eyes up and down his slight frame. 'Fortunately, you don't look too heavy. I should be able to carry you back to the car no problem. Come on, follow me.'

The unnatural light of the autopsy room was stark, intrusive and headache inducing. There were no windows to let in light from outside and the sound of air conditioning and extractor fans was a constant hum of annoyance. The ceiling was low, adding to the oppressive atmosphere. It was cold. It was quiet. It was grim. Death stalked the hallways and lurked behind every corner. The bank of refrigerators either side of the long corridor added to the macabre mood.

'I don't think I can do this,' Finn said quietly to his boss.

'You don't have a choice, I'm afraid. This is part and parcel of the job. You'll have to attend a great deal of these in your career; you may as well start with a bad one.'

Matilda showed Finn where to go in order to suit up. Matilda was an old hand at this and, to her, the oversized green scrubs, the gloves, face mask and wellington boots slipped on with ease. Finn kept everyone waiting.

Finn's role was as exhibit officer. His relief at not being in the main autopsy room was palpable. He was in the anteroom where he would record any evidence that was found on the body.

In the main room, a single table was welded to the floor. In the middle, Keeley Armitage's small body was covered by a white sheet. At the back of the room, a workbench contained all the tools Adele would need to perform the post-mortem.

The sheet was removed, revealing Keeley's naked body. She looked younger than nine years old. She was pale. Her skin was smooth and soft. She didn't look real.

The photographer stepped forward and began taking pictures of the child from every angle while Matilda, Adele, and the pathological technician, Lucy Dauman, stood to one side.

'When you're presented with a child, you really begin to question why you decided to do this job,' Lucy said to no one in particular. 'I mean, any murder victim is upsetting, but a child. She's nine years old for crying out loud. What could she have possibly done to someone to make them kill her?' Her voice broke and she wiped away a tear with the back of her hand.

'You can't think like that, Lucy,' Adele said. 'It's incredibly sad what's happened to her, but we're helping to find out who did it so they can face justice. We've been here so many times before. We know to keep our emotions in the locker. This is just any other post-mortem.'

'It's not, though, is it?'

'I'm sorry, Lucy, but it is. It may sound harsh and insensitive, but if you keep thinking of the person they used to be, it will eat away at you.'

Within seconds of Adele inserting the scalpel to begin making the traditional Y-shape from behind each ear to meet at the breastbone, a thud was heard from the anteroom. Finn had fainted. A technician helped him out of the room, and another stepped in as exhibit officer and the post-mortem continued.

Matilda didn't usually struggle with post-mortems, but she couldn't get what Lucy had said out of her mind. It was difficult to leave emotions at the door and see the victim as an object. She wouldn't be doing her job justice if she didn't have sympathy for the person who had been killed. Only a cold-blooded psychopath could approach the autopsy of a nine-year-old with icy disdain. She watched Adele out of the corner of her eye, searching for any signs of humanity. She didn't see it in her face, which was partially covered, but she saw it in her shaking hands as the scalpel cut into the flesh. As she recorded her findings into the microphone hanging from the ceiling, her voice was distinctly higher than usual, and she had to keep swallowing to compose herself.

Despite the digital autopsy showing no bones were broken during the strangulation, Adele needed to be certain. There had to be a complete dissection of the neck which included the full removal of the larynx including the hyoid bone, with the tongue still attached. They were individually examined for signs of contusion and haemorrhage.

Matilda stood well back from the table to allow Adele, Lucy, and the other technicians space to move freely around.

'I shall now begin examining the body for evidence of sexual assault,' Adele said into the microphone.

Keeley's legs were spread open wider and Adele stepped back to allow the photographer to visually record any evidence. There was a remote chance there could be semen present which would help Matilda in tracking down the perpetrator. How long ago Keeley was assaulted would determine how old the sample was and whether it was any use to test. This part of the post-mortem would be more intricate and precise.

In order to check a victim for evidence of sexual assault, dissection of the pelvis involved removing all of the pelvis organ *en bloc*. The pubic bones were sawed a few centimetres on each side and the perineum deeply dissected to remove the vagina, rectum, anus, uterus, tubes and ovaries for a more detailed dissection. Adele was looking for any signs of haemorrhage or contusions. She found them. She looked up at Matilda and their eyes met. It was the first time Matilda had ever seen Adele cry during a post-mortem.

'I'm so sorry,' Finn said as he sat in Adele's office with a mug of water in his hands.

'Don't worry about it. You're not the first person to faint at a post-mortem and you certainly won't be the last.'

'Does it get any easier?'

Matilda thought for a moment. 'No. It doesn't. You need to become hardened, though. Find a way that works for you to be able to get through these, because you'll be attending a lot more in your career.' She looked up and saw Adele approach. Her face was grim. 'You head back to the station. I'll be along later.'

He placed his mug carefully on the table and walked out with his head down.

'He's a nice lad,' Adele said.

'Yes. Once he's lined his stomach with steel, he'll be fine. Go on then, give me the worst.'

'I'm sorry to say that the digital autopsy was correct in its findings. Keeley was indeed sexually assaulted, on more than one occasion. However, she wasn't assaulted on the night she was taken. These are old injuries that haven't quite healed.'

'Please tell me there were semen samples or a hair or something.'

'I'm afraid not. I can tell you that Keeley wasn't drugged.'

'How do you know? I thought toxicology took weeks to come back.'

'Haven't I shown you my new toy? Follow me.' Adele led Matilda out of her cramped office and into the main autopsy suite.

At the back of the room was a neatly arranged table with all the equipment required for a post-mortem. Adele picked up a sealed foil packet and tore it open. She removed a small piece of plastic, no bigger than a credit card and showed it to Matilda.

'It's called Intelligent Fingerprinting. See this little pad here? This is the application pad. We press all ten fingers on the pad firmly for five seconds each. Give me your hand, I'll do a practice on you.'

'Really?'

'Yes. It doesn't hurt.'

'Isn't it a waste of resources?'

'I've opened the pack now. I may as well use it. Not nervous or anything, are you? You haven't been sniffing coke or injecting yourself with heroin lately?'

Matilda proffered a sarcastic smile then held out her hand. Adele pressed her fingers firmly on the pad then closed a protective window over it when she'd finished.

'Usually I'd record all your details on the back, but as this is just a demonstration, I won't bother. This innocuous looking machine is actually very high-tech,' she said, moving over to a small and unimpressive looking piece of kit. 'It's called the Reader 1000. I open the drawer, insert this wee cartridge, press a few buttons and within ten minutes I'll know whether you're a coke head or not.'

'That's all it takes, ten minutes?'

'Yes. It will tell me if you have any drugs in your system. If so, we'll do a full toxicology and that'll take the usual couple of weeks to come back. However, if this little puppy says there are no drugs present, there's no need to do a tox screening and waste all that time waiting.'

'So, you did this on Keeley and found no drugs.'

'That's right. I'll include the printout in my report.'

'That's amazing.' Matilda smiled, suitably impressed.

'I know. There aren't many of these in the country; we're one of the lucky ones.'

The reader signalled the results were ready. Adele looked at the screen. 'Your secrets are revealed. According to this you spend your evenings smacked off your tits on nose candy, drinking Baltic tea and singing the hits of The Manhattan Transfer.'

'Your machine isn't all it's cracked up to be as it was Jefferson Airplane last night,' Matilda smiled.

Adele ejected the cartridge and handed it to Matilda. 'You may keep this or destroy it. Your choice.'

'Thank you. My own personal drug test.' She placed it in her pocket. 'Listen, going back to the sexual assault thing, can you tell how long ago these injuries were inflicted? Are we talking years or what?'

'Not years, no. There's bruising and bleeding. The hymen has been torn and there are abrasions on the vulva. They're not old, but they're not new either.'

'You're not helping.'

'I'm sorry. If there was a date stamped on the hymen, I would have told you.'

'I know. I'm sorry. It's just . . . I don't want to ask the questions I need answers to.' Matilda took a sip of her coffee and pulled a face at the cold liquid. 'Sexual abuse of a child is usually from someone she knows and trusts: an older sibling, uncle, father, grandfather, favourite teacher, neighbour. I have three suspects: a child rapist who is no longer in prison and seems to have disappeared, his brother who was Keeley's teacher, or her father.'

Chapter 34

'DC Deshwal?'

Ranjeet looked up from the dated glossy magazine he was bored of reading. A small, well-turned-out woman in a dark grey suit stood in front of him with her right hand out.

'I'm so sorry to keep you waiting. I've only just been told you were here.'

Ranjeet had been waiting for almost half an hour. 'That's fine,' he smiled.

'I'm Poonam Asan. I'm Calvin Page's parole officer. Would you like to follow me?'

Ranjeet followed the tiny woman as she clacked down the corridor to her office. She kept looking back over her shoulder and smiling at the DC. She opened the door to her office that was no bigger than a cubbyhole.

'I'm sorry about the mess,' she apologised again and pointed to Ranjeet to take a seat in front of her desk which was laden with cardboard files and an old, chunky laptop in the middle. Poonam sat in her seat with a deep sigh. 'So, how can I help you?'

'What can you tell me about Calvin Page?'

She rifled through a pile of files on the edge of her desk before pulling one out. 'You'd think these would all be on computer, wouldn't you? Calvin Page was released on January 14th this year after serving six years of a thirteen year sentence.'

'He was only sentenced to thirteen years after raping three girls?'

'The case involving the third girl was thrown out of court at the trial due to a lack of evidence.'

'Even so . . .'

'I know,' Poonam interrupted, holding up her hand. 'I just deal with the aftercare. I've nothing to do with sentencing.'

'I'm sorry. I didn't mean to imply . . .' he waffled. 'When was the last time you saw him?'

'Blimey, let me see,' she pushed the file to one side and turned on her laptop. 'The office may not be paperless, but I try to be as much as possible. My whole diary and schedule is on here. It's a bit slow, sorry.'

'Did you speak to Calvin about his crimes? How was he?' he asked while waiting for the computer to come to life.

'One of the reasons for his early release was because he showed remorse for his crimes. While in prison he went through several courses of therapy and treatments. He was a model prisoner.'

'What was the motive for his crimes?'

'Wouldn't you know that?' she asked with a hint of a smile.

'I know what it says in the files. I wondered what he said after six years in prison.'

'Calvin has an attraction to young girls,' Poonam said, leaning forward on the desk and folding her arms. 'Actually, I should probably say that in the past tense. He knows what he did was wrong. He knows how he felt is wrong and he has been treated accordingly.'

'So, what are you saying, he's suddenly cured?'

'Not suddenly, no. His treatment is ongoing. He has regular therapy sessions and takes medication to contain his feelings and emotions. He is also on the sex offenders register for life and is banned from ever working with children. Ah, here we are,' she said, looking at the laptop. 'Now, the last time I saw him was Thursday 12th of April.'

'Really? Why so long ago?'

'Well, I had to cancel our next appointment as I was on my honeymoon. The appointment after that was the 12th of June but Calvin cancelled because he was ill.'

'How did he let you know he was ill?'

'He sent an email.'

'You didn't speak to him?'

'No.'

'So, how did you know he was ill?'

'Erm . . . well, I didn't,' she said.

Ranjeet rolled his eyes. 'And the appointment after that?'

'I couldn't fit him in until late July.'

'And you didn't see him then either?'

'No. He emailed asking for permission to attend a wedding in Brighton.'

'Jesus!' Ranjeet uttered.

'Look, do you have any idea how busy I am? I'm doing the work of three people. The parole office is seriously understaffed and underfunded.'

'Shouldn't you have alerted police to Calvin as a no-show?'

'No. As far as I was concerned, he wasn't a no-show.'

'You haven't seen him since April. It's now September. What address do you have for him?'

She looked down at her laptop. 'I have an address in Malton Street in Pitsmoor,' she said, sheepishly.

'Really? We have a house in Hillsborough. Malton Street is where his brother, Sebastian, lives.'

'Yes. He said he couldn't settle in Hillsborough. He didn't like living on his own so he was moving in with his brother.'

'But we have that property under surveillance. He hasn't been seen anywhere near that. Do you have any further contact details for him?'

'I have a mobile number and an email address,' she said, not making eye contact with Ranjeet.

'May I have those?'

'The thing is . . . when you called asking to see me, I phoned Calvin and sent him an email.'

'Go on,' he prompted.

'The phone kept ringing out. It didn't even go to voicemail.'

'And the email?'

'Bounced right back.'

'Shit.'

'I'm sorry.' She ran her fingers through her hair and rested her head in her hands.

'So, you have no idea where he is and no way of contacting him?'

'No.'

'He's a convicted paedophile and you've left him go off-grid since April.'

'I haven't purposely—'

Ranjeet stood up and left the room, slamming the door closed behind him. He'd liked Poonam on sight; she was a very attractive woman and was wearing a sweet smelling perfume. He sympathised with her for being overworked but she should have alerted police to Calvin being unreachable. He would not like to be in her shoes when Matilda found out.

* * *

Sian, Rory, and Scott were having a break in the HMET suite. Scott made the them all coffees while Rory rifled Sian's snack drawer for chocolate. Sian was finishing a phone call.

'The Armitage family are known to social services, but that's only because of Riley and any help they may need for him,' she said, hanging up.

'Are we really suggesting Craig raped and killed his own daughter?' Scott said, sniffing the milk before pouring it into the mugs. 'He works two jobs; seven days a week. He raises all that money for charity. He's had the house modified to accommodate Riley. He's like the perfect father.'

'There's no such thing,' Sian said.

'What about your Stuart?' Rory asked.

'Where do I start? He dropped Belinda twice before she was even one year old. He left Anthony at the park and came home with a different child. He laughed when we were called in to school by the head when Danny set off a fire extinguisher in the middle of an assembly. I could go on.'

'Please do, these are funny,' Rory smiled.

'All I'm saying is that there's no such thing as a perfect parent. We're all just bumbling along trying to do our best to make sure our kids survive and don't bring the police to the door.'

'But why would he work so hard at making sure his family have as normal a life as possible when he's abusing his youngest daughter?' Scott asked, bringing the mugs to Sian's desk.

'To cover what he's doing. We've all met child abusers before. They're masters in manipulation. Just because he plays the part of a doting father doesn't mean we should take it at face value and believe everything we're being told.'

'Has anyone told Ellen yet?' Scott asked.

'Yes. I have,' Sian said. 'She's basically echoed what you've just said. 'He loves all three of his children and can't imagine him hurting them. Although . . .' she paused while she thought. 'Ellen did say that she couldn't warm to them.'

'What does that mean?'

'I asked but she wouldn't elaborate. She just said there was something strange she couldn't put her finger on. I'll ask the DCI to have a word with her.'

'So, where do we go from here?' Scott asked. 'How do we break the news to the parents that their daughter was sexually abused without saying we actually suspect one of them?

'We give them the facts and interview them separately,' Sian said.

'There's a task I'm not looking forward to,' Rory said, throwing a Bounty wrapper away and taking a Tunnock's Tea Cake out of Sian's drawer.

'Surely there's someone else in Keeley's life who could have assaulted her,' Scott said, his hands wrapped firmly around the mug. 'There was something definitely dodgy about that teacher and his brother who seems to have vanished.'

'Until we find Calvin and can question him, there's not much we can do there. We don't even know if they've ever met. Sebastian is the link between the two, but there's no motive or anything.'

'If this was a horror film, Calvin Page would turn up in the final act with his throat cut,' Rory said.

'Do you think we should try to find out who Calvin was friends with in prison? Maybe see if any of those are either out now or know anything about him his parole officer doesn't?' Scott suggested.

'Worth a try, I suppose. I don't think it will be difficult to find something the parole officer doesn't know,' Sian said. 'According to Ranjeet, she was absolutely clueless.'

'Do you ever get the feeling that the whole justice system in this country is completely arse about face?' Scott asked.

'You're not getting disillusioned about your job are you, Scott?' Rory asked.

Sian's mobile rang. She picked it up and stepped away from her desk before answering.

'No, of course not. It's just . . . well, the papers are full of stories about light sentences, criminals re-offending and not going back to prison, people flouting the law and our hands being tied because we're short of money and officers, or some smarmy solicitor finding a loophole. It just pisses me off sometimes.'

'I'm afraid you were wrong, Rory,' Sian said, disconnecting her call.

'Sorry?'

'That was Christian. I think we're a long way from the final act and Calvin Page has just turned up.'

'Really? Where?'

'The ski village.'

'The ski village? But that burnt down ages ago. What was he doing, hiding out?'

'No. Well, someone was hiding him. He's had his head caved in.'

Chapter 35

The Sheffield Ski Village was opened in Parkwood Springs in 1988. The first slope proved to be so popular that within two years a further seven slopes were added making it one of the largest artificial ski villages in Europe. Ski lodges, bars and shops were added, and some slopes redesigned to enable a variety of skiing activities.

In April 2012, the main building was destroyed by fire and the site was closed to the public. The fire was ruled to have been started accidentally. There were further fires, and by August 2016, the site had suffered from approximately fifty arson attacks.

Since 2012, the ski village had stood derelict and been blighted by significant fly tipping, used as a gypsy traveller site, been subject to theft, vandalism, and further arson attacks.

Matilda pulled up as close as she could to the entrance in her Range Rover. It was getting dark but she could see where she had to go by the artificial lights that had been erected around where the body had been found.

Parkwood Springs was high up and gave wonderful panoramic views of Sheffield. Matilda shivered as a gust of cool autumnal wind blew around her.

'Good evening boss,' Rory smiled. 'Did you ever use the ski slopes?' he asked with a smile.

'I can't say I did, no. You?'

'No.'

'Isn't it supposed to be getting developed?' She asked, looking around at the ruined site as they made their way to the crime scene.

'Apparently so. I was looking online in the car on the way over. Some extreme-sports company is wanting to build on it. They'll have their work cut out judging by the state of the place.'

'Tell me about the body.' Matilda stumbled over uneven ground and Rory caught her just in time before she fell. 'Cheers.'

'From what we can tell, it's Calvin Page. We may need dental records though to formally identify him.'

'What happened?'

'According to Dr Kean he's been repeatedly hit over the head with a blunt object.'

'So, if we need dental records to identify him, how do we know it's Calvin Page?'

'He has a tattoo which reads "Calvin Page. Pure Sheffield Steel" on the inside of his left arm.'

'Oh. That's very considerate of him. Maybe more people should have it done in case they get brutally murdered,' she said with a hint of a smile in her voice.

'Who found him?'

'Sian called them a courting couple,' Rory smiled. 'I don't think they were doing much courting.'

Against a backdrop of a stiff breeze and the uneven terrain, Matilda struggled into the white paper forensic suit. She pulled open the entrance to the tent and stepped in, squinting at the harshness of the lights.

'What can you tell me, Adele?'

Adele looked up and smiled. 'Well, Lucy was just telling us

all a delightful story about an ex-boyfriend who brought her up here for a romantic evening of outdoor sex a few years back.'

'Adele! That was private,' Lucy said. Behind the face mask, Matilda could see she was blushing.

'We're in a tent made out of paper and you're not the quietest person in the world, Lucy. I bet the majority of the forensic team heard you.'

'I heard you,' Rory said.

'Oh my God,' Lucy turned away, embarrassed.

'I thought it was hot, actually,' he said. 'You, Adrian Pritchard, a bottle of prosecco and a Fiat Punto I think you said.'

There was a ripple of laughter from around the tent.

'Oh, bloody hell. I knew I should have phoned in sick today,' Lucy said.

'One of these days, Lucy, I'll buy you a drink and tell you some bizarre and eye-opening stories about Adele,' Matilda said, putting a comforting arm around her shoulders.

'You do and I'll tell your team about why you and James had to cut your honeymoon short.'

Matilda thought for a brief second. 'Sorry Lucy, you're on your own.'

'I'd love to know why you had to cut your honeymoon short,' Rory grinned.

'Well—'

'One more word out of you, Adele, and you'll be joining Calvin Page here in the mortuary,' Matilda interrupted.

'I think we should move on, don't you?' Adele said.

'Good idea. Back to my original question: what can you tell me, Adele?'

Adele squatted next to the battered and broken body. 'As you can see, he was savagely beaten about the head. If you look here,' she pointed to the base of the skull. 'You can see an indentation of a circular object, small in size. I think you're looking for something like a hammer, maybe. The blows are random. A couple from the front to take him down, then the killer couldn't stop. The back of the head is completely caved in.'

'Jesus,' Matilda uttered. 'Was he killed here?'

'No. If he had we'd be looking at blood spatter all over the place. This was a violent attack. The killer showed no mercy. The first couple of blows would have been enough to kill him, but this was relentless. I'll do the PM tomorrow morning about ten o'clock.'

'Thank you.'

Matilda turned to leave the tent. As she reached the exit, she stopped, turned to Lucy and said, 'By the way, Adele was once thrown off a ride in Blackpool for having too much fun with her . . . what shall we call him? . . . companion.'

Lucy laughed as Adele gasped.

'Matilda! I told you that in strictest confidence.'

'Oh sod off, it made the local paper.'

'That's so funny,' Lucy said.

Matilda left the tent with the sound of laughter in the background. It might seem insensitive laughing and joking at a crime scene, especially over the body of a murder victim, but Matilda, Adele, and their teams saw the worst of human behaviour on a daily basis. They came into contact with evil and depravity as regularly as the sun rose. If they took everything to heart, allowed it to weigh them down, and took the death, murder, rape, and assault home with them, they'd be raging alcoholics queuing outside a therapist's office.

Nobody ever made fun of a murder victim. They were always respected, no matter who they were, but, from time to time, the lightness had to break through the darkness.

'Rory, give Ellen a call. I want you to find out if Craig has been at the house all day today. If so, has he made any phone calls or has anyone been round to visit?'

'You think he may have done this?'

'I don't know. It seems strange that a girl is killed and then the brother of her teacher, who happens to be a child rapist, is found dead within twenty-four hours. Also, bring Sebastian Page back in for questioning too.'

'Tonight?'

'No. First thing in the morning. I've had my head bitten off about overtime spending lately. If the Chief Constable only wants to pay us for office hours, he can only expect us to work office hours too.' She began peeling off the forensic suit. 'Go home, Rory. Have an early night.'

'I was planning on seeing Natasha, actually.'

Matilda turned back and saw the smirk on his face. 'Oh. Well, I'm sure you'll still be having an early night.'

Once behind the wheel of her Range Rover, Matilda took her phone out of her pocket. She had two missed calls from her mother, a missed call and a voicemail from Pat, a text from her sister and two texts from Daniel. She paused, not knowing who to respond to first. Her mother could definitely wait until last.

She decided she didn't want to see Daniel tonight. She liked Daniel a great deal and wanted him in her life, yet she didn't want a second husband. She didn't want a replacement for James. She enjoyed being by herself. Yes, she did get lonely occasionally, but didn't everyone? Matilda decided that she and Daniel needed to have a succinct chat about where they were going. She wanted to be more than friends but didn't want him moving in or leaving a toothbrush in her bathroom. Unfortunately, she wasn't in the mood for such a conversation tonight and ran off a quick text telling him a body had been found and she'd be at the crime scene until the small hours. A little white lie was harmless.

Ellen Devonport couldn't wait to leave the Armitage house. She'd received a long text from Christian bringing her up to speed on the finding of Calvin Page's body and the possibility of Craig Armitage sexually abusing his youngest daughter. She knew she should question the family more, but she had stayed well past her time and wanted to go home, sink into a hot, deep bath with a bottle of wine and fall asleep watching *Fleabag* on iPlayer.

The problem, and the cause of her headache, was that her feelings towards the family were conflicted. She admired Craig and Linda for everything they did for their kids, especially Craig. He worked all hours every day for his kids, to give them the best they could afford. They had been dealt a rotten hand with Riley's illness, now Keeley's murder, and facing questions about sexual abuse had the potential to destroy the family completely. However, she couldn't hide away from the fact that the majority of children murdered were killed by a parent or family member. She really wanted Craig to be innocent.

As she was leaving, she gave Craig a hug which had lasted longer than she intended. When she stepped back, she noticed Jodie was watching them from the kitchen. She said her goodbyes and quickly left, telling them to call her anytime. She was on call twenty-four hours but hoped she wouldn't be needed. She felt physically drained after spending a whole day in that house among the grief and despair.

Outside the house, bunches of flowers had been arriving all day. By now, most of the front garden was awash with colour.

Ellen glanced at them; the waft of various scents tickled her nostrils. The local florists would be having a bumper month.

She pulled the collar up on her coat and put her head down. She tried not to make eye contact with any of the journalists parked up on the pavement.

After the storm last night, there was a distinct coolness to the air. A stiff breeze was blowing, and the sky was darkening with a swirl of angry clouds over Sheffield. She lifted the collar on her thin jacket and headed for her car.

'Excuse me? Hello? Can I have a word?'

Ellen looked up and saw a woman trotting towards her. She was in her late fifties and wearing black trousers, a white jumper and a cream coloured cardigan which she held in place with her arms firmly crossed over her chest.

'Are you with the police?'

'Yes.'

'I was wondering if I could have a quick word with you.'

'Of course.'

'The thing is,' she said, looking around her. 'I want to do this anonymously. It's been weighing on my mind for a long time, and, well, since Keeley went missing, I suppose it's brought it back.'

'I'm sorry, I don't—'

'No. I'm waffling, aren't I?' the woman interrupted. She was shorter than Ellen. Her dull blue eyes were starry and flittered from side to side. 'It's just . . . I really don't know how to say this.'

'If you think you have information about this case, or any case, you have a duty to report it, no matter how difficult it may seem.'

'I'm aware of all that. Oh God, this is hard,' she licked her lips and swallowed hard a few times. 'If I tell you something, will you promise that my name won't come up?'

'Well, as you haven't told me your name, it won't be able to come up.' Ellen smiled. She looked over the woman's shoulder and saw the front door of a house three doors down from the Armitage family was open. It wouldn't be difficult to find out her name.

'That's true. Good. Well, I think you need to be looking closer at the family. I've read the story in the local paper tonight about how loving and caring they are. The thing is, people are always made out to be saints when they're involved in a tragedy, aren't they? The Armitages, they're not all they're cracked up to be.'

'In what way?'

'Look into Riley's illness. Find out how he came to be brain damaged.'

'We know about his seizures.'

'But what caused his seizures?'

'He has epilepsy.'

'Does he?'

'What are you saying?'

'You can get access to medical records. Talk to his GP. Who witnessed his seizures? I'm not telling you how I know this as I'll get them into trouble and I swore I'd never repeat what I heard, but with Keeley dying, I can't keep quiet, and this isn't me being a gossip, this is me being concerned for the people in that house. Find out who witnessed Riley's seizures.' She turned and walked away.

'Wait,' Ellen called out.

The woman didn't wait. She took long strides back to her home and slammed the front door behind her.

Ellen remained standing in the middle of Acorn Drive with the wind whipping up around her. She looked to the Armitage house. What the hell was happening with this family?

Chapter 36

With another murder and the prospect of interviewing Linda and Craig tomorrow about their daughter being sexually abused, Matilda had hoped for a night to herself. She was going to open a bottle of wine, read the transcript of the interview with the supposed Carl Meagan in France, and then have an early night with a good thriller.

The house soon warmed up once the wood burner was lit, and while the microwave was heating up a bowl of soup she changed into comfortable pyjama bottoms and an old sweater. She could smell the chicken and vegetable soup as she came down the stairs and her grumbling stomach told her just how hungry she was.

With her bowl of steaming soup, a couple of crusty breadcakes and the emailed transcript of the interview, she settled on the sofa and began reading.

Transcription of the interview between Detective Patrick Platini (PP) and Detective Eric Desailly (ED) with "Carl Meagan" (CM). From child protection, Detective Suzanne Beltrame (SB), acted as appropriate adult.

Detective Patrick Platini: Can you tell us what you're doing here in France?

Carl Meagan: I'm on holiday.

PP: Alone?

CM: No.

PP: Who are you with?'

CM: I'm supposed to call them my mum and dad.

PP: What are their names?

CM: I don't know. They only speak English when they talk to me. When they talk to each other they speak in a different language.

PP: What language do they speak in?

CM: I don't know.

PP: Is it French?

CM: I'm not sure. I don't think so.

Detective Eric Desailly: Where are you living? Here in France?

CM: No.

ED: Can you tell us anything about where you're living?

CM: No. I don't understand the words they use or anything of the language.

(Detective Suzanne Beltrame suggests a five-minute break be taken here as "Carl" starts to cry.)

PP: Can you tell us about the night you were taken, March 25th, 2015?

CM: My parents had gone out for the night. My nan was looking after me. We played games and watched films before I went to bed. I was asleep and was woken up by my bedroom door opening. A man came in . . .

PP: Did you know this man?

CM: No. I'd never seen him before.

ED: What did he look like?

CM: I don't know. It was dark and he had a mask on.

ED: What kind of mask?

CM: It was black and it had holes for his eyes and mouth.

PP: Ok. What did he say to you?

CM: Nothing. He just grabbed me by the arm and pulled me out of bed.

PP: What happened next?

CM: I was carried downstairs and out of the house.

SB: Where was your nan while all this was happening, Carl?

CM: I don't know. I could only hear Woody barking.

ED: Who is Woody?

CM: My dog. He's a golden Labrador. He's only a puppy.

PP: What happened when you were carried downstairs?

CM: I was put in the back of a van.

PP: Can you describe the van?

CM: It was white. It was dirty and smelly inside.

PP: What did it smell of?

CM: I don't know. It smelled like a garage, I think.

PP: Was there anyone or anything in the van with you?

CM: There was a mattress. It was dirty and cold.

PP: How long were you in the van for?

CM: I don't know.

ED: Where were you taken?

CM: I don't know. I don't remember getting out of the van. The next thing I remember is opening my eyes and being in a strange room with just a single bed in it. Can I see my mum and dad now?

(SB recommends another five-minute break. CM is becoming agitated and upset.)

PP: *What can you tell us about the people you're living with?*

CM: *They're friendly. They're looking after me, but they're quiet. I'm not allowed to talk much.*

PP: *Do you go to school?*

CM: *Sometimes. The woman I'm supposed to call mum teaches me at home. When I do go to school, she is with me all the time.*

ED: *Do you have any friends your own age?*

CM: *No. I'm not allowed out without Mu— The people looking after me.*

ED: *Are they the ones who took you from your home?*

CM: *No.*

ED: *Then how did you come to live with them?*

CM: *I was driven to them. We were driving for a very long time. More than a day as it went dark and then light again. I was taken out of the back and the woman came to hug me and put me in*

*the back of her car. We drove again for a very long time to the
house they said was going to be my home from now on. Can I see
my mum now? I want to speak to my mum.*

End.

Matilda threw the printed email onto the coffee table and leaned
back on the sofa. She hadn't touched her soup. She wasn't happy
with what she read. She would have liked to have heard a
recording of the interview, to listen to the words of the boy
calling himself Carl Meagan. She wanted to hear his voice, his
accent. The questioning didn't go deep enough for Matilda's
liking either. They didn't challenge his version of what had
occurred on the night he disappeared. Which way did he turn
when he left his bedroom to go down the stairs? Was the living
room on the left or right as he made his way out of the house?
What was he wearing when he was put to bed by his nan? They
were all questions Matilda knew the answer to that had not
been made public. She would know if he was really Carl or not
by his level of detail.

What had happened to the couple he was living with? Had
they been traced and interviewed? Where was he staying while
in France?

Matilda was not happy at all, and she wasn't convinced the
boy in Marseille was really Carl Meagan. If not, there were two
questions she wanted answering: who was he, and why was he
doing this? There was also something else to consider: who put
him up to this in the first place, and what dark motive could
they possibly have?

It wasn't long before Matilda's mind began to wander. The
cases of Carl Meagan and Keeley Armitage weren't dissimilar

– a child taken, seemingly for ransom, which is then botched, for some reason. But while Carl is spirited away, never to be seen again, Keeley turns up dead. Were the crimes similar because they were perpetrated by the same people? If so, was Carl dead too, lying buried in woodland in an unmarked grave? Was Carl lying less than a mile away from home and he just hadn't been discovered yet? She hoped to God he wasn't.

There was no doubt in Matilda's mind that she would catch Keeley's killer. If she did, would she be catching Carl's too?

Chapter 37

Friday 14th September 2018

Matilda slept through the night without waking once. That hadn't happened for a long time. Usually her sleep was interrupted by random thoughts and echoes of conversations she'd had years ago that returned to plague her: old cases, cold cases, relationships with former colleagues that had ended on a sour note, the sight of DC Faith Easter falling to her death and Matilda being unable to do anything about it. Last night, however, she'd fallen asleep within moments of her head touching the pillow and hadn't woken up until the alarm sounded at six o'clock the following morning.

She woke to find two text messages from Daniel Harbison. The first was from just before midnight wishing her a good night. The second had arrived a few minutes ago, asking if she wanted to make any plans for the weekend. She did want to make plans; she wanted to tell him how she felt and where she wanted this relationship to go. Hopefully, he wouldn't run a mile.

After a quick shower, a light breakfast of a black coffee and two pieces of fruit, she left the house. The long, deep sleep had been exactly what she needed. She felt buoyed and determined. Today would be a good day. She could feel it from within.

Ellen Devonport was waiting for Matilda outside her office. She paced the floor and had a look of worry on her face.

'DCI Darke, can I have a private word before I have to go around to the Armitages's please?'

Matilda could sense the urgency and stress in her voice. So much for today being a good day. It seemed to be going downhill already.

'Sure. Come on in.'

Matilda switched on her laptop and asked Ellen to begin while she rifled through the colourful Post-it Note messages that had been left on her desk overnight.

Ellen cleared her throat and filled her in on what the neighbour had said about a mystery surrounding the origins of Riley's illness.

'What did she mean?' Matilda asked, leaning forward, a heavy frown on her face.

'I don't know.'

'Didn't you ask her to elaborate?'

'She didn't give me chance. She said her speech then ran off back to her house.'

'What did you interpret it to mean?' Matilda asked. Ellen knew the Armitage family better than anyone else. She was keen to test her judgement.

'Well, I thought she was raising doubt as to Riley's condition in the first place. But, I mean, you've seen him, there's no getting away from the fact that he's suffered severe brain damage.'

'Do you think the neighbour was saying that perhaps his condition hadn't been caused by epilepsy?'

'But how else . . . oh,' the penny dropped for Ellen. 'You mean Linda injured him in some way?'

'I suppose it's possible. We need to look at Riley's medical records and talk to his GP as well. I'll get one of the team to look into it. Meanwhile, you go to the house as normal. I'll be coming along later this morning, anyway.'

Ellen scratched her forehead and rubbed at the worry lines. 'I've been thinking about this all night; I've hardly slept. From where I'm sitting, there are only two possibilities: either Riley's condition was caused by negligence or he was deliberately injured. If it was deliberate, then maybe whoever did it could be responsible for Keeley's death too.'

Matilda nodded. 'Look, Ellen, do you want to take today off? I can send someone else to the Armitages's for the day.'

'No. I'm fine, honestly. I'm just . . . Riley's really sweet,' she said with a hint of a smile. 'And Jodie is too. They really put on her. I want to be there for them.'

'Ok. But you can't take any of this personally. We're working on a case here; keep your eyes open at all times. And if you feel uncomfortable, or like you're in any kind of trouble, call me straight away. Understood?'

Ellen nodded. She stood up and left the office, quickly walking out of the HMET suite with her head down.

Matilda's feeling had changed. Today was not going to be a good day.

'Sebastian Page has gone missing,' Rory said, bounding into the open-plan office.

All eyes turned to him, then to Matilda who was about to start the morning briefing.

'What?' she said.

'I've had a call from the team observing his flat at Pitsmoor. He hasn't been there for two days and, according to the head at Mary Croft, he hasn't been back there since he fled on Tuesday.

His bank account hasn't been touched and his mobile is switched off.'

'What about his car?'

'Still outside his flat.'

Matilda took a deep breath. 'Right, we need to do a door-to-door. Find out who saw him last, where and when. Sian go back to Mary Croft. I want all the teachers interviewed; what do they know about Sebastian, any places he's mentioned, friends, family, partners, the usual.'

'Will do.'

'Why would he kill his own brother?' Ranjeet asked.

'We don't know that's what's happened yet.'

'So then why run off? You only run if you're guilty. If he hadn't killed his brother he'd be in his flat, going about life as normal, because he wouldn't know about it yet.'

'Maybe he killed him because he's trying to live a normal life while Calvin's past is destroying that,' Scott said, thinking out loud.

'Is that a reason to kill someone? If you didn't want any contact with a family member you just move away, maybe even change your name. You don't smash their skull to smithereens,' DC Deshwal said.

'Ranjeet's right,' Matilda said.

'First time for everything,' Rory grinned.

'We need to approach this with caution,' Matilda continued. 'We don't know who killed Calvin Page, but a missing brother is certainly suspicious. Either he's succumbed to the same fate as Calvin and we haven't found him yet, or he's the one who killed him. Christian, put out an alert for him, distribute his description, but tell everyone to approach with caution. He could be dangerous.'

Christian nodded, scribbling on his notepad.

'Rory, Scott, I want you two to come to the Armitages's with me. Aaron . . . where is Aaron?' she asked, looking around the room.

'He's not in yet,' Sian said.

'Why not? Any particular reason?'

'Not that I've been made aware of.'

'Ok. Finn, set up interview rooms one and two and the observation room. I want you in there with me.'

'What are we doing?' Rory asked.

'We're bringing Linda and Craig in for formal questioning. I think we've left them long enough to grieve. It's time they answered some questions.'

Chapter 38

Jodie Armitage was at the sink in the kitchen. Tears were streaming down her face. She would never forget the look on her mother's face as police led her out of the house to the waiting cars.

'Are you all right?' Ellen asked.

Jodie wiped her tears on a tea towel. 'They looked like they were being arrested,' she cried.

Ellen stepped forward, put her arm around the teenager, and led her to the table.

'I know it didn't look good, but we need to ask your parents important questions that can only be done under formal conditions. Do you know when you see on the news about a dog walker or a jogger finding a body? Well, that person has to go to the police station. They have to give all their clothes to be analysed and they're seriously questioned. They're treated like a suspect, basically. From the outside, it looks bad, but it's just procedure. Your mum and dad will be home very soon.'

'Mum's not well. She's sick.'

'In what way?'

'She keeps throwing up. She's been like it for months. Dad says she should go to the doctor, but she says it's just stress.'

'Maybe she's right. It can't be easy looking after Riley all the time.'

'I help out as much as I can, but I've got school.' Jodie choked on her tears. Her face was reddening.

Ellen reached out and took Jodie's hands in hers. 'Jodie, you can't be responsible for your parents. I know you like to think of yourself as a grown-up, but you're still a child. You should be out there with your friends, not looking after your brother.'

She sniffed hard and wiped her nose on her sleeve. 'I don't have any friends.'

'Why's that?'

'They go out at the weekend to town or the pictures or to Meadowhall, and I can't go with them because I have to help Mum with Riley while she does the washing. Or I have to help clean the house, or go with Dad to do the big shop. I have to ask if it's ok for me to go upstairs and do my homework.'

'Oh, Jodie,' Ellen said, squeezing her hands harder. 'There are places that can help with children who are carers. Riley can go into respite care for a few days to lessen the demand on the family. It's a way of helping.'

'Dad's looked into that, but Mum said no. She said it wouldn't be fair on Riley.'

'Would you like me to have a word with your mum and dad for you?'

'No,' she said, quickly wiping her eyes. 'If they knew I was talking to you like this they'd go mad. We're not supposed to burden others with our problems.'

Ellen took a deep breath. 'Is there anything I can do?'

'Take me away from this place.'

Both Craig and Linda were informed that they were not under arrest and were free to leave the station at any time. They could have a solicitor present if they wished, but they were simply being asked questions about their daughter. The finger of suspicion was not being pointed toward them. They both declined legal representation.

Before the interviews began, Scott had informed Matilda that he'd finally managed to get hold of Craig's ex-colleague, Dean Oliver, who'd been bad-mouthing Craig on social media once he'd left Parcelforce. The interview had been conducted over the phone as Dean was currently sunning himself in Corfu. Matilda skimmed the transcript and handed it back to Scott, telling him to bring it up during questioning.

Craig was ushered into interview room one where DS Sian Mills and DC Scott Andrews were waiting. In interview room two, Linda sat at a desk opposite DI Christian Brady and DC Rory Fleming. From the observation room, Matilda sat next to DC Finn Cotton who had entered carrying a coffee for the both of them. The small room was filled with the aroma of strong coffee, which made a change from whatever fragrance Finn had chosen to bathe in that morning.

As arranged beforehand, both parents would be asked the same questions in the same order. It was important to see if their stories were the same. The interviews were to be taped and filmed.

'Mr Armitage – Craig,' Sian started. 'Before we begin, I have to inform you that the results of the post-mortem examination on Keeley have revealed that before she died, she was subjected to sexual abuse.'

Craig's face remained blank for a long and heavy moment while he processed the information. He swallowed hard before he spoke.

'But, that can't be. Ellen told us that she was found fully clothed.'

'We believe the sexual abuse occurred before she went missing. This is something that happened months before.'

He took a deep and shaky breath. 'What?' His bottom lip quivered. He tried to keep hold of his emotion, but he couldn't stop a single tear falling from his left eye. 'You mean, someone's been . . . with my daughter?'

'I know this is incredibly difficult to hear, Craig, but do you know anyone who may be responsible?'

'No. I mean, how can they have? She's nine years old. She doesn't go anywhere without me or her mum.'

Sian cleared her throat. She was playing with her fingers, a tell Matilda had spotted over the years that she was uncomfortable. 'Usually, when a child is abused, it's by someone they know, someone they trust, someone who has manipulated the victim into believing what is happening is perfectly normal. Is there anyone you know of who fits that description?'

Craig sat motionless. He stared straight ahead, way beyond Sian and Scott. He didn't reply.

'Craig, did you hear what I asked?' Sian asked.

He nodded. 'I feel sick.'

'This isn't easy, I know. I'm a mother myself, and I can't begin to imagine what you're going through. But we need to find the person responsible, and we can only do that with your help.'

'I know. I'm sorry.'

'There's no need to apologise. Take your time.'

In the second interview room, when Christian broke the news of Keeley being abused to Linda, she broke down. Her sobs were loud. She opened her mouth and a let out a cry that sounded like a wild animal in pain. She slumped to one side and fell onto the floor as if her spine had been torn out of her. Christian ran around to her, put his arms around her and held her to him.

'Rory, go and get some water.'

'Not my Keeley. No, no, no,' she cried into Christian's shoulder.

'Should we do something?' Finn asked Matilda.

'No. Keep watching. DI Brady knows what he's doing.'

Rory returned to the room with a plastic cup full of water. He handed it to Christian who placed it to Linda's lips.

'Here, drink some of this.' She took a sip. 'Now, take some deep breaths. Try and calm down.'

He handed the cup back to Rory and gently rocked back and forth while Linda regained control of her breathing. It took a while, but she eventually stabilised.

'Are you all right to continue?'

She nodded and he helped her up and back to the seat.

'Linda, I'm a parent myself,' Christian said as he went around to his side of the table. 'I can't begin to understand what you're going through, but I want you to know that I will do everything I can to find the person responsible.'

She looked up at him and smiled through the tears. 'Thank you.'

'Linda, the abuse on Keeley didn't happen on the evening she was taken. The injuries were months old. We believe there is someone in her life – in your life – who has been abusing her over a period of time.'

Linda shook her head. 'No. That can't be. She's only nine. She doesn't go anywhere on her own. If she's not with me she's with Craig or Jodie.'

Christian and Rory exchanged glances.

'You're not suggesting . . .' Linda took another sip of water. 'You're not suggesting that Craig . . .' She began to cry again. 'No. No. He loves all his children.' She was struggling to speak against the tears. 'He loves all of us. He'd never. He'd . . . No.

You're wrong. He . . . he . . . oh God . . . I'm going to be sick.'
She clamped a hand over her mouth.

'Rory, go and get a bucket or something.'

Rory headed for the door, but he wasn't fast enough. Linda
turned to her right and vomited. Nothing came out except for
the small amount of water she'd drunk. She heaved and retched,
but nothing more would come.

'I can't think of anyone,' Craig replied.

'Any uncles, cousins, neighbours, teachers?' Scott asked.

'No. I mean, we're a big family. I've got cousins and sisters all
over Sheffield, so has Linda, but we hardly see them. I'm working
all hours; Linda has her hands full with the kids. Any free time
we do get we like to spend it together, just the five of us.'

Sian leaned forward. 'Craig, the evidence doesn't lie. Somebody
has been sexually abusing your daughter. That someone has
had regular access to Keeley over the past few months. Now, the
only people who know that are you and Linda. So, who comes
to your house on a regular basis?'

'My sister comes around occasionally. My parents. I'm sorry,'
he wiped his eyes. 'I refuse to believe a member of my family
has been abusing my little girl.'

'Ok. When Keeley goes out to play with friends, where does
she go?'

'I don't know. I'm always working.'

'Craig!' Sian was getting irritated. 'We need to know the
people who have access to Keeley in order to find out who killed
her. You need to help us here.'

'I'm trying.'

'You're not.'

'I don't know, all right?' He shouted. 'I'm never around. I

know that makes me sound like a bad father, and I probably am, but I'm working my arse off to keep Riley in medical equipment and nappies and special toys. Jodie wants an iPad then Keeley wants an iPad too. Then Linda moans she hasn't been out of the house for three weeks and wants to go for a meal, just the two of us. Every time one of them opens their mouth it costs me money. So something has to give. I'm sorry that I don't know any of Keeley's friends. But I can't work two jobs, seven days a week, and spend time with my children.' He collapsed in a heap on the table.

'Go in for the kill, Sian,' Matilda said. The message came through the earpiece both Sian and Scott were wearing.

Scott looked down at the table.

'Craig,' Sian began. 'Have you ever touched Keeley inappropriately?'

'I'm so sorry,' Linda said.

She was sitting back in her chair with a plastic cup of water in her hand. She was taking small, gentle sips.

'I keep being sick. I don't know why. I can't seem to keep anything down.'

'That's understandable given the situation,' Rory said.

'No. It's been happening for months. I thought it was a bug at first, but I can't seem to shake it.'

'Have you been to the doctor?'

'No. I called for some advice. We have to be careful around Riley when it comes to illness and infections. His immune system is very low. I'm fine in myself, I just keep being sick. The doctor thinks it might be a nervous stress type thing.'

'When was the last time you had a holiday?' Christian asked.

'I don't know the meaning of the word,' she gave a slight chuckle.

'There are places Riley can go, respite—'

'No,' Linda almost shouted. 'I'm not palming him off onto complete strangers. He's my son.'

'I'm sorry. I didn't mean to—'

'No. I'm sorry. I shouldn't have snapped like that. I know you're trying to help. Look, can I go? I don't like being away from Riley for too long.'

'I have a few more questions I'd like to ask you first,' Christian said.

'I really should be getting back,' she ran her fingers through her greasy hair.

'Linda, we're trying to find out who killed your daughter. Now, whoever abused her is high up on our list of suspects and we need to know who that person is. Who are Keeley's friends? Where does she go when she goes out to play?'

Linda shook her head. 'She visits the children who live on the same road as us. I know it's horrible to say this, but it's nice when she goes out. There's one less child in the house. We tell her not to talk to strangers, not to go with people she doesn't know, and when to be back home. She's a good girl and always does as she's told, but . . . I'm sorry,' Linda broke down once again. 'I've no idea where she goes. That makes me sound like such a bad mother, doesn't it?'

'We're not getting anywhere here, Christian,' Matilda said into his earpiece. 'She may as well go home.'

Craig looked up from the table. His eyes were wide and steely.

'I know you have a job to do. I know you have questions to ask,' his voice was quiet and calm, but he was full of anger. 'But you're way off the mark here. I love all three of my children and I would never do anything to harm them. If you think I could have hurt my own daughter, then you are sick. I would lay down my life for all of them.' He was physically shaking as he spoke, his hands were fists and his knuckles white.

'Ok,' Sian said quietly. 'I'm sorry, but I had to ask.'

'Can I go now?'

'There is one more thing I'd like to go over with you,' Scott said, opening the thin file in front of him. 'We've been speaking to a former colleague of yours – Dean Oliver. He's mentioned you leaving your former employment under a bit of a cloud. There was talk of parcels going missing from your rounds.'

'What does this have to do with Keeley being killed?' he asked, folding his arms across his chest.

'You were overheard having an argument with Dean in a pub in which he said that if you ever went near him or his family again, you'd pay for it. Now, Dean has been in Corfu for just over a week, so he's not a suspect in the murder of your daughter, but what happened between you for him to make such a statement? Did you threaten him or his family?'

'Good questioning, Scott, but don't put words into his mouth. Let him fill the gaps,' Matilda said.

Craig couldn't sit still. He fidgeted nervously and his eyes flitted around the room. 'Dean's a jealous twat,' he suddenly said. 'He saw me making something of myself, starting up my own business and he couldn't handle it, because he doesn't have the gumption to do it himself, so he bad-mouthed me. It pissed me off. I wasn't going to sit back and let him trash my name all over Sheffield.'

'Did you threaten him?' Scott asked.

'Sort of. It was just a warning. I wouldn't have acted on it. I had to down three pints before I had the courage to have a go at him. I'm not a violent person. I hate confrontation.'

'So why was he so violent towards you? What did you do to his family for him to say you'd pay for it?'

Craig closed his eyes and took a deep breath. 'I was coming home from work one night and I saw his daughter going home from the shops. I pulled over in the van and gave her a message to give to Dean. It was a spur of the moment thing. I regretted it straight away,' he said, looking down at the table.

'What was the message?' Sian asked.

It was a while before Craig replied. 'I said that if he didn't stop trying to destroy me, I'd destroy him, and . . .'

'Go on,' Sian prompted when Craig stopped.

'And . . . I'd break his daughter's legs,' he said quietly.

'Jesus Christ!' Finn exclaimed from the observation room.

'How old was the daughter?' Sian asked.

'Eight.'

'You threatened an eight-year-old girl?'

'I didn't mean it. Like I said, it was the spur of the moment. She did ballet or something and it was the first thing that came into my head. I know it doesn't look good, but I wouldn't have done it. I'm not that kind of person. I'd never do anything to hurt a child. Ask anyone. Ask Linda. When we were on our honeymoon this bloke tried it on with her and I couldn't say anything. I'm a coward, ok? I'm all talk.' He looked away. He couldn't make eye contact with Sian or Scott.

'Cowards also target those who are vulnerable,' Finn said to Matilda.

'Let him go,' Matilda said to Sian in her earpiece.

'What? Really?' Finn seemed shocked.

'We don't have any physical evidence.'

'He's volatile. He's quick to temper. He does things on the spur of the moment. That could include killing his daughter.'

'Then find me the evidence and we'll charge him.' Matilda stood up and stormed out of the room. She was angry that she was unable to charge Craig, frustrated that they were no closer to understanding who was involved in Keeley's death. But the interviews hadn't been a complete waste of time. Her suspicions had been further aroused. It was going to take time, but the dots were being connected, slowly.

Chapter 39

It was obvious Valerie had been crying. Her eyes were red, and she could disguise the quiver in her voice by pretending to have a cough as much as she liked, but she was fooling nobody, especially Matilda. She was the queen of trying to hide her emotions at work. However, she didn't draw attention to it. If Valerie wanted to talk, she knew Matilda was always available.

'I'd like you to listen to something,' Matilda said as she scrolled through the apps on her iPad. 'Here we are.'

Craig Armitage's voice was loud as the recording started. "I know you have a job to do. I know you have questions to ask, but you are way off the mark here. I love all three of my children and I would never do anything to harm them. If you think I could have hurt my own daughter, then you are sick. I would lay down my life for all of them."

Matilda ended the recording. 'Anyone else hearing that would think he was the perfect father defending his family.'

'He didn't say he *didn't* kill his daughter,' Valerie said, wiping her nose with a tatty tissue.

'Exactly. He said he hadn't hurt her. In his head, he will have justified abusing her as a father loving his daughter. When he killed her, he wouldn't have thought he was hurting her, merely silencing her, as if putting her to sleep.'

'Then why throw her down an embankment and leave her to the elements?'

'To throw us off the scent. To make us believe we're looking for someone who strangled her, panicked, and fled.'

'Is Craig capable of that?'

Matilda sighed. 'I hate to say this, but, yes, I believe he is.'

Valerie thought for a moment. 'Ok. Where do you want to go with this?'

'I already have DC Ellen Devonport in the house as FLO, but I'm worried she may inadvertently uncover something, and Craig could turn violent with her. I'd like a car covertly parked close by to keep an eye on what's going on in the house.'

'That's fine.'

'Also, some of the neighbours have raised questions about Riley's illness. They don't seem to think he was brain damaged due to epileptic seizures. We've been on to social services and they've never received any complaints and don't have the family under their watch. I'm not sure where to go with this.'

'If it isn't pertinent to the case then it's none of our business,' Valerie said firmly.

'I'm aware of that. It's just . . . if Linda purposely harmed Riley, she may have had a hand in Keeley's death.'

'Hang on,' Valerie raised a hand. 'We're talking about Riley and Keeley, but what about the eldest daughter? What about Jodie? Has she shown signs of being abused? Why would Craig wait until he had a second daughter? Why would Linda wait until she had a third child?'

'I've wondered that myself. Maybe . . . I don't know . . . maybe something happened within the family that changed their outlook on things. I've no idea,' Matilda said. 'I feel like I'm clutching at straws here. One moment I think the parents have put on this elaborate play to cover up killing their own child, then someone says something else and it throws me off in another direction. I've never been more conflicted.'

'Has the teacher turned up yet?'

'Sebastian Page? No. Sian's back at Mary Croft today talking to the teachers.'

'And what about his brother?'

'Post-mortem is later today.'

'Have any other suspects come up within the investigation?'

'No.'

Valerie took a deep breath. 'I think you should bring Jodie Armitage in and have her interviewed with an appropriate adult present. You'll need to ask her some difficult questions.'

'Will do.'

'Now, Matilda, I saw the article in *The Star* last night from our favourite journalist. The Chief Constable said we should ignore it, let it fizzle out and hopefully you'll have an arrest soon and this whole thing will go away. However, once the press finds out about this boy in France claiming to be Carl, they'll be all over it and you. How do you want to play this?'

'Personally, I'd like to cut Danny Hanson's balls off and turn them into a nice pair of earrings, but I'm guessing the Chief Constable may frown upon that,' she said with a smile. 'I think we should leave him to write what he wants. If this boy does turn out to be Carl, then we have a good news item. If not, then we just tell the press it's another weirdo in a long line of pranks.'

Valerie nodded. 'Good thinking. Well, I shan't keep you any longer.'

Matilda stood up and slowly made her way towards the exit. She turned back. 'Any change with Arthur?'

Valerie seemed to deflate in her chair. She shook her head.

'We played him a video last night of the last time we all went away together. We went to Greece for my fiftieth. I'd not seen it myself, so it was lovely to look back. He fell asleep on a sun lounger with a paperback on his chest. He was annoyed that he had to wear a T-shirt for the rest of the holiday because of the patchy suntan.' She giggled at the memory. 'I looked over at Arthur in the hospital bed; there was nothing there. It's like he was watching strangers. I honestly don't think I'll ever get him back.'

On her way back to the HMET suite, Matilda fired off a text to Daniel telling him she'd love to see him over the weekend. Who knew what lay around the corner? Stroke, cancer, heart attack, being hit by a car, terrorist attack, nuclear bomb, anything could happen at any time. Why should she spend her evenings wallowing about being happy with Daniel when she could be dead by next week?

She entered the suite which was buzzing with activity.

'I've been to Mary Croft,' Sian began.

'Just give me a few minutes, Sian,' Matilda said, not stopping and heading to her office. *Walpole, Compton, Pelham . . . No, no, no, not this again.*

'I've been emailed Riley Armitage's medical records . . .' Scott said.

'Not now, Scott.' *Pelham-Holles, Cavendish, Pelham-Holles again . . . Stop it. Fucking stop it.*

She closed her office door and sat down behind her desk. Matilda wasn't great at marshalling her thoughts. Her head was a whirlpool of activity. It was like an internet browser with a dozen windows open, several of which were frozen – James, Carl, work, Daniel, grief, worry, isolation, loneliness. Her phone started to ring. She looked at the display and saw it was Danny Hanson calling. *Fuck*. He was the last person she wanted to talk to. He was another window open in the internet browser of her mind.

'Yes,' she answered. All she wanted was a few minutes to herself. She was constantly plagued from every angle from time thieves.

'DCI Darke, it's Danny Hanson from *The Star*.'

'Yes, Danny, I know it's you.'

'You have my number stored? I'm touched.'

'What do you want?'

'I've had a very interesting call from a member of the public.'

Matilda sat up. This did not sound good. 'Oh?'

'Indeed. I won't reveal her name, obviously, but she tells me a member of your team has abused his position as a detective to elicit an affair with a witness to a very brutal crime. Apparently, he took advantage when her resistance was low, and, now that she's pregnant, he's turned his back on her.'

Matilda could feel the blood rushing around her brain. 'What?' She looked up out of her office at her team going about their work. It couldn't be Scott as he was gay and in a relationship with her best friend's son. She very much doubted it was Finn as he constantly rambled on about his wife. She hoped it wasn't Christian or Aaron. They were both committed family men and knew it would shatter their wives to learn of their husband's deceit. Rory? It was possible. He was a habitual flirt. Ranjeet? Again, Matilda hoped not. His wife was still off work on maternity leave.

'Are you still there?'

'Yes. I'm still here. So, who is this detective?'

'Are you telling me you really don't know what's going on in the private lives of your team?'

'Danny, I'm aware this is a multiple orgasm to you, but if you don't stop pissing about and tell me, I shall have you arrested for wasting police time.'

'Ok. I'll tell you. Drumroll please.'

'Danny!'

'Ok, ok, just trying to add to the drama,' the joy was evident in his voice. 'It is Detective Sergeant,' he paused deliberately, 'Aaron Connolly.'

Matilda's heart skipped a beat and her mouth fell open. 'You'd better be one hundred per cent sure about this, Danny,' she said. Her tone was flat and cold.

'Oh I am. I've got the photos to prove it.'

'Photos?'

'Oh, didn't I mention that?' he asked, playfully. 'The woman in question emailed me a couple of snaps of the two of them together. It's so sweet. Well, it would be sweet if the detective in question wasn't married with a young child.'

'What do you want?'

'Nothing. I'm just giving you a right of reply before I run the story of a detective abusing his position of power with a vulnerable witness, getting her pregnant, then abandoning her when she needs him the most.'

'Ok, Danny, I need to have this confirmed with Detective Sergeant Connolly. You cannot run this story until I know it's not a hoax or some kind of revenge attack on my officers.'

'I'm aware of my position on this, DCI Darke. As it's Friday, I'm going to be generous and give you the weekend to mull it over. If I don't hear from you, it will be all over the front page of Monday's paper. Fingers crossed I'll be working on a national by the end of the year.'

The line went dead.

Matilda still held the phone to her ear. She wanted nothing more than Danny Hanson's testicles as earrings now. She'd rip them off him with her bare hands if she had to.

She looked out of her office and into the suite. Her team were going about their business with professionalism. Aaron always had the look of a man who had the weight of the world's problems on his shoulders, but now his frown was heavy, his head was sunken and he strolled around the office like a man heading for the gallows, which wasn't far from the truth.

Matilda had no idea what to do. Ideally, she should tell ACC Valerie Masterson, but she had enough to cope with at the moment. Professional Standards would need to get involved and possibly the Crown Prosecution Service. Depending on who the witness was and what input they'd had on the investigation, it could throw the whole case into jeopardy.

The ping on an incoming email made Matilda turn to her laptop. She didn't recognise the sender's name, but the subject line was enough to make her sit up and take notice:

DNA test results: Carl Meagan

She clicked open the email, scrolled down the greeting and the waffle to the result at the bottom of the page. Usually, it would take a long time for DNA results to return but as Carl's were already on file, this was just a case of matching the two.

Matilda's eyes ran across the screen and back again like she was engrossed in a tennis match.

'Jesus Fucking Christ,' she said.

Chapter 40

A uniformed PC entered the HMET suite carrying a large bunch of flowers. He looked over to the small group having coffee which comprised Sian, Rory, Scott, and Finn.

'Is one of you DS Sian Mills?'

'One of us is,' Rory said. 'That's all the hint you're getting,' he smiled.

Sian stood up. 'I am. I'm guessing those are for me.'

'Yes. They were just delivered downstairs.'

She took the bouquet from him and smiled as she looked for a card among the roses, carnations and lilies. 'Aren't these gorgeous?'

'Secret admirer?' Scott asked.

'I bet they're from a serial killer taunting you from his prison cell,' Rory said.

'They're from Stuart,' Sian said, reading the card.

'I was so close,' Rory laughed.

'He hopes I'm ok and not working too hard. He's pleased he's married to the most beautiful, understanding, and tolerant woman he could hope to meet, and he's looking forward to the next twenty-five years together,' she read with a huge grin on her face. 'Take a note here, boys. I've been married for twenty-five years and my husband can still surprise me with flowers. If you want to keep your partners that long, be attentive, and don't take them for granted.'

'I've been married for four years this November,' Finn said.

'I can't believe that,' Rory said. 'You're twenty-four, you look about twelve, yet you've been married for four years. It's like you've skipped freedom and gone from college straight to being middle aged.'

'If you find the person you're meant to be with, does it matter how long you wait before marrying them?' He said with a smile.

'He's only jealous, Finn,' Scott said.

'I'm not jealous. I'm in a very close relationship with Natasha. Or had you forgotten?'

'Difficult to forget when the plaster is falling off my bedroom wall.'

'Well, you won't have to put up with it for much longer. You'll be moving out soon.'

'I know,' he grinned. 'I can't wait.'

'You're definitely moving into the flat above Matilda's garage?' Sian asked, cradling the flowers in her arms.

'Yes. We're going around tomorrow to measure up.'

'Don't you think it's going to be a bit weird, trying to have sex when the boss is within hearing distance?' Rory asked.

'She won't be able to hear anything. The garage isn't as close to the house as you think. Besides, DCI Darke's bedroom is at the back of the house. There's plenty of distance.'

'I still think it's going to be awkward. Speaking of DCI Darke,' he said, leaning forward in his seat, 'did you see the way she charged out of here earlier with a face like thunder?'

'Difficult not to,' Sian said. 'I thought she was going to break the glass in the door the way she slammed it.'

'What's going on?' Finn asked.

'No idea.'

'Surely you know, Sian. She tells you everything.'

'Well, she hasn't told me this time.'

'It must be serious then. I wonder if it's to do with the ACC and her husband.'

'Could be,' Scott mused. 'If it was to do with the case, she would have told us.'

'Sian, have you got any Minstrels in your drawer?' Rory asked.

'You're banned from taking anything out of my snack drawer until you put something back in. It's running empty at the moment.'

'I'll do a shop at the weekend. I'll fill it up for you on Monday.'

'Nothing until you do. I'm going to try and find something to put these in.'

'Scott, go and steal us a Toffee Crisp or something,' he whispered once Sian had left the office.

The phone on Scott's desk began to ring. 'Do your own dirty work,' he said as he went to answer it. 'Homicide and Major Enquiries. DC Andrews speaking.'

'Hello Scott, it's Danny Hanson from the *Sheffield Star*. How are you?

Scott pulled out his chair and sat down. 'I'm ok thank you. What can I do for you?' He never wanted to stay on the phone long with journalists in case he said something he shouldn't.

'I was wondering if you could give Aaron Connolly a message for me?'

Scott looked over to Aaron's desk. 'Erm, sure. He's here somewhere in the building, I can find him for you if you want to hold?'

'No. A message will be fine.'

'Ok.'

'Tell him that Leah Mercer is having a boy.'

Scott waited for him to elaborate. He didn't. 'Is that it?'

'Yes.'

'Ok. Will he know what that means?'

Danny laughed. 'He should do.'

'Fine. I'll pass that on for you.'

'Thank you, Scott.'

The line went dead.

Scott looked down as he pondered the message he had written in his untidy scrawl.

'Rory, where have I heard the name Leah Mercer from before?'

'Bloody hell, Scott, are you losing it? Leah's family were butchered while she was away on honeymoon earlier this year.'

'Oh yes, I remember now.'

'Why?'

'I just had a call from Danny Hanson. He's told me to tell Aaron that Leah is having a boy.'

'What's that got to do with Aaron?'

'That's what I thought.'

'Where is Aaron?' Rory asked.

'I've no idea.'

Chapter 41

Aaron was in the corner of the car park talking quietly on the phone. Matilda saw him as she headed for her Range Rover. She immediately saw red and shouted his name so loud it echoed. He dropped his phone and almost jumped out of his skin.

'Sorry. I was just . . . I . . . I was taking a few minutes. It's not easy trying to make a private call when you've got Sian and Rory glaring at you,' he said with a strained smile.

'How is Katrina?' Matilda asked. She walked up to Aaron and, although he loomed over her, the expression on her face, the rage oozing out of her, definitely put her in control of this conversation.

'Katrina?'

'Yes. You know, the woman you're married to, the mother of your child.'

'Oh,' he nervously giggled. 'She's . . . she's fine, yes, everything's fine.'

'Is it?'

'Of course, yes.'

'Nothing preying on your mind, no other worries I should know about?' she asked, defiantly crossing her arms.

'No. Not that I'm aware of.'

'So, who's this woman you're having an affair with?'

His eyes widening betrayed any words that were about to come out of his mouth. Matilda raised a hand.

'Before you even start waffling, save your breath. The look on your face has given you away. Come on, get in the car.'

She pointed the fob to the Range Rover and unlocked it. She climbed in behind the driver's side and waited while Aaron tentatively walked around to the front passenger seat. He clicked the door closed carefully and sat in silence.

'We have a dead child and a missing teacher to investigate, but I can sit here all day until I get the truth out of you,' Matilda said, facing forward.

He took a deep breath. 'I've made a really big mistake.'

'That's certainly one way of putting it. Are you going to tell me who she is?'

Another deep breath. 'Leah Mercer.'

Matilda turned quickly to look at him. 'Leah Mercer? You are joking, surely.'

Earlier this year, while on honeymoon, Leah's mother, father, and brother, Jeremy, were brutally murdered. Her niece, Rachel, was the only survivor to the massacre, and responsibility for her upbringing rested with Leah. Once the funerals were over, she had moved to Liverpool, where Rachel and Jeremy had been living, to start a new life as guardian to her niece and try to make sense of everything that had happened in recent weeks.

Leah and Aaron had grown close during the case, and before she left Sheffield, they had shared a kiss. Aaron had asked if he could call her once she was settled in Liverpool and they'd swapped numbers. Within a week of her leaving, she'd called him and invited him to spend the weekend with her and Rachel. He hadn't given it a second thought.

The affair had been passionate and intense. Leah had wanted someone to hold her, to make love to her, to want her, and Aaron had been eager to oblige. Back in Sheffield, Katrina had been itching to have a second child. It had taken years for them to conceive and the pregnancy had not been an easy one with Katrina in and out of hospital. His weekend escapes to Leah's had been explained as training courses which Katrina had believed. He had treated them as mini holidays, and he had looked forward to having Leah in his arms. He had found himself smiling and relaxing in her presence.

When she'd told him she was pregnant, the life had drained out of him. He'd realised it wasn't because of the worry of a difficult pregnancy that he'd told Katrina it was a bad idea to have another child, it was because he didn't want one. He loved the bones of Dwayne, but he hadn't really developed a relationship with him. Another child would be disastrous, both for him and Katrina, and for him and Leah.

He had left Liverpool and vowed not to return. He had ignored Leah's calls, texts, and emails. It was childish, he knew, but he couldn't face the responsibility of being a father again. He had planned to tell Katrina everything. If she chose to leave him, he would deal with it, but he hoped she'd understand the pressure of his job and how he had succumbed to temptation while caring for a woman who had lost everything. He would also do right by Leah too. He planned to return to Liverpool and state that he would contribute financially towards the upbringing of their child, but he needed to be honest with Katrina first. Unfortunately, that was easier said than done.

Katrina was not an easy woman to talk to. If the conversation wasn't about her, a second child, or a holiday to somewhere exotic in the summer, she wasn't interested. Whenever Aaron tried to broach the subject – something he spent hours waffling and stuttering about – Katrina interrupted by shoving a holiday brochure under his nose or asking if he liked the names Garfield for a boy and Zandi for a girl.

He went to bed most nights kicking himself, and while Katrina slept blissfully beside him, he remained wide awake, fretting over how to open his heart to her. The words and the time had never arrived.

'He's got photos?' Aaron asked after Matilda had told him all about the conversation with Danny Hanson.

She nodded.

'They must be from the barbecue we had in the summer.'

'Do you have any idea how stupid you've been?' she asked.

'Yes. I do.'

'Not only have you ruined your marriage, but you've put the whole Mercer case in jeopardy. The case is due to start in November. If the prosecution gets hint of a detective sergeant sleeping with one of the witnesses, they'll do their level best to get this whole case thrown out. What do you think that will do to little Rachel Mercer when she finds out the murderer of her father and grandparents won't face justice because her auntie shagged one of the detectives?'

He shook his head in regret.

'Not to mention the stress the case caused your own colleagues and the money South Yorkshire Police paid out in overtime and forensic examinations. The amount of money it cost to prepare the cases . . .'

'I'm sorry,' he interrupted feebly.

'And look at what happened with Keith Lumb. He sacrificed his life to save me from Ladybower Reservoir. Four people died as a result of that case and it could all be for nothing because you couldn't keep your dick in your trousers!' she shouted.

'I really am sorry,' he said. 'I know it sounds basic, but it's the truth. I never meant for it to go this far.'

'Well it did. And the story is going to be printed in glorious technicolour on Monday.'

'Fuck,' he said as he collapsed, his head landing in his hands. He started to sob. 'Katrina shouldn't find out like this.'

'Then you have the whole weekend to tell her the truth.'

'I can't.'

'You have no choice. You've fucked up royally, here, Aaron, and you have to face the consequences.'

'I'm so sorry,' he cried.

'So am I. I thought I knew you better, Aaron. You have no idea how disappointed I am in you.' Matilda's voice was calmer, but it was still filled with venom.

The silence in the car was heavy. A light rain began to spatter on the windscreen. Matilda had a million and one things to do but she had no intention of leaving the car until she was ready.

'What's going to happen to me?' Aaron eventually asked.

'You're suspended as of now and there will be a disciplinary hearing. Professional Standards will have to be told and they'll launch an enquiry. You'll be off the HMET and either be sent back to CID or sacked altogether. I'll have to inform the CPS and the defence. Leah Mercer's evidence may be discounted in the case. Your conduct in the whole investigation may be brought into question and if there is any hint that you acted unprofessionally, they may use that to throw the whole case out.'

'But . . . I—'

'Get out,' Matilda interrupted. She was staring straight ahead out of the windscreen.

'I . . .'

'Aaron, I don't want to hear any more from you. I'm so angry with you right now. The whole of South Yorkshire Police, me and my team in particular, are going to be facing a serious shit storm, and it's all your fault. Get out of my car and go home.'

He remained seated for a few more seconds before opening the car door and letting in a cool blast of air. He stepped out and Matilda felt his eyes on her before he closed the door. She couldn't look at him.

Out of the corner of her eye, she watched as he went to his red Ford Focus, shoulders hunched, head down, dragging his feet against the tarmac. She waited until he reversed out of his space, left the car park and turned right for home before she allowed the tears to fall.

There were some people within the press who were itching for Matilda Darke to make another mistake. They couldn't wait to bring up the Carl Meagan case to taunt her. Once this got out, she'd be to blame. Matilda was in charge of the Homicide and Major Enquiries Team and the officers who worked in it. If she couldn't keep them under control, how could she possibly solve the cases the public were relying on her to investigate?

She needed a break. She could feel the knot of a headache at the back of her head and she felt physically sick.

As she drove out of the car park and headed for Watery Street, there was only one solution she could think of – she would need to keep the whole Aaron Connolly affair out of the newspapers. Unfortunately, to do that, she'd have to betray those closest to her.

Chapter 42

'I've been watching you for the past five minutes. You look like you've booked a trip on a world cruise but found out you'll be sharing a cabin with Donald Trump and Nigel Farage,' Adele Kean said as she entered her office. Her hair was wet and there was a strong scent of conditioner. She'd obviously recently showered after performing a post-mortem.

Matilda Darke had been waiting for her for around half an hour. There were so many conflicting thoughts going through her mind she hadn't registered Adele's presence. She looked up.

'Sorry?'

'Is everything all right?' Adele closed the door behind her and perched on the edge of her desk.

'No. Something bad's just happened.'

'Oh my God. Has someone on the team died?' Adele asked, slapping a hand to her chest.

'No. Nothing like that.'

Adele visibly relaxed. 'Oh good.'

'Adele, I really need your advice on something. Are you free to talk right now?'

'Yes. I've just finished Calvin Page's autopsy.'

'Shit, I forgot all about that,' Matilda said, running her hand through her hair. 'How did it go?'

'Blunt force trauma to the head, like I said at the scene. I've found samples of metal filings within the wounds. I think you're looking for something like a hammer or a wrench, perhaps.'

'Did you use your fancy-pants fingerprinting thing?'

'I did. No drugs, but plenty of alcohol. I'll send my report later today. So, come on, let's hear all this juicy gossip,' she said, pulling up a chair and trying to get as comfortable as she could in her incredibly cramped office.

Matilda filled Adele in on the whole story of Aaron Connolly and his affair with Leah Mercer and the possible snowball effect it would have when the case came to court in November.

'Bloody hell,' she said, sitting back and blowing out a breath. 'I mean, I know all men are shits, but I always thought Aaron was a true family man.'

'So did I. He's bored us for years about how much he and Katrina love each other.'

'It's always the quiet ones, though, isn't it?'

'That's why they're quiet. If they talk a lot, they end up spilling their secrets.'

'Poor Katrina.'

'Have you met her before?'

'Yes, a couple of times. She's a bit loud, but she's lovely.'

'I remember when they got married,' Matilda said. She sat back in her seat and was visibly relaxing now. Her shoulders were no longer hunched up beneath her ears with angst and worry. 'He was so nervous, more than usual for a bloke about to get married. He worried he wouldn't be a good husband, a good father, that he'd somehow ruin the happiness Katrina represented.'

'It sounds like he knew what lay ahead in his future.'

'He didn't have a very good childhood. His parents split when he was about four and the custody battle went on for years. His parents despised each other. He told me that he always said he wouldn't get married but when he met Katrina, he knew she was special. He just hoped he wouldn't turn into his father and ruin everything.'

'And that's exactly what he's done.'

'Maybe.'

'What do you mean?'

'I think I can keep this out of the newspapers and allow Aaron to deal with this privately.'

'How?'

'Well, Danny Hanson wants an exclusive. He doesn't care what the story is as long as he gets a massive front-page lead which will look good on his CV.'

'Yes. So what?'

'I just have to give him another exclusive.'

'You don't have one.'

'I do.'

'Really?'

Matilda took a breath. 'Carl Meagan.'

'What?'

'I could give Danny Hanson the exclusive on Carl Meagan being found in France.'

'But you don't know he really is Carl Meagan yet, do you? Have you had the DNA results back?'

Matilda looked away. 'Not yet.' *LIAR!*

Chapter 43

Ellen stood in the doorway to Riley's bedroom and watched as Jodie went about changing his nappy. She handled him with confidence as if she had done this a thousand times before, which she probably had. All the while she was changing him, cleaning him up and dressing him, she engaged him in conversation. He couldn't join in, but Jodie's voice was different with Riley. It was light, soft, with a hint of happiness and jollity, as if all was right with the world.

'You're getting to be a big boy, Riley,' she said as she grunted under the strain of lifting him down from the changing mat. She placed him, carefully, in his bean bag. 'Look at these big solid legs.' She held his feet and wiggled his legs which made him giggle. 'You're like a little rugby player, aren't you? Riley the scrum half.'

She turned around and saw Ellen watching. It made her jump. 'Sorry, I didn't see you there. Did you want anything?'

'No. I came to see how you are, but you seem to be doing ok.'

Jodie sat cross-legged on the floor beside Riley. She handed him his favourite penguin toy. 'It's strange but coming in here and being with Riley, it's like the rest of the world doesn't exist. Inside this room, it's all about Riley, his needs and there's no responsibility, no stress. We can sit here for hours blowing bubbles, playing with his toys, or watching the lights fade into different colours, and nothing else matters. I could honestly close that door and never leave this room again.'

Ellen frowned. The weight upon Jodie's shoulders was too great for a fourteen-year-old to contend with. She shouldn't be talking about getting away from the world. She should be out there living in it, exploring it, meeting boys, buying make-up, and trying a cheeky cigarette or an illicit sip of vodka.

'I was thinking about doing a shepherd's pie for tea,' Ellen said to fill the silence. 'Your mum hasn't eaten much today; she could do with something substantial. What do you think?'

'That would be nice. Will you grate some cheese on top of the mash? Dad likes it like that.'

'Of course,' Ellen smiled. 'Do you know what time your dad will be home?'

'I've no idea,' she shrugged. 'He's missed a lot of work lately, so he'll be wanting to put in some overtime to make up.'

'Ok. Well, I'll set a plate aside for him.'

The house was silent.

The shepherd's pie was in the oven and Ellen was washing the dirty dishes. Linda had promised to come downstairs once it was ready. She had taken to her bed after her meagre lunch. She didn't go to sleep, but the sounds of her crying and vomiting could be heard from upstairs.

Ellen should have gone home more than an hour ago, but she wanted to make sure the family had a decent meal. Linda wasn't in a position to look after her two remaining children at the moment and Craig had insisted on returning to work. Somebody needed to maintain a degree or normality for Jodie and Riley, and that role fell to Ellen.

'Riley's nodded off,' Jodie said as she entered the kitchen. 'I think I've tired him out. We might get a few hours of peace.' She spoke like a parent who had put their baby down for a nap. It was strange for Ellen to hear such words coming out of a teenager's mouth. 'Is there anything I can do?'

'You could set the table if you like. It's almost ready.'

'It smells lovely.'

'Thank you.'

Jodie went about setting the table for four people. Ellen didn't know if this was through habit of setting a place for Keeley or if she was being thoughtful by including Ellen.

'When will we be able to have the funeral?' Jodie asked out of nowhere.

'Well, the coroner has opened the inquest and adjourned it while we continue our investigation. Once he's satisfied as to the cause of death, he'll release Keeley and you can arrange things then.'

'Will that be a long way off?'

'I don't know how long these things take, I'm sorry. It all depends on how the investigation goes and if the coroner is satisfied.'

'I saw a coffin online. It's pink and you can have things put on the side. I thought it would be nice to have pictures of Disney princesses and castles. Keeley would have loved that.'

'I'm sure she would.' Ellen pulled out a chair at the table and sat down. She beckoned Jodie to do the same. 'Jodie, you can't take on all the responsibility for yourself, you know. You're still only a child. You'll need to go back to school soon or you'll fall behind in your studies. Your mum is here to take care of Riley and it's the role of your parents to organise Keeley's funeral.'

'Mum can't cope,' Jodie eventually said, wiping away a tear

before it had a chance to form. 'You've seen how she is. She's sick. I don't have a choice.'

'Yes, you do. None of this is your responsibility.'

'I don't mind, though. I like looking after Dad and Riley.'

'But who looks after you?'

'I can look after myself.'

'But you shouldn't—' Ellen was interrupted by the front door opening and slamming closed. Craig was home.

'I was hoping you'd still be here,' he said as he stormed into the kitchen. His face was like thunder. 'Jodie, go and check on your brother.'

'He's fine. He's sleeping.'

'I'll not ask you again,' he said, his voice raised.

Jodie scuttled away. Ellen noticed she went into Riley's room but didn't fully close the door behind her.

'I've been thinking long and hard this afternoon,' Craig began, leaning on the table and staring daggers at Ellen. 'Where do you lot get off questioning me and Linda like that?'

'I'm sorry?' Ellen looked genuinely scared. She remained seated at the table but leaned back as far as she could go.

'Accusing me and Linda of killing our own daughter.'

'Nobody is accusing you.'

'You lot bloody are. I work my fingers to the bone for this family. I work every hour God sends. I love all my children, and you think you can just swan in and start throwing around vicious accusations.'

'Craig, please, calm down, and I can explain how these things work.'

'I don't want to calm down, and I don't want to hear any more of your bullshit. I know why you're here; it's not to look after us and make sure we're all right, it's to fucking spy on us. You're here to try and find some shred of evidence, no matter how small, that me or Linda could have killed our daughter. Well I'm not standing for it. I want you out.'

'Craig, please. Let me give DCI Darke a call . . .'

'What for? So she can come around here and start accusing me of something else. Is she going to take the floorboards up in the living room to look for Carl Meagan under the house? I don't think so. I want you out. Now.'

'Craig . . .'

'I'm not a violent man, Ellen, but I swear to God, I will literally throw you out of this house if I have to.'

Ellen fell silent. She had never been more scared in her whole life than she was right now. Slowly, she stood up.

'I'm very sorry you feel this way, Craig. You have my number if you need anything.'

As she edged past him, she could feel the rage and anger oozing out of him. From the hallway, she collected her coat and bag she had draped over the bannister and turned back. Craig was in the same position, hunched over the kitchen table. His broad back was heaving as he took deep breaths to try and steady his nerves.

Ellen turned to leave and caught Jodie standing in the small gap she had left in the entrance to Riley's bedroom. Ellen gave her a sympathetic smile, but Jodie didn't react. Her face was blank.

Once Ellen was out of the house, she visibly relaxed. She let out a huge breath. She looked up the road for the silver Peugeot, but it had gone. So much for being protected. She'd send an email to DCI Darke and report what had happened, but she hoped she wouldn't be sent back here.

Ellen put on her coat and headed up Acorn Drive. She had parked around the corner again today. The journalists had been parked outside the house this morning when she arrived, but they'd gone now. Obviously a juicier story had come up.

The door to the house next door opened and Amanda Raine stepped out. Ellen stopped and looked over to her.

'I heard the row,' she said quietly, but in the dying light of the day, her words echoed around the empty street. 'Are you all right?'

'I'm fine, thanks.'

'He gets like that; flies off the handle at the littlest things. You should have heard the things he said to my Grant when they had a disagreement over the size of the garden fence round the back. I honestly thought he was going to hit him.'

'Is he violent?' Ellen asked, stepping closer to Amanda's house.

'I don't think so. He's more of a verbal bully. There's no wonder Linda's ill all the time. She's a nervous wreck.' A gust of wind came from nowhere. Amanda wrapped her hands firmly across her chest, closing her cardigan against the stiff breeze. 'You didn't hear this from me, but he's argued and threatened every person on this road.'

'Threatened?'

'Oh yes. He doesn't like you parking outside his house. When it's bin day, he kicks off if the bins aren't collected as soon as they're emptied. Her at number eleven, he had a go at her on the day she moved in because the removal truck was blocking the road. I've said it many times, but it's like living next door to Jekyll and Hyde.'

'Amanda, Jocelyn's on the phone,' a call came from inside the house.

'I'll have to go, that's our Jocelyn. Her youngest went into labour yesterday with twins. Ta-ra,' she closed the door before Ellen could reply.

Ellen turned and headed towards her car. As she went around the corner, she looked back at the Armitage house. There were a pair of eyes staring at her from an upstairs window, and she felt an icy chill run up her spine.

Chapter 44

The HMET suite was deserted. A skeleton staff was manning the phones in the CID and if anything important arose, the SIO on call would be informed, but budget cuts dictated that a full staff was not required to work weekends.

Matilda entered the large open-plan office and looked at the mess of desks before her. She shook her head in disappointment. Police work shouldn't be Monday to Friday. There should be no such thing as regular office hours when you were a detective. Crime didn't recognise bank holidays and weekends, so why should the police. It angered her when she heard about budget cuts to the police when governments wasted millions of pounds on unnecessary projects. How much was spent during the Brexit campaign on leaflets, posters, websites, tour buses, events and conferences? How much was being spent in the ensuing clusterfuck that followed with trips to Europe and back to hammer out a deal? MPs filled in expense forms for every single little item, but how many hours did Matilda work for free every month? Every single member of the police force put their lives on hold, and on the line, every single day to protect the public, and it was a thankless task. Politicians didn't care. Twenty thousand officers were cut and then they wondered why knife crime rose so rapidly. The solution was simple, put the twenty thousand officers back and employ twenty thousand more. Stop wasting money on a garden bridge over the Thames, planning for HS2, pissing about with Brexit, and you find your money for the extra officers needed to make people feel safe again.

She went into her office and closed the door behind her. She slumped into her chair that had stuffing coming out of the seams (no money in the budget for a replacement) and took her phone out of her pocket.

She had ignored the many texts from Adele last night and this morning, begging her to rethink her absurd plan. However, if Matilda was to go ahead with selling her soul to Danny Hanson, then she was on her own. That hurt Matilda. She had suffered a great deal in the past few years and the one thing that kept her going was knowing that her best friend was always there to help if she needed her. Now, she was being abandoned. She knew what she was about to do was wrong, but there really was no other solution.

Walpole, Compton, Pelham, Pelham-Holles . . .

A knock on the glass door made her jump. She looked up and saw Christian Brady grinning at her from the other side.

'I didn't expect to see you in this morning,' he said, opening the door.

'No. To be honest, I don't know why I'm here. You?'

'I could be super arse-kissy about it and say I wanted to put in some unpaid overtime to protect the people of Sheffield.'

'And the truth?'

'I left my phone here last night.'

Matilda smiled. 'While you're here, can I pick your brain?'

'There's not really much to pick, but you're welcome to help yourself.'

'Thanks. Put the kettle on. We need a coffee for this.'

They were both shocked when they opened Sian's snack drawer and saw there was very little left. A two-fingered KitKat, a small packet of salted peanuts, two purple Clubs and half a packet of dark chocolate digestives.

'It's not like Sian to let supplies run this low,' Matilda said.

'I think she's pissed that people are taking things out and not putting anything back.'

'Oh dear. I think I might be guilty of that.'

'I think we all are. I'll pop to Costco on the way home and buy something,' Christian said scooping up everything that was left and taking it into Matilda's office.

With the door closed, Matilda filled him in on the phone call she had had with Danny Hanson the day before and the potential fallout once Aaron's affair with Leah Mercer was exposed.

'What does the ACC say?' He asked.

'I called her last night. Her phone went straight to voicemail, so I left a message saying I needed to talk urgently. When I woke up this morning, I found she'd left me a message. Arthur's had another stroke.'

'Oh my God.'

'She said she'll see me on Monday, but I doubt she'll be in.'

'She's not the type to take compassionate leave, is she?'

'No. She should, though.'

'If there's not much for her to do at the hospital she probably thinks being at work is the best place to be.'

'The thing is, I'm up against the clock here. Danny Hanson

says he's going to run the story about Aaron in Monday evening's edition.'

'Would it really jeopardise the Mercer case?'

'Of course it would. You know what defence lawyers are like; they'll look for any chink to try and get their guy off and I will not let someone walk away from three murders on a technicality that can easily be avoided,' Matilda said. She took another biscuit from the packet and tore off a chunk. She ignored the crumbs that fell onto her chest. 'Besides, Keith Lumb sacrificed his life to save mine. I know he wasn't the most law-abiding person in the world, but I won't let his death be in vain.'

'I can understand that. So, what are you going to do?'

'I've got two options. On the one hand I let Danny run his story. The fallout would be Aaron getting sacked and the Mercer case being thrown out of court at the cost of several million pounds and the murderer of three people potentially walking free. On the other hand, I give Danny a completely different story, he still gets his front-page story which will hopefully lead to a job on a national and he can fuck off out of Sheffield, the trial goes ahead in November as planned, and all Aaron has to do is deal with Katrina and go back to CID.'

'That seems like the best option all round.'

'Exactly.'

'What story are you going to give Danny?'

Matilda took a deep breath. 'The story I plan on giving him isn't exactly moral.'

'Ah.'

'The only one I can think of is Carl Meagan turning up in France.'

'Do you have the DNA results back yet?'

She looked at her laptop. 'Erm . . . no.' *BIG FAT LIAR.*

'Then you can't give it to him.'

'I could tell him Carl's been found. He runs the story and if the DNA results come back and the boy in France isn't really Carl then it's Danny who's for the chop and not me. I'll deny everything.'

'You're not that type of person,' Christian said, looking at Matilda over the top of his cup.

'I could be.'

'And what about the Meagans?'

'That's what's causing the biggest headache. I'll be getting their hopes up for nothing.'

'I don't know about this, Mat. You know how fragile Sally Meagan is. If she thinks Carl's been found and then it turns out not to be him, who knows how she'll react.'

'I'm aware.'

'Fucking hell,' he said slowly. 'Is there nothing else you can give Danny Hanson to stop him running the story?'

'Not unless you can tell me the identity of Jack the Ripper.'

'I'm afraid not.'

'Then I have no other choice.'

'You can't throw Philip and Sally Meagan to the wolves like this.'

'I can't allow a murderer to go free either.'

'Won't Danny wait for the DNA results if you tell him you may have found Carl? It will only be for a few days and it'll buy you extra time.'

'He'll think we're stalling him on purpose.'

'I know the Carl Meagan case means a great deal to you. We all know what you went through and you have the support of the entire force behind you when the press criticises the way the case was handled. If you go ahead with this, you'll lose all that if the boy in France turns out not to be Carl.'

Matilda turned back to the laptop and saw her face reflected in the black mirror.

'Then what do I do, Christian?' She asked, raising her voice. She was clearly struggling with her inner moral compass. 'What do I actually do next?' Her voice quivered.

He slowly shook his head. 'If I knew, I'd tell you. There's no chance the Mercer killer could change his plea to guilty, is there?'

'He's pleading diminished responsibility, but I know for a fact he knew exactly what he was doing when he entered that house. He butchered three people. He cannot be allowed to get away with that.'

Christian pulled his buzzing phone from the pocket of his jeans. 'That's the wife; she'll be wondering where I am. Look, whatever you decide, I'll support you, but I can't condone you betraying the Meagan family like this.'

Matilda nodded her thanks. She was afraid to speak in case her emotions poured out. She waited until Christian left the office, watching as he walked out of the HMET suite with his head down. She looked around her. She loved how this team supported each other no matter what was thrown at it. It had taken years for her to build up the trust and respect of every member and there was a distinct possibility she was about to destroy it all and ruin the chance of a promotion to superintendent.

She scrolled through the contacts in her phone and made a call. It didn't take long for it to be answered.

'DCI Darke, a pleasure to hear from you. I trust you're having a lovely weekend,' Danny's cheerful voice chilled her to her very soul.

'We don't like each other, Danny, so cut the small-talk bollocks. We need to talk.'

'Go ahead.'

'In person.'

'You're not going to try to appeal to my better nature by telling me DS Connolly is an outstanding detective and one slip is going to ruin an illustrious career, are you?'

'Danny, you don't have a better nature. You're the very definition of a parasite. No, I have a much better story for you.'

'Unless it's photographic evidence of Theresa May snorting coke through a rolled up fifty Euro note, I doubt I'll be interested.'

'Trust me, Danny, you're going to be very interested in this one.'

Matilda felt physically sick as she arranged a time and a place to sit down and have coffee with the devil himself.

Chapter 45

Dolly Richardson had lived in the Pitsmoor area of Sheffield for more than fifty years. She had seen many changes in the suburb where she'd brought up her four children, and not one of them good. Following the death of her husband in 1992, she moved out of the four-bedroom house and into a flat above a shop on Ellesmere Road. When she moved in it was charming, quaint, and a hubbub of friendly activity. Now, it was a forgotten area. Crime was rife, abandoned cars on every street, litter piled up, and people didn't chat anymore. They went about their business with their heads down, not risking eye contact with anyone.

Dolly lived above an ethnic food store. The smells emanating from downstairs made her hungry – not that she'd ever been in. She wouldn't know how to go about cooking with pulses and chickpeas. At eighty-three, she was too set in her ways to attempt a chana masala or dhokla. Her cupboards were filled with Fray Bentos pies and tins of mushy peas.

Taking the rubbish out to her bin, she sniffed up. That wasn't the smell of spices, it was more like something had crawled into a hole and died.

The iron staircase tacked onto the side of the building was rusting and rickety. Dolly really shouldn't be living there. However, in her words, *I'll only move out of here when I'm in a pine box*. Holding onto the railing for dear life, she descended the wet stairs slowly, and tossed the rubbish bag into the wheelie bin belonging to the shop below.

She limped around the corner, glancing up to the flat next door. She reached the Peugeot she'd seen parked opposite the green for the past couple of days and rapped hard on the glass with her gnarled knuckles. The window lowered.

'You're detectives, aren't you?' she asked the young man behind the wheel.

'What makes you say that?'

'Come on, love, I live in Pitsmoor. I can spot a copper a mile off and you two stand out like a sore thumb around here.'

The detectives glanced at each other.

'If you wanted to blend in you should have worn one of those burka things. Listen, I need you to have a look at the flat next door to mine,' she said in her deep Yorkshire accent.

'We're actually on duty at the moment, madam. If you have a complaint, I suggest you dial 101.'

'And I suggest you listen to what I've got to say before you interrupt.'

The other detective sniggered.

'Sorry. Go on.'

'The flat next door to mine. I've seen you looking up a few times, and there's been uniformed coppers knocking on the door day and night lately. I might be old, but I'm not daft. There's something wrong.'

'Like what?'

'I don't know. That's what I want you to find out. There's a hell of a stink coming from it and flies buzzing around the windows. I'll bet you a pound to a penny there's a dead body in there.'

'Are you serious?' the detective in the front passenger seat asked.

'Come and see for yourself if you don't believe me, but if I end up with rats because you've not done your job properly, it'll be South Yorkshire Police who pays for the exterminators.'

Dolly walked away.

'Should we call it in?' PC Walker, who was behind the wheel, asked his colleague.

'Better take a look first,' PC Kendal said. 'For all we know there could just be a rotting chicken in there or something. We don't want to be a laughingstock.'

'Says the man who tried to arrest a priest for being drunk and disorderly,' Walker smirked.

'You'll never let that drop, will you?' Kendal said as he climbed out of the car. 'How was I supposed to know he was having a fit?'

By the time they went around to the back of the shops, they'd caught up with Dolly. She'd reached the bottom of the iron staircase.

'You live here?' Kendal asked, shocked by the conditions she was living in. A burnt-out car was inches away from her flat, the brickwork blackened by the fire, litter from the shops, fly-tipping from passing motorists who used the abandoned back yards of the flats as places to throw broken toilets, bedsteads, and busted mattresses.

'It's a shit-hole, isn't it? Never used to be. At one time there was a waiting list for people to move to Pitsmoor.'

'Why don't you move?' Walker asked with sympathy in his voice.

'At my age? My next move is to the cemetery, love.'

'Are you ok living here on your own?' Kendal asked with concern.

'I'm fine,' she smiled a toothy smile. 'I keep myself to myself, don't go out after dark and don't open my door unless I know who's calling. You want the next lot of stairs. You'll not get to his flat from mine.'

Walker and Kendal walked carefully over uneven ground, striding over bags of rotting rubbish, old engine parts, and half a bath.

They gingerly walked up the stairs which creaked loudly with every step. They made it to the landing and approached the flat. Walker knocked on the door and stood back while Kendal went over to the window, cupped his hands around his eyes and looked inside.

'Fucking hell,' he said, stepping back.

'What is it?'

'You'd better call it in.'

'Why? What have you seen?'

'What is it, love?' Dolly asked from the opposite landing where she stood outside her front door. 'You've gone as white as a sheet. I've got some whiskey if you want something to line your stomach.'

Before he could say anything, Kendal turned away and vomited.

'They don't make coppers like they did in my day,' Dolly said, folding her arms across her ample chest. 'Are you going to have a look or are you a vomiter as well?'

The call came through to DI Christian Brady. For some reason, Matilda wasn't answering her phone. He left his wife and daughters in Endcliffe Park and phoned Scott Andrews on the way to Pitsmoor.

'Sorry for calling you out, Scott. I didn't fancy going in that flat with Jasper Carrott and Robert Powell as back-up,' Christian said as Scott climbed into the car and put his seat belt on.

'Who?'

Christian looked at the face of innocence. 'Oh for God's sake,' he said, suddenly realising he was getting old.

Walker and Kendal were waiting at the bottom of the iron staircase when Christian pulled up. They both had a mug of tea in their hands. An elderly woman stood next to them, walking stick in hand, hunched over.

'Ingratiating yourself with the locals, I see,' Christian said.

'Dolly, here, alerted us to Sebastian's flat,' Walker said.

'Dolly, is it? You really are getting to know the neighbours. Lead the way.'

Walker handed his empty mug to Kendal and set off with Christian in tow. Scott followed behind.

'Bloody hell, they're getting younger,' Dolly said as she saw Scott. 'What is this, bring-your-child-to-work day?'

Christian took more offense at that remark than Scott did.

When they reached the flat, they all looked at the window next to the front door and saw the number of flies buzzing around on the inside. Christian took out a pair of gloves from his back pocket and began to put them on. Scott did the same.

'I think we can safely say that there could possibly be a life in danger in that flat, so I'm legally allowed to break down this door to investigate,' Christian said. He took a step back, lifted his right leg up and slammed it hard into the door. It buckled but didn't open.

The door was a cheap, dirty white uPVC one with a small round double-glazed frosted window near the top. It took two more kicks before the door flew open and slammed against the wall behind. All three were hit by the smell of decomposition.

Walker quickly turned away while Christian searched in his pocket for something to cover his mouth with. He found a creased handkerchief he kept on him for such an eventuality. Scott wasn't quite as prepared and pulled down the sleeve on his sweater to cover his hand and use as a mask.

Walker stayed outside while the DI and DC entered the dark property. The first door on the left, next to the front door, was closed. Looking down, Christian could see flies buzzing in and out of the gap where the threadbare carpet was. He looked at Scott whose face was screwed up against the smell.

He placed a hand on the handle and braced himself. Slowly, he pushed it down and opened the door.

It was dark in the bathroom, but there was no mistaking that a naked man in the tub full of bloody water was dead and had been for some time.

Less than an hour later, Adele Kean and Lucy Dauman were carefully lifting Sebastian Page out of the bloody bath and onto the opened up body bag on the floor. He was a tall man, and despite being slim, he was heavy – a dead weight – and the small room left very little space for manoeuvre.

Christian watched from the doorway. He looked around to make sure nobody was in earshot.

'Adele, have you heard from Matilda lately?'

'No. Why?'

'I've called her a couple of times and her phone is going straight to voicemail.'

'Maybe she's out with her new man,' Lucy said with a grin.

'Hmm,' Christian said, not convinced.

'Christian, come and have a look at this,' Scott called from the somewhere else in the flat.

The living room was dark and cluttered. The three-piece suite was old, the furniture second-hand and dated. A large mass-produced bookcase at the back of the room was bursting with DVDs and Blu-rays. The only new thing in the whole room was the widescreen television which was too big for the room.

'Any chance of opening the curtains or putting a light on?' Christian asked.

Scott flicked a switch on the wall. An energy saving light bulb slowly came to life. It was of such low wattage that it didn't make much difference.

Christian rolled his eyes. 'What am I looking at?'

'I've found this. It's not sealed down.' Scott handed him an envelope with the word 'Mum' handwritten on the front.

'Where?'

'On top of the fireplace.'

Both detectives were wearing gloves, so the risk of disturbing evidence was at a minimum. Christian turned over the cheap envelope and removed a single sheet of A5 paper folded in half. He opened it, skimmed it, and sighed.

'A suicide note,' he said.

Mum,

I'm sorry. I'm not as strong as you think I am. I know you've taken a huge risk in helping me cover everything up and I thank you and love you for it but, at the end of the day, I've killed someone, and that fact won't ever go away.

Some people will say I'm taking the coward's way out. Maybe I am, but I don't care anymore.

Tell the police it was all me. Don't let them drag you down with me. I'm dead now. They can't do anything to me.

I'm sorry for what you'll have to go through and if you're the one who finds my body, I'm so sorry and I hope you'll forgive me.

Thank you for everything you did and for trusting me by giving me the job at Mary Croft. You are a wonderful mum and I love you.

Seb.

'Oh my God,' Scott said, reading it after Christian. 'The poor bloke.'

'I know.'

'It doesn't say if Calvin killed Keeley Armitage or not.'

'No,' Christian mused. He went over to the window and pulled open the curtains. He looked out over the depressing view of a forgotten Sheffield: abandoned buildings, closed-down factories left to be targeted by vandals and graffiti artists. 'Read that last bit again for me, Scott.'

'Thank you for everything you did and for trusting me by giving me the job at Mary Croft. You are a wonderful mum and I love you.' Scott read.

'Doesn't that sound odd to you?'

'No. She helped him get a job. There's nothing wrong with using a parent's connections.'

'That's not what he says. He says thank you for *giving* me the job, not *getting* me the job.'

'What's the difference?'

'His mother gave him the job because she was in a position to do so. And who does the employing at Mary Croft Primary School?'

'I don't know, the head teacher presumably.'

'Exactly. Sheila Croft. Making her Sebastian's mother.'

Chapter 46

Ellen Devonport slept in until almost lunchtime. After emailing her daily report to DCI Darke, she'd had a late night during which she'd watched Graham Norton then the late film and eventually nodded off in an armchair. She woke up with a crick in her neck and a hangover. She knew never to drink a full bottle of red wine, as the after effects were lethal, but she could never resist a Merlot, especially when it was on special offer at Tesco.

She showered, forced herself to eat a two-day-old croissant and headed for the gym. If half an hour on a treadmill didn't sober her up, nothing would.

Unfortunately, Ellen only managed twenty minutes. Her legs felt heavy. She hadn't exercised all week, apart from rushing up and down stairs to take Linda Armitage a cup of tea while she wallowed in her own bed. She felt sluggish. Maybe once this job was over with, she should have a word with her line sergeant about moving away from the whole FLO thing. It wasn't for her.

A bottle of ice-cold water and a quinoa salad in the canteen of the gym and Ellen was feeling something close to human once again. She scrolled through her phone and replied to a few texts she'd received overnight, one of which was from DC

Kesinka Rani who asked if she was still coming over this afternoon for a visit. She'd completely forgotten all about that. Ellen wasn't overly fond of children, and never understood why people cooed over babies. They didn't do anything except lie there eating, screaming, and crapping. Where was the joy in that? However, a couple of hours with Kesinka and the baby (whose name she'd forgotten) would take her mind off the Armitage family.

Ellen had left the car at home, not trusting herself to be fully sober to drive, and popped in to the supermarket on the way to Heeley where Kesinka and Ranjeet now lived with baby what-shisname. She bought a couple of bottles of wine, a tub of mini muffins and, from the baby section, she found an adorable onesie and a little teddy bear for the child.

'Oh my goodness, Kes, I can't believe how much he looks like Ranjeet,' Ellen said as she bent over the carry cot in the living room of their two-bedroom house.

'It's frightening, isn't it? He really is a mini version of his father,' she replied.

Kesinka had conceived on her honeymoon. There was nothing else to do on a long weekend in the Lake District when it did nothing but rain for four days solid. She worried about giving up work and being a stay-at-home mum, but she'd been adamant from the start that she would returning to work the moment her maternity leave was finished.

'Where is Ranjeet today?' Ellen asked.

'He's at his father's.'

'Why didn't you go?'

'It's a long story,' she said, slumping into the armchair. 'Basically, he thinks we should have named the baby after him,

but I wanted to name him after my father who died a couple
of years ago. Ranjeet's dad has shot me daggers ever since.'

'That's childish. Maybe you can name your second son after
him.'

'You've never given birth, have you?'

'No. Why?'

'Trust me, there'll be no second child.'

'That painful?'

'Like you wouldn't believe. Would you like a cup of tea?'

'I'd prefer a glass of this if you want to join me?' Ellen said,
pulling a bottle of Chardonnay out of her bag.

'I can't. Not while I'm breastfeeding,' she said.

'Oh. Another reason to add to the list for not having kids.'

While Kesinka went to make a cup of tea, and pour a glass
of wine for Ellen, she went to the mantelpiece and looked at all
the cards of congratulations that were still there. She smiled as
she read the good wishes and tried to submit the name Hemant
to memory. She went back to the cot.

'Hello baby Hemant,' she said in a light voice.

He looked up at her with wide brown eyes and a cute smile
on his face. He wriggled his legs and made a gurgling sound.
He really was incredibly cute. Maybe the sacrifices of no alcohol
and a painful birth were worth it when you had something so
adorable to take care of.

'I've bought you a little present,' she said, taking the small
bear out of her bag. She waved it at him, and he smiled. 'Do
you like him? What shall we call him?' She frowned as her mind
went blank. 'How about . . . Ted?'

'Not very original,' Kesinka said from the doorway.

Ellen laughed. 'I'm not that great with kids.'

'Neither am I. When my mum came round to visit when I

came home, she told me she spent the first week crying her eyes out because she'd forgotten everything she'd been taught and was worried she'd drop me.'

'Oh dear.'

'I haven't dropped him yet, but the responsibility is weighing on me, especially with Ranjeet telling me about that girl who was abducted. Everything seems scary once you're a mum.'

Ellen picked up her glass of wine and sat down beside Kesinka on the sofa. 'It's horrible, Kes. I've been FLO before, but never on anything like this. I feel like I'm way out of my depth,' she said, taking a large sip.

'In what way?'

'I don't know what to do. I've offered advice and a shoulder to cry on, but there's such an atmosphere there. And then, last night . . . No, you don't want to hear this.'

'Go on.'

'No. It's not fair. You've got enough on your plate with . . . erm . . . Hemant.'

'Ellen, my days are spent listening to nursery rhymes and changing nappies. I'd love some grown-up conversation.'

Ellen leaned forward and refilled her glass. 'The father, Craig, he threw me out last night.'

'What? Why?'

Ellen told Kesinka the story of Craig's outburst. 'I don't know what to do. I felt genuinely frightened. I told Matilda, but she's not going to send a different FLO. I suppose I should cut the bloke some slack; he's lost his daughter. He's going through all kinds of things.'

'Ellen, if you're uncomfortable, you shouldn't be there, especially not on your own. If he's as volatile at you say, maybe he had something to do with Keeley dying. Don't forget, whoever did it faked a kidnapping; they're obviously sneaky and dangerous. You shouldn't be alone in that house, Ellen.'

'I know,' she said, taking another long drink of wine. She sighed and leaned back in the sofa.

Hemant started crying. 'He's as regular as clockwork when it comes to feeding. I'll be back in a bit.' She picked up the baby and went upstairs.

Ellen remained motionless on the sofa. Her eyes travelled around the room, landing on Ranjeet and Kesinka's wedding photo and the smiling faces enjoying themselves. There was a picture of the new parents holding the baby. She had never seen such huge natural grins on anyone before. This was what life should be like for a family – happy, enjoying being together. Was it possible Craig could have killed his daughter? Could Linda have caused Riley's brain damage? What kind of people do that to their own children? Looking at Hemant, Ellen couldn't understand why or how someone could harm something so precious.

When Kesinka returned and Hemant was placed on the floor to play, Ellen watched through sad eyes. Maybe it was the case, maybe it was the alcohol, but she could feel the tears rising within.

'I think I'm going to get off,' she eventually said.

'Are you sure? Ranjeet should be home soon. I could cook us something.'

'No. You want to spend the evening as a family.'

'Are you all right?'

'I'm fine,' she wiped her eyes as tears started to fall. 'Sorry. I don't know why I'm crying.'

'Oh, Ellen,' Kesinka stepped forward and hugged her colleague and friend. 'It's this bloody case you're working on. They always get to me when it's to do with kids. Why don't you take some time off?'

'I've got some days left but I don't know what to do with them.'

'Just spend them at home, have a few late nights and lie-ins in the morning. Come here and we can take Hemant to the park and have lunch.'

Ellen stepped back and wiped her eyes. 'I will,' she smiled.

'Are you all right to drive?'

'I left the car at home. I'll walk back.'

'Are you sure? It's a long way and the sky's gone dark. They've forecast more rain for tonight. Did you hear it last night?'

She didn't tell Kesinka that she'd passed out in a drunken stupor. 'The walk might sober me up a bit,' she smiled painfully. 'I should probably cut back on the wine anyway.'

'Ok. Well, it was lovely to see you, and thanks for the gifts. You're welcome any time. Text me when you get home.'

'I will.'

Ellen kissed Kesinka on the cheek and left the house quickly. She was worried more tears would fall.

She zipped her coat up and looked up at the sky. It was grey and the clouds looked heavy. It wouldn't be long before they opened and a huge downpour fell. She checked in her handbag that she had her umbrella with her, just in case; luckily she did. If it did rain, she'd be able to cry and the tears would mix with the rain drops.

Ellen walked down Well Road, under Ponsford's Jubilee Bridge and turned right onto Chesterfield Road South.

Saturday evening traffic was a nightmare. Fortunately, Sheffield United were playing away or it would have been at a standstill. The road was busy with people heading home after

Michael Wood

a day at work or shopping in town. Ellen walked quickly, head down, under the railway bridge that was splattered with bird shit and dodged the traffic to cross the road. In the distance, she could see the towers of the Islamic Centre on Wolseley Road. She needed to head up there, turn left, and she'd be home. It sounded like a short journey, but Wolseley Road was misleading when you were in a car.

She hurried past the garage that always looked closed and was about to go over Heeley Bridge when she heard her name called out. She turned around.

'Hello. What are you doing here?'

It all happened so fast. She was hit over the head with something heavy. As she staggered backwards, she felt someone grab hold of her. The background of heavy traffic and horns beeping mingled together. Suddenly, she was no longer standing on the pavement, she was airborne and then she landed with a splash in the swollen River Sheaf below.

Her vision blurred. She could taste blood. She reached out aimlessly for something to hold on to, to give her balance, but there was nothing but water crashing around her, over her, in her mouth, nose and ears. Then everything went dark and she succumbed to the flow of the river as it carried her out to God only knows where.

Chapter 47

Matilda Darke ran to her car as the heavens opened and the rain began to fall. She hadn't been able to go through with it. Try as she might, she just wasn't the type of person to throw good, decent people to a parasite like Danny Hanson. He'd sent her a text telling her he was stuck in traffic, leaving her standing outside The Cavendish on West Street with her mind whirling. She felt sick and could feel her stomach somersaulting. In the end, she decided to leave and let Danny print what he liked. She felt sorry for Aaron and hoped he'd be able to repair the damage the story would cause, but it was of his own making, and she was going to have to break Sally and Philip's heart without adding the pain of a scandalous and fictitious newspaper report.

As Matilda drove down the road, windscreen wipers working hard to clear the rain, she glanced at the pub and saw Danny standing in the doorway, sheltering from the downpour. She took some pleasure in seeing him soaked and shivering in just a thin jacket, but not much.

'I'm sorry, Aaron,' she said. 'You're on your own.'

* * *

Sheila Croft lived on Keswick Close in Loxley, not a million miles away from Mary Croft Primary School and had to pass close to the Armitage house on her way to and from work every morning.

Once Christian and Scott had established who she was in relation to Sebastian Page, they obtained her address, and despite the lateness of the evening, they decided to pay her a visit.

From the front passenger seat, Christian tried to call Matilda, but his call went unanswered as the voicemail kicked in straight away.

'It seems like she's turned her phone off,' he said as they pulled up outside the semi-detached house.

'That's not like her,' Scott said. The rain was coming down hard and he kept the windscreen wipers on full so he could see out into the quiet cul-de-sac.

They stepped out of the car and ran quickly down Sheila's drive. Thankfully, she had a small awning over the front door so they sheltered under that, though they were still getting wet by the stiff breeze blowing the rain at them.

'I've not seen rain like this for a while,' Scott said.

'Remember that case at Starling House? It was like this then,' Christian recalled.

'You don't have to remind me. I ruined a good suit in that bloody storm.'

The front door opened, bathing both detectives in a warm glow from the hallway.

'Sheila Croft?' Christian asked. She nodded. 'I'm DI Brady from South Yorkshire Police, this is DC Andrews. Any chance we can come in for a quick word?' he asked, holding out his ID with a shaking cold, wet hand.

'Of course, come on in,' she stepped to one side and ushered both detectives in.

They vigorously wiped their feet on the mat before moving on to the laminate flooring.

'Stay there, I'll get you a couple of towels.' She went into the kitchen and returned quickly, handing them both a white towel each. 'Shocking weather, isn't it?' She tried to smile, to be polite, but there was a heavy sadness in her eyes.

'Tell me about it. I always seem to get called out when the weather turns,' Christian smiled.

'So, what can I do for you? More questions about Keeley Armitage?'

Christian dried his hair then glanced in the mirror as he fingered it into place, taking care to hide his rapidly increasing bald spot.

'No. I'm afraid something else has come up. Is there any chance we can sit down?'

Sheila quickly glanced down at their feet.

'Don't worry, we'll take our shoes off,' Christian said, kicking off his scuffed black shoes.

'Thanks. I'm not usually so fussy, but it's a new carpet in the living room. It was only laid on Wednesday.'

The living room was neat and tidy, bright and warm, but it wasn't homely. The smell of the new carpet mixed with artificial air freshener and furniture polish gave a sense that everything had a place. Ornaments on the wall unit were perfectly aligned. Magazines were neatly stacked on the coffee table. Intricate antimacassars adorned every arm and head rest of the sofa and armchairs. This was a house so anally clean the slightest imperfection would be spotted immediately, which was why Christian tucked his feet beneath him as much as he could so his odd socks (one black, one navy) wouldn't be noticed.

'Do you live here alone, Mrs Croft?' Christian asked.

'Yes. I'm widowed.'

'Oh, I'm so sorry.'

She waved his apology away. 'There's no need. It happened a long time ago.'

Christian looked over to the marble mantelpiece at the framed wedding photo of a much thinner Sheila in a beautiful white gown standing beside a tall, solid man in an army dress uniform. Sheila followed his gaze.

'He went through the Gulf War, saw things in Kosovo nobody should witness, and got killed by a drunk driver on Bocham Parkway.'

'Oh,' Christian said. 'That must have been devastating, I'm sorry.'

'It was. I spent years worrying every night while he was away,' she said wistfully, not taking her eyes from the wedding picture. 'Every time the phone rang, or a knock came on the door I expected someone telling me he'd been blown up or shot down. And he ends up getting killed on his own doorstep.'

'Was the drunk driver caught?' Scott asked.

Her face soured. 'Not that it did much good. Three years for causing death by dangerous driving and a two-year ban.'

Christian didn't know what to say. He felt another apology was inadequate. The silence grew.

'Anyway, I'm sure you didn't come around here in this bad weather to make idle chit-chat.'

'No,' Christian cleared his throat and adjusted his position on the sofa. He always felt uncomfortable delivering the death message. 'Mrs Croft, why didn't you tell us you were Sebastian's mother?'

She let out an audible sigh and crumbled in the armchair. 'I wondered how long we'd be able to keep it a secret.' Her bottom lip quivered. The pain was etched on her lined face as she struggled to find the words without a torrent of emotion coming out. 'I'm guessing Sebastian told you.'

Neither Christian nor Scott replied. As always in these kinds of situations it was best to allow the witness to talk. Who knew what gems she would reveal?

'I knew Sebastian would crack first, bless him. Would you two like a drink? I think we're going to need one.'

'I'll have a whiskey if there's one going; I'm not driving,' Christian said. Despite the old adage of 'not while I'm on duty', plain-clothed detectives were allowed a drink, though never to excess. The majority never did, however.

Sheila smiled, eased herself out of the armchair and headed over to the wall unit. She pulled down a door which revealed an array of different types of whiskeys.

'Do you have a preference?'

'There's no prejudice when it comes to whiskey in my opinion.'

'Man after my own heart. I'm guessing you'd just like an orange juice,' she said to Scott.

'Yes, sure, why not?' he replied, clearly deflated.

Sheila poured three drinks and carried them over on a small silver-plated tray. She took a healthy swig before sitting down in the comfortable chair.

Christian had no intention of having a drink, as much as he'd have liked. He never drank on duty but didn't want the topic of drink to distract Sheila from what she was about to say.

'I'm guessing Sebastian's confessed.' There was a catch in her throat which she tried to clear. 'It's strange how two boys can be so completely different from each other. Sebastian was always sensitive, quick to tears. He had a few friends, but not many. He preferred to spend time in his room with his model cars. Calvin, well, he was the polar opposite: brash, loud, uncaring, a complete psychopath.' She looked over to the detectives and took in their wide-eyed expressions. 'I suppose it's not often you hear a mother talk about her own son like that. I knew there was something wrong with him from an early age. I took him to a doctor, and all he said was that boys will be boys. You wouldn't get away with that now.' She took another drink. 'When the police knocked on the door wanting to question Calvin about those rapes, I knew he'd done it. Oh, he tried to lie his way out of it; he even gave an alibi for one of them, but I could see through it. My son had raped three girls. It made me physically sick thinking about what I'd brought into this world.

'Richard had long since died, thankfully,' she looked over to the wedding picture again. 'I don't know how he'd have reacted. Sebastian was a lot like Richard. It wasn't easy for him, to have a brother who was a convicted rapist.

'I kept in touch with Calvin, while he was in prison,' she said, turning back to the detectives. 'Looking back after everything that's happened, I probably should've washed my hands of him, but, well, he's my son at the end of the day. When he was released, I wanted us to be like a normal family again. We'd been through so much drama, I just wanted us to be happy, to sit down and have a meal together like families do.'

Sheila trailed off. She stared into the distance as if into the past. A look of blissful contentment spread across her face as if she was imaging the perfect family she never had.

'Why do you have different surnames?' Scott asked to break the silence Sheila had allowed to descend.

'Croft was my maiden name. I was Page in everything else, but it was easier for work to be Mrs Croft.'

'Do the staff at Mary Croft know Sebastian is your son?' Christian asked.

She shook her head and emptied her glass. 'Would you like a refill?'

'I'm fine, thanks.'

Sheila went over to the cabinet, took out the bottle and brought it back with her.

'Sebastian couldn't get a job anywhere. When he did and people found out who his brother was, they made it difficult for him to stay there. Like I said, he was a very sensitive boy.'

'He wasn't a qualified teacher, was he?' Christian asked.

Again, Sheila shook her head. 'He was a PE teacher in a primary school. It's not like he was teaching A-level physics. All he had to do was play rounders and badminton with the kids, keep them active. It suited him. He loved the job. He loved the kids. For the first time in his life, he was happy.'

'And then Keeley Armitage went missing.'

'We couldn't track Calvin down for love nor money. He wasn't answering his phone, he wasn't at the flat, we started thinking the worst. Then he turned up here asking for money. Sebastian was in the kitchen when the knock came on the door. I answered it and in he walks, bold as brass. I told him we'd been looking for him, ringing him, but he didn't seem interested. Sebastian came storming into the living room. He had him up against the wall, demanding to know what he'd done with Keeley.' Tears had started to roll down Sheila's cheeks. She didn't wipe them away. The half-filled glass in her hands was shaking as she gripped it tight, her knuckles white.

'Like I said, Calvin was a psychopath. He laughed. He actually laughed in Sebastian's face. He said he'd not even heard of Keeley going missing. Sebastian grabbed the newspaper and showed him the story. Do you know what Calvin said? He looked at Keeley's photo and said she was hot. Can you believe that? My own son actually said a nine-year-old girl was hot in front of his mother. It made my flesh crawl.'

'What happened then?' Christian asked.

'I've never seen Sebastian like that before. But, I suppose we all have a breaking point. He just flew into a rage. He grabbed my gavel – I had a brass gavel on the mantelpiece – and he hit him. It was like the world stopped turning. Blood started to flow slowly down Calvin's face. Then he grinned. There was no stopping Sebastian. He kept hitting him over and over and over. I didn't stop him. I couldn't have even if I'd wanted to.'

'Is that why you changed the carpet?'

She nodded. 'The floorboards are stained though. You'll see when you take the carpet up. You will be careful though, won't you? It wasn't cheap.'

Christian nodded. 'Whose idea was it to take Calvin to the old ski village?'

'Mine,' she answered after draining the glass.

'And the gavel?'

'It's in the dishwasher. It's been washed so many times but I daren't take it out. I'm convinced there's still blood on it.' She stood up and went over to a sideboard. From a drawer she took out a Samsung mobile phone in a clear plastic freezer bag and handed it to Christian. 'You'll be wanting this.'

'What is it?'

'Calvin's phone. The PIN is his birthday: 1906. Not very original. Sebastian brought it back with him from the ski village. There are over three hundred video clips downloaded and saved. Prison didn't change him at all.'

Christian took the phone from her. She went back to her

armchair and slumped into it. 'I didn't think Sebastian would be able to keep it a secret, bless him. Have you arrested him? Will I be able to see him?'

Scott and Christian exchanged glances.

'Sheila,' Christian began, sitting forward. 'We were called out to Sebastian's flat this afternoon. I'm afraid he took his own life. He left you a note.'

Sheila swallowed hard and nodded her head. 'I thought he would have done. I wondered why he didn't come around last night. I was going to go around this morning, but . . . I didn't want to find him.' She looked at Christian. 'A mother always knows.'

Chapter 48

'South Yorkshire Police. How may I help you?

   'I've just seen someone being pushed off Heeley Bridge.'

'Ok. Are you at the bridge now?'

'No. I was in my car when I saw it happen. I pulled over and got out to look, but the river is flowing really fast. I couldn't see anyone. I'm back at my car now. The rain is coming down heavy.'

'The person who was pushed over the bridge, was it a man, woman or child?'

'I don't know. It all happened so fast.'

'Did you see the person who did the pushing?'

'No. They were wearing black and had a hood up. Whoever it was was slim and fast as they ran like lightning.'

'What direction did they run in?'

'They ran back down the road as if towards Ponsfords.'

'Ok, sir, can you stay with your car? I've despatched a team to come out to you.'

PCs Natasha Tranter and Gemma August drove through the busy streets of Sheffield at maximum speed. Sirens were blaring and windscreen wipers tried in vain to give them a clear view of the road and dangers ahead. Natasha, though she didn't admit it to her colleague, was nervous in the front passenger seat. Gemma lived for these conditions.

'My husband bought me a day out in Silverstone for my birthday a couple of years ago,' Gemma shouted over the sound of the engine and torrential rain. She didn't take her eyes off the windscreen as one hand was on the wheel and the other on the gear stick. 'It was absolutely pissing it down and I went round that track like Lewis Hamilton on steroids. Loved it.'

'What did your Shane think?' Natasha shouted back.

'He was fine until I aquaplaned, and he pissed himself,' she laughed. 'Best birthday ever.'

'You're a strange woman, Gemma.'

'Enjoy every day,' she grinned. 'We could all be dead tomorrow.'

'We could be dead in the next five minutes if you don't slow down.'

'Have a little faith.'

Cars pulled over on Chesterfield Road and Gemma slammed her foot down on the accelerator and entered the third of four lanes. Halfords, the car wash, and Boots opticians went by in a blur. She drove through a red light and Natasha pointed out the blue Ford Focus with its hazard lights flashing up ahead.

'That's the guy who called,' she said.

Gemma pulled up just in front of him and they both climbed out, putting their hats on to give them a modicum of shelter from the rain.

'I'm driving back,' Natasha said as she locked the car.

'Fine by me. We'll be sticking to the speed limit. Where's the fun in that?'

'Mr Lomax?' Natasha said to the man climbing out of his car. He was tall and thin and wearing a waterproof coat two sizes too big for him.

'That's me,' he shouted over the sound of the downpour.

'You say someone was pushed into the River Sheaf?'

'Yes. It was . . .'

'Would you like to tell my colleague, here, while I go and have a look?' Natasha said. She headed off in the direction of the bridge. Gripping the railings, she looked over the side and into the dangerous waters of the river below. It was almost up to bridge level. If the rain continued, it wouldn't be long before it was spilling out over the road. If someone had been thrown into the river, they would have been swept away by now.

Natasha turned on the torch attached to her uniform and leaned further over the bridge. There was nobody there, but she hadn't expected them to be. The dirty water crashed on the rough banks.

She turned her back on the railings and looked around her to see if there were any signs of CCTV on the nearby buildings. She couldn't see any.

Gemma joined her. 'Mr Lomax has got a dashcam. He played back the footage. It's only a few seconds but there's no mistaking.'

'Shit. There's nobody in the water. They could be miles away by now,' she shouted.

'Where does the Sheaf lead to?'

'I've no idea. The River Don probably.'

'We need to get a search team out here.'

'There's no way they're going to be able to look for her in this weather. I doubt even a helicopter will get up in this.'

'I'll call the Sarge. Let him make the decision.'

Gemma stepped to one side and spoke loudly into her radio while Natasha crossed the road, playing chicken with the traffic, to look over the bridge on the other side. The river was furious as it flowed. She blinked hard against the raindrops hitting her in the face, but she couldn't see anybody clinging to life or floating face down in the water.

As she turned back, a bus passed, its headlights on full beam. They bounced against something shiny on the side of the road in front of the railings where whoever had been pushed over. Risking her life against the traffic once again, Natasha ran across the road. Among the weeds and detritus at the edge of the pavement in front of the bridge, she saw a handbag with a buckle that had caught the buses headlights. She picked it up, opened it, and rummaged around inside.

'Fuck me,' she said to herself. 'Gemma!' she called out.

'What is it?' She asked back.

'Tell the Sarge to get a team out here right now.'

'Why?'

She held up the warrant card. 'It's DC Ellen Devonport.'

Chapter 49

Sheila Croft had calmly gone with Christian and Scott to South Yorkshire Police HQ. She was placed in a holding cell while Scott and Christian went into the changing rooms to dry off.

'Poor woman,' Scott said as he slumped down on the bench. He kicked off his shoes and struggled to take off his sodden socks. 'Some people seem to get all the bad luck, don't they?'

'It would appear so,' Christian said, peeling off his shirt.

'So, do we think Calvin killed Keeley or not?'

'I don't think so. She hadn't been raped and the sexual assault was old. He'd have to have had contact with her on several occasions going back months. I don't see how he could have done it.'

'So, we're back to square one with no suspects.'

'Not really. It does leave us with one.'

'Who?'

'The father.'

The Homicide and Major Enquiry suite was in darkness. Christian opened the glass doors and switched on the lights. They buzzed and flickered into life. He went over to his desk, but something caught his eye. He looked up and saw Matilda

Darke sitting in her small office. She was looking straight at him but hadn't seen him. Her eyes were wide, her face expressionless.

Christian tapped lightly on the glass, but she didn't hear him. He knocked louder but didn't wait for her reply before walking in.

'Is everything all right?'

It was a while before she realised anyone was there. 'Sorry?' She asked.

'You looked like you were a million miles away. What were you doing sitting here alone in the dark?'

Matilda looked around her as if wondering where she was. 'I just needed somewhere to think.'

'And a big farmhouse in the middle of nowhere's not good for that?'

Matilda smiled painfully.

'Have you been here all day?'

'Most of it. I had arranged to meet with Danny Hanson. I was going to give him the Carl Meagan story, but I couldn't go through with it.'

'I'm glad,' Christian smiled.

'It doesn't help Aaron, though, does it?'

'I like Aaron, I really do,' Christian said, hitching his chair closer to Matilda's desk. 'He's a good detective and a nice bloke. He's made a mistake, a huge one, but a mistake nonetheless. And he has to answer to that mistake.'

'But what about the Mercer case?'

'I was thinking about this earlier. If Leah Mercer had been an actual witness to the murder of her family, the case would be in trouble, but she wasn't. She wasn't even in the country when the murders took place. If she's called as a witness when it goes to court, all she'll be able to say is what wonderful people her parents and brother were. She can't give any evidence, because she doesn't know any.'

'But Rachel does. And while Aaron has been seeing Leah, he's been seeing Rachel. The defence could say Aaron's been coaching her for giving evidence while pretending to be a caring friend of the family.'

Christian blew out his cheeks. He hadn't thought of that. 'Ok. Ok. Rachel's evidence is a lot to lose but look at everything else. We've got the attack on you, the car chase to Ladybower, the connection between Millie Jonson and the Mercers, your evidence on top of that. The jury could be full of village idiots and they'd still see the truth.'

It was a while before Matilda responded as she mulled over what Christian said. 'You're right. I know you're right. I just don't want to throw Aaron to the lions.'

'I know you don't. Neither do I. But he's a grown man. He knew what he was doing when he began the affair and must face the consequences.'

'Christian, if you were in my position and had Danny Hanson practically blackmailing you and a detective having an affair, how would you handle it?'

'For a start I wouldn't let Danny Hanson blackmail me. I'd let him print his story and pass it on to our lawyers. As for Aaron, I'd have him in the office, ask him to explain his actions, then deal accordingly.'

'You wouldn't feel uncomfortable with Aaron being a close colleague?'

'Not if he'd made such a monumental cock-up. I'd be incredibly sad, but it's of his own doing.'

Matilda sat back and smiled.

'What?' Christian asked.

'You're going to make a great DCI.'

His eyes widened. 'What?'

'There's going to be a restructuring at some point next year. The ACC is recommending me for Superintendent, and I can't think of anyone better to take over my role.'

'Are you serious?'

'Would you be interested?'

'Of course. When is this restructuring happening?'

'I'm not sure. It'll be another year or so.'

'Oh good. I've got plenty of time to pay off my secret second family,' he laughed.

'Don't even joke about that, Christian,' Matilda smiled, genuinely.

The door burst open and a saturated Sian Mills entered the office.

'Why is it I can never break down outside a chocolate shop or a millionaire's mansion or a vineyard?' She said breathlessly.

'In Sheffield?' Christian interrupted.

'My sodding engine flooded and died on me. I look up and what's the first thing I see? The bloody South Yorkshire Police sign.'

Matilda stifled a laugh. 'Would you like a lift home?'

'Yes please. Last time we had a big rainstorm, my house flooded. I'm dreading it happening again.'

Scott pushed open the door and practically sent Sian flying.

'I'm sorry,' he said. 'Something bad's happened. Ellen Devonport's been attacked. She's missing.'

While Scott was on the phone trying to get hold of anyone on the team to come in and help with the search for Ellen, Sian was co-ordinating with sergeants and inspectors in uniform to put a search team together and find out whether the helicopter would be useful in this weather.

Christian grabbed Matilda by the elbow and pulled her to one side. He filled her in on Sheila Croft and everything surrounding Sebastian and Calvin.

'I'm worried that it leaves us with just one potential suspect,' he said, his voice lowered.

'Craig Armitage?' Matilda guessed.

'Exactly.'

'But what's his motive?'

'The historical sex abuse for a start. What if he's the one who's been abusing her? What if she threatened to tell someone and he killed her to shut her up?'

'I could understand that if Keeley was an only child, but there's Jodie to think about in all this. Why didn't he abuse Jodie when she was Keeley's age?'

'Maybe he did,' Christian said, firmly, not breaking eye contact with Matilda.

'Fuck!' Matilda said, kicking the nearest door. 'We've never had a serious talk with Jodie, have we?' They should have interviewed her. They should have taken her out of that house and asked her to give them chapter and verse on Craig and Linda as parents. If Matilda hadn't been so distracted with Carl Meagan and the worry of her reputation at another child disappearing and not being found, she would have asked the right questions of the right people and known the Armitage family inside and out by now. Once again, she blamed herself.

'It's on the list of things to do but we've been tiptoeing around them because they're grieving.'

'We still can't discount Calvin Page, though. Get his phone off to forensics and see if any of these photos or videos show Keeley Armitage. Get a sample of his DNA and run it past anything we found on Keeley's body or inside the Armitage house. Also, get a decent photo of Calvin and send it to my phone. I'll show the Armitages, see if they recognise him.' She ran her fingers through her hair, pulling tight on the strands. 'Ok, here's what we're going to do: me and Sian have spoken to the Armitage family the most, so we'll go out there now and have a private word with Jodie. I need you to get everyone out there looking for Ellen.'

'Do we think there's some kind of connection?'

'I bloody hope not, but we'll get an alibi for Craig, see if he's been out at all.'

There was a crack of thunder so loud that the lights dimmed and the walls of the station shook, causing everyone to stop in their tracks.

'Please don't tell me that's an omen,' Matilda said.

Chapter 50

A red weather warning from the Met Office was issued for parts of Yorkshire and Humberside. Power lines were down, and roads were closed. People were advised to stay indoors and not make any journeys unless they were absolutely necessary. Detaining a potential murderer was deemed as being a necessary journey.

DC Rory Fleming was the best advanced driver in the HMET. He'd come to the station to pick Natasha up but decided to hang around when he heard she was out on a call. Christian and Scott found him in the open-plan office bent over Sian's snack drawer.

'Sian's going to kill you if she finds you rooting around in there,' Scott said as they entered.

'No she won't. She'll offer to have my children,' he stood back to reveal a drawer full to the brim with brightly coloured chocolate bar and sweet wrappers.

Christian bent down to grab a bar, but Rory slapped his hand. 'Not until Sian's seen it first.'

'In that case, you can drive Sian and DCI Darke to Stannington. They're downstairs waiting for you.'

As they left the room, Rory grabbed Scott's arm. 'Scott, can you do me a favour?' He looked worried.

'Sure. What is it?'

'When you get out to Heeley, tell Natasha to be careful.'

'She will be careful.'

'I know, but, when it's one of our own, we sort of throw the rule book out of the window, don't we? I don't want her doing something that could risk her life.'

Scott smiled. 'You really like her, don't you?'

'Scott, mate, I love her.'

'Have you told her?'

'Not yet. Will you tell her for me?'

'You can piss off.'

Once they were out of the city centre, the traffic was practically non-existent as people paid heed to the warnings and stayed safely indoors. It seemed like the end of the world. It was Saturday night; the city should have been full of people heading for pubs, restaurants and night clubs, but everywhere was deserted.

Rory drove at speed. His hands gripped the wheel firmly and his arms were straight at the elbow. He frowned in concentration as he skirted around deep puddles and fords in the road.

He drove with Sian in the front passenger seat beside him. Matilda had decided to take her own Range Rover. In weather this bad, it was best to have a back-up vehicle.

'Whoever says climate change doesn't exist is a complete moron,' Sian said. 'We never used to get storms like this. Remember when Meadowhall flooded a few years back? It will do again if it doesn't let up soon.'

'We've had a hot summer,' Rory said. 'I suppose this is the price we pay.'

'They keep saying on the news we need to act now before it's too late. I think we've already passed the tipping point,' Sian said, glaring out of the window as the rainstorm drenched Sheffield as if mother nature was trying to sweep it out to sea.

Rory slowed as they turned into Acorn Drive. He slammed on the brakes when he saw an ambulance parked outside the Armitage house. The back doors were open and the blue lights were flashing, dancing in the dark.

'Oh my God,' Rory said.

By the time Sian had taken her seatbelt off and got out of the car, Matilda was already tearing towards the house.

The front door was open, and she went inside without knocking. 'Hello. Is everyone all right?'

She almost collided with a paramedic in the entrance to the living room. Matilda introduced herself.

Linda Armitage was being secured to a trolley. She was unconscious and covered in blood.

'What's going on?'

'Mrs Armitage began coughing up blood about an hour ago. I'm afraid it took us a while to get out here in this weather. We've managed to sedate her and get fluids into her, but she's lost a great deal of blood,' the young paramedic said. 'Would you like to go with your wife?' he asked Craig.

Craig was standing by the window. He had a look of pure horror on his face as he tried to make sense of what was happening to his family.

'Erm, I don't know . . . I need to look after Jodie and Riley.'

'We can sort something out, Mr Armitage, if you want to be with your wife,' Rory said.

'Thank you. I suppose I should go with her.' He began to follow the paramedics out of the room as they slowly and carefully made their way to the door.

'Daddy.'

Craig stopped and turned to look up the stairs. Jodie was sat at the top hugging her knees. There were tears running down her face. She was wearing a thick towelling dressing gown. Her hair was wet. She looked younger and more vulnerable suddenly.

'Jodie, I need you to stay here and look after Riley. I promise, I won't be long.'

'Will she be all right?'

'I hope so.'

'What do I do?'

He ran up the stairs to her and held her by the shoulders. 'Sweetheart, I need you to be a big girl. I need you to look after Riley. As soon as I can, I'll come home. I promise,' he kissed her on the forehead.

'I love you,' she said as her father ran back down the stairs.

He stopped and looked back at his remaining daughter. 'Love you too, sweetheart.'

Matilda pulled Rory to one side. 'Rory, follow him to the hospital,' she whispered. 'Find out what the hell happened here and try and get as much information out of him as possible. Ring me if you get anything.'

'Will do.' He ran out of the house, slamming the door behind him.

Matilda and Sian stood in the hallway. Their faces were blank. They had expected to come here to interview Craig and hopefully have a quiet word with Jodie.

'Jodie, would you like to come downstairs?' Sian asked in her calmest 'mother' tone. 'I'll make us a nice hot drink and you can tell us what happened here tonight.'

'Is my mum going to be all right?' she asked.

'I'm sure she will. Some of the best doctors in the world work in Sheffield. We're very lucky to live here. Come on, come down.'

'I don't want to go into the living room,' she said.

'Why not?'

'That's where all the blood is.'

Sian gave a weak smile to Jodie and left her on the stairs while she and Matilda went to the lounge. Blood was splattered on the coffee table and soaking into the carpet. She had never seen someone expel so much blood without them being shot or stabbed.

What the hell was wrong with Linda Armitage?

Chapter 51

It was pitch dark. The new, energy saving streetlights were useless for conducting a proper search and it was too windy to erect spotlights. The helicopter flew low over the streets of Heeley, shining its bright beam onto the rapidly flowing river and surrounding areas. Chesterfield Road South had been closed to traffic. It was a major road running through this part of Sheffield and would cause as much disruption as the weather. There was no alternative, however.

Natasha Tranter looked like she'd been pulled out of the River Sheaf. She was drenched from head to toe and her curly brown hair was sticking to her head. DC Finn Cotton handed her a damp towel.

'Why don't you take a break,' he shouted over the sound of the rain.

She rubbed hard at her head and wiped her face. 'I can't. We need to find her.'

Finn couldn't decipher which drops on her face were rain and which were tears. 'We will. DI Brady is sending out more officers.'

She swallowed hard. 'Finn, what if she's dead?'

He couldn't answer that.

'What if she's been swept away? What if she's drowned?'

He held her by the shoulders. 'Nat, take five minutes.'

'I can't. I'm going back down.'

She pushed by Finn and headed across the road to go around the back of a Victorian building that had been a pub for over a hundred years but was now a wood flooring centre. Finn was about to follow when he saw a car pull up. He squinted against the headlights and the rain hitting his face to get a good look at who was inside. Hopefully it would be someone of a high rank who could tell Natasha to take a step back.

DCs Scott Andrews and Ranjeet Deshwal climbed out of the car wearing waterproofs. He headed towards them and saw DI Brady get out of the back.

'Any news?' Christian asked.

'No. The bloke in the helicopter says if the wind gets any worse, they'll have to call off the search. It'll be too dangerous for them to be up there.'

'This rain isn't letting up at all, is it?'

'I think the river's going to break its banks at any moment, sir,' Finn said.

'Who's down there?'

'A few uniformed officers are taking it in turns. Sir, will you have a word with PC Tranter? She won't take a break. She's soaked and knackered.'

'I'll go,' Scott chimed up. 'Where is she?'

'She went around the back of the building.'

'I'll come with you,' Ranjeet said. 'We can relieve some of the officers, give them a break.'

The helicopter roared overhead. The searching spotlight lit them up before plunging them back into darkness. The river was raging and the blades from the helicopter weren't helping.

Using powerful torches, officers searched the overgrown banks for any sign that Ellen had been washed ashore. It was an exercise in futility; they couldn't see anything. But a fellow officer was missing so they would search all night if they had to.

'Natasha,' Ranjeet called out. She didn't hear him despite the fact he was standing right behind her. He called her name again. 'Natasha, DI Brady's on the bridge. He wants a word with you.'

'What? Why?'

'He didn't say. Don't keep him waiting. You know how short-tempered a wet DI can be.'

'Ok. Here.' She handed him her torch. 'I'll be right back.'

She looked exhausted as she struggled to climb up the embankment and back to the road.

Ranjeet and Scott walked along the edge of the river. The ground was soaked and unstable. They were wearing all the right gear, but nothing could protect them if they slipped and fell into the raging torrent.

'This is ridiculous. She could be anywhere,' Scott shouted from behind.

'Where does this river run to, do you know?'

'Not a clue. I'd say the River Don, but that's just a guess.'

'Bloody hope not. She gets in that, we really will have lost her.'

'I've never seen this river so high,' Scott called out.

'Me neither. What's that under there?' Ranjeet asked, aiming his torch across the river.

Scott squinted and pointed his torch in the same direction. 'I think it's a black bag, probably rubbish someone's dumped.'

'I thought it looked like an anorak or something.'

They trudged further on down river. When they reached the railway bridge, there was no way they'd be able to go under it without succumbing to the same fate as Ellen. They struggled to climb up the saturated embankment, ran across the tracks and down the other side. While they held on to tree branches and roots sticking out of the ground to stop them falling in, other officers on the opposite side of the river were searching from the relative safety of the narrow concrete walkway at the back of ancient offices and warehouses which had seen better days. Windows were boarded up; brick work was covered in illegible graffiti. A footbridge ran across the river acting as an escape route from the buildings; a few officers were on there, struggling with a large searchlight on a tripod. Everything was being done to find Ellen Devonport.

Beyond the footbridge, the river dropped deeper, making the water rage even faster. There was no way an officer could risk their life by wading through that to find her. Scott and Ranjeet helped each other up the embankment to the empty car park. They were filthy, soaked, out of breath and seriously dejected.

'This is futile,' Scott said. 'Even with the torches we can't see a sodding thing down there.'

'I know. We can't stop, though.'

'We could have already passed her and not realised.'

Ranjeet looked at him. 'You think she's dead?'

'The bloke who called it in said she was pushed over the bridge. If she's fallen in the water, she could have hit her head and been knocked unconscious. I mean, she could even have got snagged on something under the railway bridge. There's too many possibilities.'

'You want to just give up on her?' Ranjeet looked angry.

'Of course I don't but, like I said, we could have already passed her.'

'Fuck!' Ranjeet screamed. 'She was at our house just a couple of hours ago. Kes told her to stay for tea, but she wouldn't. If she'd have waited even another half an hour I would have been back. I could have given her a lift.'

'You can't blame yourself, Ranjeet.'

'Kes said she'd had a full bottle of wine to herself. There's no way a drunken woman could survive in this. If she's dead, Kes will never forgive herself.'

Scott was about to speak, to reassure his colleague, when a large rumble was heard behind them. They turned and watched as a large section of the riverbank crumbled and fell into the Sheaf.

Neither of them said anything, but they were both thinking the same thing: how could anyone survive in such conditions?

Scott's phone vibrated in his pocket. He struggled to get to it with wet fingers and fought to pull it out of his trouser pocket. The display told him DI Brady was calling.

'Yes?' he said loudly into it. 'What? I can hardly hear you . . . Really . . .? Are you sure . . .? Fine. I'll tell him.' He ended the call and looked down, dejected.

'They've found her?' Ranjeet asked, hopeful.

'They're calling off the search.'

'What? Why?'

'It's too dangerous. The helicopter's leaving. We can't keep searching in these conditions. DI Brady said we'll start again at first light. Hopefully the rain will have stopped by then.'

'And what if it hasn't?' Ranjeet screamed. 'What if this carries on for a few more hours? What if the river bursts its banks and the whole area floods? We'll have lost her, Scott. I'm not stopping.' He turned his torch back on and headed for the edge of the swollen river.

'Ranjeet, we've had an order to go back.'

'You do what you like. I'm not giving up on her.'

Ranjeet jumped onto the bonnet of a white Transit van and scrambled his way to the roof. He leaned on the wall overlooking the river and shone his torch. He screamed Ellen's name at the top of his voice, but even Scott struggled to hear him.

'This is insane,' Scott shouted. 'Ranjeet, come down. Save your energy until tomorrow morning.'

If Ranjeet heard him, he showed no sign of it. There were vans and cars parked next to each other. DC Deshwal jumped from one to the other, leaning over the wall and looking down into the river, searching hopelessly for his colleague.

Scott got back on the phone and rang DI Brady.

'I'm coming down. Don't let him do anything stupid,' was all he said before disconnecting the call.

Scott turned back to Ranjeet. 'Don't let him do anything stupid,' he said to himself. 'How the bloody hell am I going to stop him?'

'I've found her!' Ranjeet screamed.

'What?' Scott ran towards him at the far end of the car park.

'She's here. I can see her.'

'Are you sure?'

'Yes. She's wedged against the bridge that runs under Myrtle Road. I can see her,' he said with a wide grin on her face.

'Is she all right?'

'I don't know. I can't tell. But it's definitely her. I know it is.' Ranjeet threw one leg over the wall.

'What are you doing?'

'I'm going to get her.'

'Ranjeet, don't be stupid, you could be swept away. We can get her from the other side.'

'The way the water is storming down here, it could sweep her away before we get the chance.'

Scott ran over to the van Ranjeet was standing on. He jumped up and grabbed hold of him. 'DI Brady is on his way down. Leave it for him to make the decision.'

'For fuck's sake, Scott, this isn't about rank, this isn't about hierarchy, this is a person, a colleague, and she's in danger.'

'What about Kesinka? What about your son?'

'You make it sound like I'm jumping into an abyss.'

There was another roar and more of the saturated embankment crashed into the water.

'Scott!'

Scott turned at the sound of his name being called. He saw DI Brady and Natasha running towards him but turned back when he heard the sound of a splash. Ranjeet was nowhere to be seen.

Chapter 52

Matilda and Sian sat at the kitchen table with Jodie opposite them. Sian had made them all a hot drink – tea for her and the DCI and a hot chocolate for Jodie who had changed into jeans and an old sweater.

The house was deathly quiet. It was usually a hive of activity. The television was on constantly, or, when Linda was in the kitchen preparing a meal, she had the radio on loud, blasting out hits from the 80s and 90s. Riley was always making a noise, whether screaming or crying or calling out but now, it was silent.

'Jodie, how long has your mum been ill?' Matilda asked.

Jodie looked down into her mug. She hadn't taken a sip yet. She remained rigid, her hands cupped around it. She shrugged. 'I don't know. A couple of weeks ago she kept saying she felt sick. We have to be careful with Riley. If any of us are ill, we can't go near him. Mum went to the doctor and they said she had a stomach virus. They gave her something, but it didn't seem to work.'

'You say she felt sick, was she actually sick?' Matilda asked.

'Not at first. It was a few days after she said she felt sick when she was properly sick. We'd just had tea. Mum was in the kitchen doing the pots and I was helping her dry. One minute we were chatting and laughing, the next she just vomited.'

'How many times has she been sick?'

'I don't know. I always ask how she is when I get home from school. She says she's fine, but I don't think she is. I think she's lying.'

'Has she lost weight?' Sian asked.

'Yes.'

'Has she been back to the doctor?'

'Yes, but they said there's nothing they can do. She's not ill or anything. I mean, if she had an illness then Riley would have caught it, and he's been fine.'

Matilda frowned. She looked across at Sian who was wearing a similar expression.

'Jodie, has anyone else been sick?' Matilda asked.

'No.'

'Who cooks the meals?'

'Mum. Sometimes I do, but not often. I'm not that good.'

Matilda fidgeted in her seat. 'Jodie, is it possible your mum might have been making herself sick?'

'What?' She looked up. Her gaze switched between Matilda and Sian and back again. 'Why? Why would she do that?'

'Sometimes people make themselves ill to get attention. Your mum spends all of her time in the house with Riley and when people see her, they ask how Riley's doing. They don't ask how she is. Do you think she could be making herself sick so people will worry about her?'

Jodie thought for a moment. She looked older than her fourteen years. There was an air of sadness about her. 'But . . . with what's happened to Keeley and everything, why would she still do that?'

'I don't know,' Matilda said. 'Your mum might be more ill than we all think.'

'You think she's mad?'

'No. Maybe a touch depressed.'

'Jodie, did you ever see Riley have a seizure when he was younger?' Sian asked.

'No. They always happened at night while I was in bed. Wait, do you think she made those up too?'

'We're not sure.'

'But . . . she can't have done. I mean, Riley was born a normal boy. Now he's brain damaged. If that didn't happen because of a seizure, how else could it have happened?'

Sian looked down at the table.

'You think . . . Mum did it? How is that even possible?'

Matilda reached across the table and placed her hands on top of Jodie's. 'Sometimes, when a woman has a baby, it's not always the happy occasion it's made out to be. Sometimes, women can get a bit down.'

'I know all about post-natal depression,' she snapped. 'Mum isn't depressed. And if you think she'd purposely harm him you're wrong.

'Erm, Jodie,' Sian began, 'where's Riley?' Her questioned was loaded with concern.

Jodie's face hardened. 'He's asleep.'

'All this time? With everything that's gone on in the house, he's slept through it all?'

'Yes.'

'Lucky him,' she said, and gave a nervous chuckle.

'Maybe we should check on him,' Matilda said. 'Sian, would you mind?'

Sian stood up.

Jodie jumped from her seat and blocked Sian's exit from the room. 'No. I'll go.'

'Jodie, sit down and talk to me,' Matilda said. 'I want you to tell me more about what your mum's been doing lately. We might be able to come up with something to make her feel better. Sian's got four kids; she knows not to go barging into the bedroom and scaring him.'

Jodie backed away and stood in the doorway. 'No. I don't want you going into his room.'

'Why not?' Matilda asked, standing up.

'You'll frighten him. He gets confused with people he doesn't know.'

'Jodie, what's going on?' Matilda stepped forward.

'Nothing.' She was growing more flustered. Her eyes were darting left and right; her breathing was erratic.

'Jodie, I want you to step away from the door. I need to check on Riley, make sure he's all right,' Sian said, standing up and moving around the table slowly.

Jodie lunged forward and grabbed a carving knife from the block on the work top. She held it firmly in both hands. They were shaking as she pointed the stainless-steel blade at Matilda and Sian.

'Jodie, what have you done?' Matilda asked.

'I haven't done anything.'

'Then what are you hiding?'

Chapter 53

DC Rory Fleming had found a quiet room for him and Craig Armitage to wait in while the doctors were racing to save his wife's life. Craig was standing by the window, watching the rain teem down through the slats of the dusty venetian blinds.

'I don't think I've ever seen rain like this before,' Craig said calmly. 'It's like the end of the world.'

'Craig, can I get you anything? A tea or coffee maybe?' Rory asked. He was sitting on the nearest chair to the door.

'No. I'm fine, thank you,' he smiled. 'Do you think the world is ending?' he asked, turning back to look out of the window.

'I . . . don't think so,' Rory frowned.

'It feels like it. My daughter is dead. My wife . . .' He choked on his words. 'I've never seen anything like that before, not even in films.'

'What happened?'

'We were in the living room eating a sandwich. She's not been herself for a couple of weeks now. The sandwich just dropped out of her hands. She started retching and then she was sick, but nothing came out. Then, all of a sudden, she's choking and bringing up blood. I shouted to Jodie to call for an ambulance. I thought the tiredness and everything was down to grief. She could have been seriously ill all this time and I've not noticed.'

'This may all be down to grief, Craig. It affects people in so many different ways. You've said yourself how much she does for Riley. She's looking after him twenty-four hours a day. Then there's the house and Jodie and Keeley, and everything else. There's only so much a person can take before their body has had enough.'

'And you think that's what this is?' he asked, looking hopeful.

'I'm not a doctor, but it wouldn't surprise me if she doesn't just need a long break from things.'

Craig moved from the window and sat in the chair opposite Rory. 'Maybe we could go away for a while. Linda's always been reluctant to put Riley in respite care; this might make her see sense.'

Rory smiled at him placatingly.

The door opened and a tall woman with her hair falling out of a loosely tied ponytail came into the room. She was thin and wore black trousers and a blue and white striped shirt. The severe bags under her eyes aged her, as did her dry skin and drooped shoulders. A doctor in a busy A&E department was not a good place to work if you wanted to look after yourself.

'Mr Armitage?' She asked. There was a slight Welsh lilt to her voice that sounded calming.

Rory moved over for her to sit down. She leaned forward.

'I'm Doctor Megan Williams. I've been working on your wife since she was admitted. I'm afraid we were unable to control your wife's breathing. The levels of oxygen in her blood were far too low and she suffered respiratory failure. I'm so sorry.'

Craig looked at the doctor. His expression hadn't changed since she'd entered the room. 'Can I see her?'

The doctor looked at Rory then back to Craig. 'Mr Armitage, your wife has died.'

'Should I go home and get her an overnight bag or something?'

Rory stepped forward. He placed a hand on his solid arm. 'Craig, listen to me,' he said slowly. 'Linda didn't regain consciousness. There was nothing the doctors could do. She's died.'

'Died?'

'Yes.'

'But . . . no . . . She can't leave me. Last night she was talking about Keeley's funeral and what music we should have.'

'Craig . . .'

'There's this company that does coffins for children and you can have Disney prints put on them. We saw one that looked like a castle. She smiled. Linda smiled for the first time. She wanted Keeley to be given a funeral fit for a princess. She wouldn't just die like that. She wouldn't.'

A tear fell from his left eye. Then more followed.

'Oh my God! Oh Jesus Christ, no,' he collapsed into Rory who held him tightly and allowed him to sob and wail and scream into his shoulder.

Chapter 54

Ranjeet plunged into the dirty water of the River Sheaf. The rain was starting to die down, but the river was still raging. As soon as Ranjeet hit the water, he disappeared beneath the surface and didn't emerge.

Scott jumped on top of the van and scrambled to the wall.

'Don't even think of following him,' Christian shouted, his voice filled with rage.

Scott ignored his superior officer. 'Nat, get up here, bring your torch.'

Natasha hesitated for a second before following Scott. She slipped on the wet van and Scott had to pull her up to its roof. They leaned against the brick wall and shone their high-powered torches over the top into the angry waters below, searching for their colleagues.

'Ranjeet!' Scott shouted. It was no use. Against the sound of the breaking waves crashing against the wall, his cries were drowned out.

They shone their torches in every direction, but they couldn't find Ranjeet.

'Is that Ellen over there?' Natasha pointed.

'Yes.'

'Sir,' Natasha turned to DI Brady. 'Ellen's stuck on the other side and the water is rising. We need to get round there before she's swept away.'

'I'm on it,' he said, turning his back on them, his phone to his ear.

'Where the bloody hell is he?' Scott said through gritted teeth as he leaned as far as he could over the wall without falling in.

Hitting the water feet first, Ranjeet landed with a thud on the hard riverbed. His left ankle twisted and snapped. He opened his mouth to cry out in pain, but the water filled it before he could make a sound. Instinct caused him to swallow and he started to choke. He tried to breathe, but it was no use. He scrambled with his arms, flailing them up and down to try and get to the surface but his body was weakened as he ran out of oxygen. With his one good leg, he kicked hard and broke the surface of the water with a gasp. A blinding spotlight immediately caught him.

He coughed and his body panicked as it tried to take in lungfuls of air. He heard his name being called, but he couldn't isolate where the sound was coming from. It wasn't long before he realised he was moving. He was being swept away down river, and he was gaining speed.

Ranjeet's mind focussed as oxygen returned to his brain. He had a task to do. He needed to get to Ellen before it was too late. He tried to find something to grab hold of, but there was nothing there. No rocks, no branches, no trees, nothing. He wasn't in a river in the middle of the countryside with trees hanging over for him to grab on to; this was the Sheaf, running through the heart of Sheffield, surrounded by factories, warehouses, and abandoned buildings. He kicked harder and managed to get to the side of the river, his fingertips holding on to a broken off piece of brick in the river wall.

He looked up and saw a blurred image of Scott staring down at him from faraway upriver, shining a torch in his face. His mouth was moving, but he couldn't make out what he was saying. He seemed so distant. Had he moved or had Ranjeet drifted too far downstream to be able to make a rescue attempt without putting his own life in danger?

Scott had asked Natasha to find a rope from somewhere once Ranjeet had emerged from below the water and started drifting. They ran to the last van in the row of vehicles in the car park, tied the rope around the front bumper and threw the other end over the wall into the treacherous waters below. It didn't land anywhere near Ranjeet and Scott couldn't tell if he had even seen what they were trying to do. The rope started to drift. He pulled it out and tried to throw it closer to their stricken colleague again. This time, it landed within a few feet of Ranjeet and drifted towards him on the surface, but he didn't make any effort to grab hold of it.

'Come on Ranjeet, for fuck's sake,' Scott shouted.

'Maybe he's frightened of letting go of the wall.'

'He has no choice. He either grabs for the rope or he floats off downstream. We need to get closer,' Scott said.

'We can't get any closer.'

'Fuck. Ok, pull the rope out. We'll throw it again. Give him a few more seconds to find his bearings.' Scott curled up the wet rope in his hands. 'Hold on to me, Nat, I'm going to lean out as far as I can.'

'You can't lean any further without falling in. We can't have three of you in there.'

'Just . . . hold on to my legs or something.'

'Shit. I don't think I can get any traction, you're all wet.'

'We don't have any choice. Here, Nat, just do it.'

Scott leaned over the wall as far as he could go. He heard DI Brady shouting something from the safety of the ground but couldn't hear the exact words. From the tone of his voice, he wasn't happy with this plan. Three quarters of his body was hanging over. If he fell, he'd suffer the same fate as Ranjeet. He hoped Natasha had a good enough grip. With as much energy as he could muster, he lobbed the rope. It landed close to Ranjeet who leapt for it and grabbed it with both hands.

'Pull me back up,' Scott screamed.

He heard Natasha groan as she pulled her colleague back. He pushed himself off the wall and they both fell back on the roof of the van.

'Are you all right?' Natasha asked.

'I think I've just seen my whole life flash before my eyes.'

'Blimey, I bet that was boring,' she smiled, though her face looked frightened.

'Cheeky cow.'

Looking back over the wall, Ranjeet had tied the rope around him as best he could and started swimming against the surge. At first, he hardly moved, but soon he built up a momentum and headed for Ellen.

'Come on Ranjeet, you can do it,' Scott screamed, hoping the encouragement would help him to keep going. 'Nat, keep an eye on the rope. We don't want it coming undone.'

Ranjeet powered on through the raging torrent that was pummelling him from all sides. He swallowed more water. He could hardly see as he had to keep closing his eyes against the spray that hit him in the face. Every time he looked up, he didn't seem to be getting any closer to Ellen. He could hear the muffled cries of his colleagues, urging, spurring him on. Failure was not an option. To fail would mean death for Ellen and himself. He couldn't leave Kesinka without a husband and Hemant without a father. His failure would lead to so much sorrow and tragedy. He couldn't let those who were counting on him down.

He kicked against the water, swam hard against the tide. His limbs were tiring, his lungs were hurting with every breath and he could feel his heart beating faster to keep him going. How much longer would his body be able to take such a battering before it gave up?

He made it to the other side of the river and dug his fingers into the saturated bank where the concrete had long since crumbled away. He pulled himself further along. He could see Ellen. He was getting closer.

Above, a brilliant white torch light beamed down. He looked up and saw several officers waiting hopefully, their faces pictures of expectation and worry.

At last, he reached Ellen. He heard cheering, as he turned her over and looked into her pale, wet face. Her eyes were closed. He placed an ear against her chest but over the sound of nature, he couldn't hear a heartbeat.

A rope fell from above, hitting him on the head. He looked up. 'Tie this around her. We'll pull her up. Then we'll get you out.' Someone shouted.

Ranjeet was rapidly losing energy. It was a struggle to get the rope around Ellen's waist, but he managed it and gave the nod for the officers to pull her carefully up the embankment. She was safe, and he began to relax. He was spent. He leaned against the bridge where Ellen had come to rest. His breathing started to slow down. He'd been victorious. He was a hero. He smiled and closed his eyes.

Chapter 55

'You don't understand. Nobody would understand.'

Jodie was standing in the doorway to the kitchen. She was facing Matilda and Sian. Both hands were gripped tightly around the handle of the knife, her knuckles white, her hands shaking. Her wide eyes were filled with tears and determination.

'Jodie, we want to understand,' Matilda said. 'But this isn't helping anyone. Put the knife down, come and sit at the table, and we'll have a chat.'

'Do you think I'm stupid? As soon as I put the knife down, you'll lunge at me and arrest me.'

'We're not going to arrest you, Jodie. We've nothing to arrest you for. Look, I think you know something but you're afraid to tell us. Am I right?' Matilda asked.

Jodie's eyes darted from Matilda to Sian and back again. She nodded.

'Is it about Keeley? About what happened to her on Monday night?'

'This didn't start on Monday. It goes back years, long before you lot came along,' she said, almost quietly.

'Ok. Explain it to us.' Matilda made a show of sitting down at the table, as if they were all having a cosy chat together. Sian copied her.

Jodie remained by the door, but her grip on the knife began to lessen.

'It started after Riley was born. Mum couldn't cope. She didn't want him; do you know that? When she told us she was pregnant, Dad was over the moon. I could tell Mum wasn't. At night, they kept having arguments. Mum said she didn't want a third child, but Dad wanted a son. He was hoping for a little boy. When he was born, Mum took it hard. She got down, depressed. I had to step up and look after Keeley and clean the house and do the shopping. Then Riley got ill. He started having fits. Funny thing was, nobody ever saw these fits happen, only Mum.'

Matilda and Sian exchanged glances.

Jodie continued. 'The night he stopped breathing, Mum said she'd had a few drinks and slept through the night for the first time. That was the story she put out there to the doctors and the neighbours. It was a load of shit,' she spat. 'She drank practically every night. The night Riley stopped breathing, it wasn't because of a massive seizure, it was because Mum went into his room and shook him. She was seriously pissed. She picked him up out of his cot and started screaming at him and shaking him. It woke me up. Me and Dad ran to get her off him, but she was like a woman possessed. You should have heard some of the things she was saying about him. He was only a little baby.' Tears were streaming down Jodie's face. She was loosening her grip on the knife which was now pointing towards the floor.

'What happened?' Sian asked. Her face had paled upon hearing the story.

'Dad called for an ambulance. Riley was unconscious. He put Mum to bed and told me to make sure she didn't come out of the room. He went to the hospital with Riley and didn't come home until late the next day.'

'Where was Keeley while all this was going on?'

'She was asleep. She was such a heavy sleeper. I took her to school the next morning, told her Riley had had another fit and Dad had taken him to hospital. I tried to make things normal for her.

'When dad came home, he and Mum had the row of the century. He didn't shout, he didn't scream, but you could see in his face that he wanted to kill her. I've never seen him look like that before. He frightened me. He kept asking her why and she couldn't answer. Eventually, she said she hadn't wanted him. She couldn't love him. Then she started crying and didn't stop.'

Jodie lowered her arms. The knife, in her right hand, hung by her side.

'Everything changed when Riley came home,' she said. 'We all had to change. Mum was doing everything to make up for what she'd done. She gave up work and became Riley's full-time carer. Dad took on a second job and started raising money to adapt the house. I was never asked, but it was expected of me to do everything else – the cooking, the cleaning, looking after Keeley, taking her to school and bringing her home, and making sure her homework was done. She was allowed to continue being a child, but I wasn't.' She wiped away the tears with the back of her hand. 'Do you know what I did for my twelfth birthday?'

'What?'

'I was at school watching Keeley playing the recorder, badly, in the school band, because Dad was working, and Mum was here. I knew then that was what my life was going to be like.'

'Didn't you tell your parents you were doing too much?' Sian asked.

'I tried, but they made me feel guilty that I was moaning about nothing when Riley needed all the attention. I told Mum one time that he wouldn't need all this attention if she hadn't got pissed and tried to kill him.'

'What did she say to that?'

'She didn't. She slapped me. Hard.'

'Oh my God,' Sian looked disgusted.

'I kept quiet after that.'

'Jodie, do you know who abused Keeley?' Matilda asked.

She nodded. 'We'd just finished school for the summer holidays, and she came into my bedroom one night. She'd been crying. She said that Dad had been going into her room at night and getting into bed with her. He'd asked her to touch him and play with him and she didn't like it. The lying slut,' she seethed.

'What?' Sian asked, frowning. 'You think she was making it up?'

'Of course she was.'

'Why do you think that?'

'Because Dad loves me. Not her.'

The house fell silent. Matilda's mouth opened in shock.

'You mean, your dad was abusing you?' Sian asked.

'It wasn't abuse. He loves me. I love him.' For the first time, Jodie had a genuine look of happiness on her face.

'How long has this been going on for?' Sian asked.

'It started after the incident with Riley. He was upset. No, he was devastated. Mum slept in their room and Dad slept downstairs on the sofa. I used to hear him crying. I'd go down and sit with him, cuddle him. It made him feel better. We'd both fall sleep together. It was beautiful.'

'When did he first abuse you?'

'It wasn't fucking abuse!' Jodie screamed, pointing the knife at Sian. 'Stop calling it that.'

'Sorry. I'm sorry,' she held her hands up.

'Tell us what happened, Jodie,' Matilda said, calmly.

'You won't understand. Dad said nobody would ever understand.'

'Help us to understand. I know you want to tell us, Jodie. It's been burning up inside you, hasn't it?'

She nodded. 'I heard Dad crying one night. I think he'd been drinking. I went into his room and asked him what was wrong. He said he was angry at Mum, that he hated her. He didn't think he'd ever be able to forgive her for what she'd done. I said I didn't think I could either. He asked me to get into bed with him, to give him a cuddle. He held me. Then he kissed me on the lips. It felt amazing. He stopped and said I should go, but I stayed. We made love.'

'Oh my God,' Sian stood up and walked over to the window, turning her back on them. 'Jodie, he wasn't making love to you—'

'Sian, don't,' Matilda interrupted. 'Jodie, how long did this go on for?'

'A while,' she smiled coyly. 'Most nights we'd kiss and cuddle, or I'd . . . you know . . . but we saved the love making for special occasions. He said I was the only person he truly loved. I was the only one who understood him. He's right.'

Sian's face was thunderous. Matilda glanced across and could see she was seething and was only just managing to keep her emotions under control.

'Had it stopped before he turned his attention to Keeley?'

Jodie's face hardened. 'He said one night that we had to stop. He just came out with it from nowhere. I said we shouldn't as we loved each other and wanted to be together. I'm not naïve. I know people wouldn't understand us being together like a proper couple, but we could make it work.

'I didn't believe Keeley at first. I thought she was just saying it to get attention. She was always doing things for attention, like when she said Mr Page was watching her in the changing rooms. Why would he look at her? Anyway, one night, I stayed awake. I heard the creaking of the floorboards on the landing and went to have a look. There was Dad going into Keeley's room. He shut the door behind him. I went over and put my ear against it and listened. She was right. He was telling her exactly the same things he told me.' Jodie shook her head. Her face reddened in anger. 'She was always dressing up as a princess and skipping around the house and sitting on Dad's lap. She was flirting. She was encouraging him. How dare she steal him away from me?' she screamed. Her fingers were wrapped tightly around the handle of the knife.

'Jodie, you're not thinking clearly. Your mind has been warped,' Matilda said.

'No. It hasn't. Why would you say that? My dad loves me. I love him. That's all that matters now.'

'It's not love, Jodie,' Sian said. She turned from the window and went over to the fourteen-year-old. She grabbed her by the shoulders. 'He doesn't love you. He's never loved you. He's been using you for his own sick pleasure and he's tricked you into believing you've consented to this all along. He's manipulated you. It's what paedophiles do.'

Sian gasped. Her mouth fell open. She looked down and saw the carving knife sticking out of her stomach.

The room fell silent. Slowly, Matilda stood up and went around to their side of the table.

'Jodie,' she said quietly.

'Oh my God! What have I done?'

'Jodie, very carefully, I need you to stand up, let go of the knife, and step away.'

'I didn't mean to,' she said, not moving, keeping hold of the knife.

'I know you didn't.'

'It's when she called Dad a paedophile, it made me angry. He's not a paedophile.'

'It's ok. I know you're upset. I just need you to be calm,' Matilda said. She held her hand out beneath the knife, ready to replace Jodie's hold on it. 'Now, let go of the knife.'

'I'm sorry,' she said as tears ran down her face.

'I know you are. Everything's going to be all right.' Matilda looked at Sian whose face had started to pale.

'Oh my God, I've stabbed someone,' Jodie said, the delayed shock and panic setting in. 'I've stabbed her. Oh God. What do I do?'

'Jodie, calm down. I'm right here. I just need you to . . .'

Jodie pulled the knife out of Sian's stomach. Blood started to escape through the gash. Sian slapped a hand over the wound, but the blood poured through her fingers. Her legs gave way and she collapsed to the floor.

'Oh shit!' Matilda said. She ran to the dresser and grabbed a tea towel. She went back to Sian and dropped to her knees and applied pressure. 'Jodie, call for an ambulance.'

'I'm sorry. I'm so sorry,' Jodie cried. She'd jumped up from her chair and was standing at the back of the kitchen, glaring at her red hands. 'I didn't mean to. I'm so, so sorry.'

'Jodie, call for an ambulance right now,' Matilda shouted.

'Where's my dad? I want to see my dad. He'll know what to do. He always does.'

'Sian, I need you to relax and take slow deep breaths,' Matilda said. 'Everything is going to be all right.' She looked over her shoulder and saw Jodie rambling to herself while studying her bloody hands.

'Jesus!' Matilda fumbled in her pocket for her mobile. It slipped out of her hands a few times which were red with Sian's blood, but she managed to swipe it to unlock and dial 999. 'This is DCI Matilda Darke of South Yorkshire Police. I need an ambulance to Acorn Drive in Sheffield. I have an officer down. She's been—'

Matilda felt the cold steal of the blade against her neck.

'Drop the phone,' Jodie said. She leaned in close from behind. Matilda could feel her hot breath in her ear.

'Jodie, please . . .'

'Drop it. Now!'

Matilda did as she was told.

'Good. Now, I want you to take me to my dad.'

'I can't just leave Sian here like this. She'll die.'

'I don't care. I need to see my dad. Move!' She screamed.

'Go,' Sian struggled to say.

'I'm not leaving you,' Matilda said, a tear rolling down her cheek.

'Just go,' Sian said.

'Listen to her. We leave right now and there's a chance she'll live.'

Matilda hesitated. She proffered a sympathetic smile to Sian. 'Keep pressure on the wound. Hopefully, they'll trace the call, and someone will come out for you.'

Tears rolled down the sides of Sian's face. 'Matilda, tell Stuart . . .'

'I'm not telling him anything,' Matilda interrupted. 'You're going to be fine. You can tell him yourself.'

'Come on,' Jodie grabbed Matilda by the hair and pulled her away from Sian.

Matilda left the kitchen, taking one last look at Sian as she lay on the floor in a pool of her own blood. She hoped this wouldn't be the last time she saw her friend alive.

Chapter 56

'Craig, is there anything I can do for you?' Rory asked.

They were sitting in the relatives' room. The storm outside had abated, the rain wasn't as intense, and the room was silent. Rory had his arm around Craig who was slumped forward, his head on his chest.

Craig had stopped crying. The anger had drained out of him. He was numb. 'It's all over now,' he said quietly. 'We said some horrible things to each other over the years. I stopped loving her a long time ago.'

Rory hushed him. 'Don't, Craig. You're grieving. Don't say something you'll regret in the morning.'

'She wanted to have an abortion when she fell pregnant with Riley. I wouldn't let her. I kept going on about how everything would be fine. I didn't realise how close to the edge she already was.'

'Craig, come on, let's get you home. Jodie and Riley will be waiting for you. They'll need you right now.'

'I don't think I can face them.'

'You have to. I know it may sound heartless, but you need to be strong for them.'

Craig sat up and looked at Rory. He wiped his eyes. 'You're right.'

'You've done a great job bringing Jodie up. I'm sure she'll give you all the help and support you need.'

'She will. She's a good girl,' he smiled.

'Do you honestly think your dad is going to welcome you with open arms when he finds out what you've done?'

'He will. He loves me.'

'You're deluding yourself.'

'So you say.'

'Did you push Ellen Devonport over Heeley Bridge?'

It was a while before she nodded. 'I had no choice. She was trying to take my dad away from me. I saw the way she was with him, touching his arm, laughing at his jokes, tossing her hair back.'

Matilda was driving with Jodie in the backseat, sitting at an angle with the bloodied knife aimed at Matilda's stomach.

'You'll go to prison for the attempted murder of two detectives and your father will go to prison for sexual abuse. You'll never see him again.'

'You're wrong. I know exactly what to do. I've been making important decisions for years. I've paid bills. I've done the big shop. I've attended Keeley's parents' evenings at school when they couldn't. I took her on play dates and sat with other parents.'

Matilda drove carefully. Although the rain had stopped, the roads were still slippery, and some were flooded in places.

'So, what is this plan of yours then?'

'We'll just drive somewhere. We don't need possessions. We don't need things. It'll just be the two of us, together,' she said with a huge grin on her face.

'You've been groomed, Jodie. Can't you see that?'

'We can't help the people we fall in love with. We're not on this earth for a long time. When you find someone to love, someone who makes you happy, you should grab it with both hands and screw the world.'

Rory drove out of the hospital car park with Craig in the passenger seat. He was staring straight ahead out of the windscreen, not blinking, his face expressionless. Rory felt sorry for him. In the last week he'd lost his youngest daughter and now his wife. How was he going to break this news to Jodie? How was he going to cope as a single father working two jobs and Riley needing twenty-four-hour care?

'Do you have any other relatives who can help you?' Rory asked. His question went unanswered. 'Brothers or sisters? Your parents?' There was no reply.

Rory drove carefully and below the speed limit. He was in no rush to get Craig home. With the news he had to break to his children, it wouldn't matter if they took the long way home, to buy Craig more time to marshal his thoughts and try to find the right words to use.

Matilda drove along Stannington Road. Jodie was sitting back in her seat, Sian's blood drying on her hands, the knife held firmly, not letting go. Matilda looked across and tried to read her expression, to figure out what was going on inside her head, but there was nothing there. Jodie wasn't all to blame. She was the product of an abusive father who had convinced his daughter their relationship was one of pure love.

They drove in silence. The streets were empty, and a light rain had started to fall. Matilda racked her brain to think of something to stop Jodie and Craig from meeting. Craig would want to cover up his involvement in the abuse of his daughter. He would lie and twist the situation to make it seem like it was all in Jodie's head.

Ahead, she spotted a car coming towards them. She didn't dare risk flashing her headlights or sounding the horn in case Jodie lunged at her with the knife. The closer they got, Matilda was able to make out who was driving, it was Rory, and Craig was in the passenger seat. She didn't have time to think. She slammed her foot down on the accelerator, waiting until both cars were level then swung the steering wheel.

She knocked into Rory's car, forcing him off the road. Jodie must have sensed what Matilda was planning to do when the car sped up. She grabbed the steering wheel and pulled it the other way. They left the road, drove onto the saturated grass, smashed through a fence, and Matilda slammed the brakes on just in time before the car crashed into Stanwood Methodist Church.

Jodie banged her head on the side of the door. Concussed, she swung her right hand towards Matilda, aimlessly trying to stab her. Matilda reached out to stop her, grabbing the knife by the blade and cutting open her palm in the process. With her other hand, she slammed Jodie's wrist onto the dashboard, causing her to drop the knife. Matilda quickly picked it up, opened the driver's door, and fell out.

'What's going on? Matilda? Is that you?' Rory asked, running towards her.

'Rory, arrest him,' she shouted.

'What? Who?'

'Craig Armitage. Arrest him!'

'Why?' He asked, looking confused.

'For sexually abusing his daughters. Just arrest him.'

'Fucking hell,' Rory turned and ran back to the car. He opened the door, but Craig was nowhere to be seen.

Matilda went around to the passenger side, opened the door, and, with the handcuffs from her back pocket, she handcuffed Jodie to the handle above the door.

'Jodie Armitage, I'm arresting you for the attempted murders of Ellen Devonport and Sian Mills. You do not have to say anything, but it may harm your defence if you do not mention, when questioned, anything you later rely on in court. Do you understand?'

Jodie looked straight ahead at Matilda and smiled.

Chapter 57

Matilda spoke at speed as she tore her sleeve from her shirt and used it as a bandage around her bleeding palm. She told Rory to wait in the car with Jodie until back-up arrived. She commandeered his phone and asked him for the pass code. She was already dialling as she ran for his car.

Matilda called for an ambulance to go to Acorn Drive and was told one was already there, thank goodness. She called Christian and told him to put out an alert for Craig Armitage, then to send back-up to Rory somewhere on Stannington Road. He mentioned something about Ranjeet and Ellen, but Matilda had already hung up. She needed to get to Sian and see what condition she was in.

Acorn Drive was lit up with a sea of blue flashing lights. Neighbours were on their doorsteps in dressing downs, standing in their doorways to shelter from the rain, yet eager to see why the emergency services had come to the Armitage house for the second time in less than an hour.

Matilda pulled up on the garden. She could see a hive of activity in the house through the open front door. She jumped out of the car and ran straight into the house and the kitchen.

Sian was on the floor, unconscious. Surrounding her, a team of paramedics worked to stem the flow of blood.

'Sian? How is she?' Matilda asked anybody who would listen. She received a few glances, but nobody said anything. 'I'm DCI Darke from South Yorkshire Police. She's DS Sian Mills,' she barked.

'She's unconscious, but stable,' a paramedic said, standing up. She was a small woman with a thin face but looked chubby beneath the layers of uniform she was wearing. 'She's got a strong heartbeat, but she's lost a great deal of blood. We're trying to stabilise the wound before we transport her to hospital. Are you hurt?' She asked looking down at Matilda's hand and the blood seeping through the makeshift bandage.

'It's nothing.'

'Stab wound?' She asked.

'Yes.'

'I want you to come with us in the ambulance. We'll get you patched up.'

'Will she be all right?' Matilda asked, not taking her eyes from her stricken colleague. She could feel the tears welling up in her eyes.

'Providing she remains stable and we get her to hospital quickly, she should be fine. The knife wounds don't appear to have struck any major arteries or organs. She's incredibly lucky.'

Matilda visibly relaxed. 'She really is.'

'Come and sit down.'

The paramedic led Matilda to a seat next to the table.

'Oh my God, Riley,' Matilda remembered.

'Sorry?'

'Riley. Where is he?'

'Who's Riley?'

Matilda stood up and headed for his bedroom. The door was closed. She didn't want to open it for fear of what had happened to him.

'Who's in there?' The paramedic asked.

'A four-year-old boy. He's severely disabled.'

Matilda placed a hand on the door handle and pushed it down. She opened the door and stepped into the darkness of the room. She couldn't hear any breathing. There was no ambient lighting or mellowing music playing. She feared the worse.

She scrambled on the wall next to the door for the light switch and flicked the main light on. The room lit up in a brilliant white and both women squinted. The bed in the corner of the room had the side railings raised to stop Riley from rolling out of bed while he slept. They couldn't see from the doorway whether he was in there or not. Tentatively, Matilda stepped closer. It seemed to take an age to walk less than three feet to the bed. All the while, Matilda listened for any sound of the young boy sleeping, gurgling, snoring.

She took a deep breath and looked inside. Riley lay motion-less on the mattress. His face was pale, his eyes wide open, his lips blue.

Matilda felt herself being pushed aside as the paramedic stepped forward and began the futile task of attempting to revive him. Matilda couldn't take her eyes from the poor boy. There was something otherworldly about looking into the eyes of a dead child. It was an image Matilda would never forget.

'I'm so sorry,' she said to herself as warm tears pricked her eyes.

Chapter 58

In the ambulance to the Northern General Hospital, Sian's heartbeat began to slow and she went into ventricular fibrillation as the ambulance pulled into the bay outside A&E. There was nothing Matilda could do but watch as she was rushed into theatre.

Matilda stood in the entrance, watching the doors close on her colleague and friend. She couldn't lose Sian. She was one of the good guys.

'Matilda, what are you doing here?' Christian came out of nowhere, making her jump. He saw her hand hastily wrapped in a makeshift bandage. 'What happened to you?'

'Long story. Sian's been stabbed.'

'What?'

Matilda couldn't speak as tears began to fall down her face. Christian placed his arm around her shoulders and led her to the waiting area. Between sobs, she filled him in on everything that had happened at Acorn Drive.

'I should call Stuart. He should be here with Sian.'

'I'll do that.'

Matilda nodded and fell silent. 'Shit, how's Ellen?'

'Concussed. She also inhaled a great deal of dirty water. They're going to keep her in for observation. She'll live, that's the main thing.'

'And Ranjeet?'

'He's fine. He's had to have his stomach pumped and he's broken his ankle. Kesinka's with him reading him the riot act.'

Matilda briefly smiled. 'I'm not surprised.'

'He did well. They all did. Scott and Natasha. They should get a commendation for this.'

'I'll have a word with the ACC when . . . oh my God, I haven't spoken to her for ages. I don't know how Arthur is. What time is it?'

He looked at his watch. 'Just coming up to midnight.'

'Is it still Saturday?'

'For a few more minutes, yes.'

'It's been a long day.'

'Let's go and get your hand seen too. You're starting to drip.'

'I feel sick.'

'That's what happens when you lose blood. Come on.'

Matilda's wound had been cleaned up. She'd been given a tetanus injection and something for the pain. She lay back on the bed, her palm facing upwards waiting for it to be dressed. She closed her eyes. She was shattered and wanted to go to sleep. Everything was a mess. She'd assumed Craig had been abusing Keeley but hadn't had the evidence to charge him. She'd had no idea how deep his vile vindictiveness ran. Poor Jodie. She'd been used, brainwashed into thinking she was in a loving relationship. Had the signs been there? The more Matilda thought about it, yes, they had been. Why hadn't she seen it?

The curtain was pushed back and Adele stepped into the cubicle.

'I've put in a request with Sheffield Teaching Hospitals to have one of these cubicles named in your honour.'

Matilda looked up and smiled dopily. 'Injured in the line of duty.'

'You shouldn't be, though. You're supposed to send the younger ones out to do the leg work. You're supposed to be behind a desk pulling your hair out about overtime and arrest targets.'

'That sounds dull.'

'Safer than getting stabbed,' she said, looking closely at her injury. 'That doesn't look too bad. I don't think it will affect you holding a glass of wine.'

'Can you check up on how Sian's doing?'

'She's in ICU. Her stomach wall was ruptured. She's lost a great deal of blood. The next twenty-four hours will be critical.'

'Jesus. Is Stuart here?'

'Yes. He and the kids are in the relatives' room.'

'I should go and see them,' Matilda said, trying to climb off the bed.

'Don't even think about it,' Adele pushed her back down. It didn't take much effort. 'Listen, do you want me to call Daniel?'

'What for?'

'To tell him what's happened.'

Matilda thought for a moment. 'No. Don't call him.'

'He'll be concerned.'

'I know. That's why I don't want you to call him.'

The curtain was pulled back again and a nurse stepped in. 'Right then, Mrs Darke, time to get your wound dressed then you can go home.'

'I'll wait outside,' Adele said.

'Is she your sister? She can wait if she wants.'

'No. We're not sisters,' Adele said.

'No. She's my lesbian life partner,' Matilda said with a grin.

Chapter 59

Sunday 16th September 2018

Matilda sat at her desk with a forlorn expression on her face. She had hardly slept, despite the number of pain-killers she'd taken for her hand, and the two glasses of wine she had been advised against drinking when she arrived home. Wide awake at seven o'clock, she'd quickly showered (with her hand wrapped in a plastic bag) and headed for South Yorkshire Police HQ. Jodie Armitage was being interviewed this morning and Matilda had plenty more questions for her to answer. What had happened to Keeley on Monday night? How had Riley died? What had caused Linda's illness? It was far too much of a coincidence for Linda and Riley to have died so close together for it to be natural causes.

There was no doubt in Matilda's mind that Jodie had murdered her little sister. In her warped and twisted mind, Jodie would have seen that Craig was trying to replace Jodie as his "lover" with Keeley and she would have done everything in her power to stop that from happening, even if that meant killing a defenceless child.

* * *

Matilda Darke sat in the observation room overlooking interview room one. Next to her was DC Finn Cotton.

'How's the hand?' he asked.

'It's fine, thank you,' she smiled.

'Is there any news on DS Mills?'

'She's had a comfortable night, apparently; whatever that's supposed to mean.'

The door in the interview room opened and Jodie Armitage was led in. She was wearing a grey jogging suit which was a size too big for her. Her hair was pulled back firmly in a ponytail. She walked with her head down and shoulders hunched. She was shown where to sit by a uniformed officer. An appropriate adult sat next to her. They didn't speak to each other.

Matilda observed Jodie's behaviour. Her eyes were red with heavy bags beneath them following a night of crying and very little sleep. She looked scared and played with her fingers on her lap.

DCs Scott Andrews and Rory Fleming entered. They started the recording of the interview and stated who was present.

'Finn, is there any word on Craig Armitage yet?' Matilda asked while the formalities were taking place.

'No. Uniformed officers have been camped outside the house all night and he hasn't returned. DI Brady's doing the round with his family and anyone who might know where he is.'

'Jodie, tell us about the events of last Monday evening,' Scott asked, leaning on the table with his pen poised over a blank pad.

It was a while before Jodie answered. 'What do you want to know?' Her voice was quiet, hardly above a whisper.

'What happened when you picked Keeley up after school and went to the Co-op on Oldfield Drive?'

'I bought Keeley an ice cream as it was a hot day. She hadn't finished it by the time we reached the Co-op, so I told her to wait for me outside. I told her not to move and not to talk to people she didn't know.'

'How long were you in the Co-op for?' Scott asked.

'I don't know. Five, maybe ten minutes. Not long.'

'And when you came out, she'd gone?'

Jodie nodded. 'I thought she might have gone on home without me. I was annoyed because I'd got a lot of shopping and could have done with some help carrying it. I managed to get it home without dropping anything though.'

'Was Keeley there when you arrived home?'

'No. Mum said she hadn't come home.'

'So then what happened?'

'I went out to look for her.'

'Where did you look?'

'I walked back the way I came home. I asked people I knew if they'd seen her. They said they hadn't. I went into the park, too, but she wasn't there.'

'She's lying,' Matilda said.

'What makes you think that?' Finn asked.

'She's refusing to look Scott in the eye. Look,' she said, pointing to the video monitor that was showing Jodie's face. 'Her eyes are all over the place.'

'Do you think she's covering for her father?'

Matilda left the question unanswered.

'How long did you stay looking for her?' Scott asked.

'I don't know.'

'And what happened when you returned home?'

'Mum was crying. The woman from next door was round. She said Mum had received a phone call saying Keeley had been . . . she'd been . . .' Her words were lost to the tears and she lowered her head to her chest.

'She's lying. She's fucking lying,' Matilda kicked a wastepaper basket in the HMET suite which toppled over and spilt its load. 'She lured her sister to Stows Wood and she killed her.'

The interview hadn't lasted ten minutes without Jodie being unable to talk through her tears. The appropriate adult had requested a break.

'We don't know that's what happened,' Finn said.

'And if it did, she's not going to admit that, not without evidence,' Rory said.

'Somebody must have seen her. I want house-to-house enquiries on every route possible from the Co-op to the woods. All we need is one person to say they saw Jodie and Keeley together and we've got her. Finn, bring up the CCTV footage from the Co-op again.'

The lights were lowered, and the screen pulled down from the ceiling. They all stood around watching as the silent film began. It showed Jodie walking to the entrance with Keeley behind, licking her ice cream. Jodie turned and waited for her sister to catch up. She stood her by the door, squatted down to her height, and spoke to her before standing back up and entering the Co-op.

'Rewind it,' Matilda barked.

The video played out for a second time.

'Stop,' she called out. 'Rewind and play it from when Jodie squats down in front of Keeley. There. Pause. Can you zoom in on Jodie?'

'Yes. Hang on.'

'There. Look.' Matilda went over to the screen and pointed. 'Jodie is looking directly up to the camera. She knew they'd be caught on CCTV. She wanted this to be the last point Keeley was seen alive, so it looks like she's playing the saintly sister.'

'Can't we get a lip reader to have a look, see if they can find out what Jodie's saying to her?' Scott suggested.

'We can try, but the quality of the footage isn't great.'

'She knew what she was doing from the start. What a manipulative bitch,' Matilda said, fuming in frustration. *Why didn't you spot this before? It's so obvious*.

'Where do we go from here?'

'We need to keep interviewing her. There'll be holes in her story, there has to be. Also, I want the house stripped. I want the whole place torn apart and every computer, tablet and mobile phone analysed.'

'Forensics have been through them all.'

'Then get them to check again. Come on, break time's over. Get her back in that interview room and tell the appropriate adult to keep her mouth shut. I decide when she needs to rest.' Matilda stormed out of the HMET suite but had to stop suddenly as she felt light-headed. *Bloody medication*.

'Jodie, tell us about the relationship you have with your father,' Scott said as the interview resumed.

Jodie took a tissue out of her pocket and dabbed at her eyes. She sniffled. 'I love my daddy. He trusts me to look after Keeley and Riley, and Mum when she's ill.'

'That's a lot of responsibility for someone your age.'

'I don't mind.'

'Jodie.' Scott leaned forward. 'After Keeley was found, we ran some tests and discovered she'd been sexually abused. We've spoken to a lot of people who knew her, and we think your dad may have been responsible. Can you tell us anything about that?'

She nodded and wiped her eyes again. 'Daddy used to abuse me. He did it for years. He stopped when I started with my period. I didn't know he was abusing Keeley too. I just thought he'd stop.'

'The lying bitch,' Matilda seethed in the observation room.

'Did you tell anyone about the abuse?'

'No. Daddy said if I told anyone he'd kill me and Keeley and Riley. I didn't want him to hurt them.' She choked on her tears and put her head down to her chest. 'But he did anyway, didn't he?' She looked up at Scott with big, tear-filled eyes.

'Are you saying your father killed your family?'

'He must have done. He would probably have killed me next,' she cried and wiped her eyes again.

'Jodie,' Rory leaned forward. 'How do you explain what happened at your house last night when you stabbed DS Sian Mills?'

'Oh God. I don't know what came over me. I'm so, so sorry. Is she going to be all right?' Her words were barely audible over her tears.

'We think so.'

'Daddy kept telling me that if I told anyone what he'd done to me, he'd kill me and that I should stop anyone who questioned me about him because he'd end up in prison and Riley would be put away in a care centre because Mum wouldn't be able to cope on her own. I was so scared DS Mills and that other one were going to take Riley away.'

'Jesus Christ,' Matilda uttered. 'She should get an Oscar for this performance.'

'What are we going to do?' Finn asked.

Matilda remained quiet as she chewed her nails. 'Until her father turns up, there's not a damn thing we can do. It's her word against mine.'

Chapter 60

Three people were dead, murdered, Matilda assumed, by Jodie Armitage, and the only thing she could charge her with was the stabbing of DS Sian Mills. She kicked open the door to the HMET suite in frustration and charged to her office. Her face was red with anger. The Mercer case in November could collapse and the killer get away with four deaths. She was not going to allow someone else to get away with murder. There had to be some evidence of Jodie committing her crimes.

Matilda looked out of her window at the uninspiring view of Sheffield's grey and unimaginative buildings.

'Penny for your thoughts?' Christian asked from the doorway.

'I don't think they're worth that much,' she said without turning around. She could see Christian's reflection through the window.

'Jodie's certainly given this a great deal of thought, hasn't she?' he said, sitting down.

'She's a liar, a manipulator, a murderer, and a psychopath, and she's playing the part brilliantly.'

'She'll have made a mistake. They always do.'

'Only in crime dramas when the writer's looking for an easy way out. I doubt Jodie's made a single error. Craig, on the other hand, he may have done.'

'What do you mean?'

'Craig has managed to convince his daughter that they're in love,' Matilda said, going over to her desk and sitting down. 'He's been able to keep that going for many years. Now, when you're in love with someone, and it's an intense and passionate affair, what do you do?'

'Please don't tell me you're asking for positions.'

'No. But, to keep her quiet, Craig will have bought Jodie treats. The neighbours have said that they've seen Jodie in designer coats despite them having to raise money for Riley's care. He'll have been buying her silence with presents.'

'But even if we find jewellery and designer gear in her bedroom, she could say they were Christmas and birthday presents. It's not evidence.'

'No, but love letters are. Don't forget, they'll have had to keep what they're doing a secret from everyone. They won't always have been able to have private time alone, so what better than sending each other illicit texts or emails.' She was clutching at straws, she knew that, but there was nothing else to go on.

'We've been through every device in the house: phones, tablets, laptops. We'd have found them.'

'Every device that we know about. Like I said, she's a manipulator, a liar, a psychopath; she's not going to leave a mobile with sexual messages from her father on her bedside table, is she? She'll have hidden it.'

'Where?'

'I don't know. But I want that house torn apart. I want the floorboards lifted. I want false walls taken down. I want the garden dug up if necessary.'

'We can't do that without a warrant.'

'We're searching for Craig who we suspect of murder. We

need to find him. We have every right to be in that house. I know it's Sunday, but I don't give a toss about overtime. Get Scott, Rory, and Finn and pull that fucking house down if you have to.' Matilda's voice grew louder with every word as anger and frustration took over her.

A fleet of police cars, marked and unmarked, drove at speed into Acorn Drive. They pulled up outside the Armitage house, and, led by DI Christian Brady, they went inside to begin dismantling it from the floorboards upwards.

The search of the house began in Jodie's bedroom. As a great manipulator, she wouldn't have kept anything incriminating so close, but if she believed she was in love with her father, surely she would have wanted something personal to hand, to hold, feel, smell, in bed at night. That was the assumption Christian was working on, which was why he sent the team upstairs.

Wearing full scene-of-crime suits, Rory and Finn led the team by searching through the chest of drawers, taking them all out of the pine unit, before removing the chest itself to look behind it. They did the same with the wardrobe and the desk. They emptied the drawers in the single divan bed and searched through every pocket in every item of clothing, all to no avail.

'There's nothing here,' Rory said, slightly out of breath.

'Take everything out of the room and pull the carpet up,' Christian said.

'Really?' Rory frowned.

'Really.'

'But say if she has hidden something under the carpet beneath the wardrobe, how is she going to have been able to get access to it with something so heavy on top?'

'It might not be under the wardrobe. And if it is, maybe there's a tunnel she's able to put her arm through to get to it. We're dealing with a complete psychopath here, Rory. Everything out, carpet up, floorboards up. Do it,' he said firmly and stood back as Rory and Finn took the strain of the wardrobe.

Christian stepped out onto the landing to give them room. He looked across the hallway and saw Scott in Keeley's room. He was tentatively looking in drawers and cupboards.

'Scott, I need you to be more thorough than that,' the DI said. 'You need to pull this place apart, piece by piece.'

Scott looked up. His eyes were red. 'It's the first time I've been in this room. Have you seen some of her things? She was just a child, nine years old. She watched *Frozen* and drew pictures. Why did he have to . . .?' he trailed off.

'I've no idea, Scott. Some people are pure evil. Look, I've been going through Ellen Devonport's daily reports that she emailed to Matilda. She mentioned she saw Craig in the living room repairing the floorboards the morning after Keeley went missing. It could be innocent, but maybe he wasn't repairing them. Maybe he was hiding something. Pop down and have a look.'

Scott smiled. He knew DI Brady was allowing him an easier task than rooting through a dead child's belongings. 'Thanks, boss,' he said. He couldn't leave the room fast enough.

Downstairs in the living room, Scott dragged the coffee table to one side, kicked up the rug and bent down to try to raise the carpet from in front of the window. A quick jimmy with a Stanley knife and the carpet came away with ease. Putting on a pair of blue latex gloves, he pressed on the boards to see if any were loose.

'Sir?' he called out over his shoulder.

DI Brady appeared in the doorway. 'Found something?'

'I'm not sure. I thought you might want to be here when I

lift these up, just in case. The three boards in front of the window aren't secured.'

'Go on.'

Scott lifted the boards and looked down into the dark and grime beneath the house. He turned on a pen torch he took from his pocket and pointed the light into the hole. He dug around aimlessly until his hand caught on something. He turned to Christian and smiled.

'What have you got?'

Scott pulled out a plastic zip-lock bag, inside of which were three iPhone 4s.

'Bingo,' Christian said with a grin.

The phones were protected by either a PIN or a fingerprint. Without Craig Armitage, they'd be useless.

Hillsborough Park was virtually empty. The storm last night had left the ground saturated and only the hardiest of joggers and dog walkers had decided to come out.

Leslie Cox was on the wrong side of sixty. A recent heart scare had forced her to re-evaluate her lifestyle. She'd ditched the chips, the chocolate, the crisps and the fried food and adopted a vegetarian diet. She went swimming twice a week, had joined a walking club which met twice a month and at the weekends she went for a light jog in the park near her home. In the last six months she'd lost three stone in weight and had never felt healthier. With Bonnie Tyler singing loudly in her ears, she set off at a brisk pace, focussing on her breathing. She ran past the playground, turned right at the pond and felt the coolness of the air as she ran under the oaks and the birches and out of the sunlight. She looked up, saw a man hanging from a tree, and screamed so loudly she scared the birds from the trees.

Chapter 61

Matilda stood back from the hive of activity and watched as Craig Armitage was cut down. She had been hoping he would have turned up somewhere and confessed, chapter and verse, to abusing his daughters. At the back of her mind, she always knew it would end like this. Abusers were cowards; they targeted the vulnerable members of society to exert power over them, but when faced with the responsibility of their actions, they took the easy way out. Craig wouldn't have coped in prison, especially when it was revealed he had raped two of his three children. She wondered what had gone through his mind as he tied a rope around his neck and jumped from the branch. Matilda blinked. She realised she didn't care what he'd been thinking. His actions had led to his daughter killing her mother, little sister, and brother. He had destroyed his whole family.

'Are you all right?' Adele asked, walking towards her and pulling her gloves off.

'Not really.'

'You wanted him alive, didn't you?'

'I want all of them alive. People should face justice for their actions. He should have rotted in prison for the rest of his life. I suppose it's too much to ask that there's a note in his pocket admitting everything.'

'We haven't found anything. If it's any comfort, it wasn't a quick death. There's no broken hyoid bone. His fingernails are torn and there are scratches around the neck. He'll have strangled himself and every instinct in his body would have been telling him to get the rope off, but he couldn't.'

'It might be a comfort to me, but what about poor Keeley and Riley?' she asked, turning and walking away.

Adele followed. 'We've sent samples from Linda Armitage off to be tested – blood and stomach contents. They'll take a couple of weeks to come back.'

'Your new gadget worked?'

'Of course,' she said with a hint of a smile. 'Riley died from asphyxiation. There was a piece of food lodged in his throat.'

'Accidental?'

'I don't know. Was he able to feed himself?'

'No.'

'Then I doubt it. Whoever fed him will have known how mashed up his food needed to be. On its own it could have looked like an accident, but when you take everything else into account, it was obviously murder. A clumsy attempt at a natural death.'

Matilda shook her head. 'What threat did Riley pose, for crying out loud? He was four years old and severely disabled. Even if he had witnessed something he wouldn't have been able to tell anyone. Why the fuck did he have to die?' She turned and walked away, her heavy shoes squelching on the sodden ground.

'Are you sure you're all right?' Adele asked, following and placing a hand on Matilda's shoulder.

'I don't know.'

'You shouldn't have come in today.'

'I need to see this through.'

'You are not to blame for any of this. You were never going to find Keeley alive.'

'I know. It's just . . .'

'Carl Meagan?'

Matilda nodded. 'I'm haunted by him every single day,' she said, choking on her tears.

Adele pulled Matilda into an embrace and held her tight while the DCI cried on her shoulder. For the first time since returning to work following the death of her husband, she didn't care if anyone saw her crying.

Chapter 62

Scott Andrews tentatively pushed open the doors to the mortuary and stepped inside. He felt the chill straight away and shuddered. It wasn't the cold; it was the thought of all those dead bodies stacked up in the fridges. He couldn't understand how someone as warm, kind and funny as Adele could spend her working days elbow deep in organs and stomach contents.

He walked slowly down the corridor. There was nobody about and he was hoping he'd had a wasted journey and would have to return to the station with his task incomplete.

'Jesus, you scared the life out of me,' Lucy Dauman said as she entered the corridor from a side room. She tucked her blonde hair behind her ear.

'Sorry Lucy. Is Adele around?'

'Yes. She's just washing up. Anything wrong?'

'No. Why?'

'You've got the look of someone who's been caught with their hand in the till.'

'Oh. I'm fine.'

'Ok,' she smiled.

Adele smelled of soap and perfume. She was sitting at her desk peeling a satsuma and leaning in close to her computer screen, reading intently. She caught something moving out of the corner of her eyes and looked up.

'Hello Scott. Have you come to ask for my son's hand in marriage?'

'Marriage?' he asked, startled. His eyes widened. He even took a step back. 'No. No. Nothing like that. No.'

'Calm down, Scott, I'm only teasing,' she smiled. 'What can I do for you?'

'I'm afraid I need your help with Craig Armitage.'

The only way to unlock the three phones found beneath the living room floor was by using his fingerprint on the home button. Unfortunately, as Craig was dead, his fingers would need bringing up to body temperature in order for them to work to unlock the phone.

Craig was wheeled out of the fridge and Adele handed Scott a pair of latex gloves.

He stood holding all three phones in his shaking hands.

'You want *me* to do it?'

'*You're* the one who wants the phones unlocked,' Adele grinned.

'What do I do?'

'You take his finger, wrap your hand around it, and wait until it warms up,' she said in a mock tone as if talking to a five-year-old.

'Which finger?' he asked, glaring down at the blue hand with a look of revulsion on his pale face.

'I don't know. Shall we ask him?'

'You're enjoying this, aren't you?'

'Just a tad.'

'You're a ghoul, do you know that?'

'Oh yes,' she smiled. 'Well, come on, get on with it. Craig

Armitage might not have anything else to do today, but I certainly have.'

Scott hated dead bodies. He hated gruesome crime scenes and he would sell his own mother to get out of attending a post-mortem. He swallowed hard, took a deep breath and stepped forward. He put two of the phones on the side of the trolley, held one in his hand, and wrapped his other hand around Craig's solid cold thumb.

'Oh my God,' he said quietly.

'I think he likes that,' Adele said.

'What?'

'Look, he's smiling.'

'Fucking hell!' Scott screamed and jumped to the other side of the room, much to the joy of Adele and Lucy who were bent double laughing.

Once the phones were unlocked, Scott changed the settings so they were permanently unlocked, then quickly left the mortuary. He didn't even say goodbye to Adele and Lucy who he thought he could still hear giggling from Adele's office.

In the car, he took one of the phones out of the evidence bag and scrolled through it. There were very few numbers stored in the phone book and the one identified as 'J' he guessed to be Jodie's number. There was nothing in the messages app either; all had been erased. That wasn't a problem; forensics would always retrieve them. Craig had WhatsApp downloaded. There was only one conversation listed, but there was no name attached. He opened it and scrolled up. The conversation had been going on for years by the look of the number of messages. When he came to a photo, he stopped scrolling. The picture was a selfie Craig had taken of himself at the wheel of his van. He was smiling. It was an innocent enough photo. Scott pressed 'All Media' and every photo sent to and from this person came up.

What he saw was worse than anything he'd seen at a post-mortem.

Chapter 63

'DCI Darke!'

Matilda was in the kitchen of the Armitage house in Acorn Drive helping herself to a glass of water in order to take a couple of painkillers. The last time she was here, Sian was lying in a pool of blood on the floor. The smudge of drying blood was still there.

At the sound of her name being called, she put the glass down and went to the bottom of the stairs. She looked up and saw Rory looking down at her.

'We've found something.'

Jodie's room was a shell. Everything had been taken out and put in other rooms or abandoned on the landing. Matilda looked at the walls: posters of *Stranger Things*, Harry Styles, and Thor with his impressive arms. This was the bedroom of a normal fourteen-year-old. Teddy bears had rested on shelves, Harry Potter books were neatly in order, a dream catcher dangled from the handle on the window. Appearances were deceptive. The person who slept in here was no normal fourteen-year-old.

There was a large hole in the floor where floorboards had been taken up beneath the window. Matilda stepped forward.

'The board directly under the window was loose. As was the carpet in this area,' Christian said. 'Look what we found.'

Matilda peered forward and into the blackness. Lying in the framework of the house among the dust and insulation was an iPhone 4S.

Matilda closed her eyes and sighed with relief. 'Get it bagged up and sent to that strange bloke in tech. I want it tested for prints and everything downloaded,' she said calmly before turning and leaving the room.

Visiting hours at the Northern General Hospital had ended more than two hours ago but Adele and Matilda, being familiar faces among the medical staff, were allowed a late-night visit.

Sian was in a side room. Sitting by the bed, keeping an all-night vigil, was her husband. Stuart was unshaven, his hair unkempt, and his eyes were red from crying. He looked up when he heard the door opening.

'How is she?' Matilda asked quietly.

'They managed to repair her stomach. She's had a blood transfusion and she's heavily sedated. The doctor said she should make a full recovery.'

Matilda and Adele visibly relaxed.

'Oh, that's wonderful news. How are you?' Matilda asked, placing an arm around his shoulders.

He swallowed hard and it was several seconds before he was able to talk. 'I thought I was going to lose her.'

'Before her big party? No way,' Matilda said with a hint of humour. 'It'll take more than a knife wound to stop her being the centre of attention.'

'Are you bad mouthing me, Matilda?' Sian said almost inaudibly from her bed. Her eyes were closed as she spoke. She turned her head slowly to face her visitors and carefully opened her eyes.

'Bloody hell, I can't even talk about you when you're in a coma.'

Stuart jumped up from the hard plastic seat and leaned over his wife, taking her hand in his and squeezing hard.

'How are you?' he asked quietly.

'Numb,' she replied. 'Am I going to be all right?'

Adele looked up from the chart at the bottom of the bed she was reading. 'It says here you're already showing signs of malingering and milking your injury to get attention,' she said with a grin.

Sian smiled painfully.

'I thought I'd lost you,' Stuart said through tears.

'Not a chance,' she whispered.

'Look, we'll get off,' Matilda said. 'Sian, I'll come and see you tomorrow at some point.'

'Jodie?' she asked.

'Just concentrate on getting better. I'll fill you in when you're more lucid. Stuart, ring me if you need anything,' she said, placing a hand on his broad shoulder.

'Thank you.'

'They're a lovely couple,' Adele said as she and Matilda slowly walked down the quiet corridor.

'I know. It's almost sickening how happy they still are after twenty-five years of marriage.'

'I wonder what their secret is.'

'Sian said it was separate bathrooms.'

Adele laughed. 'Are there any more of your colleagues you'd like to see while you're here?'

'They'll be sleeping now,' Matilda said, looking at her watch. 'Kesinka said Ranjeet should be allowed home tomorrow and they're keeping an eye on Ellen. They want to run a few more scans on her head.'

'I'm so glad I don't work on your team,' Adele said, putting her arm through Matilda's. 'There's always at least one of you taking up a hospital bed.'

'I'm not sure if we're dedicated or stupid.'

They both looked at each other. 'Stupid,' they said together, laughed, then headed for the exit.

Matilda's phone started to vibrate in her pocket.

'DCI Darke? It's Freddie Whishaw from forensics here.'

'What can I do for you?'

'I'm sorry to call you so late, but I was told the iPhone that was brought in was urgent. I've found something I thought you'd want to know about now rather than wait until morning to hear.'

'I'll be right there.'

'Right where? It's not twenty-four hours since you were in this hospital. You should be resting, too,' Adele chastised.

'I've had a called from forensics; something's come up.'

'Can't it wait until tomorrow?'

'Something tells me it can't. Do you mind making your own way home?'

'Story of my life,' she muttered.

Chapter 64

There was a change in atmosphere at South Yorkshire Police HQ. Matilda felt it the moment she opened the door and walked in. People were subdued, walking along corridors with their heads down, talking in hushed tones, falling completely silent when anyone approached them. As Matilda approached the HMET suite and saw several members of her team hunched over newspapers at their desks, she realised why. Danny Hanson had written the story about Aaron Connolly. She immediately felt sorry for the detective sergeant she had known, respected, and admired for years. There was nothing she could have done about the story getting out. She pushed open the glass doors and walked in.

'Is this true?' Rory said, looking up.

'I'm afraid so.'

'I can't believe it. I always thought he and Katrina were so happy.'

'Let me give you some advice about men, Rory, that perhaps your mum didn't tell you when you were growing up. They have two brains. One inside their head, and the other in their pants. The one in their pants often talks louder than the one in their head. Unfortunately, listening to that one gets them into a whole lot of trouble.' She patted him on the back as she headed for her office.

'Is he off the team?' Rory called after her.

She stopped and looked back. Others were looking at her for the answer. She nodded. 'Look, Aaron is a great guy and a brilliant detective. There's no reason why he shouldn't continue in his career. I hope this so-called news story blows over quickly. I also hope Aaron and Katrina are able to sort out their differences. In the meantime, Aaron is still our colleague. If I hear any jokes, snide remarks, or see any evidence of you ostracising Aaron, you'll have me to answer to. Is that clear?' she said, addressing the whole room. There were slight nods of ascent. 'Good. Now, we all have work to do and we're a few members down. So, put those in the bin where they belong and do what you're paid to do. Christian, a word.'

Christian closed his newspaper and slipped it into his drawer. He'd take it home for Jennifer to read later. She'd met Aaron and Katrina a few times and liked them. She'd be devastated.

'I'd ask if you had a good weekend, but we didn't really have one, did we?' Christian said, entering her office and closing the door behind him.

'Not really.'

'So much for cutting back on overtime.'

'I know. Valerie's going to kill me when she comes back.'

'Any news on when that will be?'

'No. I'll give her a call later. Now, late last night, I had a call from forensics. They've been through the three phones and the one found under Jodie's bedroom floorboards. I want you to interview her with me.'

'Oh. Why?'

'Because she's a manipulator and I don't want her getting her claws into an inexperienced DC. When she knows she's up against a DCI and a DI, hopefully she'll crumble.'

'I wouldn't have thought she was the type to crumble.'

'She will be when she finds out what I know.'

In interview room one, with Finn and Rory in the observation room, Jodie was sitting at the table with her solicitor next to her and an appropriate adult to one side, keeping an eye on proceedings and making sure Jodie wasn't too distressed by the questioning.

Jodie was wearing a navy tracksuit. Her hair was neatly tied back. She looked like she'd lost weight overnight, despite the duty sergeant telling Matilda she'd wolfed down her breakfast. Her eyes were sunken and surrounded by black circles. Had she suffered a sleepless night in a cell due to the remorse she was feeling for her actions, or was she one of the greatest actors never to grace the London stage? She hadn't been told about her father's death, yet. Matilda wanted to break that news herself.

Christian turned on the recording equipment and stated who was present while Matilda made herself comfortable and put the plastic box containing the evidence she was going to show Jodie on the floor beneath the table.

'Jodie, before we begin, is there anything you would like to tell us about the deaths of your brother, sister, and mother?' It pained Matilda to speak in a sympathetic tone. However, she wanted to surprise Jodie when the time was right.

'No,' Jodie said without looking up. Her head was down, her chin on her chest, acting the perfect victim.

'Jodie, there is no easy way for me to say this: I'm afraid your father was found dead yesterday morning in Hillsborough Park. He hanged himself.'

Jodie didn't move. Her face was hidden. All eyes were on her as she sniffled a few times. The appropriate adult stepped forward and offered her a tissue which she took. She wiped her eyes, but the tissue came away dry.

'Are you all right? Would you like to have a break for five minutes?' Matilda asked. She was pretending to play into her hands.

Jodie blew her nose loudly and looked up. She cleared her throat. 'No. I'm fine.'

'Ok. Any time you want to have a break, let me know,' she smiled and gave the same mock-sympathetic smile to the solicitor whose face remained stoic.

'Jodie, in searching your house yesterday, we found three mobile phones. All iPhone 4s which belonged to your father. Do you know why your dad had three mobiles?'

'No,' she replied with a catch in her throat.

'For the benefit of the recording, I am showing Jodie the three phones.' Matilda lifted all three phones from the box at her feet. They were in plastic evidence bags. She lined them up in front of the fourteen-year-old. 'On one of them we found the numbers of your mum and other family members, and your father's friends. The texts are as you'd expect, as are the photographs and internet history. The second phone is one he used for work-related purposes. This third one, however, only has one contact in the phone book and he seemed to use WhatsApp more than anything else. There's one conversation that has been going on for a number of years in which your father appears to be having a very intimate relationship with someone who isn't your mum. Unfortunately, he doesn't have the number assigned to anyone, so we don't know who that person is. Can you shed any light on who it might be?'

'No,' she replied quickly.

Matilda pulled a cardboard file from the box. 'We've printed off the conversation. It's incredibly detailed and sexually explicit. Your father describes sexual activities he and this other person have done together, what he'd like to do in the future, and he's even sent photographs of parts of his body.'

'I don't think my client would like to hear what her father has been getting up to, DCI Darke,' the solicitor interrupted.

Matilda ignored her. 'The receiver of these messages replied in a similar vein. At times, she's even more explicit, and the photographs she sent of herself are, quite frankly, highly disturbing. There's even a four-minute video of this person, though we can't see her face.'

Jodie bit her bottom lip hard. Her eyes darted around the room. She was unable to look at Matilda.

'Is any of this relevant?' the solicitor asked.

'Jodie, are you the person your father is messaging?'

'No,' she replied quietly.

Matilda brought out another phone from the box beneath the table. 'I'm showing Jodie Armitage an iPhone 4S that was found in her bedroom under the floorboards by her bed. The carpet was loose there as if it had been pulled back many times. Do you recognise this phone?'

'No.'

'Are you sure?'

'Yes. It looks like any other iPhone 4. It's not mine. I've got an iPhone 8.'

'How can you account for this phone being in your room, underneath your bed?'

'Well, I can't,' she shrugged. 'I've never seen it before.'

'We've analysed this phone. There are no contacts saved but

in WhatsApp is the other half of the conversation with your father that we found on this phone which was hidden under the floor in the living room.'

'Maybe someone planted it there?'

'Who?'

'I don't know. That's your job to find out.'

'It is, isn't it?' Matilda leaned forward and picked up the phone. 'Do you know what I love about these iPhones? They're so smooth and sleek and shiny. You only need to pick it up once and you leave behind a perfect fingerprint. These are a godsend to police. We find these, dust them for prints, and we always get a good set from them. We dusted this one too. Would you like me to tell you what we found?'

Jodie sat back and folded her arms. She shrugged her reply.

'We found your prints. Well, we only found one. It was a thumb print on the home button. As you know, we took your prints for elimination purposes. They're a complete match to the one on this phone.'

'That's not possible.'

'Why not?'

'Because I've never touched that phone.'

'You have. Looking at the times and dates of the messages sent you'll have been in bed, chatting on the phone to your father in the next room and when you've sent your final message with three kisses and told him how much you loved him, you turned the phone off and hid it beneath the floorboards.'

'No.'

'Your mum slept downstairs in the extension with Riley. Your father was in bed upstairs on his own. Many times you started your messages with 'Would you like me to come in?' You volunteered to go into your dad's room and engage in sexual activity.'

'You have no proof of that,' the solicitor said. 'Even if it's true, she could have suffered years of abuse at the hands of her father, making her seem complicit to avoid other physical abuse or abuse enacted towards her brother or sister.'

'I'll let you have a copy of this conversation, including the pictures we downloaded, and the short video. Did I tell you what the video was of?' Matilda asked, a smile on her face. 'It's of a young woman, a girl, using a vibrator on herself. The message that went with it said, 'Happy birthday, Daddy'. Care to explain?'

'That wasn't me,' Jodie said, firmly.

'I'm going to put in a request to have a doctor examine you, Jodie. That doctor will be able to tell if you match the person in the video. They can tell by any veins that appear prominently on the leg, or by moles or skin defects.'

'It's not me,' she said, a little less confidently.

'Yes, your father may have instigated the abuse, but you enjoyed it. He made you believe what you were doing was perfectly normal. He forced you to fall in love with him. Then, when he turned his attentions to Keeley, you killed her because you thought she was going to replace you.'

'You're lying.'

'You wanted him for yourself so you poisoned your mother so it could be just the two of you.'

'No.'

'And you killed Riley so you could move away somewhere and start afresh. Father and daughter living as husband and wife.'

'You're seriously sick in the head.'

'You're the victim of abuse, but the perpetrator of three murders.'

'Wrong. You're so wrong it's unbelievable.'

'Then why is your thumb print on this phone?'

'It isn't because I always wiped—' She fell silent.

Matilda savoured the silence. 'You always wiped it before you put it back under the floorboards. Is that what you were going to say?'

Jodie slumped in her seat as if the life had been torn out of her. She looked down. Her breathing was slow. Eventually, she looked back up at Matilda.

'You tricked me.'

'I know. I'm sorry. I'm not proud of that.'

A silence descended. Matilda waited for Jodie to begin in her own time.

Her bottom lip began to wobble. 'I never thought what Dad was doing was abuse. He was always so gentle, so kind. He made me feel safe and wanted. When it started, it was just kissing and holding each other. The first time we had sex, I told him I wanted my first time to be special. We went for a meal, just the two of us. Keeley was staying over at a friend's house and Mum was in the extension with Riley. She never came upstairs. We made love for hours. It was . . . amazing,' she smiled as she recalled the memory. Her face was one of contentment, but tears began to run down her face.

'You must have known it was wrong,' Matilda said.

'I did. I told Dad we shouldn't be doing it, but he said you can't help who you fall in love with. He's right. We're taught at school about being tolerant towards people from other lifestyles and religions. We watched a video and there was this man who hated being a man. He hated everything about being male and changed gender. Yet, when he was a woman, he still wanted to sleep with women, so he entered into a lesbian relationship. I remember some of the lads in my class laughing at that. And I thought, yes, it is a bit weird, but he looked so happy. I was sleeping with my dad, but I was happy, so, surely that's all that matters . . . that I'm happy.'

Matilda and Christian exchanged glances. Everyone in that room felt uncomfortable. Suddenly, they weren't sitting opposite a cold-blooded killer, but a victim of prolonged sexual and mental abuse.

'You killed Keeley, didn't you?' Matilda asked, breaking the heavy silence.

Jodie lost her grip on her emotions. The tears fell in a torrent and she struggled to keep her breath. She refused the offer of a break.

'When Keeley told me what Dad had done to her,' she eventually began, 'I thought he'd finish with me and go to Keeley. I loved him so much. I just wanted him for myself. I loved Keeley, but she was getting in the way of my happiness,' she wiped her eyes with the backs of her hands.

'What happened on Monday evening?'

'I bought Keeley an ice cream from the van outside the school. Then, when we went to the Co-op, I told her to wait there until she'd finished it, then go and wait for me in the woods and I'd bring her a treat. I told her not to speak to anyone. We'd have a little picnic, just the two of us. I quickly did the shopping, took it home, made some excuse to Mum about Keeley wandering off then went to look for her. I phoned Mum not long after I'd left and pretended to be a kidnapper. Then I went to find Keeley. She was there, waiting for me by the tree, drawing in the dry ground with a stick, acting all sweet and innocent as if she'd done nothing wrong.'

'But she hadn't done anything wrong,' Matilda said.

'You wouldn't say that if you saw the way she flaunted herself around the house – dressing up like a princess, sitting on Dad's knee. It made me sick. I had to get her out of the way.'

'She was nine years old,' Matilda exclaimed.

'So? Don't let someone's age fool you. She knew exactly what she was doing.'

'What did you do?'

Jodie picked up the plastic cup of water and took a lingering sip. 'I smacked her over the head with a rock. It was easy. She didn't scream. She just fell to the ground. She wasn't dead though. I thought she was but suddenly she started to groan and squirm.'

'Go on,' Matilda prompted.

'I strangled her,' she said, matter-of-fact. 'That's harder to do than it looks in films. I made sure she was dead then I rolled her down the embankment. I came home and to tell Mum I couldn't find her, but she was in tears thinking she'd been kidnapped. It was so easy.'

'But why the fake kidnapping story?' Matilda asked.

'I have you to thank for that,' Jodie smiled. 'I knew you'd be leading the investigation; the great DCI Matilda Darke. I've read that book Carl's mother wrote. I knew Keeley would turn up dead and the newspapers would see it as a kidnapping gone wrong. Then, all the attention would be on you for screwing up another kidnapping, and not me.'

Matilda couldn't believe what she was hearing. How was it possible for such a sweet and innocent-looking fourteen-year-old to be so evil and manipulative?

'Jodie, were you behind the photos of Keeley we found on her iPad?' Matilda asked.

She smirked. 'The ones of her in make-up and acting all sultry?' Matilda nodded. 'Of course I was. Who do you think did her hair and painted her face? She thought we were just having a fun day together, two sisters messing around. I put them online hoping some paedo would get a hard-on and snatch her off the streets. No such luck.'

'My God!' Christian said. He looked utterly disgusted.

'And what about your mum?'

Jodie's face hardened. 'I hated Mum for what she did to Riley, for causing him such pain. When I was with him, playing with him, looking after him, feeding him, he'd look at me with his dead eyes and he'd be crying and yelling and I knew, I knew he was telling me how much pain he was in. He wasn't living. He was just existing. He was trapped in his own body and he wanted to be set free.'

'How long have you been poisoning her for?'

She shook her head. 'I don't remember. A while.'

'What have you been using?'

'Botulinum Toxin.'

Matilda frowned. 'What? Why? How did you even get hold of that? Wouldn't something like rat poison have been quicker?'

'Because I wanted it to be slow. I wanted her to suffer. She needed to know why she was dying. Have you seen the photos of Riley before she shook him? He was such a sweet baby, always smiling, always hugging. He was so cute. His eyes lit up when he saw me. After she tried to kill him, all that was gone. His eyes no longer sparkled. She'd ruined the most perfect little baby I'd ever seen. She had to suffer.'

'Where did you get it from?'

'Well, it wasn't easy. I spent hours and hours on the internet trying to find it. Did you know that it's the same thing they use in Botox injections? It was fascinating.'

'Why did you kill Riley?'

'I wasn't planning on killing him. My plan was to finish school and then I'd be his full-time carer and look after him and Dad.

We'd be a proper couple, a proper family. But then I started thinking . . . he'd get older, but he wouldn't grow up. I pictured him as a twenty-year-old, strapped in a wheelchair, still laughing at *Pingu*. That image frightened me. Nobody should have to live like that. He didn't suffer. I promise you he didn't suffer. I waited until he was asleep, and I popped a little piece of cheese in his mouth. He always slept with his mouth open. He didn't know what was happening.' She fell onto the table, her head in her arms. 'He never knew what was happening.'

Matilda's heart ached as she watched and listened to a four-teen-year-old girl admitting to murdering her family. There was a little remorse there when she spoke of Riley's death, but she knew the harm she had done to Keeley and her mother. Matilda was conflicted. Jodie had arrived here through years of abuse. Should she be labelled a cold-blooded killer or the victim of a perverted father?

'I don't think I've ever needed a drink more,' Christian said as he and Matilda left the interview room. He slumped against the wall and let out a deep sigh.

'Come on. I know where we can get one from.'

ACC Valerie Masterson always kept an emergency bottle of whiskey hidden in the depths of a filing cabinet for such situations.

The room was cold and empty. It seemed strange to enter it while Valerie wasn't in the building. Matilda went straight to the bottom drawer and took out the half-filled bottle and two glasses. She blew into them to clean away the dust.

'It feels naughty being in here while the head teacher is away,' Christian said, reluctantly sitting down on the comfortable armchair.

'Do you really see the ACC as a head teacher?'

'Yes. Don't you?'

She thought about it for a while and the many times she had cried on her shoulder. 'Not really.'

Matilda poured them both a healthy measure and they drank in silence.

'What will happen to Jodie?' Christian asked once his glass was empty.

'I've no idea. She certainly needs to be assessed by a psychologist. She's suffered years of mental and sexual abuse by her father and that's led to her killing three people and trying to kill Sian and Ellen.' Matilda finished her drink and poured them both another. 'You know, I went into that interview wanting to catch her out as the cold-hearted psycho bitch I thought she was.'

'And now?'

'Now, I don't think I've ever felt more sympathy for anyone than I do her. I just hope she receives the treatment she needs and she's able to recover.'

'Do you mind if I go home early today? I wouldn't mind spending a bit of time with my girls,' Christian said.

'No. Of course I don't mind.'

'What are you going to do now?'

'I need to go and see the Meagans and tell them the results of the DNA test. I've been sitting on them for too long.'

'Do you want me to come with you?'

'No. I'll give Pat a call. She'll be glad of an excuse to leave her husband in the garden centre on his own.' Matilda stood up to leave. She placed a hand on Christian's shoulder. 'Christian, do me a favour. Go home, take your wife and daughters out for a nice meal, and be a normal boring family for the night.'

'I can do that. I'm Mr Boring.'

She leaned down and kissed him on the cheek. 'I wouldn't have you any other way.'

Chapter 65

Matilda and Pat were sitting in the Meagan's living room nervously waiting for Sally to join them. She'd been in the shower when they arrived. Philip showed them in then went upstairs to fetch his wife.

Woody remained in the living room with them. He'd taken to Pat in the months she had been coming to visit and she always had a treat for him in her handbag. Treat eaten, belly scratched, he curled up on the floor beside her, his head on her foot.

Matilda looked around the clean, spartan living room. Carl seemed to be looking out at her from every picture frame. She looked at him in the silver frame on the mantelpiece in a snap taken one Christmas morning. His eyes were dancing in excitement, his smile wide as he marvelled at the mountain of beautifully wrapped presents in front of him. A picture of happiness tinged with sadness. When Matilda looked at the photo now, she saw a sad little boy, asking her, pleading, begging to find him and bring him home.

Sally bounded into the living room. She'd hastily dressed in skinny jeans and a white sweater. Her hair was still damp and tangled. It was obvious she was struggling to hide her excitement at the thought Carl might actually be on his way back to Sheffield.

'Philip said you had some news.' She sat down on the sofa opposite. Philip sat next to her and they held hands. Their mouths were agape. Philip was more restrained, but Sally had already made up her mind that Carl would be sleeping in his own bed tonight.

Matilda closed her eyes to compose herself. She took a deep breath.

'I'm so sorry, Sally. The boy in France isn't Carl.'

Sally took a deep breath and gripped harder onto her husband's hand. Her bottom lip began to wobble. She wanted to speak but was clearly afraid to open her mouth in case a torrent of emotion fell out.

'Are you sure?' she eventually asked.

Matilda nodded. 'The DNA results came back two days ago. I wanted to have a few more questions answered before I let you know. The British ambassador has been in touch with Police Nationale to find out why this boy said he was Carl when he clearly wasn't.'

'But he looked so much like him,' Sally said, her voice shaking.

'He didn't look that much like him, Sally,' Philip said.

'The boy in France has a disturbing mental illness. His parents have moved so many times they've lost count. He accuses neighbours of abusing him, school friends and teachers of hitting him. He's gone into police stations many times to say his parents have kidnapped him. He always seems very genuine in his claims so the police have had to look into each allegation.'

Sally had turned red. 'Jesus! Shouldn't he be locked away or something?' she fumed.

'Sally!' Philip chastised.

'I'm sorry, but someone like that shouldn't be allowed on the streets. Doesn't he realise what he's putting people through with his lies?' She stood up and went over to the mantelpiece. She picked up the photo of her son. 'I genuinely thought we'd found him. I really thought he'd be coming home this time.'

'I know you did. I did too,' Philip said. He went over to her and put his arms on her shoulders.

'This is heart-breaking,' she cried. 'I move on, you know. I don't forget. I'll never forget, but I'm able to function, to a degree. Then something like this happens and it's like I'm right back to square one. My son is out there somewhere, I know he is. I can feel it.'

Pat dug in her handbag for a tissue and wiped her eyes. Matilda remained impassive on the sofa.

Sally stepped away from her husband and went back to the sofa. 'So, what happens now? There hasn't been a sighting for months. The emails have all but dropped off. I'm running out of things to do.'

'I do have one idea,' Matilda said, leaning forward. 'I can arrange for you and Philip to do an interview for the media; you can talk about this past week, the boy in France, how your hopes were raised then dashed, mention the other sightings too. It will bring Carl back into the public eye and we can get the story printed in papers here and in France.'

'No offence, but it's not really a story, is it?' Philip said. 'We're not saying anything fresh. Who would be interested in printing that?'

Matilda thought of Danny Hanson. 'I know a guy who owes me a favour or two,' she said with the hint of a smile.

Epilogue

Tuesday 16th October 2018
Gothenburg, Sweden

8pm

It was dark. It was cold and a bitter wind was blowing outside. Winter had come early.

The young boy was sitting on the floor of the living room in front of the wood-burning fire. His legs were tucked up to his chest and he was engrossed in the first Harry Potter book. He'd never read it before, though he'd seen the film. Every time he turned a page he looked up at the couple on the sofa. He hated them.

The old-fashioned clock on the cluttered mantelpiece chimed eight o'clock. He didn't need telling what that meant. It was bedtime. He closed his book and stood up. The golden Labrador curled up beside him copied his actions.

'You can read for one hour more then you must turn out your light,' Marika said, looking up from her magazine.

'Ok,' he replied.

'Kiss for me and your dad?' she asked, putting the magazine down and holding out her arms.

He took a deep breath. Reluctantly, he went over to Marika, leaned down and allowed her to hug and kiss him on the cheek. Her touch felt cold and his whole bodied stiffened. Her lips were coarse against his soft skin.

'Goodnight,' she said, smiling that ugly smile. Her thin lips spread across her face and she showed her crooked teeth. It made him shudder to look at her.

In the armchair, Martin was doing a crossword. He put it down and pulled him into an embrace, squeezing him tight. He kissed the boy on the forehead, his bushy blond moustache tickling him.

'Sleep well and have pleasant dreams,' he said in broken English.

The little boy gave a smile and quickly left the room, closing the door firmly behind him. Usually he waited in the hallway, his ear pressed against the door, to see if they were talking about him; not that he could understand when they spoke in their own language. Tonight, however, he had things to do.

On the way to the stairs, he stopped and turned to go into the kitchen. The dog followed. In there, Marika had left her bag when she returned home from work. Carefully, and as quietly as possible, he opened it, removed her purse and took out a fifty krona note. He stuffed it into his pocket and replaced the purse. He stood in the silence and listened. All he could hear was his own heart pounding in his chest and Woody breathing loudly with his tongue hanging out. He was about to leave the kitchen when he remembered Martin had been shopping today. From the pantry, he grabbed a tin of tuna and a can of dog food before hurrying out of the kitchen and taking the stairs two at a time. His faithful companion ran after him.

In his cool bedroom, he closed the door and dropped to his

knees to look under the bed. He pulled out a backpack. He stored the tins of food inside. He didn't want to make the bag too heavy, but he needed there to be enough provisions as he didn't know how long he would be on the road for. He found an envelope in the front pocket of the bag and placed the fifty krona note in it. He took a deep breath and found he was shaking. His mum and dad, his *real* mum and dad, had always told him stealing was bad, but it was all he could think of if he was going to make it home.

'We've started now, Woody,' he said as he jumped on the bed with the dog and cuddled up to him. 'We'll keep saving more food and I'll wait until I have enough money. I just need to try and see Marika use her card at the cash point so I can find out her number, then I can take her card and we can leave.' He smiled warming at the dog who licked his cheek as if sharing in the conspiracy to run away.

Carl Meagan had put his plan into action when he read a story in an English newspaper at a shop in town. His parents were still looking for him. They'd suffered setbacks and had experienced heartache, but they were never going to give up. He tore the story out of the paper, put it in his pocket, and took it home with him where he read it every night and hid it under his pillow before going to sleep.

His plan was simple. If his parents couldn't find him, then he'd find them. He just needed to make sure he and Woody had enough food and money to survive the journey home as he had no idea how long it would take.

By the dim light of his bedside table, Carl snuggled down under the duvet. He read the article again. His eyes teared up as he looked at the photo of an unhappy-looking Sally and Philip with his dog in between them. He couldn't wait to get back home, to see his mum and dad, and for the two Woodys to meet.

'Look, Woody,' he said to his dog. 'This is your brother. We're going to see him soon. It's going to be a long journey, and it might be scary, but it will be worth it. We're all going to be so happy.'

Woody whined and licked his face before curling up next to him. Carl turned out the light and lay down.

Carl fell asleep with a smile on his face as he pictured the reunion. The last few years had been a nightmare, but it would soon be over. His mum and dad were going to be so proud when they found out what he'd gone through to get back home. They were all going to be so happy.

Acknowledgements

There were a number of behind the scene changes going on while writing this book, so I have a few more people to thank than usual.

My former agent at Blake Friedmann, Tom Witcomb and my current agent at Ampersand, Jamie Cowen.

My former editor at Harper Collins, Finn Cotton and the new people who are currently looking after me: Charlotte Ledger, Bethan Morgan and Hannah Todd. Also, my copy editor, Fran Fabriczki, many thanks.

As always, I've had a number of people help me with research. For the last time, Claire Green gave me invaluable insight into digital post mortems before she took early retirement. She's far too young to retire, but she deserves it so much. Philip Lumb is an eminent pathologist and I'm grateful for him for taking the time to answer my emails. Simon Browes for medical research (our text messages frighten even me at times), fellow crime writer, Andy Barrett has advised on forensic detail and a huge thank you to "Mr Tidd" for his police procedural advice. I say this every time, but any errors in this novel are purely mine. Please do not blame the experts, and remember, this is a work of fiction, after all.

Thank you to Glenis Schofield for talking to me about Stannington; my nephew, William Ricketts for driving me around Stannington and my niece, Megan Ricketts, for coming along for the ride. We really must visit Our Cow Molly again at some point.

Thanks also to the usual suspects for listening to me talk through my plots and for just being there when I've needed you – my amazing mum, Christopher Human, Scout Master Kevin, JD, and Maxwell Dog.

Finally, a massive thank you to Colin Scott. I honestly don't know where I'd be without your support. It's comforting to know that whenever I need you, you're right there, at the end of my fingertips. Yay!